REVENGE
IS BEST SERVED COLD

REVENGE
IS BEST SERVED COLD

Tracie Howard

and

Danita Carter

NEW AMERICAN LIBRARY

New American Library
Published by New American Library, a division of
Penguin Putnam Inc., 375 Hudson Street, New York, New York 10014, U.S.A.
Penguin Books Ltd, 27 Wrights Lane, London W8 5TZ, England
Penguin Books Australia Ltd, Ringwood, Victoria, Australia
Penguin Books Canada Ltd, 10 Alcorn Avenue,Toronto, Ontario, Canada M4V 3B2
Penguin Books (N.Z.) Ltd, 182–190 Wairau Road, Auckland 10, New Zealand

Penguin Books Ltd, Registered Offices: Harmondsworth, Middlesex, England

First published by New American Library, a division of Penguin Putnam Inc.

Copyright © Tracie Howard and Danita Carter, 2001

Grateful acknowledgment is made to Edwina Owens Elliot
for her contribution to the cover design.

LIBRARY OF CONGRESS CATALOGING-IN-PUBLICATION DATA:

ISBN: 0-451-20475-1

Set in Sabon

Printed in the United States of America

PUBLISHER'S NOTE
This is a work of fiction. Names, characters, places, and incidents either are the
product of the author's imagination or are used fictitiously, and any resemblance to
actual persons, living or dead, business establishments, events, or locales
is entirely coincidental.

The journey leading me to write *Revenge Is Best Served Cold* began at birth and has since been guided by unconditional love and parental wisdom. For that reason, I dedicate this book to my mother (who has also been my father, teacher and mentor), Gloria Elizabeth Freeman.

Tracie

To my parents Bill and Alline Carter. Thank you for supporting me throughout *all* of my artistic endeavors. And for creating a solid and loving family unit for Ronald, Denise and me—one that will carry on for generations.

I love you beyond words.

Danita

ACKNOWLEDGMENTS

Before a vision ever becomes reality, people—other than the creator—must see it. Even when the vision for *Revenge Is Best Served Cold* was murky at best, there were many people who were able to see it through my eyes and, thus, helped me to continually bring it into clearer focus. So, for supporting and encouraging me when, without prior writing experience, I said with a straight face, "I'm going to write a book," I'd like to thank my friends and family, in particular: Greg Anthony, Vanessa Baylor, Siddiq Bellow, Julie Borders, Ken Chenault, Keith Clinkscales, Greg Fierce, Jennifer Harper, Karen and Oswald Morgan, Oniel Morgan, Margaret Mroz, April and Ted Phillips, Erica and Antonio "L.A." Reid, Rose and Steve Salem, Judith Service, Anne Simmons and Donny and Tony Smith.

For the support that I've received throughout my entire life, I thank my mother, Gloria Freeman; my sisters, Alison Howard-Smith and Jennifer Freeman; my nieces, Chelsae Smith and Korian Young; and my many nurturing and much loved aunts, uncles and cousins.

I'd also like to give heartfelt thanks to fellow authors Veronica Chambers (for giving me the benefit of her wisdom) and most especially Crystal McCrary Anthony, without whom I don't know if *I* would have taken me seriously.

I also owe large debts of gratitude to my girlfriend and attorney, Denise Brown, who stroked my ego even after the first shaky draft, and to an extraordinarily cool editor, Audrey LaFehr, who I admire because she so "gets it"! Not to mention the incredible Penguin Putnam/NAL staff that includes Jennifer Jahner, Carolyn Nichols, Louise Burke, Liz Perl, Rick Pascocello, Richard Hasselberger, and many others. And to someone who truly without whom this wouldn't have happened: my coauthor and girlfriend, Danita Carter.

The last person that I want to thank is someone who is a visionary himself, and therefore when I put one weak sentence on the first blank page, he said, "Keep writing—you can do it." He is Scott Folks, the love of my life and the person who is always there helping to make me a better person. For all of these people, and for my health and strength, I thank God.

Tracie

First and foremost I thank God from whom all blessings flow. To my friend and writing partner, Tracie Howard, "Girl, can you believe it, our baby is finally born!"

And to the following, a big ole' warm fuzzy THANK YOU: Crystal McCrary Anthony for encouraging and believing in REVENGE before one word was ever written; Scott Folks, who read the story before it was fully fleshed out and never waned in his faith that "the Girls" could do it; our attorney, Denise Brown, for her wisdom and great advice; our editor, Audrey LaFehr, for realizing the potential in the story and the long tedious hours she and John Paine put into helping us develop it; Edwina Owens Elliott for conceptualizing an awesome cover; Jennifer Jahner for her patience in dealing with two new authors; E. Lynn Harris for the advice; to my siblings, Ron and Denise, who knew me before I knew myself; Iris Simms, my therapist-cousin-friend; Katherine Bell, Melinda Kelly, Beverly Smith Lashley, Saunté Lowe, Charlene Oliver, Charles Walton, Saundra Warren and Cathy Williams for loving the story in its infancy; Kim Russell for her faith; Daryl Myers for his French; to Danique, Ronnie, Iman, Danny, Khary and Tamille for putting up with a zany-auntie; my brother-in-law Earl Milloy for his entrepreneurial spirit; my sister-in-law Diana for the prayers; Vivian Bruce for still loving me and to the rest of my family and friends whose love and support have no boundaries.

Danita

1

New York's young, beautiful and savvy all flocked to Ocean, a trendy restaurant on the city's Upper West Side. Morgan Nelson and Dakota Cantrell soaked up the late-day sun at a window table as guests of Seth Harris, a stockbroker from Salomon Smith Barney. Other dinner guests were his overbearing wife, Dania, and a couple of her cronies, along with a smattering of Wall Street's jocks.

As the second round of drinks was served, the guys were flirting shamelessly with Morgan and Dakota, to the dismay of chain-smoking Dania. She wore her dark auburn hair swept up in a loose French twist, the ends spiking freely from the top. The carefully coiffed look was supposed to evoke a carefree, natural appearance that said, "I am so chic that I need not bother with the styling of my hair." She wore a white cotton shirt with the collar turned up, a strand of pearls and a pair of navy pleated slacks.

Smiling slyly at her friends, she asked, "So, Morgan, what do you do?" blowing smoke with barely hidden disdain.

"Excuse me?" Morgan replied. Not because she didn't hear Dania, but to put her attitude in check.

"Who do you work for?" Dania asked in a more cordial tone.

"Global Financial," Morgan answered.

"Oh. What do you do for them?" Dania asked, nodding at her buddies as if to say, "Here it comes."

"I'm the vice president of Marketing," Morgan answered.

She got the inevitable raise of eyebrows. It was never the answer that was expected. Because of her looks, people often assumed that Morgan was a model or an actress, anything but an executive in a Fortune 500 company. She wore her hair daringly short, framing her flawless caramel skin, chiseled features and beautiful brown eyes. She looked tall and svelte in her slate blue Jil Sander pantsuit.

Thwarted in her first attempt at one-upmanship, Dania then turned to Dakota. "What about you? What exactly is it that you do?" she asked, while her girlfriends lay in wait.

Dakota's look combined Wall Street conservatism with SoHo chic. Her cocoa complexion accented sharply sculptured features and a dazzling smile. She had a deep, sultry voice and wore signature black cat-eye glasses that accentuated a pair of smoldering eyes.

"I decide how much money your husband will make each day," Dakota answered evenly.

"Excuse me?" Dania nearly shouted, smoke billowing through her thin, pursed lips.

"I decide which brokers will execute orders for my Swiss clients. Right, Seth?" Dakota turned to face him with an innocent expression.

Visibly uncomfortable, he said, "Yeah. Dakota's my favorite sales trader."

Jim Elliot, a self-proclaimed "cool white boy," said, "You know, you two got it goin' on." Inserting foot further into mouth, he added, "You know, Hershey's ain't got nothin' on y'all."

Morgan and Dakota looked at each other. What was the polite response to that?

Jim's sidekick tried a different tack. "You know, some of my best friends are black."

"What a coincidence. So are mine!" Dakota replied, raising her eyebrows in feigned surprise.

Getting the joke about two beats late, Mutt and Jeff joined Morgan and Dakota in a good laugh.

"Heel, boys," Paul chided lightly, smoothing over any awkwardness. Paul worked next to Dakota on SBI's Swiss trading desk, and as usual he had Dakota's back. Grateful for the intervention, she and Morgan smiled in his direction.

As the general conversation started again, Morgan leaning toward Dakota, "Funny how 'in' it's become to be black," she whispered.

"Yeah. It's all good until you're asking for the green. Then if you're black—get back."

"Not totally true. Look at us—we're living the American dream," Morgan said, looking around at the elegant restaurant, gourmet food, expensive drinks and designer clothes. "Here's to a room with a view—the corner office, that is!" Morgan raised her bellini to meet Dakota's glass. Morgan was being considered for a promotion to senior vice president, and based on her skills and the competition, it seemed to be in the bag. She could almost taste it.

"It looks like I'm just in time. I love a celebration."

Turning to see who owned the rich tenor voice, Morgan and Dakota caught the grand entrance of a tall, charismatic man. He swept in, bowed smoothly, and kissed the back of Dania's hand. "Darling . . . how arrrre you?" he purred.

"I am well, dear. Do join us," she answered. Snapping her fingers, she called out, "Garçon!" to the waiter. "Let me introduce Blake St. James," she then announced, as though presenting a lord to her less royal subjects.

Blake was over six feet, mostly legs and model thin. He carried himself in an elegant flourish as though his arrival was the most anticipated coming since the last millennium. After dispensing greetings, Blake turned to Dania and said, "Though I would love to, I really can't stay. I've got to get home to dress for tonight. Will I see you all later at the Back Room?"

"Of course," she replied, speaking for her husband and everyone else.

Morgan and Dakota agreed to accompany them for a nightcap.

Strolling up Columbus Avenue at a brisk pace, they merged with the fast, kinetic energy of the other fashionable upscale

New Yorkers. They passed an eclectic assortment of clothing and specialty stores. New York was the only place Morgan knew of with specialty stores even for caviar and truffles.

"Don't you just love it?" Morgan said. Even though she and Miles had lived in New York for several years now, she still retained a touch of wide-eyed awe. She remembered the wonder of her first visit with her parents at the age of twelve. They'd come during the holidays and seen the magnificent tree at Rockefeller Center, then *The Nutcracker* and the Rockettes. It had seemed to Morgan that everyone in New York was glamorous and very, very busy as they strolled up Fifth Avenue wrapped in fur, with designer handbags on one arm and shopping bags draped on the other.

"There is no place I'd rather be," Dakota answered with her trademark certainty.

Halfway past a pet store with made-for-TV-cute puppies in the window, Morgan came to a sudden stop. "Ohhh, look at the babies! They are soooo cute." She pressed her face against the window.

"Yeah, until they stop being puppies and turn into dogs," Dakota said pragmatically.

"Look at the white bichon chasing his tail!" Morgan had both palms flat on the glass in unabashed love.

Dakota refused to be pulled in by the cute button noses, round puppy-dog eyes and lapping pink tongues. "Like I said, they grow up and, just like men, they turn into dogs and start chasing other tail."

Not to be discouraged, Morgan said, "But look at that face." She stood mesmerized by the tumbling bundles of energy. Pulling out her cell phone, she quickly called her husband's office. "Lauren, would you put Miles on? It's important," she said to his assistant. After a few seconds, he was on the line. Dakota watched as Morgan cooed into the phone, trying to convince Miles that a puppy was an absolute necessity. They had had this conversation before, but so far Miles had been able to hold Morgan at bay. "Oh, baby, he is so cute. It's a bichon. No, they don't get that large, only about thirteen pounds . . . I know, I've already thought about that . . . yes . . . small . . . small poop size is important . . . yes . . . I love you, baby . . . have a good trip."

"Well?" Dakota asked, with one hand on her hip. "What's the verdict?"

"He'll think about it," Morgan answered, happy that at least the subject was still on the table. When Miles got back from L.A., she'd bring him to the pet store and let him try to say no to those big brown eyes.

"With all the cooing you were doing into the phone, how could the man possibly deny you?" Dakota said, laughing.

"That's the point," Morgan answered matter-of-factly.

She and Miles were like Claire and Cliff, Ozzie and Harriet, and Lucy and Ricky, but cool. They were everything that Dakota wanted in a relationship, but had so far missed. "You two are so lovey-dovey. It's sickening really," Dakota teased.

While the Upper East Side had Park Avenue's old money, the Upper West Side was the playpen for the uptown hip crowd. It was chock-full of trendy bars and restaurants, each hipper than the next. The Back Room was a posh, upscale cigar bar on Columbus Avenue set amidst a block brimming with sophisticated lounges and restaurants, all swarming with people needing to see and be seen. It was where the sleek meet and greet. The Back Room had a cozy fireplace in the rear and a streetfront entrance that spanned its width, giving the place the feel of an elegant den. Tonight's pack was the Wall Street crowd, all abuzz about the latest IPO and full of theories on how far and fast the technology gravy train would go. Generally you could guess the number of zeros in their investment accounts by the quality of their wristwatches. Those in the caboose wore Seikos, and those that drove the train wore Boucheron's Chronographes.

Morgan and Dakota took an intimate table near the fireplace, while the other members of their party filled up a larger table. Turning to Dakota, Morgan said, "Well, that worked out well. Tell me, how on earth do you put up with those silly-ass white boys?"

With a teasing smirk, Dakota replied, "You know, girl, nothing comes between me and a check."

"Hey now!" They gave each other a light high five.

"Speaking of which, I read about your man's impending promotion in *Billboard* magazine. Why didn't you tell me, your best friend?" Dakota asked.

"Girl, you know how conservative Miles is. He insisted on not talking about it until it's final, but of course the trade magazines actually prefer the rumor mill to press releases."

"You guys must be so excited," Dakota said, beaming. She was so happy for them.

"We are. You know Miles has wanted to buy a brownstone in Harlem for a while. So, with his promotion, maybe now we can."

"You are so lucky. You've got a great career, you can eat anything and never gain an ounce, and on top of all of that you're married to a fabulous, successful and sexy man. I think I hate you," Dakota said, shaking her head in mock dismay.

"Look who's talking, Ms. Hotshot Wall Street Diva."

"The operative word there is 'Ms.' Finding a good man is like trying to find a cab at five o'clock during a downpour."

"What's going on with you and Jackson?" Morgan asked, with a puzzled expression.

"He's cool, but until the ink dries on his divorce papers, he's still 'occupied.' "

"I heard that," Morgan said, glad that Dakota's practical side still had control when it came to dating a married man. Even though Jackson was separated from his wife, technically he was still her property.

Morgan was protective of her best friend. She and Dakota had met five years earlier in Atlanta, at her cousin's wedding. They had hit it off immediately. Born a day apart, they seemed to recognize each other's genetic code, and within a few days were completing each other's thoughts and sentences. After losing touch for a couple of years, they literally bumped into each other one afternoon while reaching for the same handbag at Barneys on Madison Avenue.

Considering the extensive menu of after-dinner favors, Dakota and Morgan tried to decide between champagne or port. As if on cue, Blake St. James emerged from the smoky darkness looking like freshly minted money. He wore a blood-red velvet smoking jacket, black open-collared shirt and a burgundy, gold and cream silk ascot nestled at his neck. Effortlessly, he assumed the role of host.

"I am glad you two could make it," he said, gliding in for a landing at their table.

"I'm Morgan Nelson and this is Dakota Cantrell." Earlier Dania had failed to make proper introductions, only presenting Blake to "the group."

"You both look fabulous," he said, giving them each the once over.

"And don't you look chic," Morgan replied, appraising Blake's ensemble.

"This old thing," he said, coyly opening his arms to offer an unencumbered view. They all laughed. The jacket had to be straight out of Armani's latest collection. "What can I get for you ladies?"

Morgan glanced over at Dakota. "A port would be nice."

"That sounds good. I'd like one that's full-bodied, and rich, with character. Just like I like my men," Dakota flirted.

"As gorgeous as you are, I can't help you there." Blake laughed, confirming Morgan's earlier guess that he was gay. "But I can serve you Taylor's thirty-year tawny. It's wonderful."

As he moved on to the larger table, they watched him flawlessly schmooze the crowd. He offered his extensive knowledge of wines, champagnes, ports and cigars, along with a funny line here and there to loosen up his patrons. Casting an admiring glance in his direction, Dakota said, "You gotta love his style. He really knows how to work a room."

"He's definitely on top of his game," Morgan agreed, observing Blake as he disappeared into the smoked-glass door of the vault-sized humidor. After returning with an assortment of pricey cigars, Blake made sure that everyone ordered mass quantities of expensive after-dinner favors. "I'll bet," Morgan said, giggling, "Blake has depleted Seth's expense account by at least a grand."

Dakota bit her lip as she casually watched him. "I wish straight men were that personable, stylish and attentive."

"The problem is that you usually have to neuter them to get that effect." They broke up laughing.

"Between our Rolodexes I thought we could reach out and touch anybody worth knowing," Morgan said, enjoying the buzz from the alcohol and Blake's one-man show. "I'm surprised we haven't met him before."

"So am I. He definitely seems like someone we would know," Dakota said.

After the last sip of port, as Morgan and Dakota were saying their good-byes to the group, Blake asked for their business cards. "Sure," Morgan said, handing one over. She didn't expect to hear from him since promising "to call and get together soon" was an art form in New York.

"Well, Blake, thanks for a wonderful evening," Dakota said, starting toward the door.

"It was my pleasure. Sorry I couldn't accommodate all of your needs." He winked at Dakota with a devilish smile.

"At this point, I am feeling no pain," Dakota said.

"That makes two of us. In fact, if we couldn't find a taxi tonight, I could just about fly home," Morgan said.

"You ladies don't have to worry about a taxi. I've already called a car for you." Leaning closer to whisper, he added, "I put it on Seth's tab."

"And they say that service is a lost art form," Dakota said, smiling at Morgan.

"You know what? I love that man," Morgan said as Blake walked in front of them to open the door to the arriving black Town Car.

2

The following morning Morgan opened her eyes and immediately recalled the anticlimactic ending to the previous night. Miles was already up and moving about, starting his day.

"Good morning," she said, offering an olive branch.

"Morning," was all he tossed back.

She could tell from the abruptness of his movements and the terseness in his voice that he was serving her the blue-ball special for breakfast. If it were up to Miles, they would have sex every night, and since he didn't know what a quickie was, sex was always a full-court press. Morgan loved sex as much as the next red-blooded female, but if she missed a night or two, it wasn't the end of the world as we know it.

Still, she'd conked out on him last night. She remembered most of it. She'd floated past her doorman with a nod and a smile and breezed through the stately burl-wood lobby toward the set of brass elevators. Exiting at the twenty-fifth floor, she found the swift increase in altitude had heightened the cumulative effects of the alcohol. After willing the doorknob still, she finally managed to insert her key to open the door.

Morgan teetered lightly on her Gucci pumps, and her heels clicked along the marble of the elegant foyer as she passed underneath the dramatic crystal chandelier that hung like a celestial arrangement from the thirteen-foot-high ceiling. The polished hardwood floor led to the den with its wall of cathedral windows that beautifully framed a breathtaking view of the

East River. Holding the wrought iron railing, Morgan delicately climbed the stairs to the second level.

At the top, she first removed one shoe, then the other. By the time she navigated her way past the library and media room and into the master suite, buttons had been unbuttoned and zippers unzipped. Still giddy, she turned on the small Tiffany lamp on her dressing table and began slowly removing her clothes. Eventually, clad only in black lace underwear, she faced the three-quarter-length mirror. She began removing her bra with the smooth dexterity of one of Scores' hot, sexy strippers, while swaying slowly and seductively to the buzz in her head.

"A striptease might make up for coming home to an empty house."

Startled, Morgan spun around, defensively covering her exposed breasts with tightly crossed arms, only to see Miles propped up in bed like a king on his throne, with his arms folded comfortably behind his head.

"Oh, my God! What are you doing here? You scared the hell out of me," she panted, trying to catch her breath.

"The last time I checked, I still lived here," Miles answered, enjoying Morgan's surprise.

Recovering, Morgan walked over and gave him a kiss on his full lips. "I thought you were leaving for L.A. tonight."

"I took your advice. I delegated the negotiations so I could race home to be with my beautiful wife—only she wasn't here," Miles explained, disappointment underlying his amicable tone.

"I'm sorry, baby. After dinner Dakota and I went to the Back Room with some of her Wall Street friends. But of course, had I known you'd be here, I would've started this show hours ago," she purred, all the while suggestively removing her scant panties.

"It's never too late," Miles said, gently pulling her close.

She remembered climbing under the goose-down comforter. She remembered snuggling up to Miles until her breasts tightly hugged his chest. She had wrapped her legs firmly around his body, strategically placing his thigh in a most desirable spot. Then the bed had seemed to do a slow spin. . . . She'd passed out.

"How was your big meeting yesterday?" she tried now, sitting up in bed.

"Fine," he answered without once looking in her direction.

"Do you think you'll sign the group?"

"Maybe." Still not even a glance.

"Are they interested?"

"Dunno."

"What is this, how-many-one-word-answers-can-I-give?" Morgan asked, exasperated.

"No. It's why-did-I-rush-home-to-be-with-my-absentee-wife."

"Ohhh, my baby's mad," Morgan said, faking a pout. Getting out of bed, she walked over to Miles as he stood before the mirror. He was terrible at making Windsor knots.

"I'm not a baby," he said, tugging at the two ends of his tie.

"This is good. That was four words," she teased. Coming around in front of him, she tied a perfect knot on the first try. "I do laces too." This time the pout was pleading. "I'm sorry I got you all riled up last night and then fell asleep."

"How about passed out?" Miles said.

"I know. I'm sorry," she said, looking up at him with her own puppy-dog eyes.

"You're lucky I have on buckle-ups; otherwise you'd be on your knees."

"For you, baby . . . anything," she answered, turning to gather the trail of evidence from the night before.

"Don't start nothin' you can't finish," Miles said, watching Morgan bend over naked to pick up the strewn clothing.

Looking back over her shoulder, Morgan said, "Don't worry about that. When you get home tonight, you'll be yelling uncle." Giving Miles a deep kiss and a quick feel, she paraded into the master bath to prepare for work.

Morgan had joined Global Financial, a multibillion-dollar charge card and financial services company three years earlier.

At thirty-two, though Morgan was vice president of Marketing and one of only a handful of black executives above the position of Director in the whole company, it had been an uphill battle fought through a jungle of nepotism and politics. The company seemed to breed a culture teeming with overeducated, underexperienced know-it-alls. The only difference between them and the nerds she'd known in graduate school was that here they carried hundred-dollar Mont Blancs in place of fifty-cent pocket protectors.

Morgan's boss, Joel Durment, wore his Mont Blanc tucked firmly into his Brooks Brothers jacket pocket. He popped into her office first thing, before she'd had her first mandatory cup of coffee. Knowing that Joel rarely brought good tidings her way, she braced for one of his digs.

"Morgan, how's the report coming?" he asked abruptly. Joel was short, with wavy dark hair and thick eyebrows that met in the middle. He was the latest Golden Boy in the Corporate Division. He could do *no* wrong.

Maybe this was an innocent conversation after all, she thought. "Oh, hi, Joel. It's coming along fine. I'm waiting for the latest numbers from Finance to strengthen my projections."

Morgan had decided to create a market projection based on factual statistics massaged with market assumptions, rather than to pull numbers from thin air, as was often the case in marketing. She believed in going the extra mile, a trait passed on to her by her father. He had risen through the ranks at Coca-Cola to become a regional vice president of Operations. Morgan and her father had been very close. On the one hand, he was the doting father of a beautiful daughter, while on the other, he challenged her the way a father would the son he was grooming as his heir. When he died the year before she met Miles, he left a void in her life that in many ways could never by filled. He had always said, "Work hard and do the right thing and you'll be successful." So with her eye on the senior v.p. prize, she would leave no stone unturned.

"Who did you go to?" Joel asked.

"Bill Watson. He's having his top analyst crunch the numbers for me."

"You spoke with Bill Watson?" Joel asked, his one long brow beginning to furrow. So much for an innocent conversation.

"Yes. Why?" Morgan asked, puzzled.

"Bill is a senior vice president," Joel answered, as though that explained everything.

And what am I—minced meat? she thought. Taking a calming breath, she said instead, "I know, but there was no one else to go to, since Tonya is out and the report is due Friday."

"Morgan, I thought I'd made myself clear before," he said, frowning. "It's not appropriate for you to make requests to executives who are senior to you. Instead, you come to me and I'll see that you get what you need. That way I'm in the loop on everything, and it keeps you from looking uninformed if I already have the information."

Politics as usual, Morgan thought. Since the financial model was based on her own set of assumptions, there was no way Joel would already have the numbers. The truth was, he wanted to be able to take full credit for anything that was successful, and the less other executives knew about his department, the easier it was for him to pull it off.

Morgan shook her head and took a deep breath as he left her office. Whereas some people thrived on office politics, it was the one part of her job that she hated. People like Joel were so busy schmoozing each other and sucking up to jockey for position that customers and competitors often came in second or third. After he left, Morgan snatched up the phone on the fourth ring. Her secretary, Aimee, was yet again missing in action. She was greeted by a vaguely familiar male voice. "Hi, gorgeous."

"I didn't catch your name," she said, annoyed.

"It's Blake St. James. We met last night," he answered, sounding a little hurt that she hadn't instantly recalled him. Listening to the smooth, cultured voice, she quickly recalled the tall, handsome guy she and Dakota had met at the Back Room.

"Oh, hi, how are you?" Morgan replied. "Say, is that the *Brandenburg Concerto No. 2* in the background?" The soothing music of Bach and Blake's melodic voice sounded worlds away from her hectic work environment.

"Yes, it is. It's one of my favorite pieces. And I'm fine, just a little overworked at the moment. But more importantly, how are you?"

"Okay. Just another day in corporate America," she replied dryly, as she glanced at the thirty-page presentation before her.

"My parents tried every bait in the tackle box to lure me into corporate America. Even force-fed me an Ivy League education. But I've always been interested in the hospitality industry," Blake said almost apologetically.

"It has to be more interesting than a spending analysis of middle-aged men," Morgan offered.

"Believe me, it is. In fact, I'm planning a dinner party next week at the Plaza for the Russian Consulate. I'm having five different types of caviar flown in from Russia. It should be fabulous!" he said. "I love the thrill of planning the perfect event."

After witnessing his finesse firsthand, Morgan had few doubts he was capable of doing just that. The excitement in his voice made Morgan long for the creative fulfillment she'd found in her previous job, working for the Olympic Committee. But instead, now she felt chained to a corporate slave master. No matter how progressive and cosmopolitan blacks in corporate America imagined themselves, at the end of the day they were only "house niggers." Only these days the Big House was a massive skyscraper made of concrete and steel rather than of white planks and columns.

"Morgan . . . Morgan." Blake must have said something she missed in her distracted state. "You must be busy. Listen, why don't you and Dakota stop by the Back Room next week for a drink on me? We can chat then."

"Sure, why not?" Morgan said. Blake was charming and certainly seemed harmless enough. Besides, she thought, Miles would be in London next week.

3

The high-tech trading floor of Swiss Bank International's Wall Street headquarters was like Grand Central Station during the morning rush hour. The decibel level approached the sound barrier. Flat-screen televisions were tuned to *Market Watch* on CNBC; phones rang back to back; traders sat elbow to elbow, yelling out orders and executions. Dakota reigned over the three-monitor command center on her desk. One was linked to the New York Stock Exchange to track listed stocks, one traded over-the-counter stocks and the third was a designated-order turnaround computer, used to send small listed trades directly to the floor of the Exchange.

"Trading, Dakota speaking," she said, snatching up the phone.

"Juerg here. I have a thousand shares of Microsoft to go at the market, and I need the execution ASAP. I have an impatient client on the other line."

"No problem, Juerg. Hold on a second. I'll get you a price," Dakota said before pressing the hold button. "Todd," she yelled across the room to the over-the-counter trader. "I need to sell a thousand shares of Microsoft at the market."

"I'll hit the bid," Todd quickly yelled back.

Dakota took her client off hold and said, "Juerg, you sold them at sixty."

"That's good," Juerg said before hanging up.

Dakota thought to herself, *Damn right it's good, consider-*

ing the stock is already down two points. She then yelled across the room, "Todd, I'll bring you the ticket in a few." All around her, traders were conducting transactions at a fast and furious pace.

"Sell short a thousand shares of YHOO."

"Buy five thousand shares of PFE at the market."

"Buy thirty thousand shares of AMAT, spread it over the day."

"Put a half top on the balance of PFE."

This went on all morning, nonstop, and into the early afternoon. After things finally simmered down, Dakota walked over to the OTC area, which was made up of two rows of desks held down by resident-white-boy traders.

"Looking good, Dakota. Tell me, how do you do it every day?" Mike, the one in charge, flashed her a look that seemed anything but collegial.

"It's a no-brainer for women, Mike. Comes natural," Dakota said casually as she handed the trade ticket over to Todd for his records.

"Where do you want it?" Dakota asked, referring to the ticket.

"Right here, baby," Todd said, licking his lips and suggestively patting his lap. He looked around, grinning, trying to impress his cohorts.

Patting her crotch and looking him directly in the eye, Dakota asked, "You want it now, or at the close?"

Her sultry voice set them all laughing. "You tell 'em, D," said Mike.

"You know I was just kidding," Todd mumbled, trying to recover.

"Yeah, right," Dakota teased back, throwing him a sexy smile.

Paul stood up and yelled, "Dakota, line one."

When she reached her desk, she picked up her handset. "Trading, Dakota here."

"Dakota, this is Armin." She smiled. He was her favorite Swiss client. "I want to buy twenty-five hundred shares of Amazon, put a three-quarter top on it."

"You got it, Armin. I'll call you back with the execution," Dakota said, hanging up to call her broker at Mayer, since the OTC desk didn't trade this stock.

"Richie, Dakota here. I need to buy twenty-five hundred shares of Amazon with a three-quarter top."

"Hey, D, hold on." After a few seconds Richie came back on the line. "D, you own 'em at thirteen and a half. Thanks for the order."

Dakota called Armin back and reported his execution. "Armin, you bought them at thirteen and a half."

"Thanks."

"No problem, Armin," Dakota said, as she wrapped up the paperwork on the trade. "So tell me, when are you coming to the Big Apple for a visit?"

Armin was very conservative by nature, so coming to New York for him was like a taste of Hedonism. "I'm going to try to make it there in the next few months."

"Well, store up your sleep, 'cause when you get here, we're gonna hit the ground running, and trust me, there'll be no rest stops along the way." Dakota's Swiss clients loved coming to New York and she loved to have them. She wined and dined them all the way to the bank.

"I'll keep you abreast of my plans. Talk to you later," Armin said before hanging up.

Hans, Dakota's boss, approached her desk. With a striking build and rugged good looks, Hans looked more like a ski instructor than the managing director of a brokerage firm. "Good job, Dakota. I notice your lines are jumping off the hook."

"Thanks. It's hectic, but I've got it covered," Dakota said confidently.

That kind of confidence had made her his star sales trader. Hans smiled. "That's what I like to hear."

"Time for another jolt of caffeine," Dakota said, to deflect the praise. "Would you like a cup?"

"Actually, I could use another. Cream, no sugar. You know."

Dakota headed down the gray-carpeted corridor toward the office pantry. When she reached the doorway, she was stopped in her tracks by the sight of Jackson Evans at the coffee machine. Jackson Evans, her supposed lover.

"I thought you were in Houston," Dakota said, standing in the doorway.

He simply answered, "I was." The only minority on the research sales team, Jackson was medium height, with smooth espresso-toned skin, thick black wavy hair and a muscular build. He and Dakota had been dating for the past three months.

"When did you get back?" she asked, walking into the pantry.

"Last night. Excuse me." Jackson reached around her for a packet of Equal.

"You're excused," Dakota said, stepping aside. She then put her hand on her hip and asked, "Why didn't you call?" She wished she could've swallowed those words as soon as they escaped her lips. The last image she wanted to convey was that of the victimized, neglected girlfriend.

He tore the blue packet of Equal and dumped it into his Knicks coffee mug, then simply said, "It was late."

"That never stopped you before." Dakota distinctly remembered one late night when Jackson had called her from the car and then come by directly from the airport. They'd stayed up half the night making passionate love. That sort of thing tended to stick in her mind. But now here he was standing before her with a tired three-word excuse: It was late. Who was he kidding?

"Look, I have to get back to my desk. We'll talk later," Jackson said, making a hasty departure.

Dakota rolled her eyes in frustration and said, "Whatever."

She had walked back to her desk when Paul yelled, "Dakota, line two."

"Trading," answered Dakota.

"Hey, girl." It was Morgan.

"Hey," Dakota said sourly.

"What's wrong?" Morgan asked, picking up on Dakota's hollow tone.

"Girl, I just ran into Jackson, and the Negro brushed me off."

"What do you mean?"

Dakota recalled the episode. "He practically ran out of the pantry."

"Maybe he's really busy," Morgan said, trying to comfort her.

"Whatever. Anyway, enough of him. Have you recovered from last night?" Dakota asked. Her voice cracked a bit as she still thought of Jackson's brush-off.

"Barely. Speaking of last night, remember Blake, that tall guy? He called and invited us to stop by the Back Room for a drink next week."

Dakota liked what she saw of Blake. He was witty, cool and seemed like he'd be fun to hang out with. "Bet."

"Well, I'll set it up. What are you doing tonight?" Morgan asked.

"The company party is tonight."

"Have fun and don't let Jackson get under your skin," Morgan counseled. "Gotta run. Call me later."

The party wasn't until seven, so Dakota went to the hair salon to have her close-cropped hair styled. Afterward, she had just enough time to run home and change into black slacks and a black cashmere turtleneck. When she arrived, a fashionable thirty minutes late, everyone was warming up, on his or her way to being toasted.

Traditionally, SBI threw an extravagant private party at one of New York's hot spots the week bonuses were announced. Since this had been a banner year, the party was being held at Balthazar, an ultrahip bistro in SoHo. The decor was turn-of-the-century French with high ceilings and gilded beveled mirrors adorning ocher-colored walls. Like living, breathing art, the patrons added just as much atmosphere to the trendy spot as the decor—models in the latest catwalk getup, guys in the latest cut of trouser and everybody sporting the hippest accessories from Prada.

"Dakota," called Shelby, the executive assistant to the director of the trading floor. Shelby also coordinated the company parties. "Where's your drink?"

"I just got here," Dakota answered, scanning the room.

"Well, in that case, have a dirty martini," Shelby said, stopping one of the waiters to get Dakota a drink from his tray. "It's the house drink tonight. By the way, I love the cut of that turtleneck," Shelby said, admiring Dakota's style.

"Thanks. From the look of this crowd it seems you pulled off another great party," Dakota said, taking in the scene.

"You have no idea how much work it is," Shelby said, rolling her eyes and tossing her hair.

"I'm sure—" Before Dakota could finish her thought, Jackson approached the two of them.

"Good evening, ladies," he said.

"Hi, Jackson," Shelby said, looking him up and down the way she had a habit of doing to any handsome, eligible guy. Eligibility for her meant breathing and with bank. "Are you having a good time?"

Looking at Dakota, he said, "As a matter of fact, I am."

"Excuse me, guys. I see my boss trying to get my attention," Shelby said, before moving off into the crowd.

"Sorry I didn't call last night, but I was beat," Jackson said, rubbing the back of his neck to emphasize his claim. He looked at her more closely. "Did you do something different with your hair?"

"It's the same style, Jackson. I guess you haven't seen me in a while," she said.

"I was only gone a week."

"And you haven't called in all that time, which is just long enough for my sheets to cool down."

Dismissing her remark, Jackson said, "Look, Dakota, we need to talk."

"You said that earlier. Let's talk after we warm up those sheets," Dakota said, determined not to be sidetracked.

"I'm serious, Dakota." Jackson's usually warm eyes were calm and cool. That meant he was about to say something that she probably didn't want to hear.

"Look, if you don't want to keep them warm, maybe someone else will."

"Don't get bent out of shape," Jackson said, trying to soften his tone. "All I'm saying is we need to discuss a few things."

"Whatever, Jackson. I'm going to mingle now," Dakota said, and marched off. Let him suffer for a while. That might change his tune.

Yet she couldn't keep her mind off him. With that distraction, plus the roller coaster the Dow was riding, she was in no mood to discuss the market or office politics. So she walked through the crowd careful not to get trapped in any heavy conversations. By the time she grabbed her second martini, Dakota was starting to forget about Jackson. With all of his soon-to-be ex-wife and children problems, he was becoming too high maintenance.

As she sipped her drink, she could see Shelby working the crowd. Guys melted in her presence. Tall and voluptuous, Shelby Hanna resembled a fashion model, strutting through the room as if on a runway. She had a small waist, shapely legs that she showcased wearing Ally McBeal–type microminiskirts, and no matter the weather she always wore tight little sweaters to accentuate full, round breasts. As she walked past Mike from the over-the-counter desk, Dakota watched her purposely brush her butt against his thigh. She and Mike had had a torrid affair for months, but it ended abruptly when his wife found nude pictures of Shelby in his briefcase. Her modus operandi to lure her prey, according to the rumor mill, was giving pictures of herself in the buff.

Shelby sauntered Dakota's way.

"Don't hurt 'em, Hammer," Dakota teased.

"What do you mean?" Shelby asked, flipping her long strawberry-blond hair.

Dakota motioned toward the huddle of men Shelby had just sashayed past, who were still gawking in her wake.

"Oh, them. What can I say?" Shelby said, blinking her green eyes. "When you got it, flaunt it."

Dakota didn't want Shelby to get going on her favorite subject—Shelby—so she asked, "Is your bonus already spent?"

"I'm going to take my mom to Paris for a mini shopping excursion."

Dakota smiled at the memory of her last trip there six months ago. She had stopped over on the way to Geneva and had a fabulous time shopping and flirting with Frenchmen. "I just love Paris."

"Oh, you've been there?" Shelby asked, surprised.

"How many times, you mean," Dakota said flippantly. "I've gone at least once a year for the last five."

Shelby was impressed. "This'll be my first. Maybe you can tell me the best places to go."

For Dakota, shopping in Paris was like being a kid loose in FAO Schwarz on Christmas Eve. She loved the signature shops along the Champs-Élysées and the trendier stores in Le Marais. And there was no place like Les Halles for great vintage pieces. "Check out the boutiques on Avenue Montaigne as well as the shops on Saint-Germain-des-Prés. You'll find some great stuff."

"Thanks for the tip," Shelby said, looking amazed at Dakota's apparent knowledge of Paris. Coughing, she then asked, "Do you have plans for your bonus?"

Dakota flashed her first real smile of the conversation. "I'm having new gutters put on my grandmother's house."

This took Shelby completely by surprise. She had probably expected Dakota to tell her about a planned shopping excursion. "How generous."

"That's the least I can do," Dakota said.

Shelby looked confused. "What do you mean by that?"

When she was ten, Dakota's parents had been killed tragically in an automobile accident on the Dan Ryan Expressway.

Her grandmother had stepped in and become both mother and father. She made sure Dakota had a relatively normal childhood, involving her in everything from Girl Scouts and ballet class on Saturday to the Junior Usher Board on Sunday. Nana, as Dakota called her, had even worked double shifts as a nurse's aide to allow Dakota to live off campus in her senior year of college. So when Dakota said, "That's the least I can do," she meant it wholeheartedly. As far as she was concerned there was nothing too good for her nana. Not wanting to get into her childhood, Dakota merely said, "It's a long story."

Dakota took another sip from her drink and continued to scan the crowd. She caught sight of an unfamiliar face across the room. He was handsome, a dead ringer for Oscar de la Hoya, but taller. He was dressed in a fitted black turtleneck, emphasizing well-defined pecs, with black slacks and the baddest pair of tortoiseshell glasses. Dakota was immediately attracted to him.

"Shelby, who is the de la Hoya look-alike?" Dakota asked, scoping out the stranger.

"Where?" Shelby answered, although she knew exactly who Dakota had between her crosshairs.

"Over near the bar, in the glasses," Dakota answered, subtly cocking her head in his direction.

Shelby didn't look happy that Dakota had discovered him. "That's the new trader on the London desk. He just started a couple of days ago."

"Damn, is he fine or what?" Dakota asked.

"Yeah," said Shelby, "but he's so full of himself. I've seen him in the elevator a few times, and he hasn't spoken once." She shrugged, but Dakota could tell that she was mad about it.

"You're just used to guys falling all over you. Obviously he's immune," Dakota said.

"Nah, that's not it," Shelby replied, her ego firmly intact. "He must already have a girlfriend, or maybe he's gay."

"Maybe. You know what? I think it's time for another drink," Dakota said as an excuse to check him out at close range.

"I think I need a refill too," Shelby said, stalking the same prey.

They approached the bar where the handsome stranger stood. Before Dakota could introduce herself, Shelby turned to him, batting her eyes. "You're the new guy on the London desk, aren't you?"

"Yes, that's me," he said, seemingly unaffected. As he looked at Dakota, she saw he really was Latin—at least partly.

Forcing conversation, Shelby asked, "Where did you work before joining SBI?"

"Citigroup," he said, looking from Dakota back to Shelby.

Shelby casually put her hand on his arm and said, "I love those glasses."

The direct approach didn't work either. He just stood there until, embarrassed by his lack of response, Shelby pulled her hand away.

"Excuse me, ladies. There's someone I need to talk to," he said, as he began to walk off, headed toward a group of women who all immediately gave him their undivided attention.

"Didn't I tell you he was conceited?" Shelby said, angry.

Dakota thought, "Isn't that the pot calling the kettle black." Shelby was the most conceited person she had ever met.

"He's probably not used to being approached by two beautiful women," Dakota said. "Anyway, I'll make it a point to get his full attention at the Monday-morning briefing."

"Unless I beat you to the punch," Shelby said.

"Is that a challenge?" Dakota asked, fully aware it was.

"Call it what you want," Shelby said lightly. "You know, I think I'll go home and dust off the old camera. I'm sure it won't be long before my next photo session."

"I wouldn't buy stock in Kodak just yet if I were you," Dakota said, putting her drink on the bar and walking away.

Shelby flipped her hair and said under her breath, "We'll see about that, missy."

4

Morgan and Dakota arrived at the Back Room around six-thirty the following Monday. Considering it was before eight o'clock, the place was relatively quiet, with the exception of a few Madison Avenue–exec types sitting in wing-back chairs drinking martinis and smoking stogies.

"Oh, you came. I'm so glad." Blake greeted them with exaggerated air kisses on both cheeks before showing them to an intimate table in the back.

"I have to tend the bar until my bartender gets here. He called saying that he was running late. It's so hard to find good help these days. But I'll send over a bottle of champagne right away. You ladies look parched," Blake said, turning sharply on his Italian heels in the direction of the bar.

Morgan and Dakota exchanged smiles over his excessive and dramatic behavior. "So," Morgan said, "finish telling me about Jackson. Sorry I couldn't talk last night, but Miles was giving me that get-off-the-phone look."

Rolling her eyes in exasperation, Dakota said, "You won't believe this shit. He called after the office party the other night, totally drunk. He said he and his wife were getting back together."

Morgan was as upset as her friend. "You've got to be kidding. I thought they were separated."

Looking down at her hands, Dakota said, "They were. When Jackson and I started going out, he said they had been separated for eight months and were in the process of filing for a divorce."

"How did filing for divorce turn into a reconciliation?" Morgan asked.

Dakota took a deep breath and exhaled with a sigh. "He said a few weeks ago he went over to pick his kids up for the weekend, and his wife started talking about giving it another try."

"I thought she was the one who wanted the divorce."

"She was. He said she felt underappreciated, because he worked too much and was never home. I guess girlfriend realized that working ten to twelve hours a day afforded her the house in Westchester and the Rover in the driveway. And I guess he finally realized that it's just plain ole cheaper to keep her."

"I'm so sorry, girl. Are you okay?" Morgan asked, reaching over and touching her friend's hand.

Looking up at the ceiling, trying to fight back tears, Dakota said, "I'm just so tired of hooking up with the wrong men." The urge to cry passed. When she continued, she tried to flick it off. "I really wasn't into being the wicked stepmother anyway. Trust me," she said, trying to convince herself, "the next man I get involved with will definitely be single, preferably with no ex-wife or rugrats."

"Jackson wasn't the one, but you'll find the right man," Morgan said, thinking how glad she was to have Miles.

Dakota waved her hands in disgust. "I don't want to talk about him anymore." Suddenly brightening up, she said, "Girl, speaking of men, there's this new guy at work who is all that."

It was just like Dakota, Morgan thought, to quickly switch gears, especially when she felt vulnerable. Growing up without parents would make anybody throw up walls quickly.

"So, what's his name?"

"I don't know his name yet, but he is definitely fly. Sort of looks like Oscar de la Hoya."

Morgan frowned. "Oscar de la Hoya. Isn't he Latin?"

"What's that look for?"

"I didn't know you were planning on crossing over." Morgan shrugged. "I'm just a little surprised, that's all."

Squinting her eyes thoughtfully, Dakota searched for words. "It wasn't a conscious decision. It's strange . . . I was at the company party, looking out over the crowd, and saw him. Something about him attracted me immediately. Maybe it was the outfit."

"What did he have on?" Morgan asked.

"Your basic black. We were practically dressed alike."

"What's so special about that? Ninety-nine-point-nine percent of New Yorkers wear black," Morgan said, clearly unimpressed.

Determined to make Morgan understand, she said, "It was the way he wore it. Boyfriend had the body of life. You should have seen him. He was standing at the bar just as cool as a summer breeze."

Morgan was skeptical. "This sounds like a rebound reaction. Are you sure you want to get involved with someone so soon after Jackson? Especially someone you work with again? You should probably give yourself a time-out before jumping back into the game."

Dakota only smiled, thinking about the new fly guy. "You know what I say about the game: you gotta be in it to win it."

"I thought that applied to the lottery, not dating," Morgan said, cutting her eyes at Dakota.

Dakota said, with the sly grin Morgan knew so well, "In my opinion they are both games of chance. You win some, you lose some."

Morgan laughed. "Touché," she said, clicking Dakota's glass.

Just then Blake walked up. "So what are we toasting?"

"Men," Dakota said.

"My favorite subject. I'll drink to that," Blake said, taking the extra glass from the table and pouring himself a sip of Moët.

"Blake, how long have you been working here?" Morgan asked. "Dakota and I were just saying the other night that it's odd we've never run into you before."

"Only a short while. I returned from France not too long ago."

Dakota's interest was piqued. "Business or pleasure?"

"A little of both. I was honing my wine-tasting skills in Bordeaux," he said matter-of-factly.

"Sounds like a tough job," Morgan said.

"But somebody's got to do it," Blake added, with a laugh. "Morgan, I saw from your card that you work for Global. How long have you been there?"

"It seems like a lifetime," Morgan said dryly.

"Do I detect a little dissension in the corporate ranks?" Blake asked.

Determined not to think about Joel or Global, Morgan simply smiled. "Just your basic complaints about life in the big house."

Blake deftly switched over to Dakota. "So, how long have you been running with the bulls?"

"About five years."

"Do you like it? Isn't it hectic?"

Dakota had been asked the question before, but never by someone so charming. "It's fast-paced, but that's what I love about it. Things change from second to second. Like the other day, I bought stock for a client. Called back two minutes later, gave him the execution and wouldn't you know the stock was up twenty points," Dakota said, running her hand through her hair and shaking her head. "The energy on the trading floor is definitely electric. Sometimes I feel like the Energizer Bunny—I keep going and going and going." She laughed.

"I know what you mean. It's like that around here on the weekends when we get the bridge-and-tunnel crowd." Blake was referring to the hordes who came into Manhattan from the other boroughs and New Jersey via the bridges and tunnels.

Blake noticed a waitress walking by with a tray of martinis, and stopped her dead in her tracks. "Don't you dare serve those drinks that way. *Martinis are best served cold,*" he said dramatically, "and I can tell from the lack of condensation on those glasses that they are chilled at best." He quickly confirmed his suspicion by wrapping his long, lean fingers elegantly around one of the Y-shaped martini glasses. He then shooed the embarrassed waitress back to the bar.

After Tony, the owner of the Back Room, arrived, they settled the bill, which Blake insisted they put on his tab, and left. Strolling down Columbus Avenue, they stopped in several places along the way. In each one Blake knew the head honcho. The "King of the Upper West Side," as he described himself airily, was clearly in his glory. Tonight he was wearing a black Nehru Prada jacket with matching pipe-leg slacks. He took pleasure in the admiring stares the stylish trio drew from passersby. He prided himself on dressing in the best money could buy. As they passed Salt, he suggested they go in and have a drink.

Salt was one of the better restaurant bars on Columbus, with cozy art deco chairs and small tables near the window for those who wanted to sit and people-watch.

"Let's sit here, by the window," Blake said.

Before they could settle in, a short, stout man approached them. "Blake, good to see you," he said, giving Blake a bear hug around the waist. "And who are these lovely ladies?"

"Sam, this is Dakota Cantrell and Morgan Nelson."

"My pleasure," he said, extending his hand.

"Sam is the owner and chef," Blake explained.

"What are you guys drinking?"

"We started off with Moët, so we might as well continue with the bubbly," Blake said.

"Anything for you, Blake. And nice to meet you, ladies, but I need to get back to the kitchen."

"Nice to meet you too," Morgan and Dakota said in unison.

They looked over at Blake in question, and he said, "I gave a party for Mount Sinai's medical staff here a month ago."

"Do you give many parties?" Morgan asked.

Blake sounded slightly bored. "I grew up in an environment where my parents were always hosting one event after another." A smile touched his lips as he remembered something. "One time, to liven things up, I dressed in full drag and crashed one of their parties at the house in London."

Dakota glanced over at Morgan in disbelief. Morgan looked just as shocked.

"What did they do?" Morgan asked.

"Oh, by then they were accustomed to my antics. They found the whole episode entertaining. In fact, they treated me like any other guest, introducing me as Belinda."

"Okay, Belinda," Dakota said, laughing.

Joining Dakota in laugher, Morgan said, "That is so over the top. I bet you have a million stories."

"A million and one, at least," he said, winking.

They chatted and drank champagne until Dakota finally looked at her watch. Seeing what time it was, she said, "I better call it a night, guys."

"Me too," Morgan said. "You want to share a taxi, Dakota?"

"I'll call a car for you two," Blake said, taking out his cell and dialing. After a few seconds of conversation, Blake covered the phone and said, "The wait will be an hour. Is that too long?"

"Don't worry about it, Blake. We'll just grab a taxi," Morgan answered.

"Well, the least I can do is hail it for you," Blake said. He popped to his feet and walked out the door.

Seeing Blake heading for the street, Dakota said, "Tonight was fun."

"After being around stuffed shirts all day, Blake is a breath of fresh air," Morgan said, leaning back into her chair. "He's a traveling one-man show."

"Yeah, he's quite colorful. Too bad I can't find someone like him, only straight, to replace Jackson."

Blake appeared again. "Ladies, your chariot awaits," he said, motioning outside to the yellow taxi.

"Thanks for an entertaining evening," Morgan said.

Dakota agreed. "It was a blast."

"That is was," he purred. "Let's do it again, soon."

5

"Was that okay or should I start over?" Morgan teased, savoring the afterglow of good hot sex. Especially on a Saturday morning, buried deep under the covers.

"Uncle . . . uncle," Miles panted, still glistening from their torrid love session. Miles's dark skin glowed as he lay with both arms limp at his side. His bare chest still rose and fell rapidly from the quickened beat of his heart.

"I know what. Let's stay naked all day, order food in, and only leave the bed to mix mimosas. We can watch old black-and-white movies on DVD and snoodle." The more Morgan added to her scenario, the better it sounded.

"We might do that. But how about an abbreviated version?" Miles asked, propping himself up on one elbow.

"How abbreviated?" Morgan wrinkled her brow. She envisioned her scenario being edited, with critical scenes left on the cutting-room floor.

"How 'bout we start with the weekend ritual: the *Times* in bed and cinnamon raisin bagels from H&H. But for act two, we head up to Harlem and take a look at a brownstone that's just come on the market. Robert called yesterday; it's supposed to be a great deal."

"But it's a perfect day to spend in bed," Morgan said, pulling the covers over her head in silent protest.

"Hey, we are going to Barbados at the end of the month, remember? There we'll have a complete week of total relaxation.

And I promise we can spend as much time in bed as you want. In fact, you'll be the one crying uncle."

Morgan relented, resurfacing from under the comforter. "All right. So, tell me about the building." She knew how excited Miles was about buying a brownstone.

Jumping out of bed with newfound energy, Miles ran to the library and returned with several sheets of paper. "Better than that, I'll show you. Robert faxed over the profile," he said, excitedly spreading out the document. "It's a four-family brownstone on Convent Avenue, built around the early 1900s. It has a ground-floor English basement and all of the original details. And best of all it's still a bargain at half a million." Miles was turning the pages and playing show-and-tell like a kid going through a new toy catalogue.

"What about renovations?" Morgan asked, knowing that many of the fabulous old homes in Harlem had fallen into serious disrepair.

The pages stopped turning. "It'll need some work," Miles admitted. "But I figure we can have an architect check it out and give us an estimate of costs. I wouldn't want to put more than a couple hundred thousand in it."

"Do you think we can afford it, plus keep this apartment?" The plan was to buy a brownstone as investment property, but to maintain the East Side apartment for a primary residence.

"Once my promotion is finalized, I'll know more. It may be close. You know how stringent mortgage lenders can be."

"Yeah, but if I get the senior v.p. position, we should be fine," Morgan added, feeling confident that it was in the bag.

Tossing the papers on the nightstand, Miles got back under the covers and held Morgan tight. "Things will work out. They always do." Nestled in his arms, Morgan began thinking about just how well things had already worked out.

Before moving to New York from Atlanta three years ago, Morgan had been the marketing director for the Atlanta Committee for the Olympic Games, which was like night and day compared to her previous jobs with Johnson & Johnson and Xerox. Her department had set the tone, determined the creative direction and devised marketing strategies for the Olympic theme albums.

At that time Miles had been general manager of Culture Club, the hottest boutique label in the record business. They were consistent hit makers, the Motown of the nineties. So it was no surprise they were chosen to produce the Olympic theme R&B album.

From the start Morgan felt her temperature rise whenever she was in his presence. She remembered their first meeting vividly, at the Olympic Committee headquarters in downtown Atlanta. Her assistant had met Miles at the security entrance and, after escorting him to a conference room, had run back to tell Morgan how fine Miles Nelson was.

"Even if he isn't, I'm sure he thinks he is," Morgan said, never looking up from her desk. Having heard so much about the record industry and its throngs of groupies, she was definitely not interested in a record industry executive. Besides, most of the ones she had met were unprofessional and full of themselves. But what she found when she entered the conference room wasn't a street-smart know-it-all. Miles was handsome, intelligent and smooth as satin sheets.

Suddenly she was glad to be wearing her burgundy Thierry Mugler suit. The tailored jacket was cinched at the waist, with a princess-cut bodice, and the skirt contoured to midthigh, dramatically displaying long, sculptured legs that ended in a pair of black Prada pumps.

Miles, sitting with legs crossed, leaning back slightly, watched Morgan intently as she outlined her vision for the album. The man was a hard read. On the one hand, he was the perfect gentleman, saying just the right thing, while on the other, his longing looks told a far different story.

Morgan said, "For the opening ceremonies, I think Iris would be fabulous. Maybe a throaty, hair-raising, inspirational ballad. One that captures triumph, high spirits and deep passion."

"Iris could be right. She's in the studio now. I'll need to check the production and tour schedule for her availability."

Morgan was also considering availability—his.

She asked around and found out that since he'd moved to Atlanta from L.A., Miles had been on every single woman's radar screen. He had been seen around town with one beautiful woman after another, but so far no one serious. Or white, which was too often the case for young, high-profile, successful black men.

During an interdepartmental meeting, to discuss the album's roster, she took a seat on the same side of the conference table. Morgan "innocently" wore a midthigh-length skirt. She was pleased to notice Miles repeatedly crossing and uncrossing his legs. He pretended furtively not to notice the cause of his growing distress. "I suppose he likes what he sees," she thought, smiling wickedly to herself. Either that or his briefs were too tight, which also had nice implications.

After three months of cat and mouse, Miles invited Morgan to Atlanta's music industry event of the year, an invitation-only birthday bash for the president of Culture Club.

She debated with Karen, her cousin, for days over just what to wear. Finally they headed to Neiman Marcus at Lenox Square. In the floor-length mirror of the dressing room, she appraised her tight, slim figure. "As much as I'd love to show him a couple of things," she said, thrusting out her chest with mischief written across her face, "I really should wear something conservative. In my position I can't afford to be seen as some starstruck hoochie."

"Morgan, get real," Karen replied. "He obviously doesn't think that, or he wouldn't have invited you as his date."

"You are probably right," Morgan said, still torn, "but Miles is one of the most eligible bachelors in the city. I certainly don't want to be seen as one of the gazillion man-hungry women starving here in Atlanta, all clawing for crumbs tossed by any available man. So, there's no way I'm going to embarrass myself by coming on to someone like him. I have to consider my image." She turned away from the mirror. "Besides, he probably needs a full-time secretary just to keep up with his social calendar. I don't need that kind of drama. Plus, I wouldn't call it a date since I'm meeting him there. He probably invited me as a professional courtesy. You know how social the entertainment business is."

Karen gave her a shrewd look. "Morgan, if this was a business invitation, don't you think he would have invited your boss instead? And remember this, sweetie: if you like him *at all*, you've gotta come ready. You know those babes will be armed for bear, pulling out the big guns," Karen said, mimicking a 38D bra size.

"No doubt." At the last industry function she attended, Morgan recalled yards of black spandex and tons of silicone.

Eventually she and Karen compromised, and Morgan selected a blouseless Mizrahi tuxedo pantsuit that hinted at her full cleavage. It was a titillating, sophisticated look, which was sexy but didn't say, "Come fuck me."

The party was held on the fiftieth floor of the Four Seasons Hotel. The ballroom had an outdoor wraparound terrace that presented a panoramic display of Atlanta's skyline. At the cocktail party, she mingled while sipping a glass of champagne, deftly moving in and out of various conversations, all the while scanning the crowd for Miles.

Just before dinner he appeared in a tailored charcoal-gray suit, with an oyster-white shirt and steel-gray tie. He looked like a sleek panther on the prowl. Spotting her from across the room, he made his way slowly but deliberately in her direction, warmly greeting his staff and guests along the way.

"Morgan, I'm so glad you could make it," he said, with an appraising smile.

"Thanks for the invitation," Morgan answered, completing her own once-over.

"Would you join me for dinner? My table is this way." Miles motioned toward the center of the regal ballroom.

"I'd love to."

With his hand gently resting at the small of her back, Miles led Morgan across the crowded room. She felt the eyes of a horde of women on her, all taking aim with venomous darts. If looks could kill . . .

"So tell me, what occupies your time when you're not playing hardball in conference rooms?" A smile played suggestively along the corners of Miles's full, sexy mouth.

Without the obstructing veil of business, it was clear to Morgan that Miles was attracted to much more than her marketing plans. "I like all types of games. Intellectual and physical," she replied.

"Judging by what I see, you're obviously a master of both." Now that they were rubbing elbows, with candlelight instead of harsh office lighting, and engaging in conversation instead of negotiation, the pull between them was unmistakable.

"You only live once," Morgan said, momentarily thinking about her father, "and I plan to see and do as much as I can. Which is why I also love to travel."

"Me too. In fact, I just got back from Amsterdam." Miles brightened at the memory. "Whenever I visit a foreign country, it always whets my appetite for more."

Unconsciously licking her lips, Morgan was aware of her own growing appetite—for the intriguing man seated next to her. Though her hormones were saying, "Go for it," her brain was saying, "Be cool . . . easy, girl."

To prolong the magical evening, they headed to Buckhead's Café Intermezzo for a nightcap. Once settled in the dark ambience of the intimate nightspot, Miles raised a glass of Dom Pérignon and said, "Let the games begin." And it was clear he was *not* referring to the Olympics. With his arm draped around the back of her chair, Miles gently caressed Morgan's shoulder. He leaned over and softly kissed her parted lips. Morgan eagerly responded, tasting the champagne that lingered on his.

At the end of their fourth date, they were in the foyer of Morgan's apartment when an innocent good-night kiss erupted into something much more provocative. Morgan had began to pull away to open the door for Miles when he suddenly embraced her tightly, backing her up against the wall. As their lips searched and tongues teased, their breathing became more shallow, their heads much lighter. As they tasted each other hungrily, Miles slowly began rubbing his hardening groin urgently against her, letting her feel his growing hunger. Stirred by the erotic image of being pinned against the wall by Miles, Morgan let go of any remaining reserve. Starved herself, she began seductively grinding against him, lifting one leg to wrap it around his back, getting her fill.

No longer was Morgan concerned about her image, only the demanding girth of Miles's bulge and the increasing damp-ness of her own hot sex. Taking a half step back, she stared through sultry eyes into his, as she seductively unzipped his pants to unleash his throbbing penis.

With his head tilted back, a slow moan escaped his throat. "Ooh, baby."

"Umm, it's nice to meet you too," she whispered into his ear as she continued to stroke the large, pulsing organ.

"I'd like to get to know you better," he said in a low, throaty voice. Slowly Miles began removing her clothing, like a con-noisseur unveiling a much anticipated masterpiece, to uncover full ripe breasts, a flat, taut stomach, and the sculptured curves of her hips.

He savored the sight of her standing naked in four-inch pumps before him. Following his lead, Morgan grabbed the knot of his tie, pulling the remaining length through. Playfully she tugged the two ends, pulling him closer, so she could whis-per in his ear. "You should loosen up a bit," she purred seduc-tively, before darting her tongue inside, causing Miles's body to tense and shudder with the promise of pleasure.

She unbuttoned his shirt before pulling his belt back to release the hook and unfasten his pants, letting them free fall to meet hers on the plush Persian rug.

Walking backward, she led her willing victim by the waist-band of his silk boxers into her lair. Morgan eased across the damask comforter and reached behind her between the head-board and mattress to bring one of her trusty Trojans to the party. Tearing the packet while Miles stood at full attention, Morgan slipped on his shield.

Joining her on the bed, he again kissed her passionately, sucking her tongue, then feeding her his. All the while his hands roamed unfettered over her body, leaving a trail of erotic sensations that converged between her parted legs.

She squirmed in delicious anticipation, her body rising anxiously to meet his probing fingers, which played her clitoris like those of a master pianist. Not wanting the music to ever stop, Morgan clasped her legs together, locking his hand firmly in place. Miles stroked her until she was suddenly overcome by an orgasm so unexpected and deep, she grabbed fistfuls of the soft comforter to brace her return to earth.

While bliss orbited behind the lids of her eyes, Miles rubbed her flowing love juices over the top of her pert nipples and prepared to feast. At first he gently teased her with tongue and teeth, before devouring her mounds of flesh. The aroma of hot sex hung in the air like a seductive vapor. Without releasing his mouthful, Miles arched his back and guided himself like a missile between Morgan's open legs. When she thought the emptiness was full, he fed her more, opening her until she flowered like an award-winning rose. Behind her closed lids was a symphony of spectacular fireworks.

As conscious thoughts began to return, she felt Miles quicken his pace before releasing a torrent with a growl that started low and rumbled in waves. It was a while before they both could speak.

"Do you have a permit for that?" Morgan asked.

"Only during hunting season," Miles said, wiping the sweat from his brow.

"Well, I hope you have an extra round of ammunition," she teased.

"For you, baby, it's an automatic."

"From my position, it's looking like an Uzi."

"What about the bagels?" Morgan murmured, when she felt the familiar stir that lying spoon-style always caused.

"Later, baby," Miles whispered into her ear. As he nibbled the sensitive spot at the back of her neck, she felt the tickle of his morning stubble adding to the pleasurable sensation.

"Then there's the *Times* to read and mimosas to drink," she said halfheartedly before turning to face him to intertwine her legs with his.

"Do I hear an uncle coming on?" Miles challenged.

"Not a chance," Morgan said, before again disappearing under the covers. But this time to do some nibbling of her own.

6

Dakota was dressed to impress. She was wearing a French-blue shirt, sterling silver cuff links, and a navy-blue pin-stripe suit. For added drama, she broke out her Alain Mikli tortoiseshell glasses. After arriving for the Monday morning meeting, she nonchalantly scanned the room for John Doe la Hoya. Just as she picked up her daily stock report, he strolled in, taking a seat at the opposite end of the oval conference table. Right behind him appeared Shelby, wearing a mauve sweater that was so thin, her nipples nearly winked. Her skirt looked like a Band-Aid around her hips. Sashaying past Dakota, she walked directly up to John Doe and asked, "Is this your pen?" holding up a black Mont Blanc. She glanced over at Dakota.

He looked at the pen and said, "No."

Leaning in closer to him, but speaking loud enough for Dakota to hear, she asked, "Are you sure?"

"I'm sure, but thanks for asking," he said with a smile.

Dakota rolled her eyes up toward the ceiling, thinking to herself, *If she gets any closer to him, he'll have to breast-feed.*

Shelby stood there another second, then walked out of the conference room.

The meeting began with analysts from the biotech, semiconductor and pharmaceutical sectors, each making recommendations based on either new and improved products, or positive end-of-quarter earnings.

"I'm Parker Emilio from the London desk," announced John Doe la Hoya. "Do you expect second-quarter earnings for

Merck to be in line with earlier predictions?" he asked the pharmaceutical analyst.

"Yes, we expect the numbers to be right on point."

"So his name is Parker," Dakota thought. "That's different."

When the meeting finally ended, there was still no way to make a personal introduction without appearing Shelbyesque. Passing Dakota in the hallway, Shelby said, "I bet he still didn't introduce himself."

"Not yet, but he will," Dakota said, hiding her disappointment.

"You think so? Maybe we should see who gets the first date with him," Shelby said, and walked on, her hips swaying back and forth.

"Bitch!" Dakota muttered to herself.

On the way back to her desk, she stopped to grab a cup of java. Maybe the caffeine would jolt her creativity. She had to think of a new strategy to meet this mysterious man. Something about his aloofness was making him even more out-of-the-blue desirable to her. Like the old saying about wanting what you can't have. Then he walked into the pantry as she was pouring half-and-half into her coffee.

"Hi, I didn't get a chance to introduce myself earlier. I'm Parker Emilo," he said, extending his hand.

"Dakota Cantrell," she said.

"What desk do you work on?"

Looking into his turquoise eyes, she said, "I'm on the Swiss team."

"Funny, you don't look Swiss," he chuckled.

"I'm not, but I do a mean yodel," she shot back.

"A little Swiss Miss," he replied, looking her up and down.

"Ja, ja," Dakota said in a Swiss accent, at which they both laughed. "Well, nice to meet you, but I need to hop."

There was that killer smile again. This time Dakota noticed he had a dimple on his left cheek. He said, "The pleasure was all mine."

Dakota sat down at her desk and logged on to her computer. It was 9:20, ten minutes to "good and plenty." That was her pet name for the market opening—good stocks, plenty of money. Alan Greenspan, the Federal Reserve chairman, announced that interest rates would hold steady, with a neutral bias, which meant stock prices would not plummet anytime soon. This fueled a buying frenzy. So the morning went by so fast, it was a blur.

The afternoon, as usual, was uneventful for her due to the six-hour time difference between New York and Switzerland, so by one o'clock her phones had quieted down. Dakota read e-mails, full of the usual interoffice mumbo jumbo.

"Hmmm, what have we here?" she asked herself, looking at an e-mail address she didn't recognize. When she opened it, the message simply said, "By the way, nice frames."

She knew immediately whom it was from. She replied, "Thanks."

Dakota was debating if she should send him a message complimenting him on his glasses when her line buzzed.

"Trading, Dakota here."

"Kota—hi, baby. You busy?"

This was a surprise. Dakota suddenly forgot all about Parker. "I'm never too busy for my nana. How you doing?"

"I'm doing," Nana said in the loving, sweet voice that had comforted Dakota throughout a turbulent childhood. She still had a hint of the Southern accent from long before moving to Chicago.

"Did you get the check for your new gutters?"

"Thanks, baby, I got it yesterday, but that's not why I'm calling."

Dakota felt worry flies beginning to flutter in the pit of her stomach. They always came when she thought something was wrong with her grandmother. And Nana rarely called her at work. "What is it, Nana? Are you okay?"

"I'm fine, baby, but there is something I need to talk to you about."

"What is it, Nana? You're scaring me."

With a warm chuckle, she said, "Oh, baby, I didn't mean to give you a fright. It's just that . . . ." Nana paused.

"Nana, will you please just tell me what's going on?" Her grandmother had a way of beating around the bush when she knew that Dakota wouldn't like what she had to say.

"Well, it's Li'l Bit." Li'l Bit, whose real name was Patricia—or Tricia, as she so often corrected everyone—was Dakota's first cousin, Nana's youngest grandchild. Patricia had been born a month premature and only weighed five pounds, two ounces. Tricia's mother, Nana's oldest daughter Sara, nicknamed her Li'l Bit because she was so tiny.

"What about Tricia?" Dakota knew that if Tricia was involved, it had to be bad news. Tricia was full of get-rich-quick schemes. A few years back, she opened a frozen yogurt shop, but overcharged and within four months was out of business. Then she went into partnership with her boyfriend de jour to open an Afrocentric card store. They bought greeting cards, bamboo picture frames and African masks of various sizes—all of which Tricia still owned because they spent all the money on inventory before a commercial space was leased.

"She wants to move in here with me."

"She what!" Dakota nearly screamed. Paul looked over at Dakota, as if to say, "Are you okay?"

"I knew you were gonna hit the roof. That's why I didn't want to tell you."

Now lowering her voice, Dakota asked, "Why does she want to move in with you? Why can't she stay with Aunt Sara?"

"Sara sold her house and is moving to Florida. She said she can't take this cold weather no more."

"Why can't she get an apartment like every other grown person I know?"

"Baby, she trying to save her money, said she wants to open her own beauty parlor."

"That's a bunch of bull," Dakota said, snatching off her glasses in frustration.

"Watch your mouth, Dakota," Nana snapped.

"Sorry, Nana. Anyway, when did she start doing hair?"

"She been going to Pivot Point, up there near Evanston, for

about eight months, said she going to open her own place once she finishes."

"You mean if she finishes." Li'l Bit was also famous for starting her latest "great idea" and never finishing it.

"Why you so hard on her, baby?"

"It's not that I'm hard on her," she said wearily. "I'm just sick and tired of her getting money from you and Aunt Sara to flush out her pipe dreams. She needs to get a real job and stop sucking the life out of this family."

That put Nana's back up again. "I didn't raise you like that, Dakota. She is the only cousin you got. We need to stand by each other in bad times as well as the good. That's what families do."

Dakota rolled her eyes and thought, *God give me patience.* "So what are you saying, Nana, that you're going to let her move in?"

"What choice do I have? She don't have no place else to go."

"Nana, what do you mean, no choice?" Dakota said, finally losing patience. "It's your house."

"You're right, it is my house, and I can open it up to any-body I see fit. I'm a let you go now 'fore you say something I don't wanna hear."

"Nana," Dakota warned, "I'm not finished talking about this."

"But I am, and that's the end of it, Dakota. I'll talk to you later," Nana said, and hung up.

Dakota sat holding the receiver, totally frustrated. Her grandmother was right—it was her house and Dakota had no say. But she knew it was just a matter of time before her no-good cousin stepped out of line. And she would be the first one there waiting to yank her back in.

7

With Bach easing out of the high-tech Bang & Olufsen stereo system, Blake sat at the Queen Anne secretary in his bedroom suite going through pictures from his recent trip to Europe. It had been entertaining, but it felt good to be back home, Blake thought as he sat pasting photographs into his travel diary. He was disturbed by a loud knock at the door.

"Come in," Blake said, still preoccupied.

"What's up, bro?" Justin asked, moving unsteadily over to the ivory chaise and unceremoniously plopping down.

"You're drunk," Blake said, disgusted. Justin smelled like a distillery. Blake could almost see the alcohol seeping out of his toxic pores.

"No shit, Sherlock."

"Before I left for Europe, Father was taking you to rehab. What happened?"

"I jumped off the wagon," Justin said, laughing. Blake simply shook his head. "Rehab was his idea, not mine," Justin explained as he leaned back in the chaise. "Anyway, I can quit anytime I want."

"Famous last words," Blake said. He liked to get his drink and party on as much as anybody, but he did try to maintain some degree of couth, especially around the family.

"You sound just like the old man," Justin said, closing his eyes.

"I would appreciate it if you would not fall asleep on my

chaise. In case you haven't noticed, it is covered in velvet and I don't want it stained by your dribble."

Justin was outraged. "Fuck you, Blake. You uppity—" He stopped short as Mattie, their live-in maid, appeared at the door.

"Blake, your father wants to see you in the living room."

"Tell him I'll be right there, Mattie," Blake said, then turned around to Justin. "Don't be here when I get back. I don't have time for your shit."

Blake walked down the marble hallway, where exquisite paintings with discreet security sensors lined the walls. What did his father want to talk about? he wondered. The living room displayed a panoramic view across Central Park. Among other antiques flown in from Europe, near the window sat an elegant mahogany Steinway piano with solid-gold inlays. Biedermeier chairs were arranged on a Persian rug that faced an overstuffed hunter-green sofa, where his father sat smoking a Partagas cigar.

"I see you dressed for the occasion," Dr. St. James said, referring to Blake's smoking jacket and ascot.

"Like father, like son," Blake said, sitting across from him.

"Not quite," Dr. St. James said, expelling a perfectly formed smoke ring.

"What do you mean by that?"

"When I was your age," his father said, pointing his cigar, "I was well on my way to making my first million, outside of family money. Not carelessly gallivanting around the globe wasting an Ivy League education in dead-end jobs." His tone was patient but nonetheless condescending.

"Father, I assure you, my gallivanting days are over," Blake said solemnly. "I've given a lot of thought to what I want to do with the rest of my life, and I've come up with a business idea that will utilize both my education and social skills."

His father looked over with a raised brow. "What type of business, Blake?"

"I'd rather wait until I have my proposal ready to present to you, so you can see for yourself how serious I am."

His father waved him off. "How many times in the past have I heard that from you? I've stopped counting."

"No, no, this time is different. You'll see," Blake said, desperate to convince his father.

"I just hope it has nothing to do with Tyrone."

Blake stiffened in his seat. "Why would you say that? I haven't even seen him since I got back."

"The last time you had a bright idea, you let Tyrone sidetrack you. Remember the restaurant you were going to open?" his father reminded him.

"Well, I guarantee you, Tyrone has nothing to do with this."

"Son, I hope you're right." Dr. St. James set his cigar in the crystal ashtray at his side. "When can I take a look at this proposal of yours?" he said, rising to leave.

"I've just begun the outline. As soon as it's complete, you'll be the first to know."

Dr. St. James headed for the door. "Don't keep me in suspense too long."

As he strolled out of the room, Blake sat there and muttered, "I'll show him this time." Why did his father always doubt him? Actually, he knew why. It was because of his wild, flamboyant side, not to mention his past involvement with Tyrone. They had grown up in the same house since Tyrone's mother Mattie was the St. Jameses' live-in housekeeper. Blake walked over to the French windows and gazed out at the park.

"Blake, do you need anything before I turn in?" It was Mattie.

"No, thank you. I'm fine."

Turning to leave, Mattie said, "Well, good night then."

Blake thought for a second, then asked, "Oh, Mattie, how is Tyrone? I haven't seen him around lately."

At the mention of his name, Mattie seemed to suddenly grow tired. "That boy of mine is doing okay, I guess. Got hisself another job. Says he likes this one better than the last one. I sho hopes he stays somewhere long enough to collect a pension one day."

Blake, seeing the worried look on Mattie's face, walked over and put his arm around her shoulder. "I'm sure he will."

"You think so?" She shook her head. "I remember when

you two was boys, doing everything together. I knows you did yo share of partying, but it seems like you trying to get yoself together. I pray Tyrone will do the same."

"Me too, Mattie."

"Well, time will tell—that's for sure. 'Night, Blake," Mattie said, turning to leave.

"Good night, Mattie."

As Blake walked back to his room, he thought, "I hope Tyrone makes something of his life, but I can't concern myself with him anymore. The smartest thing I can do is to avoid him like the plague."

8

Morgan gathered her presentation, notes and planner, stuffing them into her briefcase before quickly heading for the bank of elevators. She could not be late for the division meeting. This quarterly gathering of directors and vice presidents often made or destroyed careers. In theory, it was an opportunity for Rob Fallon, the president of Global Financial, to review progress and plans from various departments. In reality, it was a prime opportunity for crab-crawling, snake-slithering, and backbiting in their highest forms.

On the way she passed her boss in the hallway. "Hi, Joel."

"You're not going to embarrass me up there today, are you?" he joked weakly.

Morgan was on today's agenda, presenting a proposal for market segmentation. She had absolutely no intention of embarrassing anyone, least of all herself. She had spent three weeks completing a thorough analysis of Global's client portfolio and developing a creative strategy to cross-market and further penetrate the market based on physicographical typing.

"Joel, you have nothing to worry about. When have I *ever* embarrassed you?" she asked, fixing him with sharp eyes.

He was too obtuse to back down. "Well, there's a first time for everything. And with the added pressure of the promotion, you know, some people crack." As far as Morgan was concerned, the timing couldn't be better. As her father always said, "Work hard and do the right thing, and you'll succeed."

"Not to worry," Morgan said, continuing down the hall.

This meeting would provide the stage for her to shine in front of the entire senior management team, especially Mark, the hiring executive v.p.

Not only was Morgan well prepared—she looked like a star. She knew her stylish look was more haute couture than conservatively pinstriped, and that could be an asset or a liability, depending on her audience. Since other women in her division considered Ann Taylor high fashion, she was constantly aware of the need to tone down her image. So, for today's meeting, she'd chosen a blue Michael Kors pinstripe four-button suit and a white Sea Island cotton shirt. For accessories she wore her Tiffany diamond stud earrings and Baume & Mercier Hampton bracelet watch. Her appearance was sedate from afar but sophisticated up close. Just the look she wanted.

When Morgan stepped into the elevator, she saw Brian Greenville with a group of his happy-hour cohorts. Brian was also being considered for the v.p. slot. A junior member of the good-ole-boy network, he had a passive, sedentary look that bespoke years of privilege presented on silver platters. Not that Morgan was anti-elitist, but Brian simply was not the sharpest knife in the drawer. He always had to be spoon-fed information repeatedly, so sooner or later he would regurgitate what little he managed to swallow.

"Good morning, Brian, John, Sam. You guys headed up to forty-eight?" Morgan asked, referring to Global's elite floor. This was where Rob's office was and those of his executive vice presidents. The quarterly meeting was always held in his private wood-paneled conference room.

"Nonstop," Brian replied with a smug expression. "I hear you're on the agenda today," he added, surveying Morgan from head to toe in one sweeping motion.

"In fact I am. So stay tuned," she answered with a poker face.

Morgan smoothly exited as soon as the doors opened. Yet, as she made her way to the conference room, she couldn't help but wonder how Brian knew she was on the agenda. Joel had confirmed her slot only yesterday afternoon.

Though she was five minutes early, the conference room was already half full. Morgan took a seat toward the head of the long oval conference table, making sure she was facing the entrance. There was no way she would have her back to the door in this cageless zoo. She discreetly watched her colleagues as they entered in small groups, signifying their standing or alliances. Brian and his drinking buddies sat together toward the front of the room, on the side facing the full-wall window. With them it didn't matter; someone *always* had their backs. Jill Hunter and Helen Bentley, two of her team members, sat together. Jill was of the belief that it was more productive to tear others down as a means of keeping herself built up. She and Helen were also vice presidents and as thick as thieves. They were as quick to turn on each other as the next person, but somehow always seemed to reunite for the next heist. Joel walked in with another senior vice president, both swinging their dicks.

After everyone had taken seats, Rob Fallon entered the room and sat at the head of the imposing table. The room was the physical embodiment of power. It was paneled in rich mahogany, with recessed lights highlighting the oil landscapes that adorned three walls. Yet the paintings could not begin to compete with the picturesque view of the vast empires that made up Manhattan's skyline. The conference table seated twenty-two and had built-in microphones at each place. The floor was covered in a plush, handwoven wool carpet with the familiar insignia of Global Financial embedded in its design.

As Rob looked around, Morgan observed that everyone increased his or her personal wattage. If they were slumping, their posture became picture perfect. If they wore a scowl, miraculously their facial expressions became thoughtful or good-humored.

"Good morning. Glad all of you could make it." Morgan smiled to herself. *As if any of us wouldn't.* "Before we begin our update, I would like to extend my personal thanks to each of you and your staffs for delivering a first quarter that showed resounding results. Pretax income was up fifteen percent, while

year-over-year sales were up an astounding twenty percent, and
I'm also happy to report that the new-business pipeline is also
flush with potential. This is the type of stellar performance that
will allow us to honor our commitment to shareholders and
make sure our stock price maintains its current momentum. So
again, sincere thanks to each of you for your outstanding
efforts. Let's keep up the good work!"

Everyone in the room glowed from the praise, as if they had
each single-handedly accomplished the results. Quickly changing gears, Rob continued. "As great as all of that sounds, the
outlook could change swiftly and without warning. As you all
know, many of our competitors are ratcheting up efforts to
attack our customer base. We have to be smarter about attain-
ing customers, we must ensure they are profitable once attained,
and most importantly, we must figure out ways to further maximize our customer relationships."

As she listened to his last words, Morgan's heart skipped a
beat. Her segmentation strategy dealt specifically with customer
maximization. She couldn't wait to strut her stuff.

"In order to meet these and other challenges, we must
employ a more disciplined approach to problem solving to
power-boost our products into the marketplace and continue
our dominance of the credit card business."

Rob's comments were followed by a boring update from
Risk Management on plans to minimize losses by creating better models to predict credit patterns, followed by a presentation
on new technology to improve customer service. Then it was
Brian's turn. He was giving a presentation on Global Financial's
advancements with its Smart Card beta test.

Morgan could sense his anxiety build as his curtain time
approached. His manner changed from cocky confidence to
timid trepidation. He repeatedly cleared his throat, while nervously fiddling with his black Mont Blanc fountain pen. Though
the room was a touch cool, she detected a sheen of perspiration
forming on his furrowed brow and thin upper lip. He looked
like a lamb headed to slaughter.

"Good morning," Brian started nervously. "Today I want to

talk to you all about Global Financial's progress with Smart Cards." He then placed his first transparency on the overhead projector and launched into an overrehearsed, dry-as-dust spiel. "Smart Cards. What is a Smart Card? What are the benefits of Smart Cards? And why is Global Financial pursuing this product? These are the topics I will address in today's presentation. The first topic, What is a Smart Card?" He stopped short when he finally realized that his audience had puzzled looks on their faces. Sensing danger, he turned and saw that the image on the projection screen was upside down. As his panic increased, he quickly flipped the transparency over, only to realize the reflection was now backward and he should have reversed it instead.

The size of the hole he'd dug for himself was deepening by the second. Desperately, he tried to claw his way out. After several more awkward attempts, he finally managed to get the image right, but by then he was reduced to a bundle of nerves. His hands shook visibly under the glare of the bright light as he feebly attempted to maneuver the remaining slides on the large screen. Looking meekly to his cohorts for a much needed boost of confidence, he saw they were now fastidiously avoiding eye contact. Somehow, he collected himself enough to fumble his way through what was left of the butchered presentation, skipping several slides to bring a faster end to his public humiliation. Embarrassed sidelong glances from the audience moved through the room like the Wave as Brian retreated to his place at the table. He was even spared the prolonged agony of the ritual question-and-answer session.

As Brian was slithering to his seat with his tail tucked tightly between his legs, Rob cleared his throat to break the ice that had formed during Brian's painful presentation. "Now Morgan will present a new cross-marketing segmentation strategy. Morgan."

Though she felt sympathy for Brian's humiliation, she also knew it could only help her cause. So she confidently slid the file with her notes from her briefcase and strode to the front of the room. Twenty-one pairs of eyes focused like laser beams on her.

As she approached the podium, she reached for a slim silver

remote and aimed it at the back of the room. The lights dimmed until the recessed points were a burnished glow, with one focused directly on her. Picking up a second palm-sized remote, she turned on a hidden computerized projector that was pre-loaded with her presentation. With the staging complete, Morgan scanned her audience, making eye contact across the room.

"As Rob noted in his remarks, it's more essential than ever in the twenty-first century, with its rapidly changing pace of technology and heightened competition, that we devise strategies to maximize our customer relationships to ensure retention *and* profitability. This morning I will review for you a robust three-pronged strategy that meets those objectives."

Using a laser-tipped pen, she highlighted significant points on the overhead slides as she moved flawlessly through her presentation. When she finished, a chorus of approval rose from everyone in the room, including Rob. Her ability could not be denied. She was the lioness, and Brian was the wildebeest.

Not one to sit back and watch a coup, her colleague Jill proceeded to pepper Morgan with a series of pointed questions designed to find flaws with her strategy. Instead, they only emphasized the depth and breadth of her thorough analysis. When Jill finally surrendered, Morgan was able to relax. She knew that if Jill had drawn blood, the rest of the pack would have circled in for the kill. Instead, her presentation was an undeniable success. She glanced at Mark, the hiring v.p. for her position, and he smiled in approval. "You worked hard," she told herself. "You did the right thing, and you *will* succeed!"

After the meeting, everyone congratulated Morgan on her stellar performance. Elated, she headed to the powder room before going to her next meeting. She had noticed a small snag in her hose as she stood to leave and decided to change into the emergency pair she always kept in her briefcase. Needing more room to change than the regular stalls offered, she popped into the larger one for handicap access. While cursing Donna Karan for the short life span of panty hose, she heard the door open and two pairs of high heels clicking on the tiled floor.

"The presentation was very good. I was impressed," said one pair of heels.

"So was I, but she still won't get the promotion," said the second pair. It was Jill and Helen, and they were talking about her!

"Why do you say that?" asked Helen.

"It doesn't matter how smart, smooth or attractive Morgan is. She still can't compete with Brian," Jill answered from inside one of the stalls.

"From what I saw, she didn't have any competition. You saw Brian. He bombed!"

"It doesn't matter. Brian's father—who, by the way, is the president of Firstbank—sponsored Mark's father for membership into the Tuxedo Park Country Club decades ago. The families go way back. Brian's family is in banking, and Mark's is in real estate. There is no way that Mark would sever years of family ties to hire Morgan or any other black female. It'll never happen, trust me," Jill said.

Morgan's heart sank as she listened to her hidden fears spoken aloud so matter-of-factly. After waiting for the two she-wolves to leave, she walked out feeling like a babe in the woods.

9

Dakota and Morgan were waiting for their new friend Blake in the lobby of the Royalton Hotel, one of Ian Schrager's boutique hotels on West Forty-fourth Street. The lobby also served as a bar area, with wheat-colored velvet sofas, chaise longues and asymmetrical chairs.

"Girl, you seem down. What's wrong?" Morgan asked, noticing Dakota's sober mood. She had decided not to mention the Jill and Helen conversation, for fear that speaking of it would help make it a reality.

"It's Tricia."

Morgan knew Tricia's tainted track record. "Oh, what did she do now?"

Dakota had the look of someone itching for a good fight. "She's moving in with Nana. I don't feel good about it. You know it's just a matter of time before she'll hit Nana up for money." She was so antsy, her fingers were drumming on the table. "I've been thinking. Maybe I should pop in on them over the weekend. If Tricia knows I'll drop in at a moment's notice, maybe she'll stay on the straight and narrow."

"That's a good idea," Morgan said, nodding.

"Plus, you know if I tell Nana I'm coming, she'll just put up a fuss about me wasting money flying in for only two days."

Morgan tried to lighten Dakota's mood. "Girl, if she only knew the money you'll spend on a ticket to Chicago is less than you spent on those Gucci loafers."

"Isn't that the truth," Dakota said with a slight chuckle.

"Well, tonight should be fun. Once Blake gets here, we'll head over to the Back Room, then go to the video shoot Miles is doing for one of his groups."

Dakota perked up. "Which group is it?"

Morgan smiled. She knew how to get Dakota going. "A female trio called Ecstasy. Miles said they're going to be the next TLC."

"How exciting. I loved TLC's last CD. If Ecstasy is as hot as them, they'll be huge."

"That's what Miles said. Anyway, he wants me to come down. I'm always asking why it takes forever to shoot a video. He said it's best that I see firsthand. Especially with this director. He has a reputation for being extremely temperamental."

"Hi, kittens, you both look delectable," Blake purred. He sat down in the empty chair facing them and signaled the waitress to order a drink. "Let's skip the Back Room tonight. Tony has a little attitude problem. I may go in later, but *only* if I feel like it." Blake had the air of someone whose toughest decision was espresso or cappuccino.

Surprised at his problem with Tony, Morgan said, "I thought you two got along great." Although Blake seemed more like the owner of the bar than Tony, the arrangement seemed to work fine, since Tony was the quiet, serious type.

"He's intimidated by me," Blake announced haughtily. "People love me, while they don't even know he exists."

"If I were Tony, I wouldn't care who customers love, as long as they brought their expense accounts," said Dakota, as usual getting right to the bottom line.

"Those jealous witches he has working there are even worse," Blake said theatrically. "Natalie would scale Mount Everest if she thought Tony's bedroom was at the summit. If only she knew, he is not my type. And if he was, she wouldn't stand a chance!"

"Stand a chance? Tony is straight." Morgan looked at Blake questioningly, as if to ask, "Isn't he?" Tony was a dark, handsome Italian. There was a mysterious sexiness about him that didn't seem at all gay.

With his head firmly cocked to one side and eyes slightly bulged, Blake responded, "We all start out that way." He crossed his long legs and raised his thick, perfectly arched brows. "Over the years, I've all too often seen masculine, bona fide ladies' men transform right before my eyes into closet queens."

Morgan cut her eyes at Dakota in response to his comment, and as if on cue Dakota said, "Not the men we know."

"Honey, you'd be surprised."

Dakota looked over at her friend, and Morgan continued. "No, we wouldn't. Dakota and I have built-in gaydar that detects the switch hitters."

Blake laughed. "I haven't heard that term in a long time."

Since her schedule had not allowed for lunch, Morgan was starving. "Let's grab dinner at Rain." She called the waitress for the check and paid the tab since Blake had so graciously taken care of the sizable one left at the Back Room the week before.

Rain was one of the more inventive restaurants on the Upper West Side, serving an interesting combination of Eastern cuisines. The scene was every bit as interesting as the food. Young, sophisticated, but definitely cutting edge. The women wore sexy little T-shirts with snug hip huggers, strappy sandals and those cute but overpriced Kate Spade handbags. The guys were a more diverse blend: either sporting the Woody Allen look, replete with polyester shirts and oversized black frames, or going for body-accentuating T-shirts.

When they hopped out of the taxi, Blake whisked them straight into the restaurant past the peons waiting outside for tables. Of course Blake knew the maître d'.

"Steve, darling, how are you?"

"Great, Blake. You still running the show at the Back Room?" Steve asked.

"You know it. Steve, pardon my manners. Morgan, Dakota, meet Steve Brandon."

After exchanging pleasantries, Steve asked, "Can I get you guys a table, or are you here for drinks?"

"A table for three in the bay window would be nice," Blake said, pointing his slender, manicured finger at the choicest available table in the restaurant.

Once settled, Blake took charge, ordering Vietnamese spring rolls with glass noodles and Thai beef jerky for appetizers. He was brilliant with his food choices, knowing the most intimate details about the preparation of each dish, down to the smallest ingredient, Morgan had noticed.

"Today must be my day for attitude problems," Blake announced after ordering for the table.

"Who else gave you fever today?" asked Dakota.

"My grandparents arrived this afternoon from Paris," Blake said dramatically, "and believe it or not, in four hours my grandmother managed to upset the entire house. She put on a white glove—God only knows where she got *that*—and went from room to room, in a six-bedroom apartment, inspecting every piece of furniture for specks of dust! Which of course she found and used as evidence to indict our live-in maid, who was so insulted, she stormed out of the penthouse. Meanwhile, Momsy was plotting to ship Grandmother back to Paris ASAP and poor Grandfather was trying his best to stay out of the line of fire."

"Talk about a soap opera," Morgan said, exchanging looks of wonder with Dakota.

"You have no idea. Say, what are you guys doing for the weekend?" Blake asked expectantly.

"I'm heading to Chicago," Dakota said, sipping her Cosmopolitan.

"Miles and I are going to Barbados for the week," Morgan answered.

Looking disappointed, Blake said, "I was planning to invite you both to a party I'm planning at Ocean. It's going to be fabulous!" His eyes suddenly lit up and he proceeded to describe the plans in glorious detail. "I am transforming the whole space into the Garden of Eden, with fig leaves strung from the ceiling and baskets of apples on every table. The invitation is serpent-shaped and says, 'Cum taste the forbidden fruit.'" The provocative invitation seemed more than appropriate coming from Blake.

"What a clever idea," Morgan said, envious of Blake's enthusiasm for his work.

"Blake, why are you working at the Back Room?" Dakota asked, abruptly posing the million-dollar question. "With your contacts and experience, you should start your own event-planning business."

Blake had a ready answer. "I've always wanted to, but for now a party here and there will have to suffice. Besides, first I have to convince Father to loosen the purse strings. To him, event planning is just another excuse for me to party every night. He and my mother are both from families of doctors and are of the opinion that if you aren't playing God in the O.R. or making life-and-death decisions, your life is meaningless. And after I spent last year studying a fifth language in Hong Kong, on top of degrees from the University of Pennsylvania and Wharton, he is now expecting a return on his investment. Imagine that!"

Morgan couldn't imagine wasting a top-shelf education. "Blake, you don't realize how fortunate you are to have had the opportunity, not to mention the funds, to attend such prestigious schools."

"You sound just like my father," Blake said. "I'm not wasting it. Trust me. I will put it to good use in the very near future." With that, he settled into eating every morsel of food on his plate. He had, both Morgan and Dakota noticed, a huge appetite for someone so thin.

After dinner, they jumped into a taxi and headed downtown for the video shoot, which was being held at the Tunnel, a nightclub near the West Side Highway. As the taxi neared the club, it could barely squeeze down the street between the massive trailers lined up for the artists. Groupies were also lined up crowding the entrance, trying to get a peek at the singers.

Morgan, Dakota and Blake fought their way through the crowd to reach the security guard who protected the entrance.

He was decked out in black fatigues with an exposed holster armed with two cell phones, a walkie-talkie and three pagers. "I'm Morgan Nelson. Miles is expecting us," she said to the burly guard.

"Come right in, Mrs. Nelson," the guard said, after referring to his list. "He's just to the left on the other side of the large screen." He pointed them in the direction where the cast and crew were shooting.

The webs of cables and electrical tape covering the floor indicated they were headed the right way. Dakota nudged Morgan in awe as they approached the glamorous set, which was dressed to look like a Monte Carlo casino. It featured crystal chandeliers, slot machines, roulette wheels and blackjack tables manned by extras in tuxedos. The four singers were dressed elegantly in ivory-satin evening gowns of the same fabric but designed differently. The lead singer's hair was coiffed in a tight bun, giving the illusion of a sophisticated lady from an old black-and-white movie, while the three backup singers wore short bobs. All had on enough ice to give Harry Winston a run for his money.

Dakota watched the makeup artist reapply concealer under the eyes of Keikei Jones, the lead singer. "Girl, look at the luggage under those eyes."

"David Copperfield would have a hard time making those bags disappear," Blake said.

Miles glanced over to where they were standing and nodded hello. He then walked over to the makeup artist and said, "Are you almost finished? We're already on our eleventh take and the clock is still ticking. Time is money."

The makeup artist finished with a final dusting of powder on Keikei's face and walked off the set. Miles asked, "Is everybody ready?"

Lei Kym, the Asian director, yelled, "Action." The music started, and the girls began to lip-synch.

Blake whispered to Morgan, "I didn't realize they mouthed the words."

"I didn't either—it looks so real on television."

The girls shimmied in the middle of the set, while a troupe of male dancers in tuxedos gyrated around them. All was going well until Keikei turned to her left, when she should have turned to the right, and found herself out of step.

"Cut, cut," yelled Lei. "Keikei, what was that? Didn't you girls even rehearse this number?"

"It wasn't me. They the ones who turned on the wrong foot."

"You a lie," said Nikki, the alto of the group, her head rotating.

"Who you calling a lie?" Keikei said, coming within inches of Nikki.

"Y'all need to stop tripping." That was Anjee, the mediator of the group.

Miles stepped up and asked, "Do you ladies need to take ten and go over the routine?"

"Naw, Miles, we got this," Anjee said, looking over at Keikei and Nikki for confirming nods.

The director yelled, "Take twelve." The camera began to roll, and the girls fell right into step, doing an updated rendition of an old Supremes move.

"Cut," said the director. "Keikei, don't look directly into the camera."

Keikei rolled her eyes and mumbled something inaudible.

"Roll tape. Take thirteen. Action."

The video had been rolling no longer than thirty seconds when Lei Kym stormed onto the set, waving his hands and screaming at the top of his lungs, "Cut, cut, cut! Keikei, how many times do I have to tell you not to look directly into the camera?"

"I heard you, but I wanna look at my peeps," Keikei said, sucking her teeth and gyrating her neck in total contradiction of her sophisticated costume.

"I can't work like this," Lei Kym shouted. "I'm the fucking director, and if I say don't look directly into the camera, that's what the fuck I mean."

"Who the fuck—" Keikei was about to make a break for Lei's neck, with Anjee struggling to hold her back.

Keikei didn't get far. Miles stepped in and took control. "Look, guys, let's take a break. I think we could all use one. We've been at it for five hours now. Lei, come with me a second." Miles calmly walked the director away from the escalating confrontation with Keikei.

"Miles just has that natural ability to defuse tight situations." Morgan beamed proudly.

After calming everyone down, Miles walked over to Morgan, Dakota and Blake.

"Hey, guys," Miles said as he leaned over and kissed Morgan lightly on the lips. He then gave Dakota a hug. "Hey, D, how you doing?"

"I'm good. Thanks for letting us come down. It's exciting to see the music world in action."

"Miles, this is Blake," Morgan said, smiling. "Remember, I told you all about him."

"Hey, man," Miles said, obviously not remembering.

Blake didn't seem offended. "Miles, it's so good to meet you. You really handled that scene well. Are all directors and singers that testy?"

"Every group is different," Miles said. Always the diplomat.

"You must have the patience of a saint to deal with them."

"You could say that," Miles said, unmoved by Blake's flattery. In fact, he seemed slightly irritated. "Babe, can I speak to you for a minute?"

Miles walked Morgan over near the corner. "Who is that?" he asked, referring to Blake.

"Didn't I tell you Dakota and I met Blake the night we went out with those brokers?" Morgan asked.

"I don't think so," Miles said. "I was only expecting you and Dakota. I told you how temperamental this director is, and the last thing I need is a set full of people to further distract him."

Morgan touched his arm softly and said, "I'm sorry, Miles, but I thought it would be fine. Blake's real cool. Actually, he's a great guy."

Miles glanced at his watch. "Listen, I've got to get back to work. I'll probably be here all night, considering how long it's taking." They headed back over to where Blake and Dakota were standing. "Take it easy, D. You too, Blake," Miles said, cutting his eyes, as though not sure what to make of Blake.

Morgan felt like a kid who had been chastised by her father. "Let's get out of Miles's hair."

"I'm not ready to go home yet. I'm too wired," Blake said. "All this energy has me pumped."

As they stepped back over the taped cables, leaving the shoot, they could hear the director yell action for the umpteenth time. Dakota looked back and saw Keikei, Nikki and Anjee resume their positions. She was a bit disillusioned by the girls. On the surface they seemed the epitome of class, but the image was shattered the instant they opened their mouths.

"Come on, let's go dancing," Blake said, once they were out in the night air.

"You guys can hang out. I'm going home," Morgan said, looking for a taxi.

"Come on, Dakota, let's hang. I know this great little club not too far from here," Blake said, nudging her on the arm.

Dakota looked at her watch. It was eleven o'clock. "I'll go for about an hour."

Blake flagged down two taxis, one for Morgan and one for him and Dakota.

"Girl, you sure you don't want to go?"

"I'm sure. You guys go on and have fun."

Dakota looked at Morgan and asked, "You okay?"

"I'm fine, just a little tired. Now go on—your cab's waiting." Morgan kissed Dakota and Blake each on the cheek and got in the taxi.

Once inside the cab, Dakota asked, "So, Blake, where is this club?"

"It's in the meatpacking district," Blake said, matter-of-factly.

"Meatpacking, huh?" Dakota joked. "Must be a gay club."

"You don't have a problem with that, do you?" Blake asked.

"Please, I just want to dance, not romance."

"Well, I wouldn't mind some of both," Blake said with a devilish gleam in his eye.

Not long after, the taxi pulled up in front of a nondescript building. Blake paid the driver, and he and Dakota stepped out.

"It's pretty desolate around here." Dakota looked warily around at the closed butcher shops with corrugated metal grating covering the fronts. Out of the corner of her eye, Dakota saw a cat scrounging around for scraps. "Blake, are you sure we're at the right place?"

"Of course I'm sure. Follow me," Blake said, confidently walking toward the back of the building. As they walked down a cement gangway toward the entrance, Dakota could hear the beat of the music. The doorman cast a look at her that said she was in the wrong place. As if on cue, Blake said, "She's cool, man." He was clearly a regular.

Inside, the Slab was painted a bright fuchsia with 1960s lava lamps behind the bar and zebra-covered stools set in front of a crescent-shaped aluminum bar. The dance floor was illuminated by neon lights, reminiscent of *Saturday Night Fever*. Pink feathers blew from a fan high above the dance floor and floated down on the dancers, who were jamming to Q-Tip's "Vivrant Thing."

"Come on, Blake, let's dance. I love that song," Dakota said, walking toward the dance floor. She fell right in to the mix of dancing bodies with Blake in tow. To her surprise she saw that Blake had rhythm. She had assumed, because he was from the Upper East Side, he would be as stiff as a surfboard, but he grooved like a brother from Harlem. The DJ was playing a remixed version of the song, which seemed to last forever. Soon she and Blake were jamming so hard they drew a crowd of onlookers.

"I feel like we're in a dance contest," Blake shouted over the music as he took her hand and spun her around. He then began to vogue. The dance had originated in the gay community but was popularized by Madonna. He expertly did a series of quick poses as if on a photo shoot.

Dakota shouted, "You go, boy," and began to dance freestyle by herself.

She became so caught up in the frenzy of the groove, with her head tilted back and every muscle feeling the beat, that she didn't notice Blake working his way to the other side of the dance floor with someone else.

The man was handsome with strong masculine features. Blake came up close, trying to be heard over the loud, throbbing music.

"How long have you been back?" Tyrone asked, looking Blake up and down.

"Not long."

Tyrone twisted his mouth and asked, "What are you doing here?"

"Dancing."

"I can see that. Who are you with?"

"A friend, and you?"

"Nobody important," Tyrone answered, shifting his eyes, looking around.

"You want to get together over the weekend?" Blake asked.

"I'm busy."

Blake frowned. Any other time, Tyrone would be eager to get together. "Well, I'll see you around. I gotta go," Blake said. Getting together with Tyrone was the last thing that he needed anyway.

By then Dakota had noticed. She started making her way toward Blake to tell him she was leaving, but before she said anything, he asked, "You ready?"

"Who was that?"

"A blast from my past," Blake said, wiping the beads of sweat from his forehead and looking behind him.

Noticing Blake's sudden change in attitude, Dakota asked, "You okay?"

"Yeah, just a little worked up from dancing. Let's get out of here," Blake said, grabbing Dakota by the arm and leading her toward the exit. Dakota looked back, wondering who that guy was and how he had made Blake so upset.

10

Tyrone slammed the door of the seedy five-floor walk-up, his androgynous features twisted in a grimace. "It sounds like somebody's got a little attitude," Jimmy called out from the tiny bedroom. His high-pitched voice echoed annoyingly off the grimy surfaces of the sparsely furnished apartment. The decor was early urban decay with dirty bare walls, old plank floorboards and a gritty linoleum kitchen. The view out the cracked window was of overflowing garbage bins in a rat-infested back alley.

"I ran into Mz. Thang St. James at the club last night," Tyrone said, disdain oozing like sludge from each syllable.

Tyrone used to have a finely furnished apartment full of Italian leather and art deco chrome. His closet had been stuffed with the latest designer clothes, all compliments of a certain wealthy gentleman. By day, Mr. Benefactor was a happily married man and model citizen with three lovely kids and a thriving empire, but after hours he was a cross-dressing closet queen. In exchange for being a kept man, Tyrone was at his beck and call twenty-four/seven. That was, until he was busted answering someone else's beck and call. Then he was unceremoniously kicked to the curb—minus most of the finery. He only managed to escape with as many clothes as he could stuff into his luggage.

And of course earlier the St. James family had been a nice meal ticket for him. Until Blake outgrew him. Oh, Blake had tried to pretend that nothing had changed between them, but it was as if all of a sudden Blake woke up one day and realized they were different. Tyrone thought to himself, "No shit. Hmmm, let's see, his family is worth about a gazillion bagillion dollars, and if that weren't enough, my mother cleans their fucking toilets. He went to Wharton while I was kicked out of City College. He travels the world on a whim, and I'm lucky to get a token for the subway ride back up to this godforsaken hellhole. By all accounts, I'd say we are different."

"So how is Mz. St. James?" Jimmy asked, peeking out of the bedroom, his head cocked to the side, beady eyes wide.

"Same ole. But now he wants to get together." Tyrone rolled his thickly lashed eyes. He had a love-hate relationship with Blake. He loved his money, but hated the way Blake had discarded him.

"So are you?" Jimmy asked expectantly. He had come into the front room, where Tyrone had sprawled out on the weary ancient sofa.

"Hell, nah," Tyrone said. "I've been fucked over enough by Mr. High and Mighty. I don't think I'll be bending over for him anytime soon."

"Honey chile, you might want to reconsider that," Jimmy counseled as he walked behind the sofa to massage Tyrone's back. "With all of his bank, your problems could be a thing of the past."

"That's where you're wrong. Blake ain't got shit. It's all his ole man's money," Tyrone corrected, as he rolled his neck three-hundred and sixty degrees.

"I thought all rich kids had trust funds," Jimmy said, digging his bony fingers into Tyrone's deltoids to rub his back.

"They do, but Blake blew through his wad parading around the world drinkin' expensive wine and shit." Every few months Tyrone would get a postcard from some exotic place that only emphasized the stark contrast to his tired, bleak existence.

"It must be nice to have family money," mused Jimmy, looking around at their dilapidated excuse for an apartment.

"Either have it or marry it, which is what Carlton's money-grubbing wife, Roshumba, did. I'm sure that bitch has nubs for nails after all the gold digging and social climbing she's done.

And Carlton likes to play the intellectual, even though it took him three times to pass the bar exam." Tyrone shook his head, as though he most certainly would have passed the first time.

"How's your mom?"

"Still workin' like a Hebrew slave. I hate seein' her shufflin' behind that family. That's the way it's always been, though." He twisted his neck to get it loose. "Blake and I may have grown up together, but I was always reminded of my place. While he dressed for fancy parties given by his parents, I was sweatin' and workin' like a dog in the kitchen, helping my mother." The memory cast a heavy sadness over Tyrone's fine features. "When the chauffeur was driving him to Collegiate, I was huffin' it and bussin' it to a run-down public school. Lest I forget, at Christmas, FAO Schwarz backed up the truck for Blake, while I was lucky to get his hand-me-downs."

"You in hand-me-downs?" Jimmy said with a tight smirk. "Speaking of which, I thought we'd dress up real pretty and hit the club tonight."

"You got my pills?" Tyrone asked, turning to face Jimmy.

"Yeah, girl," he said, a bit hesitant. "My supplier is getting tight wit' it, but I got ya covered." Followed by Tyrone, Jimmy sashayed to the bedroom. Reaching under the beat-up mattress, Jimmy picked out two small pills from a stash stored in a crumpled plastic Ziploc bag.

"Now I can get my party on," Tyrone said, popping the pills and chasing them with New York tap.

Later, as he sat perched in the sleazy, rusty little bathroom shaving his legs, Tyrone wondered exactly where things had gone so wrong. He'd gone from Central Park West, doormen and antique rugs to a back alley, drive-bys and holdups. All things considered, though, he was still fine, and men were as attracted to him as bees were to honey. Maybe not as many as when he was younger, but he could still turn some heads, and soon he'd be right back on the gravy train.

After dressing, he looked in the mirror admiringly and said, "Chooo-choooooo."

11

Dakota left work early Friday to catch the American Airlines two o'clock flight to Chicago. With the one-hour time difference, she would arrive at O'Hare by 3:20. That was enough time to rent a car, sit in traffic on the Kennedy Expressway and make it to the South Side by six o'clock, just in time for dinner.

Once off the highway, she drove down Martin Luther King Boulevard, which was the main drag through her old neighborhood. Twenty years ago it had been a thriving shopping district with predominantly small, white-owned businesses, banks, and boutiques. The once well-kept neighborhood had changed, though. It was now a trash-strewn strip of dilapidated buildings housing storefront churches, liquor stores and corner groceries owned by Arabs. The street pharmacists conducted their business on the corner.

The only block that maintained a resemblance of the past was the one Dakota had grown up on. The older residents still managed to keep their lawns mowed and houses painted on a semiregular basis. As Dakota parked the burgundy XJ6 in front of her grandmother's two-story bungalow, she noticed stares from her childhood crew. They were sitting on the porch next door. Reaching into the backseat, she grabbed her weekend Prada duffel and hopped out. A chorus of questions rang out from the porch.

"Damn, girl, you rollin' like that?" asked Kevin, who still lived with his parents.

"How's the Rotten Apple?" asked J. B., Kevin's toothless sidekick.

"Girl, you can give me that bag. Is that a Paraada?" asked Jasmine, Kevin's overweight girlfriend in the too-tight jeans.

Dakota didn't know who to answer first. "Yeah, it's a Prada, and I think I'll keep it," she said. "New York is New York, John-Boy," she said, calling J. B. by his given name, which he hated.

"It's J. B. I told you the last time you was home to call me J. B," he said, irritated.

"And as for the car, it's a rental," Dakota said, to answer Kevin's question.

"Where you rent that from? It's phat," Kevin said, walking toward the car to get a closer look.

"Budget."

"I didn't know you could rent Jageewars," J. B. said.

Dakota replied, "You can rent just about anything, if you have the funds." She didn't mean to come off as uppity, but she was tired of the twenty questions every time she came home. She had been tight with these guys as children, doing everything together, but as they grew up, they grew further apart. Dakota was ambitious and always dreamed of making a life outside the neighborhood. Her childhood friends seemed content staying within the confines of the familiar.

Dakota walked up the steps to her grandmother's house, smiling as she noticed the spanking-new gutters.

"Well, Ms. New York, let's get together before you leave. You still drink Ole Eight?" Kevin asked.

"Bet. We can do that," Dakota said, trying to remember the last time she drank Old English 800 malt liquor. *For old times' sake, I will*, she told herself.

Dakota put her key in the lock, but before she could turn it, the door opened. "I thought you was going to stand out there all day running your mouth," said Dakota's grandmother. Dakota smiled at her impatience. "Now, get in here and give your nana a big hug." The arms that had protected her as a child encircled Dakota. She closed her eyes and inhaled the familiar combination of Wind Song and fried catfish.

"Aren't you surprised to see me, Nana?" Dakota asked.

"I knew you was coming home. Child, I know you better than you know yourself," Nana said, releasing her granddaughter. She headed down the long hall toward the kitchen. Following behind, Dakota could smell a lemon meringue pie, her favorite, baking in the oven.

"I made your favorites—catfish, spaghetti, cole slaw—and I even baked you two lemon pies, one for here and one to take back," Nana said, deftly turning over a piece of fish in the sizzling hot skillet.

"Nana, you know I can't take pie on the plane," Dakota said, looking around. The yellow kitchen was the same, with the original stove, refrigerator and Formica dinette set. She remembered making popcorn in that same cast-iron skillet. They would stay up late watching *Creature Feature* and eating burned popcorn.

"Oh, I forgets how important you are now. Driving fancy cars, living up there in Sin City, and wearing them 'spensive clothes," Nana said, mocking Dakota's jet-set lifestyle.

"Nana, please. You know I have to be in New York because that's where I work. Plus, my job allows me to send you a little somethin'-somethin' every month," Dakota said, kidding with her grandmother.

"Okay, Miss Somethin', go wash your hands and get ready for dinner." Nana had more of a stoop in her back than Dakota remembered from her last visit.

"Speaking of dinner, is Miss Tricia joining us, or do I have the pleasure of dining alone with you?" Dakota asked, looking around for signs of her cousin.

"She's upstairs. Go tell her dinner is ready."

"Where is she?"

"In your old room," Nana said as she turned back to the stove.

"Nana, why did you put her in my room?" It came out as a little girl's whine.

"Because I turned the guest room into my quilting room."

Dakota drew herself upright in the kitchen chair and asked, "Where am I supposed to sleep?"

"On the pullout in the den."

"That's still my room. Put *her* on the pullout."

"Listen, Dakota," Nana said, turning around to face her granddaughter. "You know this will always be your home, but Patricia needs a little help right now to get back on her feet. So I'm asking you to be patient. Before long you'll have your old room back." Nana walked over and kissed her on the forehead, then teased, "Not that you need your old room anyway, Ms. Manhattan. Now go on and tell your cousin dinner is ready."

Dakota reluctantly walked up the stairs toward the room she grew up in. Faced with a closed door, she suddenly felt like a stranger. She knocked and waited. There was no answer. "I know that heifer hears me," Dakota said, and knocked again. Still no answer. She put her hand on the knob and slowly opened the door. Tricia was lying in the middle of the queen-sized canopy bed with her eyes closed, listening to Dakota's stereo through the earphones and singing off key to Tina Turner's "What's Love Got to Do with It."

"Tricia," Dakota shouted, looking around. There was a bundle of dirty clothes in the corner, and the desk was piled high with beauty school notebooks. There was even a mannequin head full of spiral curls. Dakota shouted again, and this time Tricia opened her eyes.

"Hey, cuz, what's up?" Tricia sat up, taking the earphones off.

"My question exactly."

"What do you mean by that?"

Skipping the pleasantries, Dakota started in. "Look, I know what you told Nana, but I want the real deal. Why can't you get a job and an apartment like everyone else?"

"That's not your business, Ms. High and Mighty," Tricia snapped.

Dakota put one hand on her hip. "Anything involving my grandmother is definitely my business."

"You seem to forget, Nana is just as much *my* grandmother as yours." Tricia stood up and then said, "Anyway, it's not my fault your deddy fell asleep at the wheel and killed hisself and yo momma."

Tricia walked out, leaving Dakota standing in the middle of the room. Dakota felt her stomach plunge. *She's not going to make me cry, not this time.* Tricia always brought up the accident whenever she wanted to bring Dakota down. She went into the upstairs bathroom, ran cold water over her face, then went back downstairs to join Nana and Tricia for dinner.

"Come on, Kota. Let's bless the table before the food gets cold," Nana said. "Hold hands and bow your heads. Lord, thank You for letting me have my two grandbabies with me this evening. Lord, watch over us as we make our way through life's journey, and thank You for this food we are about to receive for the nourishment of our bodies, in Christ's name. Amen."

Tricia dropped Dakota's hand as soon as the prayer was over. "Nana, this food sure smells good. You keep cooking like this and I'm a gain some weight for sure."

"Li'l Bit, you could stand a few pounds. Couldn't she, Kota?"

"Not if you like the heroin-waif look," Dakota said snidely.

"You need to stop drinking Hater Ade," Li'l Bit shot back.

"Please, why would I want to look like a ninety-pound weakling?" Dakota rolled her eyes and took a bite of catfish.

"Stop it right now, Dakota. I told you to give Tricia a break. I'm not gonna have all this back and forth. You hear me?"

Dakota felt like a teenager, like those times when she and Tricia would argue toe-to-toe and Nana would step in to break it up. "Yes, Nana."

Tricia hurried through dinner and went back upstairs to Dakota's room. Dakota helped with the dishes.

"Does she help you around the house, Nana?"

"Tricia has a lot of homework."

Dakota ignored the warning tone in her grandmother's

voice. "That's the least she could do, since she's living here rent free."

"Don't start on that again. I'm tired and don't want to hear it," Nana said, handing Dakota a plate to dry.

"Well, if she helped you around here you wouldn't be so tired."

"What did I just say? You so hardheaded. I'll finish up. You go on and get ready for bed."

It wasn't fair, Dakota thought. Why was Nana taking Li'l Bit's side? She was the one that was responsible, while Tricia flitted aimlessly from one failure to another. She knew that having Tricia here was nothing but bad news. Too bad Nana couldn't see it. But she would keep her eyes peeled and watch out for both of them.

Nana woke Dakota early Saturday morning to a hearty breakfast of blueberry pancakes, bacon and eggs. She needed it after tussling with the loose springs and hard mattress in the sofa bed all night.

"Where's Tricia?" Dakota said, sitting at the table.

"She's gone to school."

"Good, at least I can have some private time with you. Tell you what. After breakfast, let's go downtown to Earl's art supply store and buy water paints and canvas. Then we can come back and make a mess like we used to when I was little."

Nana was sipping coffee out of her saucer, and she smiled at the thought. "Remember, I used to call your paintings magic? Even had some of 'em framed."

That sparked a question in Dakota's mind. "Do you still have those old paintings?"

Her grandmother looked vaguely toward the ceiling. "They're somewhere up in the attic. We can look for them when we get back."

Pleased at the idea, Dakota settled in to eat. She was crunching on a piece of bacon as she said, "Nana, I see you still drink your coffee out of the saucer."

"Cools it down."

Dakota burst out laughing. "Remember you used to let me sip a little of your coffee when I was little? But you told me I couldn't drink too much, because it would make me black."

"Guess you didn't listen," Nana said, laughing too, " 'cause you a little chocolate drop."

After breakfast, they went downtown to buy art supplies. Used to the brisk pace of New York, Dakota felt odd being back in Chicago. Though Michigan Avenue had some of the best shopping in the world, nothing compared to Madison and Fifth avenues in New York. Walking out of the art supply store, Dakota said, "Let's go over to Marshall Field's. I want to buy you a few outfits."

The old woman shook her head. "Not today, baby."

"Why not?"

She looked at Dakota uneasily. " 'Cause I don't want Tricia to feel bad. She was just saying the other day, when she start making some money, she gonna buy me a new suit for church."

"I don't understand how me buying you a new suit is going to make *her* feel bad."

"Because she can't afford to do for me the way you can, and it makes her feel uncomfortable."

That was no reason, not as far as Dakota was concerned. "Frankly, I don't care how she feels. It's not my fault she wastes her time on pipe dreams instead of working at a real job."

"True, it's not your fault, but I'm not gonna walk in the house with an armload of new clothes. Our shopping spree will just have to wait."

That stopped Dakota, but only for a moment. "I know. If it makes you feel better, you can come to New York. You had a lot of fun last time. We'll go shopping, go to a show. That way it wouldn't be directly in her face."

The uneasy look was back. "Maybe."

"Come on, let me plan it. You haven't been to see me in a while. It'll be fun."

"I'll let you know." A twinkle came to her eye, and she put her hand on Dakota's arm. "Now come on and buy me lunch, since you aching to spend your money."

When they returned to the house Tricia was there, with papers spread over the dining room table.

"You might want to move some of this junk," Dakota said, putting down her art supplies.

"This is my homework, and I need all of this space," Tricia said as she wrote in a notebook.

Dakota was about to argue, but she saw Nana shaking her head. "Whatever," Dakota said. "Nana, I'm gonna see what you got in that attic."

She walked upstairs and began a stroll down memory lane. Going through Nana's attic, Dakota found her old, dusty brown Girl Scout uniform, letters from a pen pal, and even her high school yearbook. While the trip was special, like most things for her, it was also poignant. The only evidence of her parents was an old blanket that her mother had crocheted when Dakota was a baby. Fingering the old stiff yarn, Dakota fought back the tears that the memory of her parents often brought on. In her remembrance they were frozen in youth, like the perfect couple you see on the top of a wedding cake.

Leaving the past behind, Dakota eventually headed downstairs with a couple of her childhood paintings under her arm. "I thought I'd take these two paintings home to bring some magic to my loft." The paintings were abstract watercolors in gold-leaf frames.

Tricia walked into the kitchen and said, "What the mess is that?" pointing at the paintings.

"That's Kota's magic."

"It look more like a tragic accident with paint." Tricia laughed.

Feeling hurt, Dakota struck back. "What would you know about art? I have an entire apartment filled with paintings. Paintings I bought, I might add."

"You always thought you was better than me. Just wait until I open my own shop and start raking in the bucks."

Dakota waved that away. "I won't hold my breath."

Tricia stormed out, just as Dakota knew she would.

"Oh, that reminds me, Nana. Here, take this, and take your

bid whisk club out to lunch," Dakota said, taking out an envelope with five crisp one-hundred-dollar bills.

"Baby, you don't have to do that. You know I always make lunch when they come over."

"Well, just take it and use it for whatever you want."

Nana still refused to take the envelope. "I don't like you spending so much money on me."

"Nana, you know it makes me feel good to do things for you. Besides, it's only money, and you sure can't take it with you."

"Okay, but don't send me the monthly check," Nana said, finally taking the envelope, knowing full well that Dakota would send the check anyway. "You're a good girl."

Dakota enveloped her in a hug. "I'm just doing for my Nana what you've always been willing to do for me."

12

After racing from the office late, Miles barely made the flight. Morgan had been at the gate monitoring her watch as though it could make him materialize sooner. When they finally settled into the first-class cabin of the DC-10, Morgan turned to kiss him. "This was a great idea."

"We both deserve it. I know you've been stressed at work lately, and getting Ecstasy's video done was like negotiating peace in the Middle East."

Morgan laughed. "Well, I for one don't plan to give my job another thought, but we do have to make a point of celebrating your promotion."

Yet as Morgan sank farther into the plush leather seats, she frowned. That conversation in the ladies' room hadn't stopped banging around in her head. She couldn't help but think that maybe Jill and Helen were right. Maybe qualifications weren't as important as pedigree.

She brought it up with Miles. When she finished, she said, "Part of me gives no credence to the babblings of two gossip-mongers, but on the other hand, they could be right."

Always the voice of reason, Miles said, "Morgan, I wouldn't give it another thought. Just stay focused on doing the great job you've always done."

"I'm sure you're probably right," Morgan said, though she still had her doubts.

Miles set aside the latest copy of *Savoy* magazine and asked,

"Since when did my girl let anybody, especially a pair of cack-ling hens like those two, mess with her confidence?"

She gave him a faint smile. "You're right. They'd be crazy to pass over me. I am the most competent person in the entire department. Hands down." Feeling the fire of confidence relit, Morgan boasted, "Brian couldn't fill even one of my Gucci pumps—with both his feet."

Now, satisfied that her career was on the right path, she opened Veronica Chambers's new book and settled in for a long flight. Not that she got very far. Before she could finish the second chapter, Morgan was in a deep sleep. Flying south past the Dominican Republic, the plane headed east over Puerto Rico, ever farther away from Gotham.

The Caribbean's world-class beaches attracted millions of visitors each year, but none was as spectacular as the white-sand beach of the Coral Reef Club, especially at sunset, which was when Miles and Morgan's limo pulled up to the main house. Having arranged for advanced check-in, they were escorted directly to one of the spacious tropical suites. By the time the porter appeared with the assorted Louis Vuitton luggage, Mor-gan was on the private balcony taking in a spectacular orange-purple sunset as it dipped into the ocean. Already in another world.

Miles moved up behind her, kissing the back of her neck while balancing a glass of champagne in each hand. Turning her head, she tasted Miles before accepting one of the crystal flutes. "What did I do to deserve all this?" she asked with stars in her eyes.

Miles clicked glasses with hers. "Just being you."

"I am so lucky to have you," she said.

Miles pretended to think for a moment, then said, "Yes, you are."

"No, seriously, I know at least a dozen gorgeous, successful, wonderful black women, including Dakota, who can't find a good man with a Thomas Guide," Morgan said, leaning onto the railing.

He struggled. "I don't understand why."

Morgan looked out over the ocean. "Most of the qualified ones are either married, gay or four-legged. Or worse, they're snatched up by a blonde with her blue eyes on his greens."

"What happened with her and Jackson? They seemed to get along well," Miles said. His interest was beginning to shift to more pressing matters, though. He hugged Morgan from behind, planting kisses behind her ears.

She tried to ignore him. "I think he now falls in both the married and canine categories."

"I don't think we have to worry about Dakota," Miles said absently. He turned her around. "Hey, what you say we check out the Jacuzzi?"

The following morning, as the sun began its dance with daylight, they ate breakfast in bathrobes on the wraparound terrace. A waiter served covered trays of tropical fruit, eggs Benedict and Belgian waffles. The smell of hibiscus mixed with gardenia floated in the air. After a quick shower, they dressed and headed to the Royal Westmoreland Golf Club, a championship course designed by Robert Trent Jones. It was a major reason Miles had wanted to come here.

Miles unloaded his set of custom-made Calloways, complete with Big Berthas, and Morgan pulled out her Cleveland irons and Cobra drivers. Seeing some older white men look at them in surprise, she could almost visualize the dialogue bubbles popping from their heads. "You know, Bob, it's one thing for us to let them in the front door, but aside from that Tiger fellow, they don't have the discipline or dexterity for such a precise sport. And by the way, how can they afford it?" Little did they know, Miles and Morgan both played excellent games. Miles had a six handicap and Morgan's was nine.

Walking the beautiful Caribbean course, with no cell phones, faxes, pagers or planners, only each other for five hours, was the epitome of relaxation. Not even her wedge shot from one sand trap straight across the eighth green into the next could spoil the mood.

After eighteen holes, they checked their clubs, showered and headed to the club's spa. Four hours of deliciously decadent pampering followed. Starting in a palm-thatched gazebo by the sea, they climbed onto twin massage tables. Island beauties in sarongs massaged them gently before slathering on cool mud from coconut bowls. Listening to strains of flute music, they both drifted off.

They were gently awakened as warm herbal water was drizzled over their bodies to rinse away mud and stress. Steamed sheets soaked in herbs were then tightly wrapped around them to remove toxins and everything else except peace and tranquillity. A sea-salt scrub served as a final exfoliate, uncovering skin as soft as a newborn's.

"You look fabulous," Miles said as they dressed for dinner, marveling at Morgan's beauty. She was wearing only eyeliner, mascara, lip gloss and a dusting of powder for a matte finish, yet she was radiant.

"Thanks, baby, and you look ravishing," she said, taking in the full view of her handsome husband. "Here, could you help me with this?"

Miles tied the straps of Morgan's backless black evening dress. The effect of so little fabric against glowing, polished skin was just what Morgan wanted. She loved the way Miles was looking at her in the mirror.

As he stood behind her, tracing circles over her smooth back, his fingers began to creep around toward the front. Morgan playfully chided him, "You're supposed to be tying me up, not stripping me down."

"We can cancel this dinner," he said, nibbling at her ear, "and have a feast right here in our room."

"Given the preparations for tonight, I'm sure that the maître d', the chef and his staff would want to fillet us if we didn't show up."

That reminded Miles of the lavish dinner they had planned. "You're right. We'd better go." After helping Miles with his bow tie and tuxedo accessories, they took one last look in the mirror. Then they headed out the door looking as if they'd stepped right off the cover of *In Style* magazine.

They were chauffeured in a white open-air Jeep with leather upholstery to a cliff that jutted out into the Caribbean Sea. As the driver led them to the private candlelit table at the point of the promontory, Morgan's breath caught at the view. The tropical sun was beginning to set, casting a radiant glow on the ocean. A table was set for two with white English linen, antique silverware, and an exotic floral arrangement of hibiscus, tiger lilies and irises. Two frosted flutes of champagne were ready for their guests.

"This is truly spectacular," Morgan said, slowly inhaling the smell of the warm, sweet air. Below them was the sound of crashing waves.

Miles took Morgan's hand. "So are you."

The head waiter appeared to greet them and discuss the food selection for each of the four courses. The first would be a mixed green salad with raspberry vinaigrette, followed by herb-crusted quail with wild rice and plantains and then an assortment of garden vegetables and curried red snapper. For dessert they were having passion fruit sorbet.

After the waiter retreated, Morgan picked up her glass and said, "I propose a toast to the sexiest, smartest and best lover that Sound Entertainment has ever had the good sense to promote to president. To your promotion, baby. Congratulations, you deserve it and more!"

Raising his glass, Miles smiled proudly. Then he leaned over to kiss her.

Sliding their chairs closer together, they held hands and watched the progression of the stunning sunset. As they moved through the courses of sumptuous food, the orange glow that had welcomed them gave way to a burnt red that faded into pinkish purple right before their starstruck eyes. No performance on Broadway could top that show.

While feeding each other tiny spoons of the sorbet, Miles said, "You know, sometimes I think our lives are about as picture perfect as that sunset. We both have great careers, a wonderful home, investment property on the horizon, and money in the bank. There's only one thing missing."

"I can't imagine what that could be," Morgan said, intoxicated by the food, view and champagne.

"A baby." She looked up at him, taken by surprise. "I think it's time we create our own natural wonder."

"Are you sure you're ready?" Morgan asked, holding her breath.

"I'm more than ready," he answered, smiling. "In fact, let's get back to the room and get started right away."

Morgan had already asked the concierge to have candles arranged and lit upon their return. With the French patio doors open, a gentle ocean breeze floated through the gauze curtains, causing the candles to flicker, seemingly in time to the soft music that chimed throughout the suite.

The candles, breeze and music said everything that Miles needed to hear. Anything else was spoken in Morgan's eyes. Without saying a word, he turned her around and began untying her dress. The light fabric floated like a summer breeze to the floor. Then he planted wet, sucking kisses down her spine, sending cascading waves of chills throughout her body. Now on his knees, with his teeth, he pulled her lace thong to join her dress in the heap on the floor. Miles then masterfully explored her natural wonders with tongue and teeth, while she stood, legs apart, head thrown back, giving him ready access.

When he stood up again, Morgan faced him naked, kicking off her four-inch satin Blahniks. She began undressing him slowly, uncovering the tastiest dish of the night. Kneeling before him, she first nibbled and licked, then tasted, before finally consuming Miles, leaving him panting for more.

Laying him on his back, Morgan continued to cover his body with tender fingertip caresses and tingling kisses, until he ached to release his building tension. Rising to meet her, Miles was gently pushed back onto the bed as Morgan mounted him instead. Working them both to a fast and furious pace, she rode him off into the sunset.

Afterward, like embers from a blazing fire, they lay smoldering next to each other, waiting for that one wild stray spark that would suddenly reignite their passions.

Suddenly, they were startled by an urgently ringing phone. "Hello," Morgan answered reluctantly after the insistent sixth ring. Her voice could barely mask the languor she was feeling.

"Morgan, it's me, Blake," he said, sniffling and gasping for breath. "I—I'm sorry to d-d-disturb your vacation, but I really needed to talk to someone, and I remembered you mentioning the resort last week. I hope you don't mind me calling."

"Blake, what's wrong?" she asked, sitting up in bed.

"My grandfather died this morning," Blake answered, bursting into tears.

"I'm so sorry. What happened?" she asked. She was concerned, but was also concerned about the damper this call was putting on her fire. She looked longingly over her shoulder at Miles as he lay in bed with a questioning look.

"He died suddenly of a heart attack at the family house in the Hamptons. He meant everything to me, and I was his favorite grandchild. Grandfather was the only one who ever truly understood me," Blake said, composing himself. "I loved him so much, but didn't get to tell him."

"I am sure he knew," Morgan said.

"I know, but it still hurts. His last words were, 'Tell Blake I love him and to make me proud.' " Blake began to cry again, but more quietly this time.

At a loss for words, Morgan said, "Is there anything I can do? I'll be back in the city on Sunday. I know, let me take you out to dinner at the beginning of the week," she offered, hoping to cheer him up.

"That's a good idea. The funeral is Saturday, so by the time you get back, the relatives should have crawled back into the woodwork and I'll need some sane conversation. So call me when you return," Blake said.

Hanging up the phone, Morgan snuggled up to Miles. "That was Blake," she said, answering his unspoken question. "His grandfather died."

"And . . . ?" Miles asked, not seeing the connection.

"And he needed someone to talk to."

Miles pulled away to look at her. "Out of the ten million people living in Manhattan, he had to call all the way to Barbados for you?"

"I think he's just in shock. They were very close."

Miles made a wry face. "So were we until he called."

"I think," Morgan said, snuggling close, "I can fix that."

13

The memorial service for Winston Alexander, Blake's grand-father, was held at a Gothic cathedral on the Upper East Side. The stately house of worship was packed with important people from many walks of life. Since the Alexanders had spent just as many years in Europe as in the U.S., the mourners looked like an assembly of the United Nations—even more so since Dr. St. James was the U.N.'s medical director. Politicians, heads of state, physicians and well-known entertainers had all come to pay their final respects to the great man.

The strains of a somber cello filled the air as the immediate family made their way to the front pew. Blake stood erect behind his older brother, Carlton, and his wife, Roshumba, as his parents entered the church on either side of his newly wid-owed grandmother. Katherine, his mother, wore a black Chris-tian Dior suit that was both elegant and understated. Her veil discreetly hid a woman of striking beauty. High cheekbones gave dimension and intrigue to a dark ebony complexion and sharp angular features. His father looked like an ambassador in that stately, rich way that only a distinguished man could pull off. His dark suit was expertly tailored, adding to his com-manding presence. He wore a thick black silk tie with subtle ribbing for texture.

Following their parents, Mr. Holier-than-thou Carlton and his money-grubbing wife made their way down the aisle. Carl-ton had not one ounce of the stature of their father. Instead, he was portly and desperately in need of his own expert tailor. As a lawyer, he also tended to take himself way too seriously and therefore could not comprehend the likes of Blake, whose place in the family hierarchy was never more clear than now.

He was paired with Justin. While Blake walked, head high, down the aisle, clad in a black Armani suit with a Versace tie, Justin floated down next to him in a suit that bore an uncanny resemblance to polyester! Blake thought the sheen was atrocious.

Behind them was an honorary member of the family, Mattie, their maid for over thirty years. Though from poor lineage, her demeanor was often more dignified than that of her wealthy employers.

As Blake approached the front pew and took his place with the family, he felt an instinctive chill roll down the pew, the source of which he detected after glancing to the last seat. There sat Tyrone. He had apparently arrived early and taken a seat in the family pew as though it was his inalienable right. Judging from the tightness in his mother's clenched jaw, Blake knew that she thought otherwise.

After Archbishop McDonald had all but anointed the deceased into sainthood, and prayers and eulogies had been eloquently delivered, the family led the exodus from the cathedral, with Blake and Justin now leading the way. Once on Park Avenue, Tyrone made a beeline to Blake.

"Hey, man, I'm sorry about your grandfather," he said, clasping Blake's hands in his.

"Thank you," Blake answered quietly.

"How you doing?" Tyrone was anxious to establish a connection now that the prospect of a will could offer a new trust fund for Blake.

"It's been tough, but we're doing as well as can be expected."

"If there is anything that I can do to help . . ." Tyrone raised an eyebrow to emphasize "anything."

"Thanks for the offer, but—"

"Do you want to get together later?" Tyrone asked hopefully.

"After we leave the cemetery, there is a reception, followed by a dinner, so . . ." Just then Katherine appeared, giving seating instructions for the limos that had just pulled up.

"Blake, you and Justin will ride with Mattie and Roshumba. Your father, grandmother, Carlton and I will ride together." Completely ignoring Tyrone, she gracefully climbed into her limo. The others followed suit, leaving Tyrone once again on the outside looking in.

"Ain't that a bitch!" he muttered to no one in particular.

Later, when Winston Alexander had been duly laid to rest, ashes to ashes, dust to dust, the family joined a reception already in full swing at their trilevel penthouse on Fifth Avenue. Mattie had arranged a small army of chefs, butlers, waiters, valets and florists to make Gramps's going-away party as good as any he'd attended while alive.

Guests meandered through the first floor, marveling at the important works of art and splendid decor. Grand floral arrangements graced the penthouse. The dining room bore a lavish display of Steuben crystal, fine bone china, imported linens and beautiful silver. Several floral arrangements and three silver candelabra adorned the twenty-four-foot dining table. Through the butler's pantry was an industrial kitchen, which was separate from the more decorative family kitchen. From there waiters served trays of appetizers and a wide assortment of beverages, including vintage French wines.

Justin took a complete beverage tray to the private library upstairs in order to save the waiters the trips back and forth. Besides, with an inheritance on the horizon, he had lots to celebrate. He was still warming up, on his third drink, when Blake strolled into the library also looking for a retreat, only to find his brother camped out drinking his firewater.

"So, if it isn't Mr. Hoity-Toity," Justin said.

"You shouldn't attempt multisyllabic words when you've been drinking. In case you haven't noticed, you're slurring badly. Not that you ever enunciate particularly well, even when you're sober," Blake shot back.

"My, my, my, aren't we testy?" Justin said, not the least bit put off.

"Considering you walked into the funeral high as Mount Everest, I don't think you've seen testy yet. Wait till Momsy gets her hands on you."

"Who are you to pass judgment on me? You think we don't all know about you and your sleazy little affairs? Not to mention, I'm not the only druggie in this esteemed family. You act all dignified around Dad, but when you strut out of this house, your Jekyll and Hyde ass turns into the freak of the week."

"What the hell are you talking about?" Blake asked indignantly.

"Don't play dumb," Justin snarled. "I know all about your little 'drug issue.' "

"I think the years of drugs and alcohol have finally caught up with you. You're delusional," Blake said, dismissing Justin's ramblings.

"Au contraire. It's you that's been caught," Justin snarled, eyebrows slowly rising. "Does San Francisco ring a bell?"

Blake's voice turned weak and shaky. "You know about that?"

Immediately the memories came flooding forward. Tyrone and Blake had been hanging out in the City by the Bay while Blake finished a monthlong tour of wineries in the Napa and Sonoma valleys. One night as they walked down Geary on the way to meet some of Blake's friends, they impulsively stopped in at a gay bar called The Tight Spot. It had been Tyrone's suggestion. He felt it would add a little "adventure" to the night. And always down for a little excitement, Blake had readily agreed. The club was thumping. True to its name, it was as tight as a can of sardines. With The Weather Girls' "It's Raining Men" feeding the frenzy, the boys were in rare form. At first glance it looked like any other club, a room full of women and men, but the women, though drop-dead gorgeous, were packing below the belt.

Preferring his meat a little tougher tonight, Blake zeroed in on a bodybuilding, strong, silent type who was leaning against the bar in Levi's and a tight white T-shirt.

"Nice crowd," Blake said as he stealthily approached his prey.

"It is now," Mr. Atlas replied invitingly.

After a few drinks at the bar, Blake hinted suggestively, "Why don't we go somewhere—how shall I say—a bit less crowded?"

"Why not?" Mr. Atlas said, eyeing Blake in all the right spots.

The Tight Spot, like many such clubs, had private rooms that allowed their customers to have more intimate parties. As Blake and Mr. Atlas made their way to one such room, Tyrone appeared at Blake's side and slid him a folded twenty-dollar bill with a gram of coke in it.

"It looks like you might need this more than I will," Tyrone said, giving Blake's catch a once-over.

"Thanks," Blake said. Being a recreational drug user with Tyrone since his preteens, he knew that sex and drugs, especially cocaine, were a kick-ass combination. He gladly pocketed the coke and kept on going.

Once inside the dark private room, he turned to get a better view of his prize for the night and instead found himself staring at the shiny gold badge of San Francisco's finest.

"You are under arrest for possession of an illegal substance. You have the right to remain silent. Anything you say can and will be used against you in a court of . . ." As the officer continued to read Blake his Miranda rights, he stared in disbelief. Blake was led away in cuffs to a patrol car that sat waiting a block away. On the way he caught sight of Tyrone at the other end of the bar and mouthed, "Help . . ."

He later discovered that the officer had seen his exchange with Tyrone. Though money had not changed hands, it looked like a drug buy. Since he already had a lead on Blake for solicitation, he arrested him, and Tyrone, of course, got away. But to his credit, Tyrone was at the jail before the ink dried on Blake's thumbprint. Since Blake had no prior offenses, he was able to post bail, later pay a fine and forget it ever happened. At least until now.

Just then Carlton walked in, his belly leading the way. Now turning his venom on him, Justin snapped, "What is this, a private family reunion? Had I known I, for one, certainly wouldn't have come here!"

"Shut up, Justin!" Blake fumed. Frowning, he wondered how Justin had found out about his unfortunate misadventure, and even more importantly, whether he had told anyone else.

"Whoa, what is this all about?" Carlton asked, quickly sensing that he had stumbled into a hornets' nest.

"Oh, nothing. Just your usual Justin drama," Blake answered, rolling his eyes.

"Well, soon you won't have to worry about seeing the next act. As soon as I get my money, I'm out of here," Justin announced, absently slugging back his fourth drink.

"What money?" Carlton, asked, warming to his role as the esteemed barrister.

"My inheritance," Justin snapped back.

"Just so you know, I looked over Grandfather's will, and you may have a bit of a problem."

"What problem?" Justin asked, suddenly sober.

"There is a drug clause which stipulates a revocation in the event of drug use by a family member."

"A re-re-revo what!" Justin stammered.

"Exactly what does this mean?" Blake asked, his own concern growing. Though he wasn't sure if Justin had already snitched to Carlton about the San Fran incident, he was sure that he could count on him to now. After all, misery does love company.

Fully in character now, Carlton replied, "A revocation, in lay terms, is a disinheritance. Right now I'm not sure in practical terms exactly what it means, but I'm sure the family trust attorneys will be looking into it." The two brothers, who seconds earlier were tearing each other to shreds, both stared, unified in disbelief. Carlton, with his civic duty done, exited stage left. Justin and Blake both felt as though the curtain had just come crashing down.

14

Morgan floated into her office the Monday morning after the relaxing week in Barbados. The time away had helped to put everything into perspective: her job, her marriage and her future. Life was good. After she settled at her desk with a mug of hot coffee, Aimee, her assistant, informed her that Mark, the hiring manager for the senior v.p. position, wanted to see her that afternoon. Immediately, butterflies began flitting about in the pit of her stomach.

Looking for reassurance, she dialed Miles's office, only to be told that he was in a closed-door meeting. So she did the next best thing and called Dakota. "Hey, girl."

"What's up?"

Morgan heard the frantic buzz of the trading floor in the background and in Dakota's rushed tone. Morgan quickly got to the point. "Mark wants to meet with me after lunch. I'm sure it's about the promotion."

Hearing a tinge of hesitancy in Morgan's voice, Dakota asked, "So what's the problem? You know you've got it."

"Sometimes I'm not so sure," Morgan confessed.

"From what you've told me, the choice is obvious."

"Yeah, but sometimes things aren't that black and white. Pardon the pun."

"There is no way in this day and age that a Fortune 500 company would be so blatantly nepotistic." Dakota, as usual, sounded so sure.

"You're right," Morgan said, instantly feeling better.

"Girl, go get your corner office. Listen, I've got to run. Employment rates were announced this morning, and the market is on a hell of a roller coaster."

"I'll call you later." Morgan hung up, feeling renewed confidence.

After lunch, she stopped by the powder room to check her makeup before heading up to the forty-eighth floor. As she exited the elevator and turned the corner, she caught sight of Brian, headed in the opposite direction. Her heart lurched. It was general practice for the hiring manager to tell the losing candidate their fate before congratulating the winner. Morgan finally allowed herself to believe she really would be the senior vice president of New Market Development, with a corner office and all the other trappings that go with the prestigious title. She took one last deep breath.

"Good afternoon, Mark," she said, striding into his well-appointed office.

"Good afternoon, Morgan. Please have a seat," he said, motioning toward the overstuffed chair opposite his leather-inlaid desk. On the credenza behind him were memorabilia from a life that had gone just according to plan. There were several awards for his outstanding service to Global Financial, framed pictures of him with the chairman and CEO, along with other markings of success. On the wall, over the credenza, were framed diplomas from Princeton and Wharton, along with a photograph of him and a gentleman who most certainly was his father. They both had the same pinkish coloring and deeply receding hairline. They stood on a pristine golf course with a black caddie in the background. A brass label beneath the picture read, "Tuxedo Park Country Club." The overheard conversation in the bathroom quickly flashed through Morgan's mind.

"Morgan, I'm sure I don't have to tell you that you are a bright and valued member of the team," he began. Morgan's anxiety started to mount. "And though your skills are considerable, I'm looking for someone with a very specific profile to be my new senior vice president of New Market Development. I really need someone with a strong financial background. For that reason I've chosen Brian as my new senior v.p."

His last words reverberated through Morgan's mind. Even though Jill and Helen had unintentionally warned her, she was nonetheless stunned. What kind of flimsy excuse was that. Since when did a marketing v.p. need finance skills? Morgan felt as if the rug had been yanked from underneath her.

Numb with anger, she stood to leave. Glaring back at Mark, she couldn't resist firing a parting salvo. "I see the good-ole-boy network is alive and thriving north of the Mason-Dixon line."

"What do you mean by that?" he replied defensively. "This decision was based solely on qualifications."

"Ooh, of *that* I am sure! Qualifications I will *never* have. Let's start with white skin and country club connections," she spat, feeling her emotions rising to a crescendo from which there could be no return.

"Morgan, please be—" Morgan never heard the word "reasonable." Neither did Mark. Instead, *she* heard the sound of his door nearly bouncing off its frame. *He* heard the reverberations as the impact temporarily rattled every artifact in the battleground that was his office. In her wake, his wall hangings were left askew—including, the framed memento from the Tuxedo Park Country Club.

Mark's assistant sat, mouth agape, as she watched Morgan storm down the hall in a blur.

With the gale safely past, Mark calmly straightened his wall hangings, lingering tenderly on the one of him and his father. Despite the squall, his long-term forecast was bright and sunny.

After the crushing defeat, Morgan sat at her desk, trying to swallow the dose of rage and despair that had just been dished out. Determined not to cry, she called Miles for a measure of strength and reassurance. She told him what happened. "What's the point?" she asked him. "Whatever happened to working hard, doing the right thing and succeeding?"

"Baby, I know it's not fair, but you have to keep your head up. Don't let them get you down," Miles pleaded.

"Now that I've had my head rudely snatched out of the sand, I see corporate America for exactly what it is—a glorified good-ole-boy's country club."

"I'm sorry, baby. But look at it this way. Now you know what you're up against, you just have to work that much harder."

"Yessir, masser. How many mo' bales a cotton you want now?" Morgan said, bitterly imitating a shuffling slave.

"Don't worry. Your time will come," Miles said with conviction.

"I don't know," she said. "I think I may have reached my glass ceiling."

A few minutes later, she experienced further fallout. Joel's secretary called to summon her into his office. Now *she* felt like the lamb being led to slaughter.

With thinly veiled composure, Morgan walked down the hall, knowing in the pit of her stomach that she was heading into the lion's den.

"Morgan, have a seat," Joel instructed, with not so much as a "how are you." Once seated, he removed his glasses as though terribly fatigued. "I just got a call from Mark. And I am terribly disappointed by your actions."

Feeling the sting of salt in her open wound, Morgan tried to defend herself. "Joel, perhaps I did get a little upset, but given the circumstances—"

Joel interrupted her. "What circumstances? Just because you didn't get a job that you thought you deserved does not give you the right to accuse a senior executive of unethical conduct. Nor does it give you the right to slam the door and storm out of a meeting." His one long brow curled across his forehead.

"But, Joel—" she started.

"There are no buts about it. I consider your behavior a serious breach of professional conduct and will document your file accordingly."

"But . . . but . . ." She suddenly felt assaulted by the flurry of blows.

"Meeting's over," he announced. He replaced his glasses

and turned his attention back to the report he had been reading, effectively dismissing her.

As luck would have it, she had to attend an after-hours retirement party for another executive that night. As much as she would have loved to go straight home for a long, hot soak, politically she had no choice. And by now she needed every political point she could muster to stay in the game.

Morgan arrived late, a couple of drinks after the appointed hour. True to form, old, stiff white men by then had completed their transformation into Austin Powers, and middle-aged white women were proving how "loose" they really were. *Just what I need*, thought Morgan, *a group of lubed-up, let's-get-friendly white folks who tomorrow morning will return to uptight, this-is-my-world-find-another-nut crackers.*

Game face on, she walked up to the bar and ordered a glass of wine. "Is that all you're drinking? Have a double vodka and tonic," slurred Joel. He had apparently forgotten about this afternoon. He tended to do that, she'd learned, at cocktail hour.

"No, thanks, I'll stick with wine," Morgan answered evenly.

"You know, Morgan, that's what's wrong with you. You're a little too uptight." Joel nodded as he slithered closer to her. So close, in fact, that his rancid breath was cutting off her air supply.

"Thanks for the advice," Morgan answered, maneuvering sideways to leave the bar. What a creep!

As she made her way through the inebriated group, her plan was to give her well wishes to the man of the hour, finish her glass of wine, see and be seen, and then leave—quickly. Experience had taught her the less time spent at these affairs, the better. She certainly was no prude, but she also knew that she couldn't get away with the antics of her lily-white counterparts. If she had two drinks, she became an alcoholic. If she danced the least bit suggestively, she became even worse—a whore. Yet if she didn't do either, she was stuck up, uptight and not a team player. Damned if you did, damned if you didn't.

As the informal round of speeches began, Morgan made her way to a table where a few colleagues were gathered, including Linda Franklin, with whom she had worked on several projects. Glad to spot a friendly face, Morgan pulled up a chair between Linda and one of the secretaries.

"Hi," Morgan said, greeting her coworkers. As Linda turned toward her, she asked, "How long have you been here?"

Linda answered, "Not long." Then she abruptly turned back to the person on her right.

Feeling slightly shunned, Morgan waited for a pause in Linda's conversation and said, "I hear that your department may be expanded next quarter." Instead of the customary exchange of office gossip, she got an indifferent shrug of Linda's shoulder and another view of her back.

Surprised by her aloofness, Morgan turned to the secretary at her left. Before she could get "How are you?" out of her mouth, the woman tossed her head, flipping mousy-brown hair within inches of Morgan's nose as she too gave the cold shoulder. Morgan gazed around the room, feeling eerily detached from the situation.

Morgan had to face a hard fact. In the white man's world, regardless of diversity training, affirmative action, or the occasional "anointed one," the rules of the game were different for her than for her pale-faced counterparts. Break these rules or cross the line and you are subject to the corporate equivalent of rollerball. And it was always a home game for them.

15

Though still in shock from work, Morgan kept her promise to Blake, taking him to Brooklyn's River Café. The restaurant was gentility combined with urban chic. The food and service were impeccable, and nothing could surpass the spectacular view from the patio, which looked out over the East River. From downtown up through midtown, Manhattan's skyline was spread out in a galaxy. Like stars, lights from the Twin Towers, the Chrysler and Empire State Buildings, twinkled off the water flowing underneath the Brooklyn Bridge.

Blake wasted no time telling Morgan the drama that had unfolded during the preceding week. "By the time I finally got to the Hamptons, the whole family was in the throes of hysteria. Momsy, the doctor, was canvassing the house with a syringe full of Seconal, sedating anybody she diagnosed as 'out of control,' including Grandmother, whom she still hadn't forgiven for taking over the penthouse and ambushing Mattie."

"How is your grandmother taking your grandfather's death?" Morgan asked. Though she hadn't met his family, he spoke of them so often, she felt she knew them.

"Not very well, actually. She traveled the world for over fifty years with him and is not accustomed to being alone, so naturally she doesn't want to go back to Paris by herself. But moving to the States would also be a big adjustment. So I'm not sure what she'll do. Me either, for that matter. I miss him already. He was the only person in the family who truly understood me and accepted me for what I am."

With a faraway look in his eyes, Blake smiled at a distant memory. "When I was thirteen, I snuck into my mother's dressing room one afternoon while my parents were out to a matinee. I had always been fascinated with Momsy's beautiful gowns and loved those gorgeous spiked heels. So that day I decided to dress in her new pink-sequined evening dress, with a pair of four-inch sandals and a black wig that I'd found in a little box tucked at the back of her closet. After putting on the wig, I got even more daring and went for the makeup too. There I was, all dolled up and practicing my sashay, when the heel of the shoe caught the hem of her long beautiful dress, sending me flailing to the floor. I landed spread-eagled, ripping a gaping hole in the delicate silk."

Intrigued by Blake's story Morgan took a sip of her martini and leaned forward to hear how it turned out.

"Grandfather, startled by the noise, ran into the room. And there I was, sitting in the middle of the floor crying. Though I know he was shocked at the sight, he picked me up, helped me out of the gown, and immediately called Chanel, ordering a replacement from the Fifth Avenue store. He never mentioned that incident again." Blake grew silent, his eyes out of focus, as though vividly reliving the memory.

"It sounds like you two were very close," Morgan said.

"We were, which is why I feel so guilty for not being there for him. He hung on for a while, asking for me just before he died. The family tried to reach me, and what was I doing? Having my toenails done! I am so disgusted with myself," Blake said despondently.

Morgan suddenly turned sad as well. "What's wrong?" Blake asked, noticing her sudden mood change.

"I was just thinking about my father. He died of bone cancer," she said, looking down. "When he was first diagnosed, I thought it had to be a mistake, and my mother was in *complete* denial. It just didn't seem fair. He had worked so hard to achieve success, so it seemed like a cruel joke for his life to be threatened at just the point when he should have been retiring to enjoy all the free time he'd earned."

"That must have been tough for you and your mother," Blake said, with a concerned frown.

"It was. You know, he put up a good fight. In fact, he braved months of radiation and chemo, but nothing worked." She shuddered at the memory of what the treatments did to him. "The last time I saw my father alive, I hardly recognized him. His face was ashen and gaunt. I tried to keep up a brave front, but that day I broke down and cried right at his bedside. And of course, his stoic facade broke, so our last day together we were unable to console each other." Exhaling deeply, Morgan said, "And the next day he died." She wiped a tear from her eye. "Let's change the subject, before I completely lose it."

Blake waited for her to recover. "I suppose I could tell you about the funeral. Only in my family would that be humorous," Blake said, trying to lighten the moment. "Well, first of all, Justin came high as a kite, wearing flammable fabric. You should have seen the polyester, girl. It was atrocious. And of course, Carlton, as usual, had his nose stuck so far in the air that he needed a control tower to navigate himself. But, worst of all, Tyrone had the nerve to crash the family pew. When we walked in, there he was, sitting front and center, like he was a St. James," Blake said, still astonished.

"What was the harm in him sitting with the family?" Morgan asked, not understanding the big deal. "Didn't he grow up in the same house?"

"He did, and at one point we were very close," Blake explained. "But Tyrone is trouble, and my parents, though they love Mattie, don't really care for him."

"Never a dull moment," Morgan said, slowly shaking her head.

"That's an understatement. But there is a silver lining underneath all that drama," Blake said, his face lighting up.

"What could that be?" Morgan asked.

"Grandfather left me a sizable trust fund. I'll have immediate access to it, which is perfect, since I can't touch my primary trust until I'm thirty-five. And given my spending habits, I could be on welfare by then." Blake laughed.

"You really should think about what you want to do with the rest of your life," Morgan said. "You're so talented, and I hate to see you waste it at the Back Room."

"You know, Morgan, I've actually given the matter some thought. For a while now, ever since returning from France, I've been thinking about an event-planning company. Something really upscale, creating high-concept events for companies and society functions. But I've had two obstacles. The first was capital. There was little chance my father would finance a 'party-planning' company for me. That would be beneath him. But now, with my trust, money is no longer an issue."

"Blake, that's a fantastic idea," Morgan said. "It's the perfect business for you. You know hospitality intimately, and with your contacts, it's a no-lose."

"There's one more obstacle," Blake added, holding his breath.

"I can't imagine what," Morgan said, "with your skills and your money."

"A partner. I've studied fine dining all over the world. Ask me anything about food, wines and cigars. But marketing and business functions are definitely not my forte."

Morgan thought he was being too modest. "It shouldn't be hard for you to find a partner. I'm sure lots of people would jump at the chance to go into business with someone as talented as you are, not to mention one that's fully funded."

"That's exactly what I hoped you'd say," Blake said, smiling broadly.

"What do you mean?" Morgan asked, not quite sure where the conversation was headed.

Leaning forward, Blake propped his elbows squarely on the table. With chin resting on the pyramid his arms formed, he answered her:

"I want you to be my partner."

16

The DJ sat perched high above the dimly lit room, pumping out hip music. Lot 61 felt more like a nightclub than a restaurant. Votive candles illuminated the tables, giving the room a seductive glow. While waiting at the bar for Morgan and Miles, Dakota surveyed the kinetic mix of Wall Streeters, artists, models, and Madison Avenue ad execs. Even on a Tuesday night, the place was throbbing.

The bar was as much a pickup scene as it was a lounge for the restaurant. All around she saw men on the prowl and women posing to be caught. Over her shoulder, she overheard the typical conversation:

"Hi, gorgeous." It was a man's deep voice.

"Hi, yourself," the woman answered, a flirtatious lilt to her voice.

"Are you here with friends? Or would you like some company?"

"Yours? Anytime." It was clear that she liked what she saw.

"Let me buy you a drink. What would you like?"

"A glass of white wine."

"Can I get a glass of chardonnay and a cosmopolitan with fresh lime juice," the deep, sexy voice behind her said over her shoulder to the bartender.

That's exactly how I like my cosmos, Dakota thought, looking over her shoulder to see the man behind the voice. She was pleasantly surprised. "Parker Emilio. Fancy meeting you here," Dakota said, in her low, vampy voice.

"Dakota Cantrell," Parker said, a large smile spreading across his handsome face.

Glancing over her shoulder, Dakota noticed that the Cindy Crawford look-alike who was the woman behind the voice was standing so close behind Parker, she seemed to be affixed to his hip.

"How are you?" Parker asked, as the bartender handed him his drinks. Before she could answer, he turned to the woman and said, "Here's your white wine. Maybe we'll see each other around." Effectively dismissing her.

The woman shot a killer look at Dakota before tossing her hair and turning to leave.

"The question is, how are you?" Dakota asked, glancing at the back of the slighted woman.

"I'm fine now," Parker answered, still smiling broadly. "Are you here for dinner or just drinks?"

"Dinner with friends." She lowered her lids slightly to add a hint of mystery as she gazed over the rim of her martini glass, slowly taking a sip. This was the look that went with the vampy voice.

Just then Morgan and Miles strolled in, looking like the perfect pair. "Hey, girl," Morgan said, greeting Dakota with a hug. "Well, I'll leave you guys to enjoy your dinner," Parker said.

"Parker, these are two of my closest friends, Morgan and Miles Nelson."

Morgan looked at Parker, sizing him up, seeing for herself if Dakota's description was accurate.

"Parker Emilio. Nice to meet you both."

"Why don't you join us?" Dakota asked. "Unless you're meeting someone?" she said, raising her brow and casting a look in the blonde's direction.

"I don't want to intrude," Parker replied unconvincingly.

"No intrusion, just a casual dinner with friends," Dakota said.

Parker smiled. "Well in that case, count me in."

As Dakota and Parker walked ahead toward the table,

Miles turned to Morgan and said, "You didn't tell me Dakota was dating a white guy."

"He's actually half Latin, and they just work together."

Morgan knew he was a little taken aback, but as always, he would be a congenial dinner partner.

Once seated, Miles asked, "So, Parker, where are you from?"

"San Francisco, but I was born in Campeche."

"Where is that?" Miles asked.

"It's a small town near the Gulf of Mexico."

"How did you end up in San Francisco?" Dakota asked, wanting to know more about this man.

"My father is from Texas and my mom is from Mexico. They started a small export business and eventually relocated to San Francisco to open a boutique."

"Do you have brothers and sisters?" Dakota asked.

"No, I'm an only child."

"So am I," Dakota said, glad to find they had something in common.

"How about you?" Parker asked Miles. "Are you a native New Yorker?"

"Yeah, I am, but I've lived in L.A. and Atlanta, which is where Morgan and I met," Miles said, looking at his wife.

Abruptly, Morgan said, "Excuse me." She stood to go to the ladies' room, eyeing Dakota to signal a time-out.

"Ladies," Miles said, as he and Parker stood to excuse them.

Once inside the dimly lit powder room, Morgan said, "Girl, he is really cute and seems nice too."

"I told you he was fly," Dakota said as she took out her lipstick to apply a fresh coat.

"That he is. But there is one small problem," Morgan said, powdering her nose.

"What's that?"

"Well, there is the race issue." She could see that Dakota was totally charmed by this guy. But she needed to take off those rose-colored glasses and see things clearly.

With her usual snap judgment, Dakota replied, "As far as I'm concerned, that's a nonissue."

"Get real, Dakota. This is America. There always has and always will be an issue when it comes to interracial dating. The bottom line is, I just don't want to see you get hurt." Morgan thought about Lisa, her college roommate, who had met and married a white guy without giving it a second thought. Until it was too late. Now, estranged from both families, they didn't fit in anywhere. And their kid had it even worse.

"Thanks for the concern, but please don't worry about me. I got this." Dakota turned to leave, a little too quickly, Morgan thought.

17

Plowed under by the weight of her crumbling career, the seed planted by Blake at the River Café began to take root. Starting a company was becoming a more and more appealing proposition. For the next few weeks Morgan researched the market to evaluate a potential business strategy for an event-planning company.

Over drinks at the Bubble Lounge, Morgan told Dakota about Blake's proposal.

"Are you sure you're not just reacting to not getting the promotion? That's no reason to go into business with someone," Dakota reasoned.

"I'm positive," Morgan answered confidently. "Even if I had gotten the job, I'd still be interested in doing something like this part-time. There's nothing like having your own."

"You aren't planning to quit your job, are you?" Dakota asked, concerned.

"No, not at all. Blake and I discussed it, and he agreed that since my involvement would be to develop marketing strategies and sales channels, I could do that in the evenings or on the weekends."

Dakota took a slow sip of her martini. "What does Miles think about it?"

"I'm not sure," Morgan answered sheepishly, lowering her eyes.

Dakota put her drink down, shocked. "What do you mean, you're not sure? You *have* told him . . . haven't you?"

"Not yet, but I will," Morgan insisted. "I just want to finish some homework before having that conversation." Shifting the topic quickly, she continued. "You wouldn't believe what I've learned already. The opportunity is huge! The top thousand companies in the U.S. spent close to three hundred million dollars last year entertaining customers and employees. Which doesn't include emerging middle-market companies. And based on my experience in corporate America, the majority of those events are planned by administrative assistants who know nothing about negotiating to maximize entertainment budgets. So basically companies are wasting big dollars for mediocre events."

"You're right about that," Dakota conceded. "Shelby plans our company parties, and I'd bet she can't even balance her checkbook."

"That's the way most companies operate," Morgan said, her eyes getting brighter. "We can take advantage of that. I can see us employing a five-year, three-phase growth strategy. Phase one would focus on New York clients that entertain locally. The second would target New Yorkers entertaining in one of ten 'feeder cities.' They would include Chicago, Atlanta, D.C., Miami, Los Angeles, London, Paris, Hong Kong, Milan/Rome and Japan. The third phase would target clients *from* feeder cities entertaining in New York."

Dakota had her chin propped on her fist thoughtfully. "Sounds like a great strategy. What services would you offer?"

By now Morgan's enthusiasm was out on the table. "The core product would be theme development, menu planning and on-site hosting as well as the design of printed materials. I also see a market for executive seminars on topics like social graces, as well as wine and cigar etiquette. These would target middle managers who are promoted to senior levels and are automatically expected to have the savvy to wine and dine clients, but often don't."

Feeling her excitement, Dakota exclaimed, "I love the concept. It's very clever. It could be a gold mine."

"I think so too. Besides, I've done my time," Morgan

announced darkly, "and if they don't appreciate me, I'll create my own Promised Land."

Later, reclined on the chaise in the library, poring over her notes, she was so deep in thought that she didn't hear Miles take his favorite place in his leather recliner. "So, what are you working on?" he asked, happy to see Morgan interested in her job again. Since being passed over for the promotion, she had been listless and uninterested in anything related to work. He had tried to make her see that although it was a big disappointment, she shouldn't take it personally. It was, after all, business.

Distracted, Morgan looked up from her papers and said, "Oh, I'm researching the feasibility of designing a corporate entertainment company."

Miles did not make the connection. "Is Global planning to diversify?"

Morgan remembered what Dakota had said. Putting her papers down, she took a deep breath and turned to Miles. "No. In fact, it's something I want to talk to you about. But I wanted to do my homework first."

Miles set aside his newspaper, as though expecting to hear all of it, so she proceeded to lay out her business strategy.

At the end he asked point-blank, "So this is for that Blake guy?"

"Yes and no." Seeing the confused look on his face, she went further. "Well, in a sense it is for Blake, but he has also asked me to be his partner."

"Partner?" Miles repeated, not quite sure that he had heard her correctly.

"Yes, partner. Blake has inherited a four-million-dollar trust fund from his grandfather's estate. He wants to use it to start this business, and he has asked me to work with him on the business-development side."

Shocked, Miles said, "Morgan, going into business with someone is like getting married. You're joined at the hip. And you certainly don't know Blake well enough to make that kind of commitment."

"You're right, but I do know that Blake is brilliant with food, wine and hospitality. He has studied it around the world. And not only have I seen it firsthand, but he has told me about some of the elaborate events he's planned. His father is the medical director for the United Nations, and many of the embassies have already used Blake. So his expertise, contacts and money, along with my brains, make the perfect marriage. Plus he's witty, charming and speaks five languages. He's the perfect partner for this type of business."

Morgan knew that Miles would oppose her plans to go into business with Blake. As wonderful as she and Dakota thought Blake was, for some reason Miles had never warmed up to him. So, just as she had suspected, he had issues, which was why she had put off telling him in the first place.

Miles had clearly been knocked for a loop. "What about your job?"

"I'll keep it. At least until we're rolling in the dough, and by then I won't need it and certainly won't miss it," Morgan said stubbornly.

"Maybe you haven't thought this through enough? You know we both have to show stable incomes to qualify for the loan on the brownstone."

"Miles, I told you, I won't quit my job until after we've purchased the building. In fact, I'll stay until our profits show consistent income at least matching my current salary."

"So, in effect you'd have two jobs. Tell me, where do I fit into these plans?" Miles asked, throwing his arms in the air for emphasis. "Not to mention our decision to have a baby. I guess you forgot about that."

Morgan had not forgotten anything. She had thought about all of these problems. "My part in building the business I could do with my hands tied behind my back. It's simply strategy work. So it won't take much of my time," she said pleadingly. "Besides, long-term it's perfect for starting a family. I'd have a more flexible schedule, so we won't have to rely on a nanny to raise our child."

Miles wasn't going to budge. "I just don't think that this is such a good idea. You barely know the man."

"Miles, trust me," she implored.

"It's not you that I'm worried about," Miles said testily.

"Miles, why can't you just support me and be happy that I've found what could be a good opportunity?" Morgan said, getting exasperated. "Why not just say, 'I'm with you and I hope it works out'?"

"I just hope you know what you're getting into," he said, gathering his newspaper and stalking out of the library.

"I am completely capable of making decisions, thank you very much," she said to his retreating back.

18

Dakota couldn't wait for the closing bell to signal the start of the weekend. By 4:04 she was already on the elevator headed home. As the doors were closing, she heard a voice yell, "Hold that!" She pressed the open button just before they clamped shut.

"Good hands," said Parker with a wide grin as he walked into the elevator. He was wearing a slate-gray suit, white shirt and muted silver tie.

"Aim to please," Dakota shot back. She looked the handsome hunk up and down, imagining where she'd really like to put her hands.

"So, Ms. Cantrell, I haven't seen you since Tuesday night. Have you been busy or are you avoiding me?" Parker asked.

Avoid you? she thought, unconsciously licking her lips. *What I'd really like to do is sop you up with a biscuit.* Instead she said, "Avoid you, never," adding, "I've just been slaving and waiting for Friday to get my two-day pass from the Big House."

"Big House? Well, that's a unique name for the office. Any plans this weekend?"

"No, just taking it easy," Dakota answered, holding her breath.

"Why don't you come with me to Bergdorf's? I have to pick up a few things, and I could use your expert opinion," he said, admiring her stylish look. "Afterward, I'll take you to dinner to cover your consulting fee. How 'bout it?"

Dakota pretended to contemplate Parker's offer as the doors opened onto the ground floor. "I'd be glad to," she said.

The men's store of Bergdorf Goodman was located on the corner of Fifty-eighth and Fifth Avenue, directly across the street from the women's store. After they entered, Parker headed for the highly polished glass cases displaying designer cuff links, studs and tie tacks. "What are you looking for?" Dakota asked as they approached men's ties. She had shopped Bergdorf's men's department before, looking for gifts for Jackson.

"I need a few shirts with French cuffs, and one or two pairs of slacks."

"Well, why don't we start with the shirts?" Dakota stopped and lifted one end of a silk Michael Newell tie. "You like this color?"

Parker squinted at it. "I do, but what color is it? It's not purple and it's not blue."

"It's periwinkle," Dakota said.

"I would have called it blurple," Parker said, laughing. "Actually, I know what color it is. I was just testing you."

An impeccably dressed salesman in a four-button navy suit walked up to Parker and asked, "May I help you?"

"No, thank you."

The salesman was unfazed. "You would look divine in a Donna Karan gabardine overcoat," he said, edging closer to Parker.

"I already have one, thank you."

Like magic, a white card appeared in his hands. "Here's my card. Please call me if I can ever assist you in the future."

Dakota raised her eyebrows and said, "If I didn't know any better, I'd say he was coming on to you."

"Trust me, men don't float my boat," Parker said, tearing up the card. "Where were we?"

"We were trying to find a blurple shirt," Dakota said. She picked up a periwinkle shirt.

"I like that. You have a sense of humor," Parker said. "I got a joke for you. This lady approaches her priest and says, 'Father, I have a problem. I have two female parrots, but they only know how to say one thing.' 'What do they say?' the priest asks. 'Hi, we're prostitutes. Want to have some fun?' 'That's terrible!' the priest says. 'But I have a solution to your problem. Bring your parrots over to my house, and I will put them with my two male parrots that I taught to pray and read the Bible. My parrots will teach your parrots to stop saying that terrible phrase.' 'Thank you,' the woman says. The next day she brings her parrots to the priest's house. His parrots are in their cage holding rosary beads and praying. The lady puts her parrots in with the male parrots. Immediately, the female parrots say, 'Hi, we're prostitutes. Want to have some fun?' One male parrot looks over at the other and says, 'Put the beads away. Our prayers have been answered!' "

They both broke out laughing.

"That's too funny," Dakota said. "I've got one for you too. There is this little guy sitting in a bar, drinking, minding his own business when all of a sudden this great big dude comes in and *whack!* knocks him clean off the bar stool onto the floor. The big guy says, 'That was a karate chop from Korea.' The little guy thinks, 'Damn,' but he gets back up on the stool and continues drinking. All of a sudden, *whack!* The big guy knocks him down again and says, 'That was a judo chop from Japan.' The little guy has had enough. He gets up, brushes himself off and quietly leaves. After an hour he comes back and without saying a word walks up behind the big guy and bangs him in the head, knocking him out cold. Then he turns to the bartender and says, 'When he comes to, tell him that was a crowbar from Sears.' "

"That's funny," Parker said, laughing and exposing a perfect set of pearly whites. "Okay. Let's get down to business. I think this shirt matches. Let's see." He walked over to Dakota to match the shirt with the tie she was holding. Yet he didn't seem satisfied. "I don't know. Here, hold the tie up against the shirt this way." Parker walked over to the mirror, took the shirt from her and held it against his chest. Dakota came up close and put the tie to his neck, smoothing out the shirt while getting in an "innocent" feel of his well-defined chest. As they stood there looking in the mirror, Dakota could feel her body heat rising. "I think it's a match," Parker said, looking at her in the mirror.

"Definitely," Dakota said with a sexy smirk. Inside, though, she was on fire. She had to get some fresh air to compose herself before she completely overheated. She had never dated a white guy before and didn't know if her nervous energy was because of the newness of it or because of Parker himself. "Look, I'm going across the street to the women's store and pick up a few things. I'll meet you out front in thirty minutes."

When they finished the minishopping expedition, they headed to Circus, a Brazilian restaurant on the East Side. After ordering a pitcher of carpennias, a potent Brazilian drink, Dakota asked, "Where did you go to school?"

"Pepperdine."

"Isn't that in Malibu?"

"It is," he said, grinning. "The campus is amazing. Going to school there was like being on a four-year vacation." Parker paused to taste his drink. "Is the carpennia too strong for you?"

"I can handle it. I'm a big girl," Dakota said, winking at him. "So tell me, how did you end up in New York?"

"After graduation I moved to London to work for Harrods. But I quickly realized I didn't want a career in fashion. So I moved to New York, got a master's in finance from NYU, worked for Citigroup for a couple of years, then joined SBI last month."

As Parker refilled Dakota's still half-filled glass, she asked, "Are you trying to get me tipsy?"

"And I thought I was being subtle."

Dakota, enjoying a warm buzz, looked around the dimly lit restaurant. There were colorful circus acts creatively painted on the walls and whimsical light fixtures throughout. The place was filled with couples of all ages who seemed to be enchanted by each other. The restaurant had a magical aura, which was only enhanced by the lethal drinks.

Parker leaned across the table toward Dakota and asked, "So tell me, why are you flying solo on a Friday night?"

"How do you know," Dakota asked in a low, provocative

tone, "that I don't have plans for later tonight?" She leaned in so close that her face almost touched his.

"Because any man in his right mind would have scooped you up right after the close."

"Like you did."

Parker looked as though he was getting lost in her big brown eyes. "Nothing gets past you, huh?"

"Not much."

Just then the waiter brought their meals. Dakota had ordered stewed lobster in a spicy black bean sauce with a plantain garnish. Parker had goat, grilled over an open fire with rice and peas baked with fresh coconut.

"You want to try some goat?" he offered.

"No, thanks. Here, try the lobster," Dakota said, sliding a forkful of the succulent dish in his mouth.

Her boldness delighted him. "Hmm, that is good."

Their verbal play went on throughout dinner, and after settling the bill they walked out to head home.

"Where do you live?" Dakota asked, feeling stuffed.

"Upper West Side."

"I'm down near the Seaport." Dakota looked up into his sexy turquoise eyes. "Parker, tonight was great. Thanks for dinner."

"Trust me, the pleasure was all mine. Can I call you over the weekend?" he asked.

"I would like that." She usually didn't give out her number on the first date. She didn't like having to wait on a call that might not come. But Parker was so charismatic, she decided to break her self-imposed rule. She jotted down her number on the matchbook from the restaurant. As she handed it to him, he took her hand and pulled her close, giving her a warm hug.

He released her to hail a cab. A taxi pulled up and he helped her in. "Talk to you soon," he said as he closed the car door. She smiled all the way home, oblivious to the frantic driving of the taxi driver. Nothing could ruin the warm glow she felt from being with Parker Emilo.

The next morning, Parker called bright and early, catching

Dakota off guard. After some chitchat, they made plans to meet in SoHo. Hanging up, she hurled aside the Saturday *New York Times*, took a last sip from her mug of almond-nut coffee, and quickly jumped into the shower. As the steaming-hot water flowed over her body, thoughts of Parker ran through her mind. She imagined his hands exploring her, finding all of her hidden treasures. When Dakota was finished showering, she decided to spice up her casual look with a sheer black nylon tee, black lace bra and leather jacket. That would give him something to think about.

They had lunch at Cipriani's, a quaint Northern Italian restaurant. Though they had choice outdoor seating, it was a little brisk for Dakota, so they sat at a table by the window, watching the endless stream of artsy natives and suburban tourists wandering by. SoHo was so different from Midtown and Uptown, it felt like a different city altogether.

After lunch, Parker suggested they hit a few galleries in the area.

As they entered the Gagosian Art Gallery on Wooster Street, Dakota said, "You know, some people at the office think you're conceited."

Parker looked expectantly into her eyes. "What do you think?"

"Well, the thought entered my mind initially," she said, trying to keep her tone as light as possible.

"Frankly, what 'other people' think dosen't concern me, but I guess I'll have to prove you wrong," Parker said, not the least bit flustered.

Together they looked around at a wall of surrealistic paintings. "What is this supposed to be?" he asked, looking at a garish mélange of oranges and purples.

Tilting her head to one side, then the other, trying to make out the weird piece, she said, "From what I can tell, it's the body of a gazelle, with a face of a woman, who's swimming in a sea of shopping bags."

Reading the price catalogue in his hand, Parker said, "And, for a mere twenty-five thousand dollars, it can be yours."

"I'll pass, thank you very much."

He elbowed her lightly and pointed toward the door. "Come on, Miss Art Critic, I know a great place around the corner that makes the best espresso."

Walking toward Prince Street, they passed a corner store with flowers of every possible color set up on the sidewalk. Excusing herself, Dakota went in to buy a pack of mints. When she came out, Parker presented her with a rainbow of two dozen flowers, wrapped in beautiful thick paper. Dakota was for once speechless. "I don't know what to say. I guess thank you will have to do."

Parker stood there beaming. "Seeing your smile is thank-you enough."

They walked through SoHo, arm in arm, with Dakota admiring the flowers. Just as they turned off West Broadway onto Spring Street, she noticed a tall, shapely blonde ahead with hands planted on her hips and mouth agape. It was Shelby. Her expression was a combination of "I can't believe what I'm seeing," and "What could you possibly have that I don't?" As they drew near, she hurriedly composed herself. "Dakota, Parker," she said. "What are you guys doing in SoHo?"

"Oh, we get around." Parker held Dakota tighter.

Shelby looked down at her oversized sweatshirt and cargo pants, undoubtedly wishing she had worn one of her too-tight sweaters.

Dakota smiled broadly, clutching her huge bouquet of flowers. Shelby was clearly floored at this unexpected turn of events. Before walking away, Dakota mumbled to Shelby, "So I guess the bets are off."

"What was that all about?" Parker asked as they walked down the street.

"Nothing. Just something we had talked about," Dakota answered, nodding triumphantly to herself.

Froth had a living room atmosphere with overstuffed sofas and velvet chairs. After settling in a corner arrangement and being served, Dakota asked the billion-dollar question: "Where's your wife and kids?"

"What makes you think I have a family?" Parker said, slowly sipping his espresso.

"From past experience," she said, thinking back to Jackson.

Devilment showed in his smile. "I'm not married, and I don't have any kids that I know about."

"So you're saying there's a possibility," Dakota said, with her eyebrows raised, "that some woman could appear on your doorstep with a kid, claiming it's yours."

"With men that's always a possibility," Parker said. "But seriously, I was engaged a few years ago."

Finally the good stuff. "Really? What happened?" she asked, leaning closer.

Looking into the espresso cup, he said, "Without getting into a long drawn-out story, I caught her with someone else."

Dakota stared at him. "That's odd. Usually it's the man who's caught with his hand in the cookie jar."

"I know. What can I say?" he said, shrugging his shoulders.

"Were you surprised?"

"Speechless."

Interested in hearing the juicy details, she asked, "So what did you do?"

With a far-off look in his eyes, he said, "If you don't mind, I don't feel like rehashing that day."

Dakota thought it strange that someone as good-looking as Parker would be cheated on, but one never knew. Every woman in the place was peeping at him, checking him out. She decided she'd have to do some more digging. Especially after the Lot 61 bar incident. It would appear that he had no trouble with women.

They strolled around SoHo some more until Parker asked, "Are you hungry?"

"I'm getting there. I know this place that makes fabulous pasta."

"Oh, yeah, where?"

"On Cliff Street," Dakota said slyly.

"Where is that?"

"Near the Seaport."

"All righty then, let's go," Parker said.

As the cab pulled up in front of her building, Parker looked over at Dakota and said, "Where's the restaurant?"

"On the tenth floor. It's called Chez Cantrell," Dakota said.

Parker's face registered surprise, followed by the look of opportunity. Anxious to see where this turn of events would lead, they rode the elevator to her loft, eyeing each other along the way.

"Nice place," Parker said, looking around.

The loft had eighteen-foot-high ceilings, an exposed brick wall, floor-to-ceiling windows with custom rose-and-gray metallic drapes that gathered into a heap on the hardwood floors. Wooden beams and imposing columns were original from the 1850s, when the building was a shipping warehouse. Dakota had covered the columns in a matte aluminum, which matched her gray velvet art deco furniture. The silver flat-screen television with its towering speakers gave the loft an innovative, high-tech look.

Dakota walked to the kitchen to find a vase for the flowers. "Thanks. What can I get you to drink?"

"How about a glass of wine?" Parker said as he followed her.

Dakota took a bottle of merlot from the rack and a corkscrew out of the drawer.

"Here, let me do that." Parker came up behind Dakota and put his arms around her waist, reaching for the bottle and corkscrew. While he opened the wine, Dakota stood with her back to him. She could feel the muscles in his arms brush against her.

"Here you go," Parker whispered in her ear once the bottle was opened.

Dakota could feel chills run up her spine. She slowly turned around, and they stood face-to-face for a few seconds before Parker closed the remaining distance by softly tasting her mouth. Her lips had parted in anticipation of their first kiss, giving him just the access he wanted. The kiss quickly grew passionate. She could feel his body responding.

Bringing her hands between them, she pushed him away before they headed down a path of no return. "Parker, Parker, no," she said, mustering the little reserve that she still had.

Taking a half step back, he asked, "What's wrong?"

"Nothing's wrong. It's just that I don't do this on the first date."

Unfazed, he said, "Well, I guess we'll just have to have more dates."

Now that sounded like a plan, Dakota thought. To her, Parker seemed like the type that was definitely into the chase. Well, not to worry. She'd give him something to run after.

19

The following Monday, Blake called Morgan at work. "Good morning, princess. How are you?" he asked.

"Really exhausted. Miles and I didn't get back from the Hamptons until late last night and, of course, I had a seven-thirty meeting this morning."

Gazing out of her forty-first-floor office window, she thought if she had to sit through one more boring meeting, she'd jump. Since Morgan's plunge from grace, her stock had fallen sharply. Her comments in meetings were either disputed or, worse yet, ignored.

"Why don't you come over after work? I'll have Mattie prepare a tray of her famous fried green tomatoes, and we can crack a bottle of Pouilly-Fuissé and chill on the terrace. After a weekend in the Hamptons, what you need *most* is a getaway." Morgan smiled as he went on. "Let me tell you, what you have there are the same people getting away from the city, on the same weekends, only to see each other again and sit in the same traffic! Come on over—it'll be relaxing. I'll send Daddy's driver down to pick you up and have him take you home later."

"Cool. Have him meet me at six." She was dying to have a peek at how the other one percent lived. She imagined the penthouse Blake had described, filled with Tiffany lamps, priceless antique rugs and original art by Degas, Renoir, Duda and Ulloa.

The rest of her afternoon, as usual, was a drain. In addition to BSs, BAs and MBAs from prestigious institutions, many of her coworkers also had PHDs—Player-Hatin' Degrees. She could afford a wardrobe full of Gucci, Prada, Donna and Jil, which would be no big deal for a blond, blue-eyed WASP from Westchester. After all, she would be "entitled" to good looks, intelligence and the finer things in life. But because she was the only black female in her group, many of her colleagues would rather she shuffled a bit.

She had been reminded of that just last week. One of her co-workers had been admiring her tank watch when she noticed it was a Cartier. Before she could censor herself, she asked, "What are *you* doing with a Cartier?"

And before Morgan could stop herself, she shot back, "Oh, they do allow blacks on Fifth Avenue these days."

"Oh, I'm sorry, I didn't mean . . ." she stammered.

"No problem. I know exactly what you meant," Morgan said evenly.

As she was about to leave the office, Blake called, breathless. "Morgan, I am so glad I caught you! Dad's been called abroad for some medical crisis in Russia. He and his driver are on the way to the penthouse to pack and catch an evening flight to Moscow. I am so sorry for the change in plans, but things are so hectic here that it would be better if we met somewhere else."

Disappointed, Morgan agreed. "Sure, but let's make it downtown." She had to think for a second. "I know, let's meet at the City Wine and Cigar Bar."

"I'll see you in about forty-five minutes."

The City Wine and Cigar Bar was in Tribeca, an abbreviation for Triangle Below Canal. The neighborhood had gone through a vast transformation over the past several decades. Old warehouses had been converted to fabulous lofts, and restaurants were growing like weeds out of deserted storefronts.

The City Wine and Cigar Bar was decorated in rich woods, with billowy drapes and a humidor the size of many Manhattan apartments. Arriving first, Morgan ordered calamari with marinara sauce and a glass of champagne to take the edge off her day.

Blake hobbled in at 6:55, short of breath. He seemed to be limping to avoid putting weight on his right ankle. Ordering champagne in two seconds flat, he began munching eagerly on Morgan's calamari. "Sorry again about the change of plans," he said between mouthfuls.

"No problem," Morgan responded, though she didn't really feel that way. The last thing she wanted after an exhausting weekend was another bar scene.

Sensing her discontent, he said, "I really wanted to talk to you about the business offer now that you've had a chance to mull it over."

That was good. He was getting right to the point. "Actually, I've given it some thought, and I think there are some innovative and interesting ways to approach it." She then began to describe the growth and product strategies she had developed the week before.

When she was finished, Blake said, "Morgan, you're brilliant. That's an incredible marketing strategy. You're awesome!"

"I'm glad *you* think so."

"Girl, those people at Global are fools for not recognizing what you have to offer." He held up a long, tapered finger. "But their loss is my gain. Between the two of us, we make the perfect package."

"I agree," Morgan said, though she knew Miles didn't.

"Does that mean you're in?" Blake asked hopefully.

"Like I said last week, since Miles and I are buying investment property, I don't have funds to sink into a business, and I also can't quit my job until we have guaranteed income," Morgan said, wanting to be clear on both points.

Leaning forward earnestly, Blake confided, "I met with my attorneys earlier today. The trust should be settled within two weeks, and four million dollars is certainly enough money, even for me. The largest costs are upfront investments in marketing, PR, and client entertainment. After that, most costs would be passed through to clients. We can maintain a small office, and since my family owns several buildings in the city, we can take a space in one of those. We'll need telecom and some office equipment, but overall the investment will be small, certainly less than fifty thousand dollars. So you see, we certainly won't need any of your money. And there is no reason you can't keep your job. As we discussed, most of your time will initially be spent developing strategy and project plans, which you can do anytime."

Glad that they were straight about the money, Morgan grew more excited, if still a little hesitant. "Before we start printing business cards, we'll need financial projections, a tactical marketing strategy and a sound budget. Why don't I finish detailing the marketing and you construct the operating and profit projections?"

"I guess I'll get to use my Ivy League education after all," Blake said.

As the waiter approached with the check, Blake began tenderly rubbing his right ankle. He explained that he had injured it the previous night while hanging out at Tops and Bottoms, a gay nightspot uptown. During all of the cavorting, he lost his jacket and wallet and broke the heel on his spiked patent-leather boots. Exactly how it happened was lost in his haze.

"Chile, I was a mess. Without money or credit cards, I limped home. Imagine me in my black Lycra catsuit with a feather boa dangling to one side. Talk about the 'walk of shame.' I had to creep past the doorman at the crack of dawn looking like a run-down drag queen."

The image of a tall, leggy Blake hobbling through the streets like a crippled giraffe in drag caused Morgan to laugh hysterically. But she did think to ask, "Are you okay?"

"It does hurt and the swelling hasn't gone down, but I'm fine," he answered, showing her the swollen ankle.

After reviewing the check, Morgan pulled out her American Express Centurion Card. He casually said, "Morgan, hold on to the receipt. Once I get the trust settled, we can treat this as a business expense and I'll reimburse you in full."

20

Dakota checked her watch every five minutes. She and Parker had had a quick drink at the start of the week, and he told her how full of client dinners his week was, but he would call her closer to the weekend to get together. Today she had gotten an e-mail from him saying, "Meet me in the lobby at the close." She couldn't wait.

So she was surprised when she walked over to the pantry and there was Shelby purring in his ear. In her hand was a white envelope.

"Am I interrupting?" Dakota asked tightly, walking over to the refrigerator.

"As a matter of fact, you are," Shelby said, her claws already extracted.

Before she could continue, though, Parker cut her off. "I was just talking about you," he said, putting his arm around Dakota's waist.

With a skeptical look at him, Dakota said, "Do tell."

He raised his hands to show he was innocent. "Shelby was saying a group of the OTC traders were going over to the Bull and Bear for drinks after work, but I told her you and I had plans already."

Shelby was stung. "Next time, Parker, I'm not taking no for an answer," she said, strutting out.

Left alone, Dakota gave him an appreciative smile.

"I need to get back to my desk. The phones are hopping," Parker said, also heading out. "But I'll see you after the close."

What the hell was that skank up to? Dakota wondered.

"Dakota—line two," Paul said, as she neared the desk.

"Trading."

"Kota, it's Nana."

"Hey, Nana," she said, sounding distracted.

"What's wrong?"

"Nothing."

"Don't tell me nothing. I hear it in your voice."

Who did she think she was fooling? "It's this guy here that I really like."

"So what's the problem? He likes you back, right?"

"Yeah, but there's this other woman here who likes him too."

"Well, I didn't raise no loser. If you want this man, don't let nobody stand in your way." Nana had long felt that all Dakota needed was a husband and some children to help settle her down.

"Thanks, Nana."

"For what, baby?"

"For always knowing what to say to make me feel better. But you didn't call to hear about my social life. What's going on?"

Hesitantly, Nana said, "I hate to bother you, but I need my monthly check a week earlier."

Dakota felt a flicker of concern. "No problem. I can send it out today. Is everything okay?"

Nana sighed heavily and said, "I might as well tell you now."

Dakota's mind began to flash through one disastrous scenario after the other. "You're not sick, are you, Nana?"

"No, baby, nothing like that. It's Tricia," Nana said reluctantly.

Rolling her eyes toward the ceiling, Dakota said, "Oh, I should have known."

"Her graduation is coming up, and she needs to pay the rest of her tuition before she can get her certificate," Nana said.

"Sounds like a personal problem to me." Thinking a second longer, Dakota said, "Did she put you up to asking me for the money?"

"No. She told me not to tell you anything about her problem."

Dakota didn't buy it. "She's so conniving, Tricia knew darn well you'd tell me. I shouldn't send it and let her suffer," Dakota said, taking off her glasses and rubbing her temples. This conversation was sure to cause her a headache.

"Well, if you don't, I'll just have to take out a second mortgage on the house."

"Nana, I'll do it," Dakota said quickly, "but tell Tricia it's not a gift. It's a loan."

"I can't thank you enough, baby. Once Tricia gets her shop, she going to make us both proud."

"Let her graduate first, Nana, before you start buying into her dreams. Let me run. I'll talk to you later."

"Okay, baby."

"Wait, Nana—have you thought about coming up for a long weekend?"

"Go ahead and make the plans. I'm sick of you nagging me about it," Nana teased.

Dakota teased back, "I wonder where I learned to nag."

"All right, smarty. Let me know the dates."

"I'll set it up. 'Bye, Nana," Dakota said, hanging up.

At fifteen seconds past 3:59, Dakota had purse in hand, and by four o'clock was on the elevator to meet "her man." Well, he wasn't technically her man yet. But Nana was right. She was no quitter; it was just a matter of time. When she reached the lobby, Parker was standing near the bank of elevators with a devilishly sexy grin on his clean-shaven face. Dakota walked right up to him and planted the sweetest, softest kiss on his cheek, while ever so slightly brushing her breasts "innocently" against his chest.

"I thought we'd start the weekend on my boat," Parker said. He grabbed her by the waist and led her out the door, oblivious to the rush of people passing them.

Dakota tried not to be too impressed. "I didn't know you

were a skipper," she said, putting on her Barry Kieselstein-Cord sunglasses as they started out into the late-day sun. "I guess I'll be first mate."

"There's a lot you don't know about me," he said with a Cheshire cat smile. "Can't give away all of my secrets at once."

"So where are you docked?" she asked casually, though inside she was excited. Dealing with Parker was like playing a high-stakes game of poker.

"At the Seventy-ninth Street Boat Basin," he answered, hailing a taxi.

When they arrived at the pier off the West Side Highway, she spotted a sleek-looking craft and, based on the direction he was walking, assumed it was his. She was right.

"That's a beauty. What is it?"

"Thanks. It's a thirty-foot Maxum 3000. Come aboard," Parker said, stepping onto the dock to help her up. "It has two staterooms, a full head and galley—basically all the creature comforts."

"I would expect no less," Dakota chided.

Parker led her into the second stateroom. It was done in red wood and chrome, with nautical watercolors and oils bolted to the walls. It felt masculine, but also very contemporary. A king-sized bed sat in its center. "If you want to get out of your work clothes, I have shorts and a tee you can change into."

Not only did she find shorts and T-shirts—there was a full wardrobe of swimsuits with matching sarongs, which all appeared to be new. "Damn, boyfriend has enough clothes to outfit a harem," she thought. Dakota chose a sexy sarong instead of shorts and replaced her bra with a thin T-shirt. She walked over to the mirror and knotted the tee to accentuate her bare breasts and taut stomach. Then she decided to slip off her panties so that the view of her full, round rear was unobstructed by panty lines. "After tonight, I'll be the only woman in this harem," she whispered to the mirror.

Dakota approached Parker provocatively as he sat on the blue cushioned seat at the rear of his boat. Stopping directly in front of him, she allowed the warm, gentle breeze to blow the sarong suggestively between her parted legs. "So what's with the boutique?"

Parker licked his lips and eyed her bare thighs, which were exposed by the windswept sarong. "My mom is always sending me clothes from their store. I think she was a Girl Scout in her last life. She said I should have a few pieces on hand, just in case." Parker abruptly reached up and rubbed a chilled glass of champagne over Dakota's pert nipples. The breeze had caused them to firm up enticingly.

Surprised, Dakota looked around to see if anyone from nearby boats had noticed, but she saw no one. Determined to act unaffected, she continued the conversation. "In case you get lucky?"

"Luck has nothing to do with it," he said, watching the effect of the cold glass against her warm skin.

"Oh, really?" she asked, taking the glass out of his hand and sliding down next to him on the cushion.

"It's all skill," he said, eyes fixed like lasers on her protruding nipples.

"Well, aren't you confident?"

"Very," he said, tasting her neck.

Damn, his lips were soft, she thought. Then he hit the tender, sensitive spot on her neck. The pleasurable sensation caused her to gasp with delight. Like a man on a mission, Parker worked his tongue from her neck to her nipples, never coming up for air or taking her shirt off. A soft moan escaped her parted lips as his tongue traveled south to her navel. She had to give it to him—the boy had some serious skills.

Well, it was time to show him a few of her own. She laced her hands into his thick dark hair, bringing his lips back to hers, her tongue doing a sensual duet with his. Parker then poured champagne on her T-shirt until the front was drenched, making her nipples stand at full attention. He sucked the champagne through her shirt as though it was his last meal.

After he'd had his fill, Dakota stood and straddled him, then realized that her nipples were not the only thing standing at attention. She could feel his throbbing penis against her moist crotch. He put his hand underneath her sarong and began rubbing her bare bottom. With her eyes closed, she thought his hands felt no different from those of the black men she had been with. Dakota then began to wonder about the myth that white men were not as well endowed as brothers, but before she could reach into his pants to check out the merchandise, he stood and picked her up, carrying her to the master stateroom. Once inside, he gently put her down and slowly untied her sarong, letting it drift to the floor.

No words were exchanged as Parker slipped out of his pants, walked over to the nightstand and took out a condom. He walked back to Dakota and handed it to her. Sitting on the edge of the bed, she slid off his boxers, praying she wouldn't be disappointed. When they slid past his hips, she smiled to herself, pleased at his size. He was at least a buck and a half. She opened the condom and rolled it smoothly onto his erectness, never taking her eyes off this fine male specimen.

When Dakota stood up to take off her soaked tee, he turned her around. He wrapped his arms tightly around her and began to grind in a smooth, circular motion into her firm, round bottom.

Dakota whispered, "Uuummmm . . . it feels so good."

"You ain't felt nothing yet, baby," he said, suddenly sounding more Latin than white. He then took one hand and spread her legs apart, gliding his middle finger into her saturated love ravine.

Dakota began to lose control as he probed his middle digit deeper and deeper. With his thumb he played her clitoris as though strumming a finely tuned guitar. "Ohhh, baby . . . I'm, I'm, I'm coming," she sang, her knees buckling as he continued to play her song.

Parker then gently laid her on the bed. Looking down, he said, "You're so beautiful. Your skin looks like smooth milk chocolate."

As he leaned down and touched her thigh, she noticed how his light skin seemed to glow against her brownness. "Have you ever been with a black woman?"

"No, it's my first time," he said as he lowered his body onto hers. "What about you?"

She kissed his earlobe, then whispered, "No."

Dakota closed her eyes as he slowly entered her. Soon all thoughts of race were erased from her mind, as their rhythm was matched by the soft waves that rocked beneath the boat.

21

Tyrone was perched on a low bar stool at the long, marble-inlaid kitchen island. Nibbling on cheese and crackers while talking to his mom, he felt like the eight-year-old who had once sat in the very same seat. All his life he'd been the kid with his nose pressed against the window of the candy store, eyeing those wonderful, enchanting, tasty treats close enough to see and smell, but not close enough for him to grab his share.

"I think I'm going to run round to the corner deli and pick up some fresh basil. Dr. and Mrs. St. James are havin' a dinner party, and I needs it for my special marinara sauce." Mattie was busy at the butcher's block, deftly kneading dough, which shortly would be filled with a tantalizing assortment of custards. While she skillfully worked the dough, the flabby skin on the undersides of her arms jiggled. Mattie was what they called down South a stout woman. Everything about her was full-sized, especially her heart.

From Natchez, Mississippi, Mattie had met Katherine at Columbia Presbyterian Hospital when she was in housekeeping and Katherine was just starting her residency. Shortly thereafter she began working for Richard and Katherine, and soon became indispensable. Around the same time Katherine was expecting Blake, Mattie also turned up pregnant.

Each summer she'd go home for a three-week vacation, and it was during one of those visits that Mattie discovered she was pregnant. She had planned to get hitched and live there in Mississippi, until the baby's father hitched a ride right out of town—without her. The next Sunday at church, the sermon "happened" to be on the sin of fornication. It seemed the reverend was preaching directly to her. During that time an unwed pregnant woman down South was considered a leper, so to avoid bringing more shame on her strict Southern Baptist family, she quickly returned to New York. Katherine and Richard welcomed her back with open arms, and even had her quarters enlarged to accommodate her new baby. Tyrone Nathan Thomas was born two days after Blake.

"You know how I feel about Katherine and Richard," Tyrone said, rolling his eyes.

"Boy, if I done told you once, I done told you a thousand times. If it weren't for them, no tellin' where we'd be. You oughta be thankful, but instead you'se full of hate," Mattie said, shaking her head.

This must be what they called "indentured servitude," thought Tyrone. No matter how hard she worked, his mother still felt she owed everything to the St. James family. "Momma, you just don't understand." Sometimes he felt so close to her that words weren't necessary, but other times it seemed they were strangers speaking different languages. No matter what he said, she'd never get it.

"What's to understand? You grew up on Fifth Avenue, had clothes on your back, shoes on your feet, and never missed a meal. That's more'n a lotta folks can say."

"Correction. I grew up in maid's quarters on Fifth Avenue, wearing Blake's hand-me-downs, with worn-out shoes, and eatin' his leftovers."

She kept her back turned, and realizing he might have gone too far, he got up and gave her a big hug. He could smell the VO5 in her blue-gray hair. "I'm sorry, Momma."

Mattie wore her hair pinned up with old-fashioned black bobby pins. Her complexion was medium brown, and she had one of those female mustaches. In fact, she had more hair on her face than Tyrone, since he'd had his facial hair permanently removed with electrolysis.

"I know, baby. I just want you to settle down, get a job and be happy. You have to stop lookin' in mirrors belongin' to other folks." That had been Mattie's mantra for years, but Tyrone didn't buy it. First he was caught with drugs at twenty-one. Dr. St. James got him out of that fix. Later, he got involved in a cell phone number-stealing scheme.

"Ma, I will. I'm working on a big opportunity now that'll set me up for good." Tyrone could tell by the sudden tenseness in her body that she already feared the worst—another illegal scheme. He couldn't blame her, not with his track record.

Changing the subject, Mattie released him, patted his small, round bottom and said, "Let me fix you a nice lunch, baby." Thankfully, she was back in her comfort zone, waiting on other people.

He was polishing off the second of two turkey sandwiches and a bowl of fresh tomato soup when the front door opened. Tyrone froze, fearing either Katherine or Richard had returned from work early. But it was Blake he heard instead.

Strolling out into the hallway, Tyrone said enthusiastically, "Blake! Whassup?"

"What are you doing here?" Blake answered, before he saw Mattie standing inside the kitchen doorway. "Oh, I see."

Gesturing toward the wood-paneled drawing room, Blake said, "Well, as long as you're here . . ."

Tyrone didn't need a second invite. "It's been a while since I've been to the 'deluxe apartment in the sky,' " he sang, echoing the theme song from *The Jeffersons*.

"Yes, it has," Blake said, ignoring the lame attempt at humor.

Strolling past the oil paintings, Rodin sculptures, and Schonbek crystal chandeliers, Tyrone was counting his blessings. Blake was about to come into his own millions, which meant he could break off a piece for himself, if he played his cards right. Then Tyrone would set himself up so that he'd never have to worry about money again.

Before they reached the drawing room, Mattie poked her head around the corner at the other end of the hall. "Blake, I'm going to run to the store to pick up some groceries for the dinner party and run a few errands. I'll be back in a couple of hours. And, Tyrone, call me later, okay, baby?"

Once in the drawing room, Blake said, "I was just about to jump into the shower. Have a seat and I'll get you something to drink first."

"You go ahead. I'll grab something out of the fridge," Tyrone insisted, sashaying toward the kitchen.

Opening the mahogany-faced refrigerator, Tyrone helped himself to a healthy tray of pâté, cheeses, water crackers, olives, strawberries and grapes. He balanced his assortment with a bottle of Dom and two champagne flutes he'd quickly frosted in the freezer. He had to admit it looked marvelous. Growing up, he'd certainly seen his momma whip up a little somethin'-somethin' in no time for the St. James family.

Tyrone headed upstairs to Blake's suite. Without knocking, he nudged open the partly closed door with his elbow. After placing the tray on a nearby coffee table, he walked into Blake's bathroom with a chilled glass of champagne in each hand. Steam seeped from the oversized shower. Pausing at the vanity, he stripped down to his birthday suit before opening the shower door and entering with the two glasses.

The steam shower was Italian-tiled and the size of the average garage. A bench bordered the circumference, which was where Blake was sitting, one foot propped on the ledge, legs open while his third appendage hung over the tiled surface. Strutting over, Tyrone said nothing as he handed Blake the champagne flute. The steam had caused the condensation to quickly turn to beads of sweat as they rolled down the fluted glass. They both took long sips. Still thirsty, Tyrone knelt to swallow Blake's growing penis. Between the hot, steamy haze, cold, frothy champagne and Tyrone's proven talents, Blake was in the throes of ecstasy. Unrelenting, Tyrone turned up the heat until Blake blew his gasket.

Lounging later in thick cream velour bathrobes, Tyrone refilled Blake's glass and asked, "Can I get you anything else?"

"What more could I ask for?" Blake answered, contentedly popping grapes like kernels of popcorn.

Taking a strawberry between clear-glossed lips, Tyrone sucked it in before extracting it by the stem, a small bite missing. "I can think of a few things," he offered, chewing slowly.

"Such as?"

"If I were you, I'd be asking for my money," Tyrone said, not-too-subtly broaching his favorite subject.

"What money?" Blake asked.

"Your inheritance," Tyrone answered, batting his lashes for effect. He had subtly transformed his hard edge into a silky-smooth femininity to work his magic.

"Oh, that," Blake said, frowning.

"Girl, I'd be all over it. What you gon' do wit' it?"

"I'm starting my own business," Blake answered, without offering details.

"Is that why I haven't seen you out, except for that one time?"

"I've been lying pretty low since I got back, though I do have to let my hair down every now and then."

Tyrone felt as though Blake was trying to play coy about his comings and goings. He was probably afraid of being busted now that he was back in his parents' backyard. "I've been thinking about my future too. In fact, I could use some cash right now," Tyrone said, laying it on the line.

"I certainly can't go counting the money too soon. The trust has been held up due to a legal issue."

"Oh? And what might that be?" Tyrone asked, sensing a line of bullshit forthcoming.

"A clause in the will stipulates that if any heir is found to have used illicit drugs, he is to be automatically disinherited. And you do remember San Francisco?"

Instantly, Tyrone knew what Blake was referring to. "Are you telling me that a minor indiscretion is going to cause you to lose your inheritance?" he asked, blinking his eyes disbelievingly. He was seeing his gravy train being derailed right before him.

"Cocaine possession is anything but minor, particularly in my grandfather's eyes. After watching how drugs ruined Justin, he swore no more of his money would be wasted on them," Blake said solemnly.

"But, Blake, it happened over seven years ago," Tyrone reasoned, as anxious as Blake was to find a solution.

"That may be my only salvation. Although Justin knows about the arrest, to my knowledge neither Carlton nor Dad does, at least not yet. In any case a statute of limitations or something could apply."

"How did Justin find out?" Tyrone pried.

"Well, it seems he went rambling through my things, probably looking for money to buy drugs, and found private papers documenting the fine that was paid."

"That drug-addicted, lying sonofabitch," Tyrone mumbled, not caring that the same description could aptly apply to him.

22

There was something conspiratorial about the two of them huddled over tawny ports, warm and dry inside while outside Noah would have battened down the hatches. In fact, it was raining so hard you could barely see a foot in front of you. Morgan and Dakota were in Penang, a Malaysian restaurant on Columbus Avenue, in the cozy cavernous area downstairs. Groups of smartly dressed New Yorkers lounged in small coves lit by votive candles.

Morgan wore a navy Gucci pantsuit under her Jil Sander trenchcoat, with a pair of black Donna Karan loafers. Dakota was dressed in black, with a tan Michael Kors short trench and black Prada buckle-ups.

"So, fess up—how was it?" Morgan asked with a mischievous glint in her eyes.

"Can I tell you, homeboy rocked the house?" Dakota answered, fanning herself with the linen cocktail napkin. Just the memory made her hot.

"Or do you mean the boat?" Morgan asked, eyebrows raised.

"Girl, my man Parker is packin'. He must be part black."

"Too bad that's not the case," Morgan slipped, not meaning to rain on Dakota's parade.

"What exactly does that mean?" Dakota challenged.

"Nothing. It's just that you deserve a strong black man. I know Parker is a nice guy, but I just don't think he's right for you," Morgan confessed.

"Because he's white?" Dakota asked, staring Morgan down as she waited for an answer.

"No. Because he isn't black," Morgan countered.

"Morgan, what matters most is how he treats me," Dakota said adamantly. "Let's take Jackson, for instance. He's a 'strong black man' and he dogged me out. Is that what you want for me?" She leaned back in her chair and crossed her arms defiantly.

"You're right," Morgan said, relenting. "As long as you're happy. That's what matters." She reached over to hold Dakota's hand. "Don't be mad. So, come on, I'm curious. How was it afterward? Was it weird?"

"Not even," Dakota said, happy to be back on good ground. "As a matter of fact, since then we've become really close. He's a doll. He's charming, funny and, better yet, knows the difference between Boone's Farm and Beaujolais."

"And most importantly, he knows how to lay the pipe," Morgan said, completing their list of requirements.

"Girl, if he laid it any deeper, we'd both be in China." They laughed, enjoying the raunchy girl talk that guys never thought women had.

"So, tell me, how is it having sex with a white guy?" Morgan asked, taking a sip of her port.

"Correction, he's only half white. Anyway, I can't speak for the rest of them, but with Parker, it was amazing. The fact that he's partially white was the last thing on my mind," Dakota said, smiling.

She noticed Morgan was smiling too, and she thought she knew why. Huddling closer, Dakota asked, "So, how's the baby-making coming?"

"It's coming and coming and coming . . ." They both laughed. "It's a good thing there's no correlation between attempts and multiple births, or we'd be having a litter in about nine months."

Changing the subject, Dakota asked, "Now that you've told him, what does Miles think about your new business venture with Blake?"

"Like most men, as long as it doesn't disrupt his life too much, it's okay," Morgan answered.

"Just don't do anything to mess up your happy home," Dakota insisted.

"Speaking of happy homes, how's it going with Tricia?" Morgan asked.

"I could ring her little scrawny neck. I don't know why I still let her get to me," Dakota said, slamming her drink down.

"You should be used to her by now."

"True."

"She probably resents you for being raised by your grandmother."

"How do you mean?" Dakota asked, taking a slow sip.

"Well, think about how grandparents spoil their grandkids, letting them get away with murder. Always baking cakes and stuff. Tricia probably thinks you've always had it easy growing up with Nana."

Dakota's expression looked as if a lightbulb had just come on. "I bet you're right. That would surely explain why she's always trying to irritate me."

"It also explains why she feels justified in moving there. I'm sure she feels like it's her turn to soak up the one-on-one grandmother time she missed as a kid."

Nodding slowly, Dakota said, "Thank you, Dr. Freud. You really hit the nail on the head."

"My bill will be in the mail," Morgan teased, taking a sip of her drink.

Just then Blake came downstairs, spotted them in the corner and made his way over. He was carrying a copy of the twenty-page strategy document Morgan had given him. "Whew! It's a mess out there," he announced, shaking out his fedora and removing his Burberry trench coat. He bent down to kiss both sets of cheeks. "But don't you girls look toasty."

"What took you so long?" Morgan asked, looking at her watch. He was thirty minutes late, which was fine since she and Dakota had had a chance to catch up, but he had to be on time once they started getting clients.

"Man problems," Blake answered sourly.

"Happens to the best of us," Dakota offered, taking a warming sip of the smooth port.

"Who is he? Do tell," Morgan insisted, leaning in for the juicy, intimate details.

Blake didn't take the bait. "No one important, really. He's just become a bit of a nuisance lately. He shows up at the house unannounced and doesn't take the hint to leave."

"How about just showing him the door?" Dakota asked, in her no-nonsense manner.

Lighting a cigarette, which he placed in a long, black onyx holder, Blake took a deep drag and quickly expelled the smoke toward the tiled ceiling. "It's so complicated," he said wistfully, shaking his head. "He's smelling the scent of freshly minted money." He looked directly at one, then the other. "The trust," he explained with an exaggerated leer.

"Why do you put up with him?" Morgan asked.

"We've been together, off and on, for so long, I suppose I feel a sense of obligation. I'm not quite sure how to end it," he answered.

"There must be some way out," Morgan said, thinking, *It must be the pipe.* That was the only reason that someone like Blake would put up with the likes of this mystery man.

His half-closed lids shielded his eyes from the drifting smoke. "Sometimes I think there is only one way out . . . *one of us has to die.*" Their hearts stopped until he raised his brows in a Groucho Marx gesture. "And since it's my idea and all . . ." He roared, laughing at the hanging punch line and the fact that they had taken him seriously.

"You know, Blake, you really are sick," Dakota said, laughing nervously at his twisted sense of humor.

"That's one reason to have two doctors for parents," Blake replied. He waved a hand. "Let's talk about something more exciting. Tell Dakota the name you came up with for the company," he said, turning to Morgan.

Looking at Dakota with a gleam in her eyes, Morgan explained, "I wanted a name that was highbrow and oozed sophistication. So I thought of Caché. It has a high-end feel, and it spells sophistication in any circle."

"It's brilliant! And it has a certain *je ne sais quoi,*" added Blake, like a proud parent. They clinked glasses, giving conceptual birth to Caché.

"Oh, isn't that . . . ?" Blake had seen a woman he knew from the Back Room. He swiftly stood and went over to her table in the corner. Denise was medium height with shoulder-length ash-blond hair and a pale complexion.

"Denise, darling, how are you?" Blake asked.

"I'm fine. It's good to see you, Blake," she said, recognizing him immediately.

"Come over and meet some friends of mine," he said, leading her over to the table.

"Denise, this is my business partner, Morgan Nelson," he said, proudly presenting Morgan, "and this is our dear friend, Dakota Cantrell. Morgan, Dakota, meet Denise Milloy."

"Hi, I'm pleased to meet you both," Denise replied, shaking their hands.

"It's nice to meet you as well," Morgan said, noting her firm handshake.

"Please join us for a drink," Blake said, motioning toward the empty fourth chair.

"I'd love to. In fact, I was meeting a friend for drinks, but she just called and had to cancel."

After Blake ordered a fresh round of cocktails, Denise said, "I thought you were still at the Back Room, but I heard you introduce Morgan as your business partner. What are you up to?"

"We've actually just started a business. So I left the Back Room to give it my full attention. That was only something to keep me busy while I decided what I really wanted to do with my life," Blake explained.

"So, what did you decide?" she asked, casually sipping her sauvignon blanc.

"We've started a company called Caché. It's a high-concept event-planning company." Blake proceeded to describe the business concept Morgan had developed, while flipping through Morgan's strategy document.

Knowing how cutthroat business in New York was, Morgan was apprehensive about sharing business strategy without a preceding confidentiality agreement, but Blake seemed totally comfortable, and Denise appeared to be a nice woman. She wore the standard female adaptation of the male power suit: blue, nondescript, with cream shirt and two-inch pumps. She probably didn't give a second thought to fashion or style. "That's a brilliant concept, and I love the marketing strategy," Denise said after perusing the document.

Her enthusiasm piqued Morgan's curiosity. She asked, "Denise, what type of business are you in?" She didn't mean to pry, but she did feel the need to level the playing field, because at the moment it was totally one-sided.

"I work for Jon Atkins PR and Advertising Company," Denise answered. Morgan and Dakota looked at each other. That was the largest advertising and public relations company in New York. Their clients were a list of who's who in fashion, entertainment and finance.

"In what capacity?" Morgan asked, now prying.

"I am the chief financial officer," Denise answered. Both Morgan's and Dakota's eyebrows rose.

Denise glanced at her watch. "I'm afraid I really have to be going now. But I am impressed with both your concept and your approach. You two make a great team."

Flattered by her comments, Morgan said, "Thanks, I appreciate your feedback," while Blake smiled broadly.

As they exchanged business cards, Denise added, "If I can do anything to help, let me know, and by all means keep me posted on your progress." Although Morgan was as cool as a California chardonnay outside, she was as bubbly as French champagne on the inside. This was the first time they had gotten totally unbiased feedback on the concept. She viewed it as an endorsement of her marketing and strategy abilities. And after the beating her professional ego had taken lately, it meant a lot.

"Well, gang, I think I have to be going too. I've got to get up early tomorrow," said Dakota.

When the check came, Blake insisted on paying. Then he raised his glass to propose a second toast. "This is to what separates the haves from the have-nots . . . Caché."

A minute later, the waiter approached their table with a strange look on his face. "Excuse me, sir, but your card has been declined."

"What do you mean, declined? Try it again. You're obviously doing something wrong," Blake said, in a snooty but hushed tone, trying not to cause a scene.

"I've already tried it several times, sir," the waiter said firmly.

"Look, Blake, it's no problem. I'll get the check," Dakota said, giving the waiter one of her many cards.

With a frown twisting his handsome features, Blake raised his glass again and snarled, "To eliminating man problems. Like the one who apparently ran up my Visa."

23

Not one to let a contact grow cold, Blake phoned Denise the next afternoon to set up a meeting. On the appointed day, Morgan arrived dressed to the nines in a black Dolce & Gabbana pantsuit, a tan TSE tee and black Prada loafers. Her look was poised and elegant. Blake wore a navy jacket, tan slacks and his signature ascot. He looked every bit the sophisticate.

Denise's office was on the fifty-first floor of an expansive tower in Midtown, where the air was indeed rarefied. As they exited the elevator, they were greeted by rich mahogany walls, exquisite abstract art and exotic fresh flowers. They approached a starched security guard posted just inside the foyer.

"We're here to see Denise Milloy for a twelve-thirty appointment," Blake announced.

"If you'd have a seat, I'll ring her office," he replied, gesturing to a guest library, done in rich, supple leathers.

While enjoying the wondrous midtown view, they were interrupted by a hostess dressed in all black, offering a variety of beverages, English biscuits and pastries. Morgan asked for distilled water with a lemon, while Blake ordered hot tea, a croissant and a pastry.

"Hungry, are we?" Morgan asked, raising a brow.

"Actually, I'm famished. Mattie had the morning off, and I ran out without grabbing anything to eat." He looked around, taking in the ambience. "If I didn't know better, I'd swear we were in a private club."

Thinking about the requirements to reach this level at Global, Morgan replied, "Oh, but we are."

The hostess returned with a tray carrying their refreshments and led them into Denise's office.

Greeting them at the door, Denise said, "I was so glad you called, Blake, and thanks again for letting me crash your party the other night. It was a wonderful evening."

The way she gushed, Morgan couldn't help but think, *Obviously she doesn't get out much.*

"The pleasure was all ours," Blake insisted.

"Come, have a seat," Denise said, leading them across the spacious office to an arrangement of chairs nestled near a marble fireplace. The office was tastefully done. Her massive mahogany desk, polished to a high shine, was set on an exquisite Tibetan rug in the center of a beautiful hardwood floor. The room was accented with a Matisse and Kimmy Cantrell sculptures, carefully arranged in spotlit niches.

The hostess set their refreshments on a marble-and-glass coffee table before disappearing through double doors.

"You two look like you've just stepped off the cover of a fashion magazine. On the other hand, I don't know if the page would be big enough for me."

A little uncomfortable with such a healthy dose of praise, Morgan smiled and said, "Oh, I can think of a few reasons to trade places with you."

Looking around, Denise replied in a hushed tone, "Don't tell anyone, but it's really not all it's cracked up to be. At this level it's pretty much nuts-and-bolts stuff. Not much creativity, which is why I'm so excited about your plans."

Blake said smoothly, "I think we're really on to something. I was discussing the business with my parents last night, and they are really excited about it. In fact, Dad's going to provide us entree into the various consulates at the U.N. And you know how much they entertain."

"Your father works at the U.N.?" Denise asked, surprised.

"Yes, he's the medical director," Blake answered matter-of-factly.

"Oh, how nice," Denise replied, obviously impressed.

"It makes for fun dinner parties," Blake said. "A couple of weeks ago we had a formal one at the penthouse. There were twelve people, all from different nations." Warming to the tale, Blake continued. "Anyway, the guest of honor was Japan's cultural ambassador, who spoke only a little English and a smidgen of French. And of course, of all times, en route up Fifth Avenue the interpreter had to be rushed to Mount Sinai, suffering from acute appendicitis, leaving my father frantic, since he speaks only French, Italian and Spanish."

Leaning forward in her chair, Denise asked, "So what did he do?"

"He sends Mattie, our maid, racing to my wing, insisting that I dress in formal dinner wear and interpret for the ambassador and his multilingual guests, none of whom spoke Japanese."

"You speak Japanese?" Denise asked, eyes wide.

"As well as French, Italian, Spanish and Cantonese," Blake answered immodestly. Morgan sat back smiling, enjoying the show.

Enthralled, Denise asked, "So what happened next?"

"It was a riot. First of all, for once in my life I had the upper hand on Father. And of course, I took complete advantage of the situation. After a few sakes, the ambassador and I were exchanging dirty jokes in Japanese, while my father and the other guests looked on, not knowing how to react or what to react to." Denise and Morgan both laughed.

Denise was intrigued by Blake, who was cultured and at the same time humorously outrageous. After twelve-hour days surrounded by number crunchers and buttoned-up senior executives, Morgan sensed she and Blake were a welcome distraction.

Always ready to leverage a situation, Blake continued to enchant Denise with long, chatty stories, and in spite of her hectic schedule, she always made time for him. In fact, they spoke on the phone almost daily, he reported to Morgan. After several dinners and meetings, Denise volunteered to act as a consultant for Caché. Morgan was thrilled with her interest in their company.

Over drinks one evening, Denise went over their hit list of companies to target within various sectors. They had come up with a who's who in New York, and were discussing personal and business contacts that might be helpful.

"You've forgotten one very important company," Denise announced.

Looking puzzled, Morgan and Blake both said, "Who?"

"Why, only the largest PR and advertising company in New York. Jon Atkins, silly!" Blake's and Morgan's mouths dropped open. Looking at their expressions, she went on. "For two savvy networkers, you both missed the most obvious opportunity."

"We are so appreciative of your help, especially with the financials," Morgan said sincerely, "that we never thought about you as a prospect, only a friend."

"Well, that's what friends are for," Denise said. "I can't promise yet, because I do need to run it by a few people to make sure that I don't step on any toes. But it should be okay. The fact is, right now we have a Christmas party to be planned."

Morgan could hardly contain herself until Denise left. "Blake, this is incredible! Do you know how much they probably spend on the Christmas party alone? Probably half a mil, which means our commission would be about fifty thousand dollars, for our first job!"

"Fifty thousand dollars!" Blake nearly screamed. "Let's crack open the Dom!"

"Whoa, whoa, let's just put it on ice for now. It's not a done deal yet."

"Speaking of done deals, I spoke to my accountant today. He's fine with the business plan and feels like fifty thousand should be sufficient to launch Caché."

"I thought it was completely *your* decision," Morgan said, not wanting any financial problems, especially now that things were under way.

"It is, but of course I have a team of advisers who routinely look over my investments. So don't worry. We'll have the money within a couple of weeks."

"Just be sure to stay on top of it. I've already charged over fifteen hundred dollars for business meals, car services, and other expenses to my credit card." Though she hadn't told Miles yet, Morgan had agreed to temporarily consolidate Caché's expenses on one of her cards until the trust was liquid, since Blake's cards were linked to his father's accounts, which meant they wouldn't later be able to write the expenses off for tax purposes.

"Be sure to keep all receipts, and I'll repay you in full and finance all other expenses from operating capital. Later you can reimburse me fifty percent of the total outlay from incoming profits."

"I can't believe everything is moving so fast!" she said.

Blake looked at her, winked and, imitating Humphrey Bogart, said, "Stick with me, kid, and you'll go places."

24

It was 4:05 on a glorious Friday afternoon; there was a man on the horizon, and both the Dow and the NASDAQ had closed up over one-hundred-and-fifty points. Life was good. Just as Dakota was racing out the door, the phone rang. "Trading."

"Dakota, sweetie, I'm so glad I caught you. I know how you Wall Street types like to bolt on Fridays," Blake said.

"Yeah, the trading floor already looks like a ghost town. What's up?"

"Calling to see if you want to have dinner," Blake asked.

"Sure," Dakota said. "I don't have any plans." Parker was in London on business.

"Okay, let's meet at Mary Ann's on Broadway around seven," Blake said, before hanging up.

Mary Ann's was a Mexican restaurant on the Upper West Side. Arriving first, Dakota selected a choice outdoor table, then ordered a frozen strawberry margarita. While enjoying her drink, she people-watched, which was an Olympic sport in New York. One was likely to see almost anything. Two nights ago she had been headed home from an opening at the American Gallery in Alphabet City. While sitting in the taxi waiting for a light to change, she saw a monkey hanging from scaffolding two stories up. Thinking she must have had one too many glasses of champagne, she shook her head, only to realize that it was a real live monkey—he was actually swinging from the scaffolding dressed in a black tuxedo jacket, white shirt and black tie, as if out for the evening. Dakota chuckled to herself. Only in New York.

Looking up, she saw Blake's leggy frame hobbling down the street. "What happened to you?" Dakota asked as he made his way to the table.

"It's a long, sad story, but the short of it is, I was getting jiggy wit' it in my spiked four-inch boots and sprained my ankle."

"Why does that not surprise me?" Dakota asked with a half smile.

When the waiter approached the table a minute later, Blake said testily, "Do I have to die of thirst before I get a drink? I'll have a grande frozen margarita with a salted rim. Dakota, are you ready to order? I'm starving." He must be, she thought, because he was already munching away on the chips and salsa on the table. Before Dakota could answer, he proceeded to order for himself. "I'll have the quesadillas and beef enchiladas. You can bring them out together." Clearly, he was about getting his eat on. Dakota ordered chicken tacos.

"Here, look at this." Blake fanned out color brochures from several special-event companies he'd gathered to research Caché's competition. After looking over the brochures, Blake confidently summed up their competition. "We have nothing to worry about. After all, they don't have . . . Caché."

When the waiter brought the food, Blake scarfed down his meal. "When was the last time you ate?" she asked, watching him in amazement.

"Girl, I've been running all day, meeting with lawyers and accountants, and just didn't have time to eat anything. You know how it is when you're caught up in the moment. Food is the last thing on your mind." Blake motioned the waiter over. "We'll have two more margaritas."

Turning back to Dakota, he said, "Morgan has come up with some really savvy marketing campaigns. One is, 'Do your clients expect you to have . . . Caché?' and 'Not everyone has . . . Caché. Shouldn't you?' "

"That's hot!" Dakota said, loving the slick double entendre.

"That's not all. After dinner let's walk over to Central Park. I want to show you Bethesda Fountain and my concept for an outdoor Caché event."

Dakota was finishing her second taco when Blake excused himself to go to the men's room. Upon returning, he scanned the restaurant, asking, "Where's the waiter? I'd like to pay the bill."

"Don't worry. I've already paid it."

Dakota was feeling slightly buzzed as she stood up to leave. They sauntered down Seventy-ninth Street, heading toward Central Park just as the sun was beginning to set, turning the sky an artful combination of burnt orange and crimson red.

"Let's take a shortcut," Blake said as they crossed Central Park West heading into the park. Even with Blake's bandaged ankle, he still managed to outpace Dakota as he led her through a narrow wooded path and up a slight incline that overlooked a miniwaterfall.

"I've never been this way before," Dakota said. The effects of the alcohol and trying to keep up with Blake, whose every long stride equaled two of hers, was becoming a test of her stamina.

"It's a shortcut. You'll see in a minute. We're almost there."

"I certainly hope so," Dakota said sarcastically, looking down at her dusty new Jimmy Choo sandals. "Had I known we'd be roaming the enchanted forest, I would've worn hiking boots."

Soon they arrived at Bethesda Fountain, an impressive sculpture of a winged goddess with water cascading into a massive circular base. Even though it was in the heart of Central Park, it felt to Dakota more like the Left Bank in Paris. Blake explained how he and Morgan could throw a spectacular party, making a grand entrance descending the two magnificent staircases that faced the fountain, while a string quartet played in the background. By the time Blake finished expounding on his grandiose ideas, the sun had set completely, turning the sky a deep cobalt blue.

"Come on, Blake, let's get out of here," Dakota said anxiously. "It's getting late, and I'm a little nervous about being here after dark."

"Chile, please, it's not that serious. You're just being paranoid."

Dakota was indeed paranoid. Even the most blasé New Yorkers were cautious about the park at night, and she thought that Blake would be a lot less cavalier about it.

Fortunately, before long they were headed out of the park. They walked through a section heavily populated by men, and she noticed one sitting on a bench under a lamppost, looking as though he were reading a book.

"How could he be reading in the dark?" Dakota asked, looking at the man suspiciously.

"Girl, he is *not* reading. He's waiting to get picked up."

"You mean as in *picked up*?" Dakota asked, amazed.

"I mean *picked up*," Blake confirmed.

"How do you know?"

"Because this is the 'Meet and Greet' section, if you know what I mean. He'll sit there pretending to read, and another guy will come and sit next to him. They'll strike up a conversation, and the next thing you know, as Chris Rock so eloquently puts it, 'Somebody's salad is being tossed.' No telling who you might see out here. You might even see one of your Wall Street boys," said Blake, with a come-hither smile.

Dakota thought he seemed a little too familiar with the park's pickup scene and wondered if his knowledge was first-hand. As they reached the low wall bordering Fifth Avenue, she asked, "So, Blake, how do you know so much about all of this?"

"Chile, let me school you on a few things." He motioned for her to sit on a bench. "Sometimes when I can't sleep, I'll come over here and check out the scene. Most people think because I'm from money, I don't know what's going on in the real world. I know more than you think, thanks mostly to Tyrone. Of course, I could never talk about these things in front of certain people, like our girl Morgan. But I feel like I can let my hair down around you. You're probably used to hearing some of everything on that trading floor," Blake said.

As they sat on the bench, watching people coming in and out of the park, Blake continued explaining what he referred to as "The Park After Dark."

"See that guy getting out of the cab? He's going in to get picked up, and I'll bet he's married with two-point-five kids. Probably told his wife he was going out to meet the guys for a few drinks. What he'll be drinking, though, doesn't come prepackaged."

Dakota's eyes widened at the thought. "What about that delivery boy?" she asked, noticing a guy on a bicycle peddling into the park with what looked like Chinese food in the front basket.

"See, these boys use cell phones to call and order takeout," Blake explained.

"How do they know where to deliver?" Dakota asked curiously.

"They'll use a familiar landmark like the statue, or they'll come and meet the delivery guy halfway."

Dakota decided she'd had enough "schooling" in this particular area, and she glanced at her watch. "Well, Professor St. James, thanks for Central Park 101. You learn something new every day." She got up and headed across the brick sidewalk to hail a taxi.

"Can I drop you off?" she asked.

"No, I'm going to sit here and enjoy the night air," said Blake, looking quite content.

"Okay. I'll talk to you later."

When she got in the taxi, she turned around to wave 'bye, but Blake was gone. Maybe he was on his way to toss a few salads. As the taxi maneuvered its way through the maze of traffic, Dakota thought, "Wait until I tell Morgan she's going into business with a freaky beast."

25

Morgan and Miles had to receive more mail than any two people she knew. Between the stacks of catalogs, piles of offers for "interest-free" credit cards, and the steady stream of bills, surely the mailman must look like Santa hauling it in every day.

After discarding every catalog except for Nieman's and Barneys, and all solicitations, especially those offering bonus miles to switch phone carriers, Morgan sat down to pay her debts to society. She did this twice a month, and it was akin to enduring a series of root canals.

Braced for the mundane, Morgan settled into the media room, which doubled as an office, in cotton PJs and fuzzy slippers, with a glass of merlot on hand if needed. In addition to balancing the books, Morgan paid all of the household and joint account bills, as well as her own personal bills. They were your usual suspects: mortgage, utilities, phone, credit cards. Halfway through the tedium, she took a much needed kitchen break to fortify herself for part two.

When she returned with her rations—a grilled cheese sandwich and chips—she found Miles standing over her desk with a bill in hand.

"What's up?" she asked, settling back in.

"By the looks of it, the balance on the American Express bill," Miles answered, looking at her. "I thought we'd agreed to keep the bills down until after closing on the brownstone. You know what Robert said."

After several trips with their real estate broker, they had made an offer, which had been accepted, on the brownstone. Now the mortgage broker was trying to get a favorable rate, which was proving to be a trial. Though Miles had gotten a large salary increase, the mortgage brokers were averaging income over the past three years, so only a portion of that increase would be included to figure their debt ratio. To keep the ratio up, they were advised to keep debts down.

"I know. But most of these charges are for Caché," Morgan explained, picking up her sandwich for a bite.

"Why do you have three thousand dollars of Caché charges on our card?" Miles asked, looking genuinely perplexed as he continued to study the bill. "What happened to Blake's millions?"

"His attorneys are in the process of liquidating the trust now, but until it's done I agreed to consolidate our expenses on my card."

"Oh, you agreed. How about me? Don't you think that I should have some say in our finances?"

"Miles, it was for tax purposes," she explained calmly. "Since his cards are linked to his father's account, we would be prevented from later writing off the expenses. But it won't be for long—two more weeks at the most. Then he'll have his trust."

"I thought you said two weeks, two weeks ago," Miles reminded her.

This was a sticking point with her too, but she wasn't going to tell him that. "I know, but Blake said there were some legal issues with his brother's inheritance that's causing a bit of a delay."

"You might want to consider delaying this business until his money issues are all resolved," Miles warned.

"We can't do that. Look how close we are to getting the Jon Atkins account. That account alone could be worth a quarter of a million dollars a year."

"I understand that, but I still can't believe you agreed to

finance a company for some rich gay guy when we are in the middle of trying to get a mortgage."

"I can't believe you're being so homophobic. Blake is a great guy. You could at least give him a chance," she pleaded.

Miles was having none of that. "I'm the last person that could be called homophobic. This has nothing to do with his sexual preference, only with him. Something about Blake just rubs me the wrong way. And he *may be* a nice guy, but honestly I think you're giving him enough of a chance for both of us. Besides, I thought he had so much money," he said, arms outstretched.

"He does. It's just that it's taking his lawyers longer than expected to settle his trust," Morgan tried patiently to explain, making the delay sound perfectly normal.

"I've never had a trust fund to settle, but I'd have to think that a rich guy like him would have other sources rather than mooching off my wife's credit card."

"Mooching?" She couldn't believe how unreasonable Miles was being.

"Yes, mooching. Look at these charges: eight hundred dollars in dinners, four hundred dollars in car service charges, six hundred dollars at Office Depot and a grand to a graphic design firm!" he said, smacking the bill with the back of his left hand. Miles was not the least bit enchanted with Blake, so to him the issue was cut-and-dried.

"Miles, I don't need you to rattle off line items. I can read and add for myself. Besides, it's not mooching. Those are upfront costs to start the business." How dared he insinuate that she didn't know how to run her business?

"Costs that he was supposed to finance. If I remember correctly, that was the condition for agreeing to the partnership. Wasn't it?"

Why couldn't he just be supportive? "Yes, it was. But this delay was an unforeseen event." It was bad enough that she had to fight Joel nine to five, but now here Miles was, calling her to the carpet in her own home.

"My only question is, what else is 'unforeseen?' " Miles asked, raising his brow.

"Miles, everything is under control." She was beginning to lose her patience. "Anyway, what are you doing going through my desk in the first place?" she asked, trying to flip the script.

"I was checking to see if a credit for some returned merchandise had showed up. Not that I need to give an explanation for looking at a bill that I pay on a desk in a room in the house that *I* own!" With that, he tossed the bill back on the desk and stalked out of the room.

"Damn," Morgan said, picking up the glass of wine—it was definitely needed. Why did he have to be so difficult? Really, men were like two-year-olds, whining most when their mothers were distracted. Morgan came to the conclusion that Miles's tantrum must be the result of all of the time she'd put into Caché lately.

So she tiptoed into the library, where Miles had retreated, already absorbed in a demo tape that he was listening to on headphones. Coming up behind him, she rubbed his tight shoulders. Removing the earphone from one ear, she leaned down to whisper, "Baby, I'm sorry. I should have mentioned the plans to use the card to you earlier."

Not giving an inch, Miles turned his neck and simply said, "Yes, you should have." He then turned back around, putting the earphone back in place.

Perturbed, Morgan walked around in front of him with both hands on her hips and said, "I said I was sorry. What else do you want?"

Letting his headphones drop to hang around his neck, Miles said, "How about a little peace and quiet?" Then he put the headphones firmly back in place.

26

"Come on in," Dakota said, stepping aside to let in her Latin lover.

Parker walked in, pulled Dakota close to him and said, "Come here, you," giving her a deep French kiss. She wrapped her arms around his neck and passionately kissed him back.

After looking around, Parker said, "Your loft seems different."

"It's the candles. They give it a warm glow," Dakota said. She walked ahead of him so he could appreciate the view through her sheer sheath. She wanted to be the only woman he craved, so she had pulled out all the stops, putting on her lacy thong and the miracle bra that miraculously turned her 34B's into 36C's. "Champagne?" she asked, posing in front of the champagne bucket on the cocktail table.

"I would love a glass . . . among other things," he said, eyeing her as he sat on the sofa.

She bent over in front of him to pick up the bottle, so he wouldn't miss her cleavage. "I hope Veuve is okay."

"As long as it's wet," Parker said, winking.

"Trust me, baby, it's always wet for you," Dakota said. Suggestively, she put the champagne bottle between her legs and popped the cork.

"Let me be the judge of that. Now get over here." As she walked closer, she could see dark chest hair peeking through his sapphire-blue shirt, unbuttoned at his throat.

Setting aside the champagne for now, Dakota sat down so

she was straddling him. She began unbuttoning his shirt, running her hand lazily across his chest. The feel of the soft, straight hair turned her on. "Be careful. You know what they say?"

"No. What do they say?"

She gave him a few butterfly kisses on his smooth-shaven cheek, then whispered into his ear, "Once you go black, you never go back."

"I've heard that before, but what I want to know is . . . is it true that the blacker the berry, the sweeter the juice?" Parker asked, running his hands slowly up her smooth chocolate thigh.

"Want a taste test?"

Parker's hands made their way to the waistband of her thong. As he played with the lace band, she squirmed in delicious anticipation.

"Are you ticklish?" he asked in a hushed tone, lightly brushing her inner thigh with his finger.

She could feel her body heat rising. "Just highly sensitive," she said in a raspy voice.

His finger traveled from her thigh to the curly triangle of hair beneath her thong. He then slowly slipped his middle finger inside. After stirring her berry box for a few moments, he took his finger out and slowly put it in his mouth.

"Well?" she asked, totally aroused.

"Hmmm . . . sweet as chocolate pudding. Now that I've had an appetizer, I'm ready for the next course." Parker took his hands and put them on her small waist, lifting her to her feet. He then stretched back on the sofa. Dakota looked down and watched as he adjusted his head on the pillow. At first she wondered if he was getting ready for a nap—how could he do that?—until he said, "Take your thong off." He put his fingers to his lips and said, "Sit right here."

Not needing to be told twice, Dakota covered his hungry mouth with her pudding pie. He licked her erect clitoris with an increasing urgency. He wasn't just performing a cursory exercise. No, Parker was giving her a full workout with his tongue. Just when she thought time had stood still, he slid his tongue in and out of her quivering sex, devouring her, until she was panting through a shuddering orgasm.

Not wanting to be a "sixty-eight"—do me and I'll owe you one—Dakota got up and led Parker to her candlelit bedroom. On the nightstand was a jar of organic honey. She slowly took off his clothes and laid him on her sleigh bed so that his penis pointed toward the high ceiling. She began gently basting him, carefully smearing the honey all over his throbbing manhood. After it was completely coated, she proceeded to slowly remove the honey with her tongue.

"Oh, that's good, baby," Parker whispered.

"You like it?" Dakota asked. But there was no answer, just the steady sound of his moans. She then reached over to the nightstand and took out a condom. After putting it on, she rode the tip of his penis until he was dispensing his own honey.

"Where did you learn that?" he asked once he regained the power of speech.

"Dr. Ruth," she said jokingly, lying down beside him.

"I'm going to have to send Dr. Ruth a thank-you note," he said, snuggling up close behind her.

"What else do you like?" Dakota asked.

"I like you," Parker said, kissing her neck.

She wanted to ask, "How many other women do you like?" but decided not to. It really didn't matter because he was here in *her* bed. Instead she began to rotate her backside suggestively against him. Dakota loved it when she could feel that limp, weak mass become a force to be reckoned with. She continued to rotate until she felt sure signs of life, then reached behind her to put on a second condom. Parker entered her from behind, and they rocked gently in the spoon position until he was comfortably inside her. He then rolled her on her stomach and picked up the rhythm. Dakota arched her back so that he could go deeper and matched him beat for beat. The headboard of her bed frantically banged against the wall as they neared climax.

"Yeah, baby, that's right. Ride it, baby," Parker yelled before he came in a blur of movement.

Dakota bit the pillow to stifle her screams as she came right behind him. They drifted off into a comalike sleep, the kind that shuts down the whole body after good sex.

The next morning, Dakota was up bright and early. She showered, threw on a white terry-cloth robe and went into the high-tech kitchen with its Sub-Zero refrigerator and matching stainless-steel stove with built-in grill. She was standing at the double stainless sink, squeezing oranges and humming a happy tune, when she heard Parker coming down the hall.

He walked in wearing a matching robe and said, "I guess it's true what they say."

"What's that?" she asked, handing him a glass of fresh-squeezed juice.

"That good loving will have a woman cooking breakfast and singing the next morning," he said, kissing her on the mouth.

"No doubt. I see you found the other robe behind the door. How do you like your eggs?"

"Over easy, like I like my woman."

"Now, don't start nothin' you can't finish," she dared.

"Oh, I can always—and I repeat, *always*—finish whatever I start," Parker said, walking up behind her. He rubbed his hands on the outside of her robe, until he could feel her breasts starting to swell. Bending her over the counter, he firmly massaged her rear with his hands. The fabric rubbing against her bare bottom was such a sensual feeling, it made the tiny hairs on the back of her neck perk up.

"Baby, we need a condom," Dakota moaned, turning to face him.

"I got it covered," he said, referring to the condom already in its designated place.

Parker let his robe drop to the floor, exposing his erect penis. "I could have sex with you all day," he said, as he took off her robe and sucked her nipples.

Dakota was beginning to wonder if he was just interested in the sex. "Parker, how do you . . ."

Before she could ask him how he felt about her, he kissed

her again. Without breaking it, he lifted her right leg and held it against his hip to gain entrance. She braced herself on the sink as he pumped hard. He had already come before she had a chance to get her rhythm.

Once he had her, he then tackled breakfast.

"What do you want to do for the rest of the weekend?" he asked, taking a bite of toast.

"Well, I thought we could go over to the flea market near Twenty-seventh Street," she answered, sipping her coffee.

"Are you looking for anything in particular?"

"Yeah, those old black signs that advertised household products. You know, the ones printed on tin, from the twenties and thirties."

"Where are you going to put them?"

"On the ledge above the window," she said, pointing at the large window that looked out onto the seaport. "Is there anything you want to do today?" Dakota asked.

"Don't ask me that," he said, reaching across the table and rubbing her hand.

"And why not?" she asked.

"Because, if I had my druthers, I would stay here and make love to you for the next twenty-four hours."

Dakota thought, *I just bet you would. And so would I, but this was a taste test. Now it's time to ration the bootie.*

Parker looked over at her, waiting for a response, and said, "Well, how about it? Why don't we stay in all day?"

Before she could think of a suitable excuse, the phone rang. Dakota walked over to the gray marble counter where the portable phone was. "Hello."

"Hey, Kota."

"Hey."

"You busy?"

Dakota looked over at Parker, sitting there with his robe half open, exposing his pecs, and said, "Kinda."

Nana said, "Well, I was calling to find out if you made my reservations yet."

"Yeah."

"Why you keep giving me these one-word answers? You got company or something?" Nana said knowingly.

"Uhh, yeah," Dakota said as she watched Parker open his robe completely and slowly stroke his penis, while looking her dead in the eye. She turned away, trying not to get turned on *again*.

"Is it the man from your job?" Nana asked excitedly.

Dakota didn't hear Parker as he got up and walked up behind her. Suddenly his hands were removing her robe. Then she felt his probing penis.

"Did you hear me?"

For a moment Dakota lost her train of thought as she began to give in to her desires, but she managed to say, "Yeah, that's right."

"I can't wait to meet him. Does he favor Jackson? I know how you like 'em tall, dark and handsome." Nana was on a roll.

"Tell you what. Let me call you back."

"Okay, baby, I'll talk to you later," Nana said with a smile in her voice.

Dakota hung up the phone and turned to face Parker. "We better get a move on, before the day slips away," she said, trying to defuse the escalating situation.

He pulled her closer. "I don't know what it is about you, but I just can't get enough."

Dakota had something else on her mind besides sex. How was she going to tell her grandmother Parker wasn't black? While she hadn't meant to lead Nana on, she also didn't want to try and explain with Parker there. But one thing was for sure: Dakota had to tell Nana before her visit. She knew from comments that Nana had made all of her life that she was a believer in sticking with your own kind. Dakota thought, *I guess this is some of what Morgan was warning me about.* But it was just a speed bump on what was going to be an otherwise smooth road. She hoped.

27

They were meeting at the Boat House, a restaurant in Central Park, for Blake's thirty-fourth birthday celebration. As usual, Miles was running late and Morgan was annoyed. She was always conscious of time, yet Miles, like many native New Yorkers, seemed totally oblivious to it.

She had been ready to leave the house by 5:15 since they were due at six o'clock. Miles, on the other hand, was just stepping out of the bath. After leisurely lotioning his toned body with Molton Brown, he stood in front of the full-length mirror inside the spacious cedar walk-in closet, casually pondering what to wear. He gazed at the built-in shelving that housed his vast collection of neatly folded sweaters, then at the double rods where his army of pants and suits were lined up. He seemed to be purposely taking his time.

Morgan knew where this was coming from. He didn't really care to celebrate Blake's birthday. The other day she'd overheard him on the phone saying to one of his friends, "Man, these days the only thing that's important to Morgan is Caché. She's either buried in business plans or talking to her flaming business partner." Later that evening, Morgan had said, "Honey, I know I've been spending a lot of our private time working on plans for Caché. But please bear with me a little longer. Once Blake and I get things off the ground, we'll hire an operations manager and I won't be involved in every minute detail."

Later that night she had drawn him a hot, steamy bath.

Once he was up to his neck in the aromatic bubbles, she sat on the tiled surface of the Jacuzzi and carefully bathed every inch of his body with a large loofah, washing away the clinging feelings of jealousy and doubt. Morgan knew they had a strong marriage, and she wouldn't let anything jeopardize what they had built.

"Miles, please hurry up," Morgan urged. She had been checking her watch every five minutes.

A lazy voice floated out of the closet. "I can't find anything to wear."

"Miles, you have more clothes than any four people I know! I don't believe you can't find anything," she said, exasperated.

"Morgan, would you chill?" His tone was still easy, but a little tighter.

She ignored the warning. "What do you mean, chill? We've been home all day and you've known about this dinner for a week, so it amazes me that you are nowhere near ready."

"Maybe if you would help me, I'd *be* ready," he said.

Morgan walked into the closet with her hands on her hips and said, "Help you do what? Miles, you're acting like a five-year-old."

Miles turned around with a scowl on his face and said, "Five-year-old? No, I'll tell you who the five-year-old is. It's your boy Blake. Calling here all day, every day."

Realizing this conversation was escalating into an unnecessary argument, Morgan lightened up. "Look, Miles, I know you're feeling a little neglected, but it won't be for long, I promise. But right now you know how important it is for me to get Caché off the ground. Please understand." She walked up behind him, encircling his waist. Walking him over to the row of suits with her arms still around him, she could feel the tension leaving his body. "Now, let's get you dressed."

Finally, at six o'clock, they headed to the park. It was a beautiful Saturday in August; the temperature was hovering around eighty-five degrees, with a gentle breeze balancing out the sticky heat. Morgan was wearing a long, flowing beige skirt, brown fitted silk T-shirt, flat brown sandals and a large straw hat with a wide, dramatic brim that shielded her face from the late-day sun. Miles had finally decided on a seersucker suit with brown-and-tan spectators. Together they looked like a couple out for a stroll along the Champs-Élysées.

When they arrived, Dakota and Parker were already relaxing on a bench outside the Boat House. Dakota had on an ice-blue Michael Kors dress that stopped at her ankles, with a matching sweater tied loosely over her back. Parker's navy linen suit perfectly complemented her outfit.

As Morgan and Miles spotted them, Morgan rolled her eyes and said to Miles, "Dakota and Kyle would look so much better together." Kyle Williams was an executive who worked with Miles at Sound Entertainment.

"Why are you so bent on her being with a brother?" Miles said, looking in their direction.

"Race isn't the only issue," Morgan said, smiling as Dakota waved. "I get the feeling Parker's a player. You remember what I told you about the women's wardrobe on his boat."

Miles nodded his head and said simply, "Yeah, I remember. A ladies' wardrobe on a boat does seem a little suspicious."

Parker stood up as they approached. "Hi, guys. Here, Morgan, take my seat."

"Thanks," Morgan said, sitting down.

Dakota leaned over and whispered to Morgan, "Isn't he sweet?"

"I'm sure he is," Morgan said, looking up at Parker.

Dakota turned her attention to the men. "Miles, I love that suit."

"Thanks, D. You're looking pretty good yourself." Miles gave Dakota a hug and a kiss on each cheek.

They small-talked until Blake showed up fifteen minutes later, looking crisp in a white Armani linen suit and shirt. He was accompanied by Liz and Erik, a third couple he had invited, but without his mysterious new boyfriend, Alan. As he ambled toward them with those long legs, one wrapped at the ankle, he brought to mind a lanky pony with a leg injury.

The third couple struck Morgan as odd. He was attractive,

in that Calvin Klein model sort of way, with a sulky, pouty personality. She was a little rough around the edges, dressed in a faded black pantsuit that should have been retired about six seasons ago.

"So, how's it going, birthday boy?" Morgan asked, exchanging cheek kisses.

"It has been an incredible day!" Blake exclaimed. "Dad took the family to the Four Seasons for brunch to celebrate."

Dakota had to smile. "Where is Alan?" she asked, hoping they'd finally get the chance to check out Blake's new beau.

Blake took a handkerchief out of his breast pocket, dabbed the perspiration from his forehead and said, "Unfortunately, he has rounds at the hospital. But he's going to try and join us later this evening." Blake had been all giddy lately about his new boyfriend, the doctor, and how pleased his parents would be that he was with someone "respectable."

They walked into the rustic restaurant and were seated at an oblong table on the terrace overlooking a pond. There were gondolas docked a few feet away for after-dinner rides. From where they sat, the famous apartment towers of Central Park West seemed but a stone's throw away. As the man of the hour, Blake sat at the head of the table. Morgan sat to Blake's right, and to his left sat Erik. Quickly, the seven of them consumed the first bottle of Veuve Clicquot, toasting Blake and his thirty-fourth birthday.

"Girl, you look great," Dakota whispered, admiring Morgan's outfit.

"If you only knew what it took to get out of the house." She too was whispering.

"I know what you mean," Dakota said, leaning in. "I was partially dressed when Parker came by to pick me up. Then before I knew it, we were getting busy and I had to start from square one."

"I wish that was my problem," Morgan simply said, not wanting to go into details here. She was glad when Parker diverted Dakota's attention.

"Miles," Parker said, making light conversation, "I understand you're an avid golfer."

"Yeah, I love the game," Miles replied. "Do you play?"

"Not enough to mention. I go to the driving range at Chelsea Piers every now and then," Parker said, looking across the table at Morgan, who was watching him intently.

Miles followed Parker's gaze and saw his wife giving him the evil eye. "I know a great pro, if you ever want to work on your game."

"Thanks, I just might look into that." Parker chuckled nervously. "I have a few clients that love golf outings, and improving my game certainly wouldn't hurt business."

The conversation died, and into the silence swooped Blake. "I'd like to propose a toast to all of you for making my birthday so special," he said, raising his glass. As he did, he bumped the table a little too hard and some of the champagne spilled onto the tablecloth.

"Cheers," they all said.

Leaning toward Morgan, Dakota whispered, "Girl, is he tipsy or what?"

"It did sound like he was slurring," Morgan said.

Nevertheless, she turned to him and handed him his first gift, a large box wrapped in blue, yellow and pink tissue paper. "Now, let's open presents," she said.

"Oh, you didn't have to . . . but I'm glad you did," Blake joked, opening the box.

"It's from me and Dakota."

Blake, relishing the attention, was close to tears when he took the tissue off and revealed a sleek black master calf Gucci briefcase.

"Oh, my God, I love it!" Blake exclaimed. He was so moved, he was nearly speechless. That, in and of itself, surprised Morgan, since Blake was a man of many words.

"This is from Erik and me. It's not Gucci, but I hope you like it anyway," Liz said, handing Blake a small, festive-looking shopping bag. Blake opened the package, which was full of assorted scented candles, two Wal-Mart-special champagne flutes and a bottle of Korbel.

Liz smiled. "For when Alan makes his house call."

Blake also smiled, but it wasn't for Liz. It was for Erik, whom Blake was flirting with shamelessly. And Erik didn't seem to be putting up much resistance. As Blake thanked Liz, Morgan felt his leg abruptly brush against hers underneath the table. It was quivering. Since Erik was sitting on the other side of Blake, Morgan assumed the table footsy was for him. At that precise moment, Erik's right side seemed to lower as though he was reaching for something under the table. Morgan could only imagine the unfolding drama.

Blake, stirred by more than the champagne, proposed another toast. "I was going to wait to announce this to my partner first," he said, looking longingly at Morgan, "but I can't resist telling you all tonight. Here's to Caché's first confirmed account." Pausing dramatically, he added, "The Jon Atkins PR & Advertising Company."

In disbelief, Morgan said, "You're kidding!"

"No. Denise called last night to tell me. We're on our way," Blake exclaimed.

Dakota raised her glass. "To Caché."

Blake added, "Some of us have it"—he nodded approvingly to Morgan and Dakota—"and some of us don't."

When Morgan got up soon afterward to go to the ladies' room, Blake followed her. She found the door locked, and she had to wait in the hallway. "Girl, you look amazing," he said as they stood outside the rest room. "I love that hat. If only I had a set of those tits, I would be fierce." Blake's comment was two-thirds bubbly, as he playfully cupped his own flat chest.

"I don't know if that's exactly the adjective I'd use." Morgan laughed, taking out her perfume and lightly spritzing her neck.

"Oh, and what is that? It smells heavenly." Blake reached for the small bottle and sprayed it on his neck too.

"It's Annick Goutal," Morgan said absently.

Blake gazed into her eyes fervently. "Morgan, you just don't understand," he said. "I want to wear fabulous hats like you. I want a successful and important husband who loves me. In fact, in my next life I want to be you."

"Don't be silly. You're just tipsy," Morgan said, dismissing his flattery.

"I'm not drunk," Blake slurred. "I mean every word."

"I swear, Blake, the more I get to know you, the more you amaze me," she said, wanting to calm him down. "From cross-dressing at your parents' parties to whooping it up in your cat-suit and feather boa—now to wanting to be me. What next?"

Miles was right about one thing. Going into business with someone was like a marriage. Only now she wasn't exactly sure who her new spouse really was. While his stories and antics made for fun and entertaining cocktail-party chatter, coming from her business partner it was a mite disturbing. But on the other hand, it was part of Blake's charm and allure. It was the very thing that made him perfect for the hospitality business. No one could ever accuse him of not being entertaining.

28

The taxi dropped Morgan off in front of Dakota's building a little after seven o'clock for their regular girlfriend-slash-therapy session. Morgan never failed to notice something different about this building near the South Street Seaport. Today it was the name, Askew Imports, etched in the stone high above the entry. She assumed it was the name of the original owner. It was ironic; she had been to this building numerous times, but had never noticed its name before.

"Hey, girl, come on in," Dakota said, opening the door with drink in hand. She was wearing an oversized red-and-black Phat Farm T-shirt and black leggings. "Name your poison."

"I don't know what I'm in the mood for. What are you drinking?"

"Jack and Ginger."

"What?" Morgan asked, puzzled.

"Jack Daniel's and ginger ale."

Morgan had to think a second. "I don't feel like a mixed drink. I think I'll have a glass of wine instead."

"Red or white?" Dakota asked, walking to the kitchen.

"Red."

"I've got a Kendall-Jackson merlot."

"That's cool," Morgan said, taking a seat at Dakota's mosaic-tiled dinette table. "What a day," she exhaled. "I must have spent ninety percent of it in meetings."

"What a day indeed. I must've had at least ninety trades,"

Dakota said, handing Morgan her wineglass before taking a seat opposite her.

"At least you don't have to listen to idiots drone on about whack marketing ideas while mentally masturbating each other to absurd fantasies about their greatness," Morgan said, swirling the ruby liquid and watching for the dregs to drift down the inside of the glass.

"True, that would bore me to tears. I must admit I thrive on the excitement of the trading floor. Did you ever play Beat the Clock as a kid?"

A hint of a memory tugged at her. "I think so. You mean the game where you had a certain amount of time to do something?"

"Yeah, that's it. Well, my day is basically like Beat the Clock."

"At least it helps the day to fly by."

"That it does," Dakota said, taking a sip of her cocktail. She shifted in her chair, getting more comfortable. "I really don't want to talk about work, though."

"Me either," Morgan said, tracing her finger along the tiles' intricate and delicate designs. "You know, Miles has been tripping lately."

Dakota was surprised. "What do you mean? Miles is usually so cool."

"I've been spending so much time with Blake, I think he's feeling jealous."

"He can't be threatened by Blake. He's a queen."

"No, he's not threatened sexually. It's really the time I spend at home in front of the computer, working on marketing plans for Caché. Not to mention when Blake comes over, and you know how he is. It's as though a whirlwind has blown through the house. There is nothing low-key about Blake St. James, so his presence is all consuming and, to Miles, irritating."

Something wasn't adding up for Dakota. "What happened to your office in his family's building?"

"It's still under renovation," Morgan said, looking glumly

into her glass. "The contractor had to leave for another job, and they haven't come back yet," she said, repeating Blake's explanation.

Fixing Morgan with a pointed look, Dakota said, "Girl, you'd better get that business out of your house and take care of home."

"Yeah, I know," Morgan said. "I just wish Miles would be more understanding and patient."

"Girl, you better give that man some attention. Do you realize how many women would love to give him a little one-on-one?"

Morgan gave her a look that said, "Don't go there." It was bad enough already. "Trust me, I'm more than taking care of my wifely duties. Speaking of men, how is that man of yours? You guys sure did look chummy at Blake's party."

Dakota's face lit up. "Parker is great, and the sex is unreal," she said, fanning her crotch. "We can't seem to get enough of each other. It's like my yang was made for his yin. And he's not afraid to pet the kitty—you know what I mean?"

"I know exactly what you mean. I'd always heard that white guys were particularly skilled in that area. Something about compensation for size." Morgan laughed, getting in her dig at Parker. "But there's nothing like a man with a skilled tongue."

"Okay!" Dakota said as she put her hand out for Morgan to slap her five, letting the dig go uncovered. "He wanted to come over tonight, but I don't want him to get whipped too fast. I need to ration it out."

Morgan nodded her head rapidly at that thought. "Yeah, girl, ration it out. I don't know how Latin or white guys are, but you and I both know that brothers definitely need it rationed to keep up their appetites. Men are predators, and the minute the hunt gets boring, they're off on another chase."

"That's so true." Dakota's expression turned serious, as she thought back to Parker's harem wardrobe. "Actually, Parker doesn't seem that different from the brothers I've dated."

There she goes again, Morgan thought, *trying to wish the world away.* "Don't fool yourself. Dating someone of another race is always different. On the surface it may seem the same, but have you thought about the big picture?"

"What do you mean?"

Morgan sighed. "You know, marriage, being accepted by his family, and if you have kids how will society accept them? They'll be too black to be Latin or white, and too Latin or white to be black. Shall I go on?"

Dakota had stiffened up in her chair. "You act like I haven't thought about that. It's not like he's all Latin or white—he's already mixed."

"Well, it's the white half that you have to worry about. Let me ask you this," Morgan said, leaning in.

"What?" Dakota said, keeping her distance.

"Have you told Nana he's not black?"

Dakota suddenly became very uncomfortable. "No, not yet. Damn, Morgan, why you trying to rain on my parade?"

Morgan put her fingers up in a peace sign. "I'm not trying to."

"You sure sound like the voice of doom to me," Dakota said crossly.

"Look, girl, I just want you to realize what you're in for."

"And how would you know, Mrs. Happily Married?"

"Dakota, don't go getting defensive on me," Morgan said, hurt by her tone. "If I can't be straight with you, who can?"

"Morgan, where is this coming from? I thought you liked Parker."

"It's not about Parker per se. It's just about how racist America can be," Morgan said. "You know how my promotion was given to an underqualified white boy."

"Do you think I'm that naive that I don't know racism is not only alive but thriving?"

"I don't think you're naive, but sometimes it seems you forget Parker is not a brother." Dakota's face didn't change, and Morgan tried to explain. "You'll see. Wait until you're in an all-black situation, and brothers give you the evil eye."

"Remember, I tried the brothers, and the last one went back to his wife," snapped Dakota.

Morgan stayed cool and rational. "Try to look down the road. Say one day you marry Parker. Do you think his white father is going to accept you? Your life will totally change, and not necessarily for the better." Leaning back in her chair, arms crossed, Morgan went on. "Case in point. My roommate from college started going out with this white guy, and before I knew it she was in lust, in love, and running down the aisle to have a baby. Completely ignoring reality. We all tried to at least make her open her eyes to it. But she refused to see until she and her white husband were isolated and blaming each other. Worse yet, their five-year-old came home from preschool asking, 'What am I?' When Lisa asked her what she meant, the little girl says, 'Jimmy said I was an oreo. What's an oreo?' How do you explain that shit to a five-year-old?"

"You know what, Morgan?" Dakota said, raising her voice an octave. "You need to let me deal with this, because if Parker and I get married and have kids, it'll be *our* problem, not *yours*. Now, let's change the subject, because I don't like where this one is headed," Dakota said, getting up to refill her drink.

Morgan called after her, "Whether you like it or not, you need to take the blinders off—that's all I'm saying. That is, for now, 'cause you know I can't let sleeping dogs lie," Morgan added with a slight chuckle, trying to lighten the mood.

"Well, let's order some food while the dog is still asleep," Dakota said from the kitchen.

As she put ice in her drink, Dakota thought about what Morgan had said. She didn't want to admit it, but Morgan had brought up some good points. To hear it verbalized straight, with no chaser, made her wonder. What if she and Parker did get married and have kids? What would her nana think?

29

Tonight called for full-court-press pampering. The competition would be stiff. Tribe Publications was hosting a premiere party for their new ultrachic, glossy magazine called *The Edge*. Like the guest list, the layout was cutting-edge fashion, blended with a hip, young entertainment vibe. Models straight off the runway, hip-hoppers swimming in baggy gear, and young, freshly minted Internet millionaires posing as rock stars were the order of the day.

After a long, steamy soak in scented bubbles, Morgan sat on the marbled platform of the bathtub, massaging a sea-salt-and-oil scrub over every inch of her body, until her warm brown skin glistened. All except the middle of her back, which eluded her reach.

"Miles, sweetie, would you give me a hand?" A few seconds later he made his way into the master bath, where he stood taking in the sight of Morgan's glowing body in the glimmer of soft candlelight.

He answered seductively, "I'd like to give you more than a hand."

"Later, baby, save that thought," she said, smiling. "Otherwise we'll never make it to the party."

"I can think of worse fates," Miles replied. Careful not to get the sea salt on his Brioni French-cuffed shirt, he gently rubbed it into Morgan's skin. "I can't say that I'm looking forward to holding Ecstasy's hands through tonight's performance."

"I know, babe, but you know how temperamental they are. Without you there, who knows what untold drama might unfold."

"Key word is 'untold.' Sometimes ignorance is bliss."

"In that case," she joked, "the whole group should be deliriously happy."

Smiling in agreement, Miles continued rubbing her back. She knew he wouldn't miss this party. Ecstasy was as unpredictable as the NASDAQ, so there was no way he would let them perform for this trendsetting crowd without his careful direction. Their first single had been a hit, and the video had helped to boost sales to near gold status. The group's carefully orchestrated on-camera persona was sharp, erotic and sexy-smooth, but off camera they were more ghetto than Halle Berry in *Bulworth*.

"Speaking of happy," Morgan said as she stood to towel off, "I'm going to introduce Dakota to Kyle tonight."

"She's not seeing Parker anymore?" Miles asked.

"Yeah, but I just don't think he's right for her. And besides, Parker won't be there. He has some client dinner tonight."

"But what does she think of all this?"

"She's *not* thinking," Morgan said flatly. "That's the problem. She's dick-whipped or tongue-lashed and blinded by his looks. And meanwhile she's overlooking the fact that he's practically white and she's black, and life *isn't* some fairy tale where everyone somehow ends up happily ever after!" Wrapping the towel around her body, Morgan headed briskly into the bedroom.

"Morgan, I know how close you two are, but are you sure you should go sticking your nose into her affairs?" Miles said, as always the peacemaker. "Just because you have a problem with his race doesn't mean that everyone else does. Besides, if he treats her right and she's happy, that's what counts. Right?"

Morgan was slipping into a silk robe. "True. But remember all those women's clothes that he keeps on his boat. Of course, he claims they are things sent from his mom's store for an 'emergency.' But it sounds a little fishy to me," Morgan said, smoothing on Annick Goutal's Hadrien's body oil. "I'll bet he has a revolving door in that stateroom."

"My advice to you would be to stay out of it."

With that, Miles finished dressing. He looked edible, Morgan thought, in his dark navy Donna Karan three-button suit and square-toed lace-ups.

After carefully applying a light face powder for that buffed look, a little black eyeliner and a touch of mascara, she added Mac's lipglass to her naturally rosy and full lips. A taupe two-piece skirt with backless halter was stunning with four-inch sandals. The overall effect was seductive and exotic.

She picked up the phone and dialed. "Hey, girl," Morgan said, after Dakota picked up the phone on the third ring.

"Hey, Morgan, what's up?"

"We're heading over to the Shadow. Should we swing by to pick you up or should we leave your name at the door?"

"Why don't you guys go ahead? I'll meet you there. Oh, and would you also leave Parker's name at the door?"

"I thought he had a client dinner tonight," Morgan said, barely masking her disappointment. This was just the kind of all-black affair that she'd been trying to get Dakota to lately, and adding milk to the coffee was not what she had in mind.

"It was canceled at the last minute. It's okay for him to come, isn't it?" Morgan could hear the silent warning in Dakota's voice.

After a slight pause, Morgan said, "Sure. We'd be glad to leave his name at the door."

"Thanks," Dakota said, relieved.

"No problem. Listen, girl, gotta run. Miles is actually ready on time, if you can believe that."

"Ciao, babes."

"Check you later."

Once they got there, Miles and Morgan followed the long winding line that snaked down Twenty-eighth Street toward the corner of Seventh Avenue. As they briskly walked by the line of New York's hippest and assorted wannabes, Morgan was thankful she had an in tonight. As they approached the entrance, the pit bull–like doorman unhooked the ever-present velvet rope. That always killed her. In New York there might be only two people inside a club, and there would still be a rope and a pair of unleashed doormen. It was all about the hype.

But tonight the hype was real. The main room was full of beautiful people, striking beautiful poses. The place was abuzz with anticipation. How many celebrities would fill the house? Who had the latest boob job or whackest nose job? Who, this week, was rumored to be gay or bi? And of course, always, who was zooming who? Miles and Morgan easily navigated through the crowd, greeting a few acquaintances along the way.

After settling Morgan in the cordoned-off VIP section, Miles headed to the green room to check on his rising stars. Sugar Daddy and Jonathan, the Shadow's world-famous DJs, were working the crowd. They were one rhythmic being, dancing to the latest hot beats. The club looked like those scenes in music videos where the vibe is so tight that the energy is palpable. Masterfully, the DJs would bring the crowd to the brink, pull back, and tease some more, before taking them to yet a higher level.

The VIP section was on the second floor of the three-level club. The top was where Sugar Daddy and Jonathan surveyed their kingdom, working their magic in a glass-enclosed control booth that had enough lights and buttons to launch *Discovery*. Behind them in a mass of crates were literally thousands of vinyl records in no recognizable order—except to the two DJs. To anyone else it looked like organized chaos. Which was the best way to describe the throbbing nightclub.

The VIP section had an elevated dance floor, where usually the freaks would meet. Tonight it would also be the stage for Ecstasy's performance. The main room had a large dance floor, an expansive bar, and cozy nooks where commoners dwelt.

Though people were grooving to ramp-up music—smooth tracks, not the call of the wild—they were more about the pose. No one wanted to sweat too much yet, lest they lose that crease or melt that makeup. Morgan looked over the crowd. One model, who had just married an eccentric but loaded investment banker, was trimmed in so many diamonds that she looked like a Christmas tree threatening to blow a fuse. Playing the alpha-male roles were New York's athletes-cum-celebrities. Why did some insist on being fashion victims? Morgan spied a seven-foot basketball player in a canary-yellow suit, which made him look just like Big Bird.

Draped into a green suede lounge chair, Morgan sipped a glass of champagne, avoiding eye contact with men on the prowl. As she watched two female models unabashedly making out in one of the nooks, Dakota was ushered into the VIP section by one of the hosts.

"It's a madhouse out there!" Dakota said, adroitly slipping past those trying to finagle their way into the reserved section.

"I know," Morgan said, standing to give Dakota a hug. She stopped the host before he could disappear again and ordered a glass of champagne for Dakota.

"Where's Parker?"

"He's meeting us a little later. He had a couple of stops to make."

Looking at Dakota suggestively, Morgan said, "I don't know if you noticed, but there are some fine brothers in the house tonight."

"It's a who's who," was Dakota's noncommittal response.

Just then Morgan saw the person she'd been scanning the crowd for earlier. Motioning toward him, she waved to a tall, brown-skinned guy with a mustache and a Denzel smile. Giving his name to the VIP gargoyle, he walked over to Morgan and hugged her before being introduced to Dakota.

"Dakota, this is Kyle Williams. Kyle, Dakota Cantrell." As they exchanged pleasantries, Kyle took a seat in the third of the four-chair seating arrangement.

"Kyle works with Miles. He's an A & R executive," Morgan explained.

"What groups do you work with?" Dakota asked.

"N2Deep, Zulu Rhythmz, and I also work with Miles on Ecstasy." Kyle had a deep baritone that was sexy as hell.

"Oh, I love N2Deep, and Ecstasy is hot too. I can't wait to see them tonight," Dakota said enthusiastically.

"Morgan tells me you work on Wall Street," Kyle said.

Looking at Morgan questioningly, Dakota answered, "Yes, I do."

"That must be interesting," he said, leaning closer.

"Some days interesting . . . most days insane."

As they laughed, Dakota looked up. Parker was having an exchange with the gargoyle guarding the gate. He looked clearly frustrated and way out of his element.

Seeing him as well, Morgan went over to the guard. "He's with us." Grudgingly, the guard stood aside as Parker walked in. After greeting Morgan, he turned to Dakota with a possessive kiss, then faced the lone wolf. "I'm Parker Emilo," he said, extending his hand for a formal shake.

"Kyle Williams." Sensing a shifting of the winds, Kyle quickly beat a retreat. "I need to check on the group. I'll catch you guys later. Dakota, it was good meeting you." As Kyle left, Morgan also got up to find a host to bring more drinks. As she did, she overheard the guard mumble something about the "arrogant white boy" to Kyle, throwing a nasty look in Parker's direction.

By the time they were all settled, a tall, light-skinned hootchie type had appeared on stage in Lycra so tight, Morgan thought, that it would take surgical tweezers to remove. Though she was introducing Ecstasy, her main agenda seemed to be to show off the biggest, most rotund ass Morgan had ever seen connected to a twenty-four-inch waist. She provided every view: front, back and side. When Ecstasy's intro music started, as if on cue, she began Atlanta's Magic City booty shake. Each butt cheek began to rotate in one direction, then the other, independent from each other. Morgan leaned over to Dakota and whispered, "Now, *that's* talent."

With the crowd appropriately primed and lubed, Ecstasy made their appearance, wearing fuchsia suede with teasing cutouts in all the right places. They walked out rocking their hit single, "Name That Thang." Mimicking the video, the women did the booty shake to the chorus. The crowd went wild, singing each line of the hook like a preprogrammed chorus.

If you hit it once, it's nothin' but a thang
Hit it twice, your balls gone hang
Hit it some mo, you better give up the dough
. . . Hit it! Hit it!
name that thang
name that thang . . .
name that thang!

Ecstasy was sensational, and the crowd loved them. After their performance, Sugar Daddy and Jonathan blended their next single, "Ho's Gotta Eat Too," into Juveniles' "Back That Ass Up." The party was on.

Dakota and Parker made their way to the dance floor to join the free-form melee of writhing, pulsing and vibrating bodies. Judging from some of the dirty dancing going on, some appeared to be in heat.

When Miles joined Morgan, she hugged him. "The girls were great!"

"Thanks," Miles said, kissing her.

"Let's dance, baby," Morgan said, pulling him out to the dance floor. While they were getting their groove on, Morgan noticed Dakota and Parker dancing not too far from them. For a half-white boy, he had some rhythm.

As she watched them, she saw a stocky black guy approach Dakota, trying to cut in. Heated words started flying between the guy and Parker, and Dakota looked alarmed. Miles saw too, and they both headed over, Miles motioning for one of the bodyguards.

As they drew near, they heard the young black guy say, "Man, why you wanna dis me?"

"I don't know what you're talking about." Parker was trying to be tough, but his unease was evident. "I'm just dancing with my lady, so why don't you back off?"

"You tellin' me what to do, huh? Huh? *Huh?*" the black guy yelled. With each word, the tension level rose as the distance between the two men shortened, until the young black guy was right in Parker's face.

Before the shove came, the burly bodyguard physically parted the two men. "What's the problem?"

"I ain't got no problem," the young black guy said, never letting his eyes waver from Parker's. "I think it's the white boy here's got problems. I'm just trying to help him set them straight."

"Man, come on." The huge bodyguard took his arm and ushered him toward the exit, with homeboy turning around still staring at Parker.

Dakota was frazzled, Parker was shocked and Morgan was feeling slightly guilty.

Miles led the group back to the VIP section, where Kyle was waiting. "What was that all about?" he asked.

"Just some knucklehead trying to cut in," Miles answered, trying to downplay the situation.

Dakota's face was tight with anger, so Morgan grabbed her hand. "Let's go to the ladies' room." Without commenting, Dakota walked out behind her.

Once inside under the harsh bright light, Morgan turned to her and asked, "Are you okay?" Although she hadn't wanted Parker to come, she hadn't wanted that type of ugly confrontation either. She just wanted Dakota to meet an eligible black man.

"No, I'm not okay," Dakota said testily. "But I suppose *you're* happy now," she added, as she swiftly turned to leave.

Morgan held her by the shoulder and said, "What do you mean by that? Of course I'm not happy. Do you think that's what I wanted?"

"That's the problem. It's always about what *you* want. Because you want me to have a 'strong black man,' you set this whole thing up, didn't you?"

Morgan was shocked. "What are you talking about? I didn't even know Parker was coming tonight."

"Which is why you were trying to hook me up with Kyle. Do you think I'm stupid? 'Morgan tells me you work on Wall Street,' " she said, imitating Kyle.

Her head hung low, Morgan said, "Dakota, I only wanted to introduce you to—"

"I know," Dakota interrupted, "a strong black man." Dakota whirled around and headed for the door.

"Dakota—" Morgan started.

"Why don't you mind your business and I'll mind mine?" Dakota snapped just before the door slammed behind her.

30

The following week, Blake seemed unusually subdued when he and Morgan met to outline their plans for the Jon Atkins Christmas party. They were continuing to use the makeshift office set up in Morgan and Miles's media room. It wasn't Park Avenue, but it did have a second phone line, a computer, printer, copier and fax.

The media room was normally Miles's personal haven. It had state-of-the art audio equipment fully integrated into a surround-sound multimedia entertainment system. Not only did it play DATs, as in the studio, but it also ran laser discs and DVDs, and housed a five-hundred-disc CD player, all accessed through in-wall keypads throughout the duplex.

A couple of nights before, Miles had come home anxious to listen to some new tracks for Zulu Rhythmz, only to find Blake sprawled out on his favorite throne, with stacks of Caché files strewn about the floor. When Morgan had looked up to see him looming in the doorway with DAT in hand, she tried the sweet-talk approach. "Hey, baby, how was your day?"

"It *was* fine," Miles responded, ignoring Blake.

Ignoring his sarcasm, Morgan continued. "There's some Chinese in the kitchen." As he continued to loom, she asked, "You need anything?"

"Yeah, how about my room back?" he asked, before marching down the hall.

"Men are such babies," Morgan had said to the room at

large. That was last week, and his displeasure had not lessened.

"When will the office be ready?" Morgan asked Blake, not excited herself about the disruption of having the business in her home. Miles was skeptical enough about Caché without having it directly under his nose. Not to mention the intrusion of Blake's all-consuming presence.

"Dunno," Blake said, apologizing. "I called the contractor again last week, but he won't give me a firm date."

"I can't believe how long this is dragging on."

"I know. I'm sorry."

"Well, at least Miles is in L.A. for the next few days."

Taking advantage of his absence, they worked late into the night on the project plan for Jon Atkins. Blake had taken off his shoes, and Morgan noticed that he continually rubbed his sore right ankle. He seemed uncharacteristically distracted and very uncomfortable.

"Blake, are you okay?" she asked. She was unaccustomed to seeing him so somber. He was the most effervescent person she had ever met.

Blake's brow was furrowed as he studied logistics for the project plan. "Not really, but I don't want to burden you with my problems," he said, not looking up from his papers.

"We're partners. Your problems *are* mine. What's up?" she said, putting down her notes.

"Well, I had Mom take a look at my ankle after the swelling didn't go down, and she sent me to an orthopedist, who examined me today. I'm getting a biopsy in the morning."

"For a sprained ankle?" she asked, perplexed.

He gave a little shudder. "I'm not sure how to say this, but there is a growth in my ankle that could be malignant. The weakening may in fact be why it sprained so easily to begin with."

"You've got to be kidding!" Morgan exclaimed, shocked.

"I wish I were." Taking a deep breath, Blake struggled to hold back his tears.

All Morgan could think was that her father had died of bone cancer. "I'm sure the doctor is just being overly cautious because of your parents. There is no way you have bone can-cer," she said confidently.

Blake simply said, "I pray you're right," and continued reading his report.

"Of course I am. Don't you give it another thought," she insisted.

They continued to work late into the evening. The project plan was brilliant, and it took Blake's mind off his problem. There was plenty to get enthused about. From the theme to the decorations and entertainment, the concept was right on point. For entertainment they decided on an entourage of celebrity look-alikes to mingle in the crowd of a thousand guests. The guests would be an assortment of important clients and vendors accompanied by their spouses. After dinner, Jerry Seinfeld would do a stand-up act. All in all, it was a good night's work, especially given Blake's unexpected news.

As she began restoring some order to the room, she said, "Let me call a car service for you." This way at least Blake wouldn't have to fight for a taxi.

"That would be great," Blake said as he stood to stretch. Just then he crumbled to the floor, clutching his ankle. Tears welled up in his eyes.

"Blake, are you all right?" Morgan asked, alarmed.

"Not really. I must have walked on it too much today. It's throbbing like mad," Blake said, his bottom lip quivering.

She couldn't stand to see him this way. "This sofa converts to a sleeper. Why don't you spend the night here? That way you won't have to put even more weight on it."

"I really hate to inconvenience you," Blake said, though clearly in pain.

"It's not an inconvenience. Besides, Miles is out of town," Morgan said. For a moment she felt strange inviting another man to stay in their home. But she knew she was doing the right thing. Blake was obviously in no condition to go anywhere.

After arriving at work the next morning, Morgan had a large arrangement of flowers sent to Blake's Fifth Avenue address with a tender note of encouragement and support. Later that afternoon, they spoke on the phone. "How are you?" she asked delicately. "I tried to call, but I didn't get an answer, so I figured you were either still at the doctor's office or too exhausted to talk."

"It was quite an experience," Blake commented, laughing lamely.

"Did you like the flowers?" she asked, hoping they had boosted his spirits.

"What flowers?" Blake asked.

"I sent you a get-well arrangement," Morgan answered.

"Which florist did you use?"

"The Daily Blossom on Twenty-seventh Street," Morgan answered, surprised that they hadn't arrived. They were normally extremely reliable.

"I'll call them now and find out what happened," Blake said anxiously.

"Blake, let me call. You need to rest. I'll call you back later."

"No, I insist. I'll call them and phone you later when I get the test results. My parents had the hospital rush the lab, so I should know by five o'clock," Blake said, ending the debate.

"Blake, you've got nothing to worry about," Morgan insisted, although she was not sure if she was trying to convince him or herself.

Her anxiety rose throughout the afternoon as she waited for Blake's results. She could hardly keep her mind on her job, which was now difficult under the best of circumstances. Since the run-ins with Joel, she had resigned herself to doing her job, no more, no less. She was in at nine and out by five.

As she was packing to leave, Joel appeared in her doorway, asking for updated business stats.

Knowing that he never came with good news, she braced herself. "You know Aimee is out today. She normally compiles that information."

"Yes, I do know. But since she's not here, it's your responsibility."

"Since when is it my responsibility to back up a secretary?" Morgan asked, puzzled.

"Since I asked you to. I want that report on my desk before you leave today." Before she could think of a reply, he was already down the hall.

Damn. Instead of climbing the corporate ladder, she seemed to be in a free fall backward.

When she finally got home at 7:30 that night, there were five urgent messages from Blake. The last thing she wanted was to call him to find out what she feared she already knew. But she had to call.

"Blake, this is Morgan. How—"

Before she could finish the question, he started a low, deep sob. It was painful to hear. She envisioned his long, lean body withering away with the gauntness that would haunt his chiseled features. Just like her dad. There was an uneasy silence as he continued sobbing uncontrollably.

When he eventually calmed down, she said, "Blake, you have to be strong. Cancer is not the end of the world, not anymore. There have been incredible advances, and with your family's connections you know you'll get the best treatment available."

Between sniffles, he said, "You're right. I know, I can't let this beat me. Not now."

Morgan was so afraid for Blake that she didn't give a moment's thought to the impact on Caché. "Blake, you're not fighting this alone," she said, determined to be strong for him. "You've got your family *and* you have me."

31

It was a sedate Friday afternoon on the trading floor. The frenzied action of the morning had given way to a surrealistic calm. Dakota welcomed the lull, except it was putting her in a zombielike state. With a big weekend in the Hamptons planned with Parker, she needed a jolt of java to bring her back to the land of the living.

"I'm going to the cafeteria to get a cappuccino. Do you want anything?" Dakota asked Paul.

Looking up from his calculator, he said, "Yeah, I could use an espresso."

"Okay, I'll be back in ten."

Before turning the corner that led to the bank of elevators, Dakota heard voices and stopped within earshot.

"Did you like the pictures?" That was Shelby speaking in a deep, provocative tone.

Dakota thought, "Who is the skank propositioning now?"

"What pictures?"

Dakota's eyes widened as she put her hands to her mouth in surprise. It was Parker!

"They were in the envelope I gave you."

"It's in my desk drawer. I haven't opened it yet," Parker said matter-of-factly.

"When you do, make sure you're alone, because it's full of wonderful eye candy just for you," Shelby said, now almost whispering.

Dakota had heard just about enough of this. She bolted

around the corner. There was Shelby standing so close to Parker that she could have counted his pores. She had on skintight khakis and a thinly woven cream sweater with the imprint of her nipples in clear view.

"Hey, D," Parker said, taking a step back from Shelby.

Dakota looked from one to the other. She didn't know what to say. If she mentioned the pictures, they would know she had been eavesdropping, and the last thing she wanted was to appear insecure in front of Shelby. But she did want to let her know that Parker was off the market.

Dakota walked in between them, turned her back to Shelby, and said, "Hey, baby, what time are we leaving for the Hamptons?"

"Uh, right after the close," Parker said, cutting his eyes at Shelby.

Stepping from behind Dakota and picking up her weekend bag, Shelby said, "What a coincidence. I have a share in Quogue." Quogue was a small, relatively inexpensive town near the tip of Long Island, where those who couldn't afford the exorbitant prices of the Hamptons went for the summer.

Dakota said, "Well, Quogue is *not* the Hamptons, and Parker *owns* a house in East Hampton, so we don't have to share." Turning to Parker, she smiled. "Isn't that right, baby?"

"Yeah, I have a little cottage," Parker said modestly.

Shelby strutted over to the elevator, pushed the down button, swung around, and said, "Parker, don't forget what I said." When the elevator came, Shelby got on, and just before it closed, she winked and said, "Have a good weekend, Parker."

"That bitch," Dakota fumed.

"What is it with you and Shelby?" Parker said. "I thought you guys were friends."

Dakota shook her head wearily. "It's nothing. I'm just tired of her trying to get with every man on the floor."

"Well, this is one man you don't have to worry about," Parker said, kissing her on the cheek. "So, where are you going?" he added, as she pressed the down button.

"To the cafeteria. I need some coffee," she said, still miffed at Shelby.

"Me too." The elevator came, and they both stepped on. Alone in the elevator, Parker grabbed her by the waist and, with a roguish smile, said, "I need some caffeine to kick up my energy, 'cause I have big plans for you this weekend."

"Is that right?" she said, warming to his charm.

"Absolutely," he said, releasing her as the elevator doors opened.

Munching on the biscottis she brought back to go with the caffeine jolts, Dakota sat at her desk, impatiently waiting for the closing bell. As she tallied her trade tickets, she could hear a nearby phone urgently ringing off the hook.

"Would somebody get that?" screamed Peter, Shelby's boss. "Where the hell is Shelby?" Dakota looked up and could see him with his hand covering the receiver of the phone while he scanned the floor for his missing assistant.

"Can somebody get that?" Peter yelled again.

"I got it, Peter." Dakota picked up her phone, hit *82, and dialed in Shelby's extension. "Shelby's line."

"Hi, this is Stephan from the Plaza," an impatient voice announced.

"Hi, Stephan, this is Dakota. What can I do for you?"

"Shelby was supposed to get back with me today to confirm the ballroom for SBI's Christmas party."

"Can it wait until Monday?"

"Absolutely not. I need a firm decision today," he said curtly. "I've held this room for a week now, and I explained to Shelby in no uncertain terms that if it wasn't confirmed today, I would have to let it go. I do have a wait list, you know."

Dakota thought, *Ain't that a bitch? The skank leaves early, and I'm doing her job.* Then she said, "Hold on, let me check her book." She walked over to Shelby's desk, thumbed through her book, and found a note Shelby had written to confirm the ballroom at the Plaza. Obviously she had forgot it in her rush to start the weekend. Dakota walked back over to her desk.

"Hello, Stephan, you can confirm the room."

"I'll need a credit card number to hold it," he demanded.

This guy doesn't quit, Dakota thought. "I'm sure SBI has a house account. Check with your accounting department for the card number, and if you have any problems, call me at Shelby's extension."

When Dakota hung up, Peter walked over to her desk and said, "Who was that on Shelby's line?"

"It was the Plaza calling to get a final confirmation on the room for the Christmas party. They were about to release it to their wait list," Dakota offered.

Peter groaned. "Shelby was supposed to confirm that room earlier this week. Do you know how hard it is to get space that time of year?" He was still looking around. "Where the hell is she?"

Dakota held back her smile. "She left early. I think she's headed to the Hamptons."

"She what?"

"Don't worry. I've taken care of everything," she said brightly. "You know, Peter, if Shelby can't handle coordinating the parties, I know this great event-planning company that's not only good, but reliable."

He looked as if he'd never heard of such a thing, then shrugged. "I'll consider it, because I can't have an assistant dropping the ball on our most important function of the year."

"The company is Caché," Dakota said, ever the helpful girl. "I'll have them send you a brochure."

"Thanks, Dakota," Peter said, impressed.

Dakota thought, *That'll teach Shelby not to toy with me. Bitch.*

The closing bell finally came at four o'clock, and Dakota rushed down to the lobby to meet Parker.

"Hey, baby, you ready for the weekend?" he asked, kissing her on the cheek. "Here, let me take that," he said, reaching for her bag.

"I'm all yours for the next forty-eight hours."

"Well, let's not waste another second. My car is around the corner on Broad Street," he said, leading the way. The garage where Parker's car was parked looked like a dealership for the rich and famous. Among others, Dakota noticed a Mercedes G-Wagen, BMW SAV, several Range Rovers, Lincoln Navigators, and even a vintage Austin Healy. The attendant pulled Parker's silver convertible Porsche around, popped the trunk, put in their luggage and bade them a good weekend.

It soon looked as though it would be anything but good.

"This is going to be a long ride," Dakota said, eyeing the bumper-to-bumper traffic inching its way through the Midtown Tunnel.

"Glad I have good company," he said, flashing his flawless smile.

"You're so sweet." Dakota leaned over and gave him a kiss on the cheek. "So tell me, Parker, what's going on with you and Shelby?"

Parker turned to her with a blank look. "What do you mean? Nothing's going on with Shelby."

"You guys sure looked chummy by the elevators this afternoon," Dakota said, trying to get him to bring up the pictures.

"Chummy like you and that guy from the Shadow?" Parker shot back.

Dakota was surprised. She hadn't expected Parker to turn the tables. "What guy?"

"The one sitting with you and Morgan in the VIP section."

Dakota thought for a minute and said, "Oh, Kyle. He works with Miles."

"From what I saw, looks like he was trying to work it with you," Parker said with a hint of jealousy in his voice.

Dakota looked over at him. "You're being paranoid."

"I don't think paranoia had anything to do with it—and certainly not with that other guy trying to cut in on the dance floor. He just flat-out dissed me. I didn't mention it before, but I know he did that because I was the only white face in the club."

Dakota scowled at the memory. "He was just being ignorant."

"Ignorant or not, it was an uncomfortable situation." As if to emphasize the point, he cut sharply in front of a taxi.

Dakota was stunned. She took off her sunglasses so he could see her eyes. "Are you saying you're uncomfortable dating me because I'm black?"

Parker hit the brakes, stopping in the middle of traffic. The car in back of him blew his horn and swerved around, barely missing the rear bumper. He turned to face her square on. "Nothing about you makes me uncomfortable—not the color of your skin, the color of your eyes or the color of your hair. Nothing. You got it?"

Well, I guess I do, Dakota thought to herself. "I got it," she said quietly, putting her sunglasses back on.

Horns behind them were blowing incessantly. Parker took his foot off the brake and rejoined the slow flow of traffic. He then added, "Trust me, if I wanted Shelby, I'd have had her already."

While they were on the subject . . . "Actually, I've been curious. Are you dating anyone else?" she asked, not quite sure she wanted to know the answer.

"Why would you ask me something like that?" he asked, taking his eyes off the road momentarily to see her response.

Dakota didn't look his way. "Because I know how men are."

Parker impatiently thumped his fingers on the steering wheel. "And what's that supposed to mean?"

Dakota took a breath, exhaled, then said, "It means that, unlike women, most men are able to detach themselves emotionally and have multiple relationships at the same time."

"Let's get something straight right now," Parker said, with a fair amount of firmness in his voice. "First, I'm not 'most men.' Second, you are the only woman I'm dating, sleeping with, and desire to be with. Does that answer *all* of your questions?"

"Yes," Dakota said, now feeling a little embarrassed for the interrogation. Still, she had to know exactly where she stood, especially since her grandmother was coming to town and would no doubt want to meet the new man in her life.

Parker looked over his sunglasses at her. "Well, I could ask you the same thing. Are you seeing anyone else?"

"Not anymore. I was dating Jackson Matthews in research sales."

His mouth opened in mild shock. He turned to look at her and said, "Jackson Matthews, really? What happened?"

She shrugged. "He was separated, but decided to give his marriage another try."

"Can't blame a guy for trying to keep his family together," he said as they emerged into the sunshine at the far end of the tunnel. "If I were married, I'd do whatever it took to stay together."

This guy sounds like a keeper, she thought. Yet he still hadn't mentioned the pictures Shelby gave him, and it made Dakota wonder just how sincere he really was.

They continued to crawl along the Long Island Expressway, the world's longest parking lot. The sun dimmed from a bright citrus yellow to a mellow cantaloupe, signaling the arrival of evening. Dakota lay back on the headrest, closed her eyes, and let the breeze from the convertible caress her body. By the time they arrived at Parker's house, it was well after eight o'clock.

The house was no cottage. It was strikingly modern, with an asymmetrical roof and a two-story, glass-walled living room overlooking the beach. The furniture was upholstered in white-and-cream leather with earth-tone accents. There were bleached hardwood floors throughout. The gourmet kitchen was stark white with a marble island. A crescent-shaped stairway led upstairs to the master suite and two guest suites.

"I love your house. Looks like South Beach," Dakota said, hanging her clothes in the master suite's walk-in closet.

"That's what most of my friends say."

"Speaking of your friends, when am I going to meet them?"

"I was thinking about that," he said, hugging her from behind.

"And?"

"And I'll call and invite Christopher and his wife, Christine, over tomorrow evening. Also—"

"That's cute. Christopher and Christine. Do all of your friends have matching names?"

Parker chuckled lightly. "You haven't even met them yet and you're making fun. Anyway, I'll also call Dave and his wife, Ana. It'll be fun. I'll grill and you can mix your legendary cosmos."

That night they cuddled under the skylight in the master bedroom, watching the stars glimmer in the moonlight, until they drifted off into a peaceful sleep. The next morning they went into town and bought chicken, fish, burgers and vegetables. They spent the rest of the afternoon marinating meat and slicing and dicing vegetables to make shish kebabs for the grill. In the process they also went through a few shakers of cosmos.

"So tell me, what are the wives like?" Dakota asked, sipping her drink.

"Christine is an editor at *Marie Claire,* and Ana is a real estate agent."

"What do they look like?" she asked, still trying to satisfy her curiosity.

"Christine is tall, and Ana has dark brown hair."

"Is that the best you can do?"

Never looking up from the chopping block, Parker said, "What else can I say?"

"Men give the worst descriptions," Dakota said. "They miss all of the important details."

"Why don't you just wait and see? They'll be here in an hour. Come on, let's head upstairs to shower and change."

Parker took off his blue-jean shorts and Harley Davidson T-shirt and tossed them on the king-sized bed. Clad only in a jockstrap, he walked over to Dakota, who was standing in the closet doorway and said, "Those cosmos have me all fired up."

With her back to him, Dakota merely said, "Really?"

"Yeah, baby, yeah," he said in his best Austin Powers voice, as he nibbled on her neck.

Dakota stepped away from him. "Come on, Parker, I'm trying to decide what to wear."

Parker put his arm around her shoulders and pulled her

back to him. "It's not that serious." He put her hand on his rising organ and said, "Now, *that's* serious."

"Parker, stop," she said, taking her hand away. "I'm trying to pick out the right outfit."

He didn't understand. "It's only a casual dinner," he said, still holding on to her.

"I'm a little nervous about meeting your friends, and I want to make a good impression."

"I know just the thing to relax you."

She looked at him skeptically and said, "What do you have in mind?"

"Let's take a nice hot shower, then let me massage that tension away," he said, leading her into the bathroom.

Dakota reluctantly stepped into the oversized oatmeal-colored marble shower. As she stood in front of Parker, he began to lather and massage her back. She could feel the tension slowly washing away. He turned her around to face him and began rinsing the soap from her body with a huge sea sponge, then gave her a succulent kiss on the neck. She could feel him against her wet, slippery thigh. Giving in to her desires, she grabbed his rear and began to grind against him, whispering, "Let's get out and finish this in the bedroom."

Parker walked over to his nightstand and took out a condom. "I've got a helmet for this soldier, and baby, I'm taking no prisoners," Parker said in a deep, provocative tone.

"Well, get over here, General," she said, jokingly, "and invade my territory."

Parker pounced on the bed, causing the comforter, along with a few pillows, to fall on the floor. The once pristine linen soon became a tangled mess as they engaged in a torrid love battle.

After taking separate showers, they dressed for a casual summer evening. Dakota put on white capri pants, a white linen cropped top, and a pair of Donna Karan flats. Parker wore a pair of faded jeans torn at the knee and a white linen shirt rolled to the elbow, exposing his hairy arms. He decided against shoes, which made his overall appearance relaxed and sexy.

In the kitchen, Dakota noticed they both had on white linen shirts and teased, "Why are you trying to dress like me?"

He looked mystified. "We're dressed totally different."

"Except for the white linen tops—or didn't you notice?"

"Yeah, now that you mention it, I think we look real good," he said, leaning across the island and kissing her on the lips. "Here, put this on before you waste something on all that white," Parker said, handing her a black apron.

"Thanks. I wouldn't want your friends to think I was a slob," she said, feeling some tension creeping back.

"I'm going out to start the grill," he said, opening the French doors leading out onto the patio.

Just after he walked out, the doorbell rang, catching Dakota off guard.

"Shit, they're early," she mumbled to herself as she walked to the front door. When she opened it, she realized too late that she still had on the apron.

"Hello, I'm—" Dakota didn't get the chance to finish.

"Tell Parker we're here." That was the tall one.

"Here, put this on ice before it gets warm, and chill six glasses." That was the dark-haired one, thrusting a bottle of champagne at Dakota.

"Where are they, on the patio?" asked the tall one as she walked in past Dakota, barely glancing her way.

The four guests proceeded toward the kitchen, leaving Dakota in their wake. She sank to the sofa, still holding the champagne. *Damn, ain't that a bitch?* she thought. *Those heifers think I'm the help.*

South Side toughness began to rear up as she stalked straight to the patio to set the record straight. When she stepped out of the sliding glass doors, Parker said, "Honey, I take it that you've met everybody?"

"Not exactly," Dakota said. This was the voice she used to wage war on her enemies.

"Oh, I thought . . ." said the tall blonde. She had turned whiter than Casper the Friendly Ghost, only she wasn't so friendly.

"I know what you thought," Dakota shot back.

"I'm Ana," said the dark-haired woman, trying to extend an olive branch.

Dakota promptly put the champagne bottle in her extended hand and said, "Maybe you can put this on ice yourself! Because I have to take off this apron and freshen up before I am accused of being the help. Oh, I forgot you've already assumed that," Dakota said, walking away. She left the four guests standing on the patio with their mouths agape.

Dakota went up to the bedroom, doing a slow burn the whole way. Just as she was cursing them for all they were worth, Parker walked in.

Not giving him time to defend himself, she said, "You didn't tell your white friends that I am black?"

Ambushed, Parker said, "Wait a minute, let me explain."

She walked over to the window and looked out at the ocean. "There's nothing to explain. When I let them in, they automatically assumed I was your damn maid. How the hell can you explain that?"

"I told Dave and Christopher that I had met someone very special, and—"

"And they assumed that I was lily white."

Parker walked over to her. "Maybe I failed to mention that you are black, but that's because when I see you, I don't see a color, just the woman I love."

Dakota spun around to face him. "What did you say?" she asked, shocked at his proclamation of love.

"I said, I love you. I didn't expect it to happen so fast, but Dakota, I'm in love with you," Parker said, looking directly in her eyes.

Dakota put her face in her hands and began to cry. She felt so confused. On the one hand, here was a man she wanted to spend every waking moment with, telling her he loved her. But on the other hand, he had *failed to mention* she was black. She thought back to what he had said in the car about being uncomfortable at the Shadow. She wondered if he truly could fit in her world—or she into his?

With Parker's help, she composed herself and went back downstairs. But needless to say, the rest of the evening was a bumpy ride that went mostly downhill. The women tried to redeem themselves and make polite conversation; the men mainly directed attention to Parker.

Dakota was subdued. Now she was wondering if he had ever told his family that she was black. Did he honestly think that race didn't matter? Or for that matter, did she? After all, she still hadn't told Nana about him. All of a sudden Morgan's words came flooding back to her. *"Don't fool yourself. Dating someone of another race is always different."*

32

The initial shock of cancer subsided, and a week later Blake had developed a wry sense of humor about his illness. "How does this look?" he asked, posing dramatically in one of Morgan's large straw hats. "If my hair falls out from the chemo, I can always borrow it."

She had initially insisted that they postpone all plans for Caché to allow Blake to focus his energy solely on his treatment, but he was adamantly opposed, saying that Caché was the only worthwhile endeavor he had ever undertaken. Though concerned about his health, Morgan agreed to proceed. Keeping busy could help the recovery process.

"Actually, not half bad," she said, admiring his elegantly chiseled features. All he needed was a little mascara, eyeliner and lipstick and he'd give RuPaul a run for his money. "But let's hope it doesn't get to that. After all, didn't the doctors say they were prescribing small doses?" They were at Morgan's while she threw together an outfit to wear to the Maxwell concert that she and Miles were attending later.

"To begin with. But how the cancer cells respond to the treatment will determine whether they increase the dosage or not," Blake explained. Then suddenly he became somber as he sat on the chaise in her bedroom with his head down.

Sensing his mood change, Morgan noticed big, silent tears slowly gliding down his cheeks. She sat down next to him. "Everything is going to be fine," she said in a voice that was much more confident than she really felt. She was convinced that had she been stronger and not broken down at her father's bedside, he would have somehow found the strength to fight for his life. She had seen the resignation in his eyes as clearly as if he had spoken it aloud. With Blake, she was determined to be strong and not act affected by his health, no matter what happened.

"I'm not so sure, Morgan." Staring up at the ceiling, fighting off more tears, Blake said, "My mother's brother died of cancer at a young age. And I just learned that my great-grandfather also died of cancer. So you see, the genetic odds are stacked against me," he said, looking at her with a pained expression.

"Blake, I don't want to hear another word about it. You're going to be just fine, and that's all there is to it," Morgan declared. She abruptly stood up and continued going through her closet. "Besides, this is just a test of your fortitude, to make you more appreciative of all that you are blessed with. Given your life of privilege, you've taken way too much for granted." With that said, she headed into the bathroom to start getting ready for her evening out with Miles.

By all indications, the treatments seemed to go very well, with the exception of the sickening nausea and draining fatigue that Blake described following each weekly dose of chemo. He also said his doctors were extremely pleased with his progress and felt he should make a complete recovery.

So they continued developing plans for Caché. They had meetings with Fidelity, Salomon Smith Barney, Citicorp and several smaller but also prestigious companies. After a successful meeting during Morgan's lunch hour Wednesday with the managing director of Fidelity, she and Blake grabbed a bite at a small café near Wall Street.

"With the events Fidelity has agreed to, plus the fifty-thousand dollars from the Jon Atkins Christmas party, we'll have over a hundred-and-ten thousand dollars in revenues within the next six months. We really don't need the trust fund," Blake said.

This unexpected change in financial strategy caught Morgan off guard. "We will most certainly need funds to cover our costs between now and then. Not to mention my American Express bill, which now has another three thousand dollars of business expenses on it. Which, by the way, will be billed and due soon," Morgan said with a tinge of warning. She had already paid last month's charges, but Miles would hit the roof if she came out of pocket with another three grand.

As though dismissing the measly sum as trivial, Blake continued flipping through his notes from the meeting. He nonchalantly replied, "The money's coming soon." He looked up from his notebook. "You know, we should send a bottle of wine as a thank-you to Tom at Fidelity."

"That's a good idea. I'll stop and pick up a bottle and have it sent over," Morgan said.

"Better yet, we can call my friends Karen and Oswald Morgan. They own several liquor stores uptown. In fact, we should open a house account with them. That way we can have a bottle delivered with a phone call anytime. I'll call Karen now," Blake said, pulling the cell phone from his briefcase.

"Karen, darling . . . It's Blake . . . I am doing well, considering. The chemo is kicking my butt, but the doctors think it's working. Listen, my partner and I want to open a house account and send a bottle out today . . . um-huh . . . a nice Rhône red, or what about a Châteauneuf-du-Pape . . . that sounds good. I'll be there in a couple hours. Ciao, babes!"

He then explained to Morgan, "Karen can get a bottle delivered within the next two hours. She only needs the card imprint to establish the house account and then she'll bill us monthly."

Checking her watch, Morgan said, "I don't have time to run uptown and be back at the office for my two o'clock meeting."

Blake immediately volunteered. "I'll take the card up to her on the way to my doctor's office and get it back to you first thing tomorrow."

"Okay, but you have to get it back by tomorrow," Morgan said, tentatively handing over the card.

"We have to get together tomorrow anyway. I've scheduled a meeting with one of Denise's contacts at Bloomingdale's."

"What time?" Morgan asked warily.

"It's at noon, so that you can swing by during lunch, like today."

She shook her head. "Blake, I really can't keep doing these lunch meetings. I'm getting back to the office late every afternoon. And I already have enough issues there to begin with."

"But, Morgan, these meetings are critical, and remember, you *are* the sales and marketing person," Blake reminded her.

"My *job* is critical too," she reminded him.

Sighing, Blake said, "If you can't make the meeting tomorrow, at least find a way to make the Citicorp meeting on Friday. Denise said that they were strongly considering us based on her recommendation and last week's meeting, but wanted a presentation given to their entertainment committee. And you know that you are so much better at that sort of corporate thing than I'll ever be."

"Blake, I don't know," she said, shaking her head. Miles's leeriness of their venture loomed over her.

"Morgan, this is a big one. This account is worth at least a quarter of a mil a year." Blake dramatically leaned back in his chair. "This is where you fish or cut bait. Are you in or not?"

Thinking of Dakota's saying, "You've gotta be in it to win it," Morgan answered, "I'm in. I'll just take the day off work."

Later that night, when Miles and Morgan were changing into nightclothes, he casually asked, "What time should I have Evan and Laura come over tomorrow?"

She was thankful that Miles had his back turned. He didn't see the look of sheer panic that crossed her face. Between dealing with Global by day and Caché by night, she had completely forgotten that Miles's new boss and his wife were coming over for cocktails before dinner at Le Colonial tomorrow. To make matters worse, she hadn't rescheduled the maid, planned for cocktails and appetizers or even made dinner reservations.

"How about seven-thirty?" she said.

Turning, Miles said, "You said you're taking off Friday, right?"

"Yeah," she said hesitantly.

"Robert wants us to stop by his office to finish the paper-work for the mortgage broker. I'm free in the morning. What is your schedule?"

"You know I have that nine o'clock in Midtown," she said, careful not to mention Blake's name or Caché.

"Then I'll confirm with him for eleven. That should give you plenty of time."

"Okay." Just then the phone rang; it was Blake. "Hold on a moment," she said before leaving the bedroom to take the call in the library.

Whispering, she recounted her domestic situation to Blake as she tried to figure how to salvage her series of blunders. She couldn't let Miles get wind of this.

"Morgan, let me handle it," Blake said.

"What do you mean?" Morgan said, wondering how he could possibly help.

"I'll come over tomorrow morning with Mattie. I'll have her clean while I throw a couple of appetizer trays together."

"Are you sure?" Morgan asked.

"I'm positive. Believe me, it's no problem."

"Don't you have to check with Mattie, or at least your parents?"

"Tomorrow is her day off. I know she'll do it for me as a favor."

"Okay, if you're sure." Morgan felt tonnage lifting from her shoulders. Miles would have killed her for sure. "Blake, you are a lifesaver."

"We'll be there by eight, and by the time you get home, everything will be in perfect order. Trust me."

"No, come at eight-thirty." Morgan knew by then that Miles would be long gone.

Then she remembered his treatments. "Blake, are you sure you are even up to this?"

"I'll be fine, and besides, I would love to help out. You're

always there for me. So rest easy. We'll see you in the morning."
Morgan was so grateful. It was just like Blake to be concerned
about other people. If only Miles knew this side of him.

With Miles safely off to work, the next morning Blake
arrived promptly at 8:30 with a bag of groceries and Mattie in
tow. Morgan was running late, and she rattled off final instructions as she grabbed her jacket and darted out the door. "Blake,
the list of things to do is on the kitchen counter, and you can buzz
me at the office if you need anything."

When she got to her office, there was a note on her desk
from Joel. It read:

Urgent, see me ASAP
Need Zenon proposal for 12:30 appt tomorrow!

She couldn't believe what he was asking her to do, especially
knowing that she had asked for tomorrow off. It would take a
couple of days for her to pull a proposal together. Infuriated,
she crumbled the note into a tight little ball and tossed it angrily
across the room into the wastebasket. She then marched straight
to his office.

"Joel, how do you expect me to complete a full banking
proposal in one day? And you know I'm off tomorrow," she
asked, leaning on his door frame with her arms crossed.

He didn't even bother to look up from his desk. "Morgan,
I'm not really concerned about how you do it. I just want it
done."

Morgan tried reasoning with him. "Plus, I can't stay late
tonight. I have guests coming over." She knew that Miles would
flip if she even thought about canceling, given all the time that
she'd put into Caché.

Looking up without batting an eye, he said, "As long as I
have that proposal when I meet with their CFO, I don't care
how it happens."

"I'll tell you what," Morgan started, creating a solution in
midthought. "I'll work on it all day today and first thing in the
morning; then I'll deliver it to Zenon's office in time for your

one o'clock meeting. They're in Midtown, right? At Fifty-sixth and Seventh?"

Focused again on his desk, Joel said, "If that works for you, it works for me. Just make sure it's there." Looking back up briefly, he added, "No excuses."

Blake called her office around noon to report that everything was fine at her apartment. "Good, I'll be home by six," Morgan commented brusquely, the stress evident in her voice.

"What's wrong, Morgan?"

After explaining her latest drama, Blake said, "So what are you going to do, finish it before tomorrow's nine o'clock meeting?"

"I'll have to work on it all day today and get up at the crack of dawn to finish it before our nine o'clock meeting. But the real problem is getting it to him. I've made an appointment with Miles and our broker to tie up loose ends for the mortgage. And you know how pouty Miles has been lately. If I even think about canceling, I'll never hear the end of it," Morgan said, feeling trapped.

"Why don't you bring the proposal to our nine o'clock meeting, and afterward I'll run it over to their offices and drop it off?"

Morgan was ecstatic. "Blake, you're a lifesaver, twice in one day!"

"That's what partners are for," Blake said.

At Morgan's place, Blake was fixing up the roof deck with candles and place settings, when he spotted a prime specimen in the window directly across from Morgan's roof. Unable to stop himself, he flirted shamelessly, starting with an "innocent" backside view. Never one to miss a trick, he escalated matters once he was done setting the table. Reclining on the roof, pretending to soak up the sun, he got up from time to time to stretch, all the while bending over to provide the blond in the window a bird's-eye view from a *very* provocative position. He then sat in the chaise with his long legs spread wide apart as he stroked his chest, allowing his voyeur an unobstructed view of his growing, bulging crotch. What had started out as an "innocent" flirtation was becoming downright torrid. This went on for over fifteen minutes until Blake finally brought down the curtain of his one-man show to finish his duties downstairs.

When Morgan got home, the apartment was spotless, the appetizers beautifully arranged and the champagne and pinot grigio chilled to perfection. After greeting Mattie and thanking her profusely, the maid replied, "You're very welcome. And your apartment is beautiful!"

"Thank you," Morgan said, thinking, *It's not Fifth Avenue, but it is rather nice.*

"Speaking of beautiful, one of your neighbors is so hot!" Blake said, fanning himself.

"How would you know?" Morgan said absently.

"I did make time for a little innocent flirting today."

Not the least bit interested, given everything else on her plate, she dismissed his comment with a sigh and a roll of her eyes.

Blake then gave Morgan some last-minute instructions concerning the food and wine before leaving with Mattie. When Miles appeared thirty minutes later, raving about how nice everything was, Morgan was tempted to attribute it all to Blake, so he would once and for all realize how wonderful Blake was. But something told her that wasn't such a good idea. Particularly since she would also have to tell him that he had been alone in their home all day.

When Evan and Laura arrived, Morgan and Miles entertained them in their usual elegant manner. The music selection was hip but sophisticated, and the lights were dimmed and candles lit to enhance the tastefully elegant decor. After the first glass of champagne, they took the party up to the roof, where they enjoyed a beautiful night topped with the luminous glow of a brilliant full moon.

Everything was perfect until Morgan noticed a recurring shadow in a window directly in front of them. A few minutes later, more light began to frame the shadow. *Oh, my God!* Morgan screamed silently as her body tensed and her temperature rose another few degrees. To her embarrassment, they were in the direct view of a nearly naked man in the next building!

Eyes widening, Laura caught the spectacle before the rest. "Do you realize you have an exhibitionist as a neighbor?" she whispered to Morgan, trying her best to be diplomatic.

"Why, what on earth do you mean?" Morgan asked, feigning innocence. Before the words were out of her mouth, the man in the window seductively removed the scant G-string that was his only remaining shred of clothing and began rubbing oil suggestively over his muscled body. Morgan immediately thought of Blake's sly tone as he mentioned "flirting with a neighbor."

"This definitely takes people-watching to a whole new level!" Evan said. Morgan laughed nervously as she snuck a guilty look at Miles.

They all watched the man in the window in amazement. If only he knew the object of his desire wasn't present tonight to enjoy his reciprocal performance.

"Fortunately, we don't usually have private showings, or I'd be forced to charge a cover," Morgan said lightly. "Why don't we head out for dinner? If we catch all of this show, the rest of the night might be anticlimactic."

33

"Girl, I feel so bad about what happened at the Shadow." Because both of their schedules were so hectic, they hadn't had a chance to get together for several weeks. They'd talked on the phone, but Morgan wanted Dakota to hear it face-to-face. "The last thing I expected was for Parker to get dissed on the dance floor. Actually, I didn't expect him to show at all."

Morgan was driving her pearl-white Range Rover up the Saw Mill Parkway to the designer outlets at Woodbury Commons. She and Dakota had on their shopping uniform: nude-colored bodysuits under sundresses. This way they could slip off the dresses quickly without zippers or buttons in the way. And the bodysuit kept panty lines from obstructing their view as they tried on their prospective purchases.

Dakota looked over at her. "So, since you figured Parker wouldn't be there, you thought you'd hook me up with Kyle?"

"I didn't mean any harm. I just wanted you to meet him. He's single, no kids, makes bank, and—"

"And, most importantly he's black," Dakota said, finishing her sentence.

Morgan looked hurt. "That's not what I was going to say. Before you rudely interrupted me, I was going to say, 'And he's a really nice guy.'"

"Well, I already have 'a really nice guy.'"

Morgan reached over and touched Dakota's arm. "I'm truly sorry. I promise I'll keep my matchmaking skills to myself. Truce?"

Dakota put her hand over Morgan's. "Okay, truce," Dakota said, smiling at her friend. "Girl, you know I can't stay mad at you."

"So tell me, how are things going with you two?"

Glancing out the window at the winding road, Dakota contemplated whether she wanted to share what had happened in the Hamptons. "Really good, but . . ." She didn't want to hear an "I told you so."

"But what?" Morgan didn't sound judgmental. She just wanted to know.

"There was a little misunderstanding at Parker's house in the Hamptons." Dakota recapped the story, but downplayed it, as if it were no big deal.

"You've got to be kidding! I would have been furious," Morgan said, banging the steering wheel with her fist. "I tell you, white folks never cease to amaze me. So what did Parker say?"

Thankful that Morgan hadn't said, "I told you so," Dakota went on with the rest of the story. "Well, I stormed upstairs, and when Parker came into the bedroom, I gave it to him with both barrels. But you won't believe what he said when I asked him why he didn't tell them I was black."

"What excuse did he give?" Morgan asked, anticipating some lame explanation.

"He said he didn't see a color when he saw me. Only the woman he loved."

"What!" Morgan said, shocked. "He used the 'L' word!"

"Yep, it blew me away. I didn't know what to say."

"Well . . . ?"

"Well, what?" Dakota turned her head deliberately, looking away from Morgan.

"Do you love him?"

Dakota turned back to Morgan with sincerity in her eyes, paused and said softly, "I do. I didn't expect it to happen so fast, but I guess you can't put this sort of thing on a schedule."

This was the worst news Morgan had heard yet. "Shouldn't you guys slow it down? Give the relationship a chance to develop?" she cautioned.

"It's not like we're strangers."

Morgan took a deep breath. "If nothing else, the weekend in the Hamptons should have given you a glimpse into the future with your half-white boyfriend in his lily-white world."

"Give it a rest, Morgan," Dakota said, sounding tired. "Let's not get started on that again. I just want to have a light day of shopping and not think about all this."

Although Morgan thought Parker seemed like a nice enough guy, she still wasn't convinced he was deserving of her best friend, especially in light of the Hampton episode. Before she could go on, though, Dakota changed the subject.

"How is Blake?"

"He seems fine," Morgan said. Maybe she should give Parker a rest. "Although I've got to tell you, sometimes I think he's in strong denial. I mean, he's following the treatment plan, but he now seems to take it all very lightly. For example, he probably shouldn't be drinking, but that certainly hasn't stopped him."

"I'm sure having Caché has something to do with Blake's positive outlook. You guys have accomplished so much in so little time."

"I'm excited that things are going so well." Morgan's face turned somber. "But can I tell you, Blake can be completely irrational. Maybe it's the medication."

"What do you mean?" Dakota had seen some of Blake's wild side, but as far as she knew, it was limited to his sexual adventures.

"He asked me to meet this friend of his, Kathleen White." Morgan shook her head slowly. "Supposedly she's loaded and just needed something to do with her time and had shown an interest in event planning. He thought she could help us. So, we met at her place across from Lincoln Center." She looked over at Dakota and exhaled loudly. "Not only was she rude, but she looked me up and down so hard that it didn't dawn on her that she hadn't offered me a seat. Not that I really wanted to sit down in that place, anyway. I came dressed for the meeting in my chino suit, but she looked like someone who sat around eating bonbons all day, watching *Jerry Springer*. You should have seen her. Her hair was a mess, and her nails were dirty." Morgan's tone wasn't just dislike—it bordered on repulsion.

"Uuuggghh," said Dakota, squeamish at the thought.

"Well, here comes the irrational part. Out of the blue, Blake started talking about making her a partner!"

Dakota was shocked. "Why would you guys need a partner? You have the marketing and business skills, and you don't need her money since Blake's trust will be liquid soon. What's up with that?"

"I have no idea." Morgan's tone kicked up another notch. "Before the meeting, he talked about the contacts she had access to for some pretty prestigious events. But when I asked her directly, she talked about planning a bunch of weddings. When we left, I asked Blake, 'Did you see anything in our business plan about weddings or bar mitzvahs?' " Morgan was now fuming. Her time was valuable and she didn't want it wasted being misled.

With a contemplative look, Dakota asked, "Why do you think he was pushing her?"

They had reached the outlets. Navigating the boat-sized Ranger into a canoe-sized space near the main entrance, Morgan answered, "I have no idea. But as sure as my name is Morgan Nelson, there is absolutely no way I'm having *her* for a business partner. This time it's the good-ole-black-girl network, and that's all I'm going to say."

As they walked through the parking lot, Dakota said, "Oh, I forgot to tell you about Shelby."

Morgan's face lightened into a smile. She knew it would be something outrageous. "What did she do this time?"

"It's more like what she didn't do," Dakota said, winking.

"What happened?"

"The other week she slipped out of work early. No sooner had she left than her phone was ringing off the hook and her boss was having a conniption. So I picked up her line. It was this rude-ass man from the Plaza, talking about how it was the last day to confirm the ballroom for SBI's Christmas party. I went over to her desk, found her appointment book and confirmed the room."

Morgan gave her a look. "Why would you cover for her?"

"Wait, let me finish. When I hung up the phone, her boss came over, and of course I had to tell him that Shelby dropped the ball." Dakota smiled broadly. "Now, this is the best part. I suggested that Caché step in if he felt Shelby was too over-whelmed."

Morgan's eyes lit up like firecrackers on the Fourth of July. "Oh, that would be great if we could land SBI as a client. What did he say?"

"I told him you would be glad to send out a brochure."

"I'd be glad to meet with him. We'll give him our masterful sales pitch," Morgan said, slapping Dakota five. "Good looking out. On that note, I say we get our shop on."

Woodbury Commons was their favorite one-day trip. It was about an hour and a half due north of the city, but the drive was worth every mile. Woodbury had the best collection of designer outlets in the country. There were Gucci, Prada, Neiman's, Bar-neys, Tods—all their favorite friends. And the list went on and on. Dakota and Morgan loved fine clothing, and they loved them even more with a deep discount. Being world-class shop-pers, they had a battle plan and knew exactly which stores to attack first.

"Let's go over to Gucci. I need a black bag for the fall," Dakota said.

Usually Gucci was packed, but surprisingly, it was relatively calm. They took a walk through the store, scoping out the mer-chandise. "Is this bag great or what?" Morgan said, holding up a black master calf satchel.

"It's beautiful. You should get it."

"I really don't need another black bag, though. You should get it since you need one," Morgan said, handing the purse to Dakota.

"I think I will. It goes with my pumps," she said, rubbing the smooth surface of the purse. "I wonder if they have a wallet that matches. You know how I like my sets."

"Let's see," Morgan said, walking over to a tray full of assorted wallets. "This one matches," she said, holding up a three-fold master calf billfold.

"Perfect." Dakota looked over at Morgan. "Now, what do *you* need out of here?" Then she laughed. "Let me rephrase that—what do you want?"

"You're right. I don't need anything, *but* I could use a new weekend bag. Let's look at the luggage." Morgan walked over to the luggage section and found a chocolate-brown square piece that zipped all the way around the sides. It was as soft as butter, perfect for the weekend. They paid for their treasures and bounced out of the store, as happy as clams.

"Let's go over to TSE. I need a pashmina," Dakota said.

"There it goes again, one of our three favorite verbs." Morgan looked at Dakota and they said together: "I need, I want and I must have!"

TSE was the store for cashmere; they even had cashmere for babies. "Dakota, look at this," Morgan said, holding up a soft pink baby sweater.

"Ohhh, that's too cute. Look, there's a matching hat," Dakota cooed.

"I've got to get it. Miles is going to love it."

"Aren't you jumping the gun? Or is there something you need to tell me?" Dakota said, eyeing Morgan's stomach.

"No, I'm not pregnant. But when I bring this home, Miles will know I haven't forgotten about our plans."

"That's pink. Suppose you have a boy?" Dakota picked up a baby blue sweater and unfolded it to examine the tiny sleeves.

"Well, I guess I must have both," Morgan said, picking up the blue hat that matched the sweater.

"Need, want, and must have—our three favorite verbs!" They both laughed as they made their way to the register.

"I'm getting hungry," Dakota said, looking at her watch.

"Yeah, I could go for some McDonald's fries and a chocolate shake." The only time Morgan craved McDonald's was at Woodbury. They walked over to the food court, where a multitude of fast-food restaurants served up calories and grease by the pound. After consuming their fair share of both, Dakota said, "Let's go over to Barneys. I could use a few new suits."

The Barneys outlet was like a small piece of heaven—Madison Avenue clothes at outlet prices. They wasted no time picking out suits, shirts, dresses, and shoes, then headed to the fitting room for their dress rehearsal.

"Do you like this?" Dakota asked Morgan as she modeled a three-button Isaac Mizrahi charcoal suit she had matched with a light gray shirt.

Morgan walked completely around her to get a good look before giving her opinion. "It fits you well. You may have to get the pants taken up, though, depending on the shoes you're planning to wear." Now modeling her own ensemble, she asked, "How about this? Do you think this is too short?" Morgan said, referring to the black evening dress she had slipped into.

"It's short, midway up your thigh, but it looks sexy, not slutty. You can't wear it to an office function, but you can definitely wear it when you and Miles go out."

"You're right," Morgan said, admiring herself in the mirror.

After they tried on a few more items, they headed to the checkout counter. The woman at the register looked at their respective selections and said with a smile, "Did you ladies leave any inventory for the Sunday shoppers?"

"Actually, we tried to shut the store down," Morgan chuckled, taking out her American Express Centurion card.

After hitting a few more select stores, they decided to call it a day and headed back to the Ranger.

As she and Morgan put their shopping bags in the back of the SUV, Dakota said, "Shopping is such an exhausting job."

"Yeah, but somebody's got to do it." Morgan laughed. They drove out of the parking lot, then through the tollgate and headed back to the city, feeling like two archaeologists after a successful dig.

34

Monday mornings were always a bitch. And after a near-perfect weekend of shopping with her girl, dining out with friends and romance with her man, this Monday was especially painful. She needed just one more day to ease back into the real world. With no such luck, Morgan pacified herself with the knowledge that at least Joel wouldn't be in the office today, since he was taking a vacation.

"Have a good trip, sweetie," she said, looking up from the *New York Times* to kiss Miles good-bye before he headed out the door.

"I will, babe. I'll call you after I check into the hotel tonight."

"Love you," she called out.

"Love you too," he said.

After Miles left, Morgan dressed quickly and headed out behind him. On the taxi ride downtown, Morgan thought back to Friday's meeting. Though she had initially been hesitant about taking a personal day to attend to Caché's business, she was glad that she had. The meeting had gone very well. She and Blake were the perfect team. She was professional, organized and sophisticated, and he was creative, extremely knowledge-able and a touch flamboyant. It was just the right mix for a high-concept event-planning company.

Still mentally at Friday's meeting, Morgan stepped off the elevator and walked slowly toward her office. She noticed an unusual quiet hanging in the air. As she looked around, everyone seemed to be pretending not to notice her. Their heads bobbed down on cue like human dominoes as she passed through the corridor. It was almost as if she were invisible. Thinking that she must be getting paranoid, she stopped at her secretary's desk before walking into her office.

"Any messages?" she asked, wanting to catch up on Friday's log of calls.

"Uhmm, no," Aimee stammered before jerking her head down to study a sheet of paper, conspicuously absent of writing.

Another domino, Morgan thought.

Feeling as if she'd stumbled into the Twilight Zone, she walked into her office with a puzzled expression. Facing her as she entered was Joel, who stood in front of her desk, arms tightly folded. He was the last domino, but this one didn't fall.

"Hi, Joel, what are you doing here? I thought you were on vacation."

"Like you were on Friday?" he asked with a menacing look.

"What are you talking about? You knew I was taking the day off," she said, placing her briefcase down, then turning to remove and hang her coat.

"You were supposed to deliver the Zenon proposal to my one o'clock meeting—day off or not." She could see his pale complexion begin to turn a bright shade of pink.

Surprised, she faced him with her coat still on. "It *was* delivered," she said.

"Let me be blunt," he started, the pink turning more urgent. "I did not receive the package that you were supposed to deliver, which left me sitting in front of the CFO of a Fortune 500 company looking like an incompetent idiot. Short of doing a tap dance, I had no choice but to apologize and leave."

"But, Joel," she insisted, "I had the package delivered." She was shaking her head, trying desperately to make sense of this.

"Did you deliver it yourself?" he asked, pinning her with an unwavering glare.

"No-no," she stammered, "I had a friend drop it off."

Joel's one long brow had become a wave of indignation. "Well, your *friend* may have just cost this company a thirty-million-dollar account. And it *has* cost you your job!" Now totally red, he handed Morgan a pink slip, already filled out and signed by Human Resources.

"Joel, wait! You can't do this! It was a mistake!" she pleaded to his back as he stalked past her out the door.

Turning, within full earshot of the now-erect dominoes, he fired a parting shot. "Have your office cleared out by noon." With that, he stormed down the hall.

Morgan stood stock-still in the middle of her office, coat still on. It wasn't until she heard Joel's office door slam shut at the end of the hall that she was shaken out of her stupor. She walked zombielike to the door, closed it, then sat at her desk, trying to comprehend what had just happened, though it was painfully clear. She had been fired.

She was shocked by the suddenness of it. One second she was a successful v.p. of a major company, and the next she was a nobody. She had never contemplated such a thing happening to *her*. Or surely it would have come with some warning, not out of the blue like a renegade asteroid.

Her next emotion was fear. Having never been outside a major company's embrace, she already felt adrift, as though the protective drawbridge had been raised while she was left standing on the wrong side of the moat. Next she felt anger. She was pissed off for being used, abused, then discarded like an old piece of soiled tissue.

But the overwhelming emotion that lingered was shame. She could see her father's disappointment in her mind's eye, causing her to well up with a flood of tears. They flowed freely as she hurriedly tossed her personal effects into boxes that had "thoughtfully" been left there earlier. After she finished, it struck her as odd that her entire fourteen-year corporate career could be so neatly stacked into two small boxes. Obviously, it hadn't meant much.

Wiping away the tears, she labeled the boxes for shipping, grabbed her bags, and walked out of her office and down the hall. And in reverse order, the dominoes popped up this time to catch one last look at the parting outcast.

* * *

Walking back through the lobby of her apartment building, Morgan felt like a child sent home from school for bad behavior. Surely there was a dunce cap set atop her head. It seemed to her that everyone knew—there's the girl who just got fired—even her doorman.

Dumping her bags inside the foyer to the apartment, Morgan headed straight to the bedroom to shed her clothes and cocoon herself under sheets and blankets. Before stripping back the covers, she found a note that Miles had left earlier. It read, "Have a good day. I'll call after I check in later tonight. Love and Kisses, Miles. P.S: It looks like we might get a closing date for the end of next month!"

Oh, shit! In her despair she had forgotten about the mortgage. Losing her job would jeopardize their approval. Just then the phone rang. Hesitantly she picked it up. "Hello."

"Morgan, what's going on?" It was Dakota, sounding anxious. When Morgan didn't answer right away, she went on. "I just called your office and your bitch secretary said that you no longer worked there. What happened?"

After Morgan explained the morning's drama, for the second time today she cried a river.

"Morgan, listen, I'll be right over," Dakota said.

Sniffling, Morgan said, "You really don't have to come over." Though she could really use some moral support.

"I want to. Besides, the Swiss market is already closed, so it's really no big deal."

"No, really . . ."

"Morgan, I'll be there in thirty minutes," she insisted, hanging up before Morgan could waste time replying.

Dakota arrived with all of the accoutrements for a pity party. She had stopped off at the Soup Nazi's to get comfort food, added an assortment of doughnuts and, of course, Morgan's favorite dessert, Chocolate Delight. The only things she didn't bring were cake and candles.

They made a picnic right on the silk rug in the middle of the master suite. After Morgan recounted the story, this time with full details, Dakota asked, "So what happened to the package?"

"My meeting with Blake ended at ten-thirty. I gave him the package, and he assured me that he was on his way to deliver it right then. Later, I asked him if everything had gone okay and he assured me that he had gotten to Zenon at eleven and left it with the receptionist, giving her instructions to give it to Joel as soon as he arrived."

"So, what do you think happened?"

"I don't know. But as soon as Blake gets back from his treatment this afternoon, I will be calling him first thing to find out."

Dakota sat slowly eating her soup. Stopping with spoon midway to her mouth, she asked, "What did Miles say?"

Sighing deeply, Morgan answered, "I haven't told him."

"What are you waiting for?" Dakota asked, eyes piercing. She recognized the tone in Morgan's voice and knew that it spelled trouble.

"For one thing, he's on the way to L.A. Plus, I don't know whether I *can* tell him," Morgan said.

"Morgan, you have to tell him. He's your husband."

Twisting her hands in her lap, Morgan said, "I will tell him, eventually. After we get the check from Denise, that's when. Then at least I'll have money and more Caché clients in the pipeline."

Dakota looked at Morgan flabbergasted. "You're going to keep this from Miles until then?"

Slowly shaking her head, Morgan rationalized, "It will only be another month. Denise will cut the check ninety days out from the Christmas party. Besides, as much as Miles will be traveling this month, he'll never know. Especially since he always leaves the house before I do and he never calls me at the office."

"Morgan, your marriage is not my business," she said, the "but" hanging like lead in the air, "but I think you are making a terrible mistake. Miles loves you. Of all people, he'll support you now," Dakota pleaded.

"What he'll do is blame Caché and Blake for everything. And I can't handle that negativity right now. Caché is my only hope of salvaging anything from this. Believe me, I will tell him . . . when the time is right."

Later that afternoon, when Dakota had left, Morgan picked up the phone and dialed Blake's number.

"Hey, princess," he cooed.

"Blake, what happened to the package you were supposed to deliver to Zenon on Friday?" she asked without preamble.

"What do you mean?" he said, caught off guard. "I left it with the receptionist like you asked."

"Well, Joel didn't get it." She was growing angry all over again just mentioning Joel's name.

"I can't imagine why. I left it with specific instructions," Blake said, sounding concerned.

"Are you sure you left it at the right place?" She hated to jump to conclusions and make a false accusation, but she also had to get to the bottom of this.

"Of course. The address is 465 West Fifty-sixth Street, between Seventh and Eighth. I left it with the receptionist. She was an older woman, weighed about three hundred pounds, and had the nerve to have on a large floral-print tent. I don't remember her name, but you can go by there and see for yourself."

With all of the details, she was sure that he had in fact gone there. "I don't know what happened, but Joel didn't get it, and because of that, I lost my job today," she told him, this time valiantly fighting off the tears.

"You're kidding! Morgan, I am so sorry. But I can't imagine what could have happened. I definitely dropped it off, just like we discussed."

"I know. I just can't explain it," she said, shaking her head.

"You were probably set up."

"Set up?" She hadn't thought of that.

"You know, Joel has had it out for you for a while now—which is why he made such an unreasonable demand to begin with. And when that didn't work, he probably decided to pretend that he never got the package. For all you know, there may have never been a meeting to begin with."

"You could be right," Morgan said, reflecting, trying to put the missing pieces together in her mind. It made sense; after all, it was very suspicious that a high-level meeting like that would happen so suddenly without her knowing anything about it.

"Morgan, if I were you, I wouldn't sweat it. Now you can really put in the time to build Caché. This could be a blessing in disguise."

Morgan closed her eyes, praying she'd awaken from the nightmare. No matter, Caché had to be a success . . . It was all that she had left.

35

Ambivalent feelings clouded her mind as Dakota sat in the back of the Town Car heading to La Guardia to pick up Nana. On one hand, she couldn't wait to entertain her grandmother for the weekend. On the other, she still hadn't mentioned Parker's race. Taking out her cell phone, she dialed Morgan.

"Hey, girl, you busy?" she asked once Morgan answered.

"Just ironing out plans for the premiere party. What's up?"

While looking out the window, watching New Yorkers rush toward unknown destinations, Dakota sighed. "I'm on my way to pick Nana up from the airport."

"Why are you sounding down? Aren't you excited to see her?" Morgan said, picking up on Dakota's tone.

"Yeah, but she still doesn't know about Parker."

Morgan's voice became more cautious. "I thought you told Nana you were seeing someone."

Dakota paused, not wanting to get into the race issue with Morgan again.

Listening to the dead air on the line, Morgan asked, "Hello, are you there?"

"I'm here. I did tell her I was seeing someone. I just didn't tell her that someone is not black."

Sensing that Dakota didn't need yet another lecture on the race issue, Morgan said, "Well, you could try to plead his case since he's only half white."

"Girl, Nana thinks he's tall, dark and handsome, like Jackson," Dakota said, nervously running a hand through her hair. "When she sees that he's not black at all, there's no telling how she'll react."

"So what are you going to do?"

"My only saving grace is that Parker's in London on business, so I'll have a chance to break it to her before he gets back tomorrow night."

"Sounds like a plan."

The Town Car passed the tollbooth. Now it was only a matter of minutes before they were at the airport. "Wish me luck. I'll take her to Sylvia's tonight for dinner." Sylvia's was a world-renowned soul food restaurant in Harlem. "Maybe the smothered chicken and peach cobbler will help her to digest the news about Parker a little better."

"Call me if you need some moral support."

"Thanks, girl, I appreciate it," Dakota said, glad to finally have an ally where Parker was concerned. "I'll talk to you later."

Dakota flipped her phone shut as the car pulled up in front of the American Airlines arrival terminal. She had told Nana to meet her in baggage claim. As Dakota walked toward the luggage carousel, she mentally rehearsed how to break the news.

She was lost in thought and didn't hear Nana approach. "Kota, baby," Nana said, ambling toward Dakota with a Jewel shopping bag in each hand.

Dakota turned around and saw Nana struggling with the bags. "Hey, Nana, what is all this?" She took the shopping bags, put them on the floor and gave her grandmother a big hug and kiss.

Nana returned the hug and said, "Baby, I brought dinner."

"Nana, you know there *are* restaurants in the city. I was planning on taking you out to dinner."

"You don't need to waste your money on taking us out to dinner. Not as long as I can cook. I know all about these 'spensive New York eatin' places."

The buzzer sounded on carousel number three, indicating the arrival of her luggage. "I've got a surprise for you," Nana said, looking around.

Dakota thought about Parker. "I've got a surprise for you too."

Nana pointed toward the end of the conveyor belt and said, "There's my bag, that big green one."

Dakota reached over and picked up the large Samsonite. "Is this your only bag?"

"Yeah, baby," Nana said, still looking around.

"Come on then, let's go," Dakota said, struggling with the suitcase.

"We have to wait on your surprise."

"Well, can I at least take these shopping bags to the car?" Dakota said, picking up the Jewel bags and the luggage before struggling through the sliding doors.

The driver got out and opened the trunk. Dakota had her back turned when someone tapped her on the shoulder. She turned around, and her mouth dropped open.

"Hey, cuz." It was Tricia, dressed in a red minidress, black patent-leather waist jacket, black fishnet stockings and red spike heels.

Dakota was shocked. She looked Tricia up and down. "What the hell are you doing here?"

"Nana invited me," Tricia said, slinging her luggage in the trunk.

Her grandmother explained. "Tricia finished with her studies, and I thought she could use a little getaway. Plus, she never been to New York. I hope you don't mind."

"Yeah, cuz, I can't wait to hit the streets," Tricia said, climbing into the back of the limousine.

Not in that hideous outfit, Dakota thought.

She shot Nana a look before they got in behind Tricia. "Nana, why didn't you tell me Tricia was coming? I could have prepared myself."

"Ain't no need for preparation. We all family," Nana said. She settled herself between her granddaughters, looking from one to the other in smug satisfaction.

On the ride home, while the two visitors chattered about the different sights, Dakota was silent. The last thing she needed was grief from Tricia. The car pulled up in front of Dakota's building and the driver helped them to unload.

"This is where you live?" Tricia asked, looking at the building and turning her nose up. "It don't look so fancy to me. I thought you would have a penthouse on Fifth Avenue." She laughed.

Dakota rolled her eyes. "Whatever." The elevator ride up to the loft seemed extra slow. Dakota thought that if this was any indication of what the weekend was going to be like, it would be a *long* one.

"This looks like some kind of factory building," Tricia said when they stepped off the elevator.

Unlocking the door, Dakota said, "It used to be a shipping warehouse."

When Tricia walked into the loft and looked around, though, her tune changed. "Damn, this is fly."

"Watch your mouth," Nana said.

Tricia gave herself an unofficial tour, then came back to the living room. "Is this one of those flat-screen TVs?" she said, running her hand across the chrome finish.

"Yeah, it is," Dakota said. Despite herself, she was glad Tricia was impressed. As she walked into the kitchen to put up the food, Tricia followed her. "How much that cost you?"

"Trust me, it was expensive."

Nana appeared in the kitchen with a floral housedress on. "Kota, where is your skillet? So I can put on the fish."

"I see you didn't waste any time getting comfortable," Dakota said, tugging on Nana's dress.

"Child, move outta my way so I can get dinner going," Nana said, pushing Dakota aside. "Why don't you and Tricia go sit in the front room until dinner is ready?"

She and Tricia marched into the living room like two little girls obeying a parent. But that didn't mean Dakota was about to cozy up to Tricia. Dakota was standing at the floor-to-ceiling window, looking out onto the seaport when the phone rang.

"Hello," she said, in a soft tone, almost a whisper.

"Hey, there, were you asleep?"

She looked over at Tricia, who was tinkering with the television remote. "No, just thinking."

"About me, I hope," Parker said.

"Sort of. What are you still doing up?" Dakota asked. With the time difference, it was well after midnight in London.

"I've been up doing a little thinking myself."

"About what?"

"Thinking I can't wait to see you."

Although she missed Parker, Dakota was glad he was across the Atlantic, especially since Nana *and* Tricia were in town. "When are you getting back?"

"Sooner than you can imagine. Hold on a minute."

There was a knock at her door. "Who is it?" Dakota said, looking through the peephole.

"Florist, Miss Cantrell."

Just then he came back on the line. "Parker, did you send me flowers?"

"Uh, why?"

"Because there's a delivery guy at my door."

"Guess you found me out."

"Hold on for a second," she said to the other side of her door. She looked back at Tricia, who had put the remote down and was watching.

"What the . . .?" Dakota said as she opened the door.

The guy grabbed her, knocking the phone out of her hand. "Parker! What are you doing here?" Dakota asked, stepping back in shock.

"Can't I come see my girl?" he asked, putting away his cell phone.

"But I thought you were in London."

"I was. I wrapped up my meetings sooner than expected, and instead of staying the weekend, I thought I'd surprise you and come home early," he said, hugging her.

Tricia's mouth was wide open. "Oh, snap! Kota got herself a white boy."

Parker looked at her strangely, releasing Dakota. "I'm Parker. And you are . . . ?"

Tricia walked over, looking him up and down. "Damn, Kota, he fine for a white boy."

Dakota was in shock. This was not going anywhere near according to plan. "Parker, this is Patricia, my cousin from Chicago."

"Nana, come here! You gotta see this!" Tricia called, ready for the action.

Yelling from the kitchen, Nana said, "Can't it wait till I'm finished?"

Dakota mumbled, "What a nightmare."

Parker heard her and said, "Why are you saying that?"

She whispered in his ear so Tricia couldn't hear her. "Well, my grandmother thinks you're black."

Before he could respond, Nana came out of the kitchen, drying her hands on a dishtowel. She stopped short and gave Parker a puzzled look as if to say, "Who are you?"

Tricia didn't give Dakota a chance to introduce Parker. "Nana, this here is Kota's new boyfriend," she said, then sat on the couch to witness the drama as it unfolded. All she needed now was a bag of hot buttered popcorn.

Dakota grabbed Parker by the hand and walked him over to her grandmother. "Nana, I want you to meet Parker. Remember, I told you about him?"

Parker extended his hand. "Nice to meet you."

Nana was dumbfounded. She lightly shook Parker's hand, then said, "Dakota, come in the kitchen for a minute, will you?"

Once there, Nana turned on her. "Why didn't you tell me he was white?"

"Nana," Dakota said, trying to soften the blow, "he's actually half white and half Latin."

"And you think that make it all right?" Nana said, shaking her head.

Dakota blurted out, "All I know is that I love him."

Nana didn't reply right away. Stiffly she bent over to take the lemon pie out of the oven. "And I bet he tells you he's in love with you, right?"

"Yeah, that's right," Dakota said proudly.

Nana put the pie on the counter with a slight bang. "Don't fool yourself, girl. They'll say anything to bed you. But trust your nana—he ain't gonna never marry you."

Tears sprang to her eyes. "Why are you being so mean?"

"I ain't being mean. I just know from experience."

"What are you talking about?"

Nana started opening cabinets until she found the plates. Then she turned to Dakota. "I never told you this, but when I was a young girl, I was in love with this boy who was so light he could pass. Well, his white momma told him that if he married me, our children would be too dark to pass for white. One day I went by his house, and his momma told me that he was gone. Said she had sent him away 'cause she wasn't going to let him ruin his life by marrying a little darkie."

Dakota could see the pain in Nana's eyes, even after all those years. "Nana, that was back in the day," she protested. "Things have changed. Give Parker a chance. You'll see he really is a great guy."

"I'm just trying to keep you from getting hurt," Nana said, starting to fill three plates. "It's best to stay with your own kind. I wouldn't tell you nothin' wrong."

"No disrespect, but I think you're wrong about this," Dakota said, wiping the tears from her cheeks.

Nana found the right drawer and took out silverware. "I been on this earth long before you were ever thought of, so don't you tell me I'm wrong," she said, slamming the drawer shut.

Dakota composed herself and said, "I see we're not going to agree. Let's just drop it." She walked out of the kitchen before Nana started in again. When she reached the living room, there was Tricia sitting across from Parker, dangling her crossed legs so he could see her thigh.

Parker stood up and pretended to stretch. "I'm going to go home. I'm a bit jet-lagged."

She walked him to the door and stepped out in the hall, closing the door behind her. She put her hands up to his face, looked longingly into his eyes and said, "Parker, I love you."

The tension in his face eased a bit. "I was beginning to wonder."

"Wonder what?"

"If you loved me back. When I told you a few weeks ago, you didn't say anything. And now this . . ."

As a tear silently fell from her eye onto her cheek, she said, "To be honest, it took me off guard."

"Actually, my feelings surprised me too. I didn't expect to fall in love with you, but I did." He wiped the salty liquid from her cheek. "What did your grandmother say?"

Dakota dropped her head. "I don't want to get into it."

Parker said knowingly, "She's upset because I'm not black, isn't she?"

Dakota began to cry. "She said you're never going to marry me, because I am."

Not quite sure what to say, he simply said, "Oh."

Dakota hadn't expected to blurt that out, but she couldn't help reflecting on what Nana said. Maybe Nana was right. Maybe Nana and Morgan were both right. Was she just deluding herself?

"I'll call you tomorrow," Parker said, kissing her on the forehead.

Dakota walked back into the apartment, with Nana's words ringing in her ears. *He ain't gonna never marry you.*

Tricia and Nana were at the dining table eating dinner. "Come on, Kota, sit down and eat," Nana said.

"I'm not hungry. I'm going to bed."

36

Morgan was sitting in her home office, reviewing notes from a Caché meeting, when Blake called. Before he could start in with more grandiose ideas, she cut him short. "Blake, we've got to get this trust thing settled *now*. It was supposed to happen last month, then last week, now it's 'any day now.' Meanwhile, I'm looking at another four-grand credit-card bill!" Her tone became curt as she drove her point home.

"Morgan, don't worry about it. I will get the money," Blake insisted.

"That's not good enough," Morgan replied testily. "I don't doubt that you will eventually. But I need it now."

Blake sounded shocked by Morgan's urgency. "I'll tell you what. I'll call my brother and borrow the money from him. Just a minute," he said, placing her on hold.

A few minutes later, he came back on the line. "Carlton will meet us downtown at the Bubble Lounge around six-thirty, and he's bringing the money with him," Blake gladly reported.

"Great. I'll see you then," Morgan said with a sigh of relief. "But I can't stay out late. Miles will be back from Paris this evening."

She hung up the phone, feeling a twinge of guilt for her nasty attitude, especially in light of his medical condition. But truthfully, Blake didn't seem too concerned about the cancer anymore, and he did treat money as if it grew on trees, especially hers. It was a shame that she had to get indignant to get some money out of him.

*   *   *

Morgan settled downstairs in the Bubble Lounge, in one of its cavernous nooks. The exposed-brick walls and heavy velvet drapes matched her dark, somber mood. Blake walked in, wearing a debonair chino suit, with a cream mock turtleneck sweater. After greeting her with kisses on each cheek, Blake promptly ordered from the beautiful but haughty French waitress. *"Bonsoir, mademoiselle, comment allez-vous?"*

"Très bien, et vous?"

"Bien. Nous commencons avec une bouteille de champagne et alors apportez-nous du saumon et des moules et du caneton, pour deux, s'il vous plaît," Blake said in perfectly accented French.

"Absolutement," she replied, impressed.

Not mincing words, Blake beat Morgan to the point. "Please don't worry about the money. You know I'm good for it," he said, as if anyone would ever have reason to doubt that.

"That's not the issue," Morgan said, feeling herself bristle. "I have already lost my job and stand to lose a mortgage, not to mention the damage that's been done to my marriage."

Looking hurt and insulted, Blake said, "Wait, are you blaming all that on me?"

"I'm not placing blame. But without question, this trust issue is making a bad situation worse."

"It'll soon be over," Blake said.

Glancing at her watch, Morgan asked, "Speaking of soon, where's Carlton? It's seven o'clock already."

"He left his office at six and was coming over the GWB from Saddle River, so he should be here within the next fifteen minutes."

While waiting, they went over the final project plan for the upcoming Christmas party. The theme they had selected, "Season of the Stars," was nonreligious and therefore wouldn't offend any of the various ethnic groups that would be present.

The execution called for clients to walk down a red carpet as they descended the forty stairs from the top of the festively decorated Winter Garden in the World Trade Center into the elegant main room, while "paparazzi" lit the room with flashing lightbulbs. At the bottom, a Joan Rivers look-alike would interview each "star" while guests watched on eight video monitors strategically placed throughout. The main room, with its grand eighty-foot-high ceiling would be transformed into a winter wonderland filled with snow-covered Scotch pines, three hundred poinsettias, and sixty large luminescent stars hanging from above. While Jennifer Freeman filled the air with jazzy seasonal selections, celebrity look-alikes such as Marilyn Monroe, Sting and Toni Braxton would join the guests, adding drama and excitement to the special evening. Later, Jerry Seinfeld would entertain the crowd with one of his witty monologues. Denise had approved the last draft and would finalize the contract in two weeks, after her return from vacation.

"Did I tell you I'm keeping Denise's puppy, Duffels, while she's away?"

Not amused, Morgan turned up her nose. "I've heard of going all out to get an account, but scooping someone else's puppy poop is where I'd draw the line."

Turning his head as though flipping imaginary hair, Blake said, "I've never really worked for anything in my life. It's all been presented on a silver platter. But because of Caché and this bout with cancer, I finally have an appreciation for the meaning of hard work." With the conviction of a reformed addict on the eleventh of his twelve-step program, he added, "So, if I have to shovel a little shit to redeem myself, I am not above it."

Ignoring his soapbox spiel, Morgan said, "Blake, it's almost seven-thirty. Are you sure Carlton is meeting us here? Does he have the right address?"

"I'll call him now," he said, pulling out his cell phone. "Hi, Carlton . . . where are you . . . you're kidding . . . did you try Eleventh Avenue? . . . okay, how much longer do you think it will be? . . . hold on." He cupped his hand over the receiver and said to Morgan, "He said traffic is horrific. He's stuck on the West Side Highway and thinks it'll be at least an hour before he gets anywhere near downtown."

"Blake, I can't wait that long," Morgan said, exasperated. "I have to get home. Why don't you meet him, get the money, and I'll get it from you tomorrow?"

"That sounds good. I'll call you first thing in the morning," Blake said, finishing his last swig of champagne. "Oh, Morgan, don't forget to leave your card so I can settle the bill. After all, this is a business expense."

The mere mention of her card made the short hairs on the back of Morgan's neck bristle. "Tell you what," she shot back. "I'll settle the bill on the way out, and when Carlton shows up, *he* can buy your third round."

Morgan was livid all the way home. The nerve of Blake to ask for her card so that he could sit up in the Bubble Lounge and eat and drink on her. She was sick of his cash-flow problems. He never had cash for anything—cabs, cars, drinks or food. And he had never replaced his lost Platinum card that was attached to his dad's, vowing to get his own once his famous trust was settled. And the Visa—who knew what the story was between him and his mysterious male friend?

Once home, she stomped up the stairs to the office to drop off her briefcase. As she walked through the doorway, she was startled to see Miles sitting in the dimly lit room, staring solemnly up at her.

"Hey, baby," she said, happy to see him.

"Where've you been all day?" he asked abruptly, fixing her with a penetrating stare.

"Working," was her one-word answer. Sensing trouble, she started her retreat back out the door.

"Working where?" he persisted.

"I had meetings," she tried.

"Morgan, stop bullshitting me!" he said, suddenly standing to his full six-foot height.

"What are you talking about . . ." she started, although she knew full well where this was going.

"Well, let's see. For starters, how about the fact that you no longer *have* a job?" He swung his arms in the air, an incredulous, hurt look distorting his face. "I guess from there we could cover a lot of ground. For instance, not only did you *not* tell me, but you lied about it to cover it up. Not to mention that I had to find out from Robert." He was screaming now. "Not even a friend or family member, but a fucking real estate agent!"

Unable to defend herself, Morgan just shook her head, searching for words that would not come.

"It's bad enough that we are going to lose the brownstone," Miles said ominously, "but what's worse is that I've lost something that I thought I would have forever—trust in you."

Morgan felt as if she'd been kicked in the stomach. Reeling from the blow, she began weakly, "Miles, you don't understand . . ."

"Understand?" he cried. "Oh, I do understand. I understand that you've let some weird fairy spin you a tale of a nonexistent trust fund for some business scheme, destroying everything that we've built."

"But, Miles, it's not Blake's fault or Caché's," she pleaded.

"Well, whose fault is it?" Miles asked, pinning her with an unwavering stare.

Trying desperately to explain the fiasco, Morgan answered, "Joel asked me at the last minute on the day before my day off to pull together a proposal for a meeting the following day. Because of my appointments with Citigroup and ours with Robert, I wouldn't have been able to finish it the next morning *and* have time to drop it off before his meeting. So Blake offered to deliver it for me. So you see, it's Joel's fault. The whole thing was probably a setup to begin with." Morgan looked at Miles pleadingly, hoping that this rush of words explained everything.

Shaking his head, Miles asked, "And you really believe that?"

"That's what happened," Morgan said, her eyes teary.

Miles said sarcastically, "Oh, sure. The conspiracy theory. Global, Joel and Zenon all conspired to have Blake drop off a proposal which never gets there. Wake the fuck up!" He began pacing furiously, his rage fueled by Morgan's apparent naiveté. "Don't you see? Blake undoubtedly set you up. That's the conspiracy. Now there is nothing in the way of your building the business that he has put very little into. Least of all money!"

"That's not true." The hot, burning tears were now falling freely.

"If that's not true," Miles said, turning abruptly to face her, "what happened to the office on Park Avenue?" He looked angrily at Caché's stuff strewn about his media room.

"It's being renovated," she said between sobs.

"Oh, okay. Meanwhile all of this shit gets dumped in my room." He stalked around the room, picking up Caché files and tossing them dismissively to the floor. In his tirade he came across Blake's jacket, left from a previous visit. Sneering at it, he yanked it off the chair and turned to Morgan. "You want it?" Throwing it at her feet, he said, "Well, you got it!" and stormed out the room.

Sobbing uncontrollably, she moved toward the door, blinded by stinging tears. "Miles . . ." She nearly tripped over Blake's crumbled jacket and kicked it savagely aside. She finally made it out the door and down the hall when she heard the finality of the front door as it slammed shut.

Devastated, Morgan cried until her eyes were swollen and her chest hurt from heaving. Not knowing what to do, she instinctively called Dakota. Her voice choking, she said, "Miles . . . he's gone . . ."

"Morgan?" Dakota could barely understand what she was saying, nor did she recognize her friend's voice.

"He's gone . . ." Morgan repeated, this time unleashing another torrent of tears. "Dakota, he's gone."

37

It was Wednesday, over-the-hump day, and Dakota was still in her blue mood. She and Parker had talked only once since the disastrous weekend. Thankfully he hadn't called the next day, and she was relieved, since she couldn't really talk with Nana and Tricia around. Dakota wasn't much of a host. She had stayed in her pajamas most of the weekend. Nana didn't care to go anywhere, either. She was content staying in, waiting on Dakota. Tricia spent the weekend in the mall at the Seaport. Dakota gladly gave up one of her credit cards, just to keep Tricia out of her face. When Sunday came, Dakota had called a car service to take them back to the airport and out of her world. On top of everything else was Morgan's blowup with Miles.

"I'll be right back, Paul. I'm going to the ladies' room." Dakota decided to take the shortcut, which coincidentally was near Parker's seat. As she walked toward his desk, she saw Shelby leaning over him. From what she could see, they were looking at something. Dakota assumed it was the nude pictures of Shelby. Instantly Nana's words rang loudly in her head: "It's best to stick with your own kind." Maybe Nana was right. From where she stood, Parker and Shelby sure did look cozy. Dakota hurried past his desk. She was in no mood for Shelby's antics today.

"Dakota, line two," Paul said, once she returned.

"Trading."

"It's me. You busy?" Parker asked.

"Just tying up a few trades," she said, too casually. "What do you want?"

"Excuse me," Parker said, sounding put off by her tone. Then he asked, "What are you doing after work?"

"No plans," she said carefully.

"You want to go to dinner?"

"Sure, why not?"

Parker breezed ahead, as if to overcome her reluctance. "I have clients coming in from London tomorrow, so I have to go by Cartier's first to pick up a few gifts. It won't take long."

She wanted to say, "I could care less about your damn clients," but instead said, "Whatever. I'll meet you at the elevator after the close." Dakota hung up and continued to calculate average prices on her trade tickets. His call did not lift her spirits. All it did was make her apprehensive. Where were they supposed to go from here?

Twenty minutes after four, she moseyed to the bank of elevators. Parker was already there waiting.

"What's wrong?" Parker asked, seeing the solemn expression on her face. "You look like you just lost your best friend."

She lied and said, "Nothing. Just one of those days."

Disguising his voice like Billy Crystal's *Saturday Night Live* character, he said, "It's not how you feel, it's how you look, and darling, you look mahvelous." When she didn't lighten up, he added, "I love that suit."

Dakota did not smile. "Thanks. I got it when Morgan and I went up to Woodbury."

In the taxi on the way uptown, they rode in silence for a while. Finally he asked her, "How's your grandmother?"

"She's fine." Dakota thought for a moment, then asked, "Parker, have you told your parents about me?"

He didn't respond.

"Did you hear me?" she asked, becoming pissed off.

"I heard you."

"Well?"

"Listen, honey, let's talk about it over dinner."

When the taxi pulled up to the red awning, Parker got out

and held the door for her. She marched right past him directly into the store.

"Let's go to the executive gift department," he said after hurrying in behind her. "I called ahead, and they should have the gifts engraved, boxed, and ready to go."

Dakota stood silently next to Parker as he dealt with the salesperson. As he handed over his credit card, she thought, *I have a few choice words for Mister Man once we get to the restaurant. How dare he put me off like that?* The least he could do was answer her question. Though she was sure he hadn't told his parents anything.

They were walking to the exit when Parker suddenly stopped and said, "Dakota, come here. Take a look at this stone."

She walked over to the counter where Parker was standing and looked down into the case.

"Isn't it beautiful?" When she didn't respond, he asked the salesperson, "Can you take it out of the case, please?" She took it out, and he handed the ring to Dakota.

"What do you think?" he asked.

"It's gorgeous," she said, truly impressed. It was a three-carat princess-cut diamond set in platinum. The stone appeared flawless and unbelievably brilliant.

"Try it on," the salesperson urged.

Slipping the expensive gem on, she held her hand up. She watched the light reflect off the diamond, creating a fire of red, blue and yellow. The ring seemed to radiate its brilliance to Dakota, instantly improving her mood.

After admiring it on her finger, Parker asked, "You ready to go?"

"Yes," she said, reluctantly taking it off. "Thank you," she said, handing the ring back.

He smiled at the salesperson, thanked her and said to Dakota, "What do you have a taste for?"

"It doesn't matter," Dakota said, her somber mood returning.

"Let's go over to Jean Georges and see if we can get a table."

"What? You know it takes months to get a reservation there." She twisted her mouth, then said, "We'll just be wasting our time."

"Don't be a pessimist. Come on," Parker said, hailing a taxi. Just as they were getting in, he realized that he had left his credit card with the salesclerk. After running in to retrieve it, they headed to Jean Georges, across the street from Central Park in Trump's International Hotel. It was one of Manhattan's premier restaurants. The world-renowned chef and owner Jean Georges was an award-winning master in the kitchen, which partly explained why it took months to secure a reservation.

While Parker talked to the maître d', Dakota excused herself and went to the ladies' room. When she returned, the maître d' miraculously showed them to a corner table. The restaurant had a romantic feel, with billowy ivory drapes covering floor-to-ceiling windows, fresh flowers, and dim lighting.

"How did you manage to get a table?" Dakota asked once they were seated.

"I just pulled a few strings. Nothing's too good for my girl." With that, he signaled the wine steward to order a bottle of Cristal.

While the champagne was being presented, Dakota scoped out the restaurant and noticed that most of the women had on evening dresses. She looked down at her outfit and was glad she had worn her new suit. "Parker, we need to talk. I've been thinking—"

"Hold that thought for a second. Let me just check to make sure the store engraved everything, just in case I need to call them before they close."

Dakota did a slow burn. Why was he avoiding the subject? She thought, *It's because he knows I want the real reason why he hasn't told his parents about me.* The fact that she had never gotten around to telling Nana herself only made her madder.

Parker took out one of the red leather boxes from the shopping bag and examined the pen for engraving. He then handed her the bag, saying, "Would you do me a favor? Look and make sure the other gifts are done."

She snatched the bag from him and took an oblong pen box out of the bag. Sure enough, the pen was engraved. She took out pen after pen and each one had SBI in small block letters on the gold retractable bar. When she got to the last box, she noticed it wasn't oblong. "Probably an engraved money clip," she thought. But when Dakota opened it, she stared in disbelief. Winking up at her was the three-carat diamond ring she had tried on in the store.

"Dakota Cantrell, will you marry me?" Parker asked, taking the ring out and putting it on the third finger of her left hand.

"I—I don't know what to say." Tears welled up in her bottom lids, then fell onto her cheeks and slid gently down onto her chin.

With a tear in his own eye, he whispered, "Just say yes."

"Yes, yes, I'll marry you," she said, looking at the engagement ring on her hand. It was as if the fire from the diamond melted all of her doubts away.

His chest swelling with pride, Parker raised his glass and said, "To my bride-to-be."

Dakota let his words linger in the air before she said anything. She wanted to bask in his love as long as possible. After a few moments she raised her glass to his and said, "To my handsome fiancé."

38

The week after Miles learned of Morgan's cover-up, she felt as if there'd been a sudden death in the family. Devastated by the loss of his trust and her job, Morgan became a shadow of her former self, barely leaving the apartment, spending most of the day in bed, even losing her enthusiasm over Caché.

Deeply concerned, Dakota had called every day to provide support and encouragement. "Morgan, you have to keep your head up, girl."

"What's the use? Miles hates me," Morgan said in despair.

"Don't be silly. He's upset, angry, even disappointed, but he doesn't hate you."

"It's just not the same," Morgan said wearily. She desperately missed the closeness they had always shared. "He gets up in the morning, goes to the office, comes home, eats, sleeps and repeats the cycle—all as if I weren't even here. I feel like I don't even exist."

That was why, as Morgan and Blake sat on the mezzanine at the Paramount Hotel discussing the upcoming premiere, she was in no mood for more of his lame excuses.

"I was livid when I found out Nancy had screwed up the money wire! Apparently she transposed two of your ABA numbers and didn't catch the error," Blake said, apologizing profusely. He was supposed to have wired the money from Carlton into Morgan's checking account two days ago.

"Blake, you have not seen livid," Morgan said, seething.

"Morgan, I will get you the money."

Struggling to compose herself, Morgan said, "Blake, I am truly sorry about the cancer and the strain I'm sure it's put on you, but honestly, I don't think being in business with you is such a good idea. Maybe we should put this all off until after your treatments. Because right now you've got more baggage than a full cargo hold." Even as she said it, though, Morgan knew that they had come way too far too fast to come to a screeching halt without wrecking everything. Not only was Denise counting on them to deliver, but Morgan was also already out over ten grand, with nothing yet to show for any of it.

Blake closed his eyes, inhaling deeply. Opening them with a pleading expression, he leaned forward to grab her hands in his. "Morgan, please don't say that." Slowly shaking her head, he said, "I know it's been hectic, but I will handle it! The biggest issue is unraveling the trust, and Carlton is working on it night and day." Brightening, he added, "But after Denise gives us the check, which is confirmed for the Monday following our premiere, we'll have $50,000 in the bank."

"Blake, listen carefully," Morgan said sternly, not blinking an eye. "I'm leaving town tomorrow, but I want my money *before* I board that plane."

"Where are you going?" Blake asked, glad to change the subject.

"To Phoenix to unwind at the Phoenician for a couple of days." Lately Morgan had been wound so tight that she felt ready to implode. Dakota had suggested a getaway to help her put things into perspective.

"If you're going out there, you should head over to San Francisco for the weekend. It's only an hour-and-a-half flight from Phoenix." Morgan looked at Blake questioningly. Going on, he said, "You can stay at my place. It's a beautiful three-bedroom Victorian on Nob Hill. There's a Beemer in the garage, and the house is completely stocked. It'd be a nice treat for you."

Dismissively, she replied, "I would, but Miles is on the

West Coast now, and I don't want to be away when he gets back Friday."

"Why don't you have him meet you in San Francisco?" Blake asked, knowing that this wouldn't happen.

"I'll talk to him about it, but I really don't think so." What were the chances Miles would want to stay in one of Blake's houses?

After a short, awkward lull, Blake returned to the subject of Caché. "So, how are the premiere plans coming from your end?"

"Fine," Morgan said dully. "The invitations went out last week." They were rolled like cigarillos and put into sleek black cigarette holders. The bands were engraved in gold with *Caché*. "So far the RSVPs are at seventy percent. What about your end?"

Blake was much more enthusiastic. "The caterer and I settled on the final menu today. We'll have the waiters serve vintage champagne and also stock a full bar. Karen and I are still working on the final wine selection."

Morgan excused herself to the bathroom to freshen up. When she returned, the bill was settled. She grabbed her briefcase, thinking someone in that strange household must have doled out some cash to Blake, since for once he had paid a bill. Hallelujah!

"Be sure to keep the receipt," she said.

"I plan to," Blake assured her, hurriedly putting away his wallet.

The next afternoon, settled comfortably into the back of a long black Town Car, Morgan headed to La Guardia Airport to catch Delta's 5:40 flight to Phoenix. Blake should also be en route, since he was meeting her at the gate with a cashier's check for ten grand and the keys to his house in San Francisco. Things had been so awful lately that she was really looking forward to being pampered at the Phoenician. After considering Blake's offer, she'd thought twice and decided that time away with Miles might be just what they needed to rekindle their cool relationship. After much pleading, he had agreed to meet her. And besides, it would be nice to chill out before the rush of events.

The premiere was the week following their Sunday night return, and the Christmas party was one month later. These events would be followed by a series of wine seminars for Fidelity that began in early January. This schedule excluded the other events they had booked and the rigorous round of holiday parties and social functions that she and Miles were personally obligated to attend.

On the way to the gate, Morgan stopped at a bookstore to pick up some light reading for the five-and-a-half-hour flight. Looking through her wallet, she realized she was missing a credit card. She had the American Express Centurion and the Visa, but was somehow missing her MasterCard. The last time she had used it was a few days ago. She had stopped at Bergdorf's to pick up panty hose and lingerie. *Hmm*, she thought, *maybe Miles has it*. But that didn't make any sense. He had a wallet full of his own.

The only other person who would have access to her bag was Blake. He was often considerate enough to carry her heavy briefcase when they were out, and he knew that she kept her wallet in the zippered side pocket. But why would he take her card without asking? She'd certainly ask him when he got to the gate.

She arrived five minutes before boarding, but there was no sign of Blake. She sat through the First Class and Million Miler advanced boarding, patiently waiting for him to show up. This was virgin territory for Morgan. She had so many airline privileges and such high mileage status that she hadn't watched people board for ages.

Soon every row had boarded and still no Blake. Puzzled, she checked her watch, then craned her neck to see if she could catch sight of him rushing down the concourse. Finally, with a snotty gate agent nipping at her heels, she gave up and boarded the 757 bound for Phoenix, albeit without her money.

When she arrived at the Phoenician in Scottsdale, Arizona, there at check-in was an urgent message from Blake. It read,

"Got caught in traffic, arrived at gate scant seconds after you boarded. Call ASAP!" She crumpled the note, grabbed her bags, and headed straight to her room. She made a beeline to the minibar to down a stiff drink to brace herself for the call.

"Blake, what the hell happened?" she asked, skipping the pleasantries.

"There was a five-car crash on the Grand Central, so we ended up in bumper-to-bumper traffic. I ran through the airport as fast as I could, but by the time I got to the gate, you had just boarded. I begged them to let me on, and of course they wouldn't. I am so sorry." Blake's words tumbled out in such a torrent that he was almost out of breath by the time he finished.

This was in stark contrast to Morgan's measured tones. "Are you sure you were at the right gate?"

"Gate B12," he confirmed.

"Yeah," she answered, relieved, thinking that at least he had really been there.

"Not to worry, hon. I'll send the package by Federal Express. Give me the address and I'll get it out first thing tomorrow. You'll have it by Thursday morning."

"All right," she said, and gave it to him. Morgan was just about to end the conversation when she suddenly remembered her credit card. "Blake, have you seen my MasterCard?"

"Yeah, I have it right here. In fact, it's in the package that I brought to the airport."

"What the fuck are you doing with my credit card?" she asked belligerently.

"Monday night when we were at the Paramount, I knew you were in a hurry to get home, so when you went to the rest room, I took it out of your wallet to settle the bill so that we could leave as soon as possible. When the waiter returned, I simply forgot and put it in *my* wallet instead of yours. Please don't yell at me—it was an accident!"

"Blake, I want my money, my card, and the keys on Thursday." You could have cut the spaces between Morgan's words with a knife. Click. Dial tone. No good-bye.

She called Dakota to tell her the latest news. Dakota heard

the exasperation in Morgan's tone. "What's wrong? I thought you were going to the Phoenician to relax, not to get wound up."

"It's Blake. This is the third time he was supposed to give me the money he owes me, and there's yet another excuse. And on top of all of that, he took my credit card from my wallet."

"What?" Dakota said, shocked. "What excuse could he possibly have?"

Morgan proceeded to give her the litany, from Carlton stuck on the West Side Highway, to transposed ABA numbers and a five-car crash on the Grand Central.

"Well, at least he did get the money from his brother," Dakota said, hoping to calm Morgan down.

"Or so he says."

After hanging up with Dakota, Morgan had another drink before calling Miles. She didn't want him to hear the tension of another Blake-related incident in her voice. "Hey, baby."

"Hi," Miles said, sounding distracted.

"I just wanted to let you know that I made it. I checked in not long ago."

"Great. Listen, I'm running late for a meeting, but have a good stay. I'll see you in a couple of days."

"I love you, sweetie," Morgan said, hopeful.

"I'll see you in San Francisco," he said coolly.

39

Over the next two days, Morgan enjoyed all the Phoenician had to offer. Amidst two-hundred-and-fifty acres of beautiful desert terrain at the foot of the Camelback Mountains, the Phoenician was one of Morgan's favorite luxury resorts. The rooms were spacious and elegant, with rattan furniture and wool Berber carpets. The baths were tiled in Italian marble. The resort boasted a two-acre cactus garden and a multimillion-dollar art collection. Not to mention a plush twenty-seven-hole golf course and a comprehensive menu of spa services, many of which Morgan indulged in, from massage and body therapies to European mineral scrubs and body packs.

When Morgan returned to her suite on Thursday, fresh from a day of full pampering, she removed her terry-cloth sweat suit, and began running her bath for a long, leisurely soak. Not until she saw the *USA Today*, which had been delivered while she was out, did she even think about the package she was expecting from Blake. She checked with the concierge, the bell desk and even the mailroom, only to find out she'd had no deliveries. She could feel her blood start to slowly boil. She took ten deep breaths, picked up the phone and called Blake.

"Hi, princess," Blake answered cheerfully.

"Blake, where is the FedEx package?" she asked.

"It's not there?" he said, surprised.

"If it was, I wouldn't be asking you, now would I?" she answered testily.

"Morgan, I sent it out yesterday morning," he insisted.

"Blake, it's not here, and I'm bored with this fucking shell game. There is no way it should take two weeks for you to give me a check. First your trust was being settled, then your brother was bringing it, next it was being wired, after that it would be at the gate, followed by a FedEx which doesn't arrive!" Now that her temper had flared to a raging boil, she was having a hard time putting a lid on it.

"Morgan, I realize you are angry," Blake said, sounding wounded, "and in my medical condition I can't take it personally. But I will call FedEx and find out what happened. Obviously they've made a mistake. I'll buzz you back in a minute."

As she sat drumming her fingers on the top of the rattan desk and trying to regulate her breathing, he called back, explaining how FedEx had input the wrong information and somehow had marked the package for two-day delivery instead of next day. "You will have the package by tomorrow afternoon," he promised.

"Wonderful, just great," Morgan said sarcastically. "I'm checking out tomorrow morning and going to San Francisco."

"I'll call them back to reroute it."

"While you're solving all those problems, what am I supposed to do about a place to stay in San Francisco, since I don't have a key to your house?" she asked. The stress she had gotten rid of over the last two days was returning with a vengeance.

"Go ahead and check into a hotel. You can check out once you get the package."

"Getting a hotel at the last minute on a fall weekend in San Francisco isn't that easy," she said. The thought of how furious Miles would be if they couldn't get a decent room was adding tension by the second. After all, he wasn't exactly the Days Inn type. So much for a romantic reconciliation.

That night she had two travel agents working frantically to find a room in one of the nicer hotels in San Francisco. It wasn't easy. A medical convention had taken over two thousand of the city's rooms. Finally she had to use the clout of her American

Express Centurion Card to practically extort a room from the Clifts Hotel on Geary.

Morgan called Blake back with the new address, and he promptly rerouted the package to the Clifts. She could expect it in the afternoon, he said, shortly after her arrival from Phoenix.

Not wanting to refuel Miles's anger about Blake, when she called later she was vague about the reason for the sudden change in accommodations, saying, "The Clifts is so convenient, it'd be a shame not to be in the middle of restaurants and shopping." As was too often the case recently, Miles had no opinion one way or the other.

After checking in at one-thirty, she took a steaming bubble bath in the oversized tub, determined to clear her mind. Afterward, she dressed in a pair of thick cream corduroys, a black cable-knit sweater and her favorite walking shoes, black velvet JP Tods. The walk through Union Square's shopping district was relaxing, and being out and about in the romantic City by the Bay made her anxious for Miles to arrive. She walked the eight blocks back to the hotel and enjoyed a glass of merlot in the beautiful Redwood Room, an elegant bar with walls covered in the most resplendent redwood, all cut from the same magnificent tree.

Miles arrived shortly after she got back to the suite. He walked in as she was tying the robe of her loungewear.

"Hi, sweetie," she said, greeting him just inside the door. "How was your trip?"

"It was fine," Miles answered, setting his briefcase and jacket aside.

"I missed you," Morgan said, walking closer and looking up at him with expressive eyes.

He somberly searched her face as though he were looking for something that was still lost. "I missed you too." But before Morgan could grab the thin thread, the bellman appeared at the door with his luggage. After tipping him, Miles retreated into the bathroom, leaving Morgan clinging to nothing but hope.

While he showered, it dawned on her that again she had not received Blake's package. Phoning the concierge, she learned that no package had arrived. She took ten more deep breaths and called Blake. "Give me the tracking number for the package," she whispered urgently into the phone. It would not do for Miles to get a whiff of this conversation.

"What?" Blake asked, taken off guard.

"I said, give me the tracking number," Morgan demanded, struggling to keep from losing her patience so early in the conversation.

"I'll call to track it and call you back," Blake said.

"Blake, I'll ask you one more time. Give me the *fucking* tracking number!"

After putting her on hold, he finally returned. "If you insist. It's A349064879." She repeated each letter and number as she wrote it down.

Before heading out to dinner she called FedEx, only to be told that A349064879 was not a valid tracking number. Fuming, she decided not to call Blake until she had a chance to calm down and figure out what the hell was going on.

That evening she and Miles went to the Grand Café in the Hotel Monaco for dinner. The fabulous dining room was done like a 1930s movie set, and Phillipe, the general manager, was a most charming host. Morgan had called earlier after remembering that Blake had once casually mentioned how good the food was and that he had learned a lot about food preparation while working there a few years ago.

As they settled at their table, Morgan felt as if she and Miles were on a tense first date. Though they were at least cordial to each other, there was still a distance between them.

After the cocktails and appetizers were served, Phillipe stopped by their table, asking, "So how is Blake these days?" The last topic of conversation that Morgan wanted.

"Besides the fact that he was recently diagnosed with cancer, he's doing well," Morgan said, feeling a twinge of guilt for raking him over the coals earlier. "But the chemotherapy has been very effective, and his prognosis is excellent."

"Cancer. I'm sorry to hear that he's out of remission," Phillipe said sadly.

"Remission? What are you talking about?" Miles asked.

"Three years ago Blake had abdominal cancer. In fact, that's why he went back East, for treatment."

Shocked, Morgan said, "Abdominal? You must be mistaken—he has bone cancer."

"He might now, but then it was abdominal. I remember because he would come to work doubled over in pain."

After Phillipe left, Morgan and Miles were both shocked by the bombshell. She turned to him and said, "Honey, I think you're right. There is definitely something wrong with Blake." Since the incident with Carlton, followed by the lifted credit card and recent antics with the package, Morgan had a growing sense of dread where Blake was concerned. Though she had wanted to ignore it, it was now staring her in the face, screaming.

Miles refrained from saying, "I told you so." He simply said, "This cancer thing is definitely fishy. I mean, I guess it's medically possible for a thirty-four-year-old man to have abdominal and bone cancer within a three-year period, but it's not very probable that they would look as healthy as Blake does."

At least now they were united in suspicion. "Blake would have certainly mentioned it if he had previously been diagnosed with cancer, if for no other reason than added sympathy and heightened drama." Squinting her eyes in contemplation, Morgan said, "And now that I think about it, I don't know anyone who has ever actually been inside his Fifth Avenue penthouse."

"It sounds like a few too many coincidences to me," Miles said.

"Wait a minute . . ." she said, having an epiphany. "What if there *isn't* a rich St. James family on Fifth Avenue? What if he made it all up?"

Wrinkling his brow, Miles answered, "Anything is possible. It's also pretty easy to verify. On Monday just call the U.N. and ask for Dr. St. James."

258 Tracie Howard and Danita Carter

On Monday morning, back home again, she placed a call to the U.N. "Dr. St. James, please."

"One moment," the operator said, transferring the call.

"Dr. St. James's office," came the brusque greeting from a woman Morgan gathered to be his secretary.

"Good morning. I'm with On Time delivery service and wanted to inform Dr. St. James that he can expect a package to be delivered to his 235 Fifth Avenue address later today," Morgan lied.

"I will be sure to tell him. What sort of package should he be expecting?" asked the woman.

Morgan never answered, she simply hung up. So there *was* a Dr. St. James and he did live on Fifth Avenue. Somewhat relieved, she then called Blake.

"Morgan, princess, are you okay? I've been trying to get in touch with you." He had left several increasingly urgent messages over the weekend.

"Blake, I didn't call to discuss me," Morgan said calmly. "What I want to know is exactly why you are lying about this money."

"Morgan, I am so sorry. You're right. I did lie. I didn't take the package to FedEx. My ankle hurt so badly from running through the airport that I asked Tyrone to take it for me. Later I found out that he never did, which is why I was trying desperately to reach you," Blake explained.

"So where are the money and my credit card?" Morgan asked, getting to the point.

"I have your card here, but Tyrone cashed the cashier's checks," Blake answered tentatively, with remorse in his voice.

"He did *what!*" Morgan screamed. So much for the calm approach.

"I know—this has gotten way out of hand. I'm going to my father to explain the whole thing and get the money from him. I'll courier the card to your apartment this afternoon."

"When are you speaking with your father?"

"He left for Switzerland this morning and is returning late

Tuesday night. So I'll see him first thing Wednesday morning. Morgan, I am so sorry for all of the trouble I've caused."

"*You're* sorry?" she said, hanging up. "I'm sorry," she said to the empty room, "that I ever *met* you."

40

Morgan had had so much turmoil in her life lately with the lost Caché job and Miles that Dakota decided not to tell her about the engagement immediately. She hated to gloat over her own happiness when Morgan was so low. Then she remembered that Morgan was in San Francisco with Miles, trying to rekindle the romance, so she figured that when she returned she would surely be in a better mood.

So Monday she decided to pick up some eats from Dean & Deluca, invite her over and tell her the good news. Maybe it would lift her spirits too.

Picking up the phone, she called Morgan. "Hey, girl."

"Hey," Morgan said, still sounding down.

"How was San Fran?"

"Interesting," was all Morgan said.

"Listen, are you busy tonight?"

"No."

"Well, come over around six. I have some good news to tell you."

Morgan's reply was glum. "I really don't feel like coming out."

"Listen, I'm not taking no for an answer."

"Just tell me over the phone."

"I have something to show you as well," Dakota said, looking down at the Rock of Gibraltar on her finger. "Come on, it's a surprise."

"All right, I'll see you at six," Morgan said, hanging up the phone.

Dakota felt like a kid on Christmas Eve. She couldn't wait to show Morgan her ring and tell her all about the night that Parker proposed. She kept looking out the window and glancing at her watch. By 6:30, Morgan hadn't arrived, nor had she called to say she was running late. Dakota called Morgan's cell. "Where are you?"

"I'm five minutes away. See you in a few."

After about fifteen minutes, Morgan knocked at her door. "Girl, you look like shit," Dakota said when she took a look at her friend.

"Gee, thanks," Morgan said, walking over to the sofa and plopping down.

"What I mean is, you don't look like your normal spry self," Dakota said, sitting across from her.

"I don't feel like my normal spry self. Since Miles found out about my job, nothing has been the same," Morgan said despondently. "Even the time in San Francisco didn't really change much."

"I'm so sorry, girl," Dakota said, now even more hesitant to share her good news.

"And on top of everything else, the charges on my card are still an issue." Just talking about it seemed to bring Morgan further down.

"Tell me this. Why did you put more Caché charges on your card?"

"Blake's trust still isn't settled, and we have to move forward."

"How did you end up floating the money to begin with?"

Morgan said despondently, "Blake lost his cards, so I just put the charges on mine. Plus for tax purposes, it made sense. I'd get reimbursed, so it really didn't seem like a big deal. Especially with a four-million-dollar trust right around the corner."

"You can't keep putting charges on your card, especially since Miles is so pissed. Girl, you already lost your job. Don't mess around and lose your man."

Morgan fought back tears. "Thanks for the vote of confidence."

Seeing Morgan's face, Dakota thought maybe she had gone too far. "I'm not trying to bring you down. All I'm saying is make sure you get the money from Blake. After all, his family *is* worth millions."

Finally Morgan snapped out of her funk. "I didn't come over here to talk about me," she said, sitting up straighter. "On the phone you said you had a surprise. What is it?"

Dakota felt a little guilty being so happy while her friend was so down in the dumps. Reluctantly she said, "Parker and I got engaged."

Morgan's mouth dropped open. "What? Are you kidding?" She looked at Dakota's left hand, trying to see the ring. "Why didn't you tell me? When did he propose? Were you surprised? What happened?"

"Wait, wait, one question at a time," Dakota said, laughing.

"I'm so excited for you. Let me see the ring." Morgan was so happy for her friend, her mood improved instantly.

Dakota uncrossed her arms and extended her hand to Morgan, showing her the ring.

"Oh, my God, it's gorgeous. How did he propose?"

Dakota crossed her legs Indian style. "He said he had to pick out a few client gifts from Cartier after work, and I went with him."

"He proposed in the store?"

The two exchanged a look and then smiled. "No. At the store he told me to look at this ring and had the salesperson take it out of the case. I tried it on and instantly fell in love with it. I thought he was going to ask me if I would want an engagement ring like that. But instead he asked me if I was ready to go to dinner."

"Then what happened?"

Pleased that Morgan wasn't interjecting her thoughts about his race, Dakota continued. "We went to dinner at Jean Georges . . ."

"Jean Georges—oh, how romantic."

"Anyway, he started looking over the gifts to make sure they were engraved, and asked me to help. So when I got to the last box and opened it, there the ring was inside. That's when he popped the question," she said, remembering as though it was yesterday.

"That's wonderful! You've gotta have an engagement party."

"I've been thinking about that," Dakota said, glad to be able to include Morgan in her happiness. "I was thinking about having a costume party for Halloween anyway, so now it'll be an engagement-slash-costume party."

"I'll help you plan it," Morgan said eagerly. "It'll get my mind off my troubles."

Dakota was uncertain. "Are you sure? I know your plate is full."

"I'm sure."

"Are you sure you're cool about Parker? I know you had some issues with me dating outside of the race."

Morgan looked Dakota in the eye. "I'm cool about it. I realize it's your life, and if Parker is your choice, who am I to say otherwise? As long as you're happy, that's all that really matters."

Dakota jumped off the sofa and went over to Morgan, giving her a hug. "I appreciate your support."

"Girl, you don't have to thank me. That's what friends are for." Morgan suddenly remembered something. "Speaking of which, I need to ask you a favor."

"Sure, what is it?"

"I called Paul, Shelby's boss, today to talk about Caché planning their Christmas party, and he said I needed to speak with Shelby, since she's still in charge of event planning. I wouldn't ask you this, but we really need the business. Could you set up a meeting with Shelby? Caché has to keep the accounts coming in, especially now that I don't have a nine-to-five."

Dakota brooded for a minute, thinking darkly about Shelby and her lewd pictures. She then looked down at the rock on her finger and said, "I'll invite her to the costume party. She's not a threat anymore, now that Parker and I are getting married."

"That sounds great. I have to prove to Miles that Caché is an asset, not a liability." To tell the truth, she felt as though her marriage, future and her life depended on Caché's success. Or failure.

41

Dakota and Parker's Halloween party was festive decadence in Dakota's loft. The art deco space, with its eighteen-foot-high gothic ceilings that majestically capped floor-length windows, had become a den of iniquity. Tonight, massive candelabra were the only source of light, and their flames danced to a rhythm all their own. The moon, visible from the wall of windows, was only a shadowy crescent, hidden by a thin veil of clouds. Vats of dry ice lazily spewed billows of foggy haze, adding to the surreal ambience.

As the bohemian crowd swayed to Outcast's "Ms. Jackson," the DJ deftly blended hit after hit. In fact, he handled the wheels of steel so masterfully that several songs had gone by before revelers finally realized that Dr. Dre was now Jay Z.

The invitations had read, "From Hedonism to Happiness. Come join Dakota and Parker as they celebrate the end of the single life." They were engraved on thick cream-linen paper with gilded edges.

Parker was dressed as Caligula, the lustful Roman emperor from the first century, complete with a leafy headdress and a tiny leather sarong. Dakota wore an ornate harem costume signifying her as the lead amongst Parker's collection of sex slaves.

Morgan arrived as Lady Godiva with a riding crop tossed over her left shoulder. She wore a skintight brown catsuit and brown spiked ankle boots, crowned by a long black flowing wig. The way it swept over her right shoulder and cascaded over her breast down past her hips caused major drama. Miles was the suicidal but brilliant Vincent van Gogh. Makeup gave the illusion of a jagged bloody gash where his ear should have been. His painter's smock and paintbrush completed the effect.

The bar served an assortment of enticing elixirs, along with a selection of red wines. The house drink was a Murky Martini, which was a combination of Absolut citron, Grand Marnier and a splash of orange/tangerine juice with a twist. Bloody Marys were offered, but Dakota had ordered that they be served only after the stroke of midnight.

Blake, the life of every party, was dressed in a traditional French maid's uniform and carried a ticklish feather duster. The tiny black skirt was so short, you could almost make out the bulge he had taped, strapped, and harnessed between his long legs. He wore a corset to minimize his already slim waist, and a pair of black fishnet hose. Masking tape wrapped tightly under each arm and across his chest along with a padded bra completed the illusion of small but perky breasts.

The pounding sound system was so intense that Blake could literally feel the music in every bone. The suggestive lyrics of "Name That Thang" by Ecstasy fed the frenzy. Blake was right at home.

> . . . *When I watch it swang*
> . . . *I wanna*
> . . . *name that thang*
> . . . *name that thang*

The music, the eclectic mix of people, and any excuse to dress in drag was a dream come true for him. But he cautioned himself: "I'll have just a couple of drinks and be sure to behave. After all, I can't do anything to cause Miss Morgan any more concern. This money problem is enough of a pain in my ass."

Speaking of asses, Blake was having a hard time keeping his wandering eyes off the tight one belonging to the blond dressed as Tarzan, who conveniently had arrived without a Jane. Looking at the imprint beneath the tiny loincloth convinced Blake he would love to swing from that limb. The song continued,

> *. . . You get any closer*
> *I'm a haf ta*
> *name that thang . . .*
> *name that thang*

Tacky divas aside, he loved Ecstasy's song. He downed his third Murky Martini, which enhanced his high, before setting off on his next adventure.

"Hey, handsome, you look like you could use a little tidying up," Blake said, with one hand on his slim hip. With the other he flicked his feather duster over Tarzan's loin.

"So what else do you do besides windows?" asked Tarzan, sounding more like George of the Jungle. But that was okay, Blake thought. His oratory skills and IQ weren't the main attraction.

"I have many talents," Blake responded, leading Tarzan by the tiny leather loincloth through the jungle of gyrating people.

> *When I watch it swang . . .*
> *I wanna . . .*
> *name that thang!!!*

How apropos, he thought. *I could have written that song to describe this exact moment.* As they danced to the suggestive lyrics, the distance between them grew shorter and shorter.

> *Get it from the front*
> *Name that thang*
> *Get it from the back*
> *Name that thang*
> *Name that thang—Name that thang*

As the last note of "Name That Thang" faded seamlessly into "Put Your Hands Where My Eyes Can See," by Busta

Rhyms, they were chest to chest and crotch to crotch. The writhing bodies were by now dripping with sweat from every pore. *Umm, this is nice,* thought Blake as he grabbed his fourth Murky Martini from one of the waiters, all of whom were dressed as hunchbacks.

Through his cloud, Blake could vaguely make out Lady Godiva and van Gogh across the room. Just then the blond jungle man reached under his skirt to massage his engorged penis. In one motion Tarzan had turned Blake around and pressed forcefully against his firm backside to the rhythm of the pounding music. This was just the way Blake liked it. Grabbing both wrists behind him, the blond whispered, "I think you could use a little tidying up yourself." Blake could barely contain himself as he felt the substantial girth of the other man's pulsating member. Out of the corner of his eye, he could see Morgan headed in his direction with Miles in tow. He had to make a move.

"Hey, big guy, why don't we find a little privacy?" Blake said as he quickly led the blond toward the back of the loft and down a narrow hallway. He recalled Dakota showing him the sleeping loft while giving him a tour of her place. He climbed the ladder, and the ceiling being so low, his head grazed the beams. But there was a small lamp in the corner and a futon on the floor. That was all they needed.

Shelby then appeared, scantily clad as a stripper from Scores, with an armband stuffed with singles, spike-heeled, thigh-high black patent-leather boots and a see-through mini-dress over thongs and a push-up bra. Dakota had only invited her so Morgan could meet her and hopefully land the SBI account.

"Shelby, this is my friend Morgan I was telling you about," Dakota said, checking out her risqué costume. The cheap ho could have at least stuffed some twenties in the armband, she thought. Dakota glanced at Morgan, who from the way she was looking at Shelby probably thought the exact same thing.

"Hi," Shelby said. "Dakota told me you and your partner have started a corporate entertainment company."

With a big phony smile, Morgan said, "Yes, we just landed

the Jon Atkins account. Our first major event is their Christmas party."

Shelby was impressed when she heard the name Jon Atkins. "I've been looking to contract out some of the parties I coordinate for the company. In fact, I just had a meeting with my boss to approve the budget, but once that's done, I'll give you a call."

"Thanks, I'd really appreciate it."

"That was painless," Dakota said, when Shelby had walked away.

"Blake and I need all the business we can get. By the way, have you seen him lately?"

Scanning the room for Blake, Dakota noticed that Shelby had worked her way over to Parker and was pulling him out onto the dance floor. "Morgan, look at that skank ho," Dakota said. She watched Shelby gyrate her hips and buttocks in front of Parker, performing a pseudostriptease, as Parker and the rest of the men chanted her on. "I'm going to put a stop to that shit right now," Dakota said, storming toward the dance floor. The record ended before Dakota reached them, and luckily Shelby walked away.

"What the hell was she doing all over you like that?" she demanded of Parker.

Looking like a kid whose hand had been caught in the cookie jar, he said, "She wasn't all over me. We were just dancing. You're the only woman I want on me," Parker said, grabbing Dakota possessively by the waist.

Dakota cut her eyes up at him. "I better be the only woman on you."

Dakota and Parker awoke the next morning with twin hangovers. Dakota couldn't begin to recall how many Murky Martinis had led to her current state. But she did realize her next move was a critical one. If she stayed in bed another sixty seconds, the combination of her horizontal position and the stabbing rays of sunlight filtering through the shutters might render her unconscious. Her other option was to actually get out of bed, but moving was also a daunting thought. As she lay there trying to make a decision, she heard a sudden loud *thunk,* followed by a sharp, high-pitched yelp, which jarred her straight out of bed. So much for choices.

By now Parker was up as well. "What the hell was that?" he asked, with a startled expression on his pasty, sleep-deprived face.

"I don't know." Dakota grabbed her housecoat from the foot of her four-poster bed.

Dakota and Parker both looked like death warmed over as they hurried as fast as hangovers would allow through the loft. Making their way clumsily down the hall, Parker glanced up in time to see a pair of black-fishnet-enclosed ankles attached to size-twelve feet sticking out of the opening of the sleeping loft.

"What the hell?" Parker stared in puzzled disbelief at the spectacle before him.

"It's just me," Blake said despondently as he leaned forward through the opening. "Last night my cancer medication made me so sick that I had to crash here. I thought I would wake up before the party was over."

Dakota was instantly concerned about his condition. "Why didn't you say something? We would have called your doctor or at least checked on you."

Blake waved the thought away. "I didn't want to spoil the night for everyone else. Plus, I'm scheduled to see Dr. Bernstein tomorrow at ten o'clock anyway."

"What was that loud noise?" asked Parker, not quite sure what to make of the situation.

"When I woke, I was a little disoriented and stood too quickly, forgetting how low the ceilings were," he said, hiding a smile. Yes, he'd forgotten to duck, but he had dodged a large-caliber bullet by having Tarzan sneak out earlier.

"Come on down and I'll fix us some breakfast," Dakota offered, thankful to have anything to distract her from the looming hangover.

"Well, I'm going back to bed," Parker said. "Maybe you guys should check the place for more human refuse."

After making his way safely down the ladder, Blake insisted on preparing breakfast for Dakota and Parker. He settled

Dakota into the chaise near the kitchen with a steaming cup of coffee and then took careful inventory of the refrigerator and cupboards. Dakota was thankful as the steam from the coffee began to vaporize the insidious core of her throbbing headache. She didn't want to get too excited, though. After all, her condition was still touch-and-go. Surprise aside, she was actually relieved to have someone to take care of her this morning. And Blake's entertaining chatter allowed her to concentrate on something other than pain avoidance. She was just sorry that he had gotten sick the night before.

He quickly prepared eggs Benedict, Belgian waffles, bacon, fresh-squeezed orange juice and a pitcher of Bloody Marys. The sight of him in her kitchen wearing a wrinkled French maid's costume with torn fishnet panty hose was way too much for eleven o'clock on a Sunday morning, especially with a hangover in effect. So while the bacon was frying, she gave Blake a pair of Parker's sweats and a large Pepperdine sweatshirt.

When she appeared with the clothes, Blake shoved a Bloody Mary into her hand. "Drink this," he instructed.

Dakota wrinkled her nose, fighting to keep down the unstable contents of her volatile stomach. "I don't think so. I really think that I've had enough alcohol to last me a while, thank you very much."

"Trust me, Dakota. You need a little hair from the dog that bit you," Blake insisted.

In her desperate state, Dakota held her nose and began taking several swallows of the suspicious liquid. Blake then took a glass to Parker, giving him the same advice. Miraculously, within thirty minutes both were cured and hungrily devouring breakfast.

After putting away the breakfast dishes, Blake said, "Well, now that I've brought you guys back to the land of the living, I'll be off. I have another house call to make."

Dakota looked over at Parker, then at Blake, raising her eyebrows. "Sounds a little risqué."

Thinking about Tarzan, he said, "Oh, it is."

42

Morgan sat in their library, which had once been their private sanctuary but was now more like a shrine of the past. On the backlit shelves were dozens of pictures in beautiful gold frames that displayed special moments captured on film. There were wedding pictures, pictures of various exotic vacations, and simple shots that eloquently showed the essence of that intangible thing called love. Morgan was immersed in the past, pulling out photo albums to help keep the present at bay.

When Morgan opened the album, staring up at her was a picture she and Miles had taken at the Opening Ceremony for the Summer Olympics. Thinking back to that day, she remembered how bittersweet it was. On the one hand they were both proud of a job well done, and on the other, it would soon be the end of their working relationship. At the time she had no idea they would end up married and living in New York. But after the way Miles had been treating her lately, she felt that maybe they'd come to the end of their happy marriage.

Morgan burst into tears. How could she have lied to him, after sharing such a rich past? She cried for what seemed like an eternity, then slowly composed herself. Once the tears dried from her eyes, she resumed her journey down memory lane, stopping at one particularly happy memory. They had taken a trip to Europe a couple of years back, and there they were in the South of France on a topless beach in Saint-Tropez. For the sake of the photo, Morgan had placed the magazine that she'd been reading modestly over her bare chest. Miles was kneeling beside her, tanned and fit, in bright yellow bathing trunks. On the opposite page, in the photo that they'd taken at the casino in Monte Carlo, they looked like stars from an old black-and-white movie. Miles was dressed in white tie, and Morgan wore an elegant long white ball gown. They both were smoking Cuban cigarillos, hers through a long black rhinestone cigarette holder. Here was the one taken with Miles's mother, Margarette, his aunt Gloria and his sisters, Alison and Jennifer.

Hours later, when Miles came home, he saw the library light on as he headed down the hall into the bedroom. Looking in, he saw Morgan curled up on the floor, asleep in a fetal position. Surrounding her were the moments of their lives. Clutched tightly in her grasp was their formal wedding picture framed in hand-cut crystal. Judging from the wads of tissue and her swollen-shut eyes, he knew she had been crying. Though he had done what men were often capable of—shut out his feelings—the sight of the ruins of his marriage left scattered on the floor caused his hardened emotions to crumble.

Stooping at her side, Miles picked Morgan up and carried her to bed, still holding the portrait. Though asleep, she instinctively held on to him as a child would a parent. Waking briefly as he tucked her into bed, she opened her mouth to speak, but Miles put his finger to her lips, insisting that words were not necessary. Instead, he held her through the night, giving them both renewed strength.

The next morning, over breakfast, they finally talked. "Miles, I am so sorry I didn't tell you about my job. I thought you would be so angry at me," she said.

Miles put his coffee cup down and looked deeply into her eyes. "Morgan, why would I be angry at you? I know how much Joel had it out for you, and how hard you'd worked for Global. Why would you think that I wouldn't understand and support you?"

"Because if I hadn't taken the day off to go to the meeting for Caché, I would have had the proposal ready to give to Joel myself. Instead, I tried to do it all, and it cost me my job and us both the mortgage."

Reaching out for her hand, he said, "Morgan, you know as well as I do that if it hadn't been the proposal, it probably would have eventually been something else. And you were entitled to take a vacation day. What you did with it had nothing to do with what happened with Joel."

"But what about the mortgage? You must hate me," she said, looking down.

"Morgan, I could never hate you. You are the most important thing in the world to me. Not some old building."

Looking up at him, she said, "Yeah, but you really wanted it, and I blew it."

"Who said that you blew it? It just means that Robert is going to have to really earn his commission. He'll just have to find another lender who will factor in more of my current income. And if not, so what? It's just not meant to be."

Taking a deep breath, Morgan hesitated, then asked, "What about Caché?" Even though it was a sore subject, she felt she might as well get it all out; after all, it was hiding things that caused all of the trouble to begin with.

"Morgan, I will support you in doing whatever it is that you want to do. I think that the business plan for Caché is excellent, and if Blake the flake can be counted on, you'll be very successful."

"So you'll support me?" she asked, wanting more reassurance. She had waited so long for any sign of approval on Caché from Miles, and she was finally getting it. His words were music to her ears.

"Of course I will," he said, leaning over to kiss her.

"I love you, baby."

"I love you too."

43

The hippest parties in New York City are like sensational plays on Broadway. And Caché's premiere party was a Tony Award winner. It was one of the most talked-about and anticipated parties of the season. The three-level penthouse they'd rented on Central Park West was where uptown elegance met urban sophistication. It was also the perfect stage for the evening's cast of characters.

Some of New York's hottest corporate executives were there, including the fat-cat Wall Street crowd and many of the most successful African-American brokers prowling "The Street." Adding glamour to the set were some of the top runway models in the world, including the statuesque beauty from Africa known simply as Amari. And of course, no party in the city would be complete without the standard mix of high-profile entertainment industry executives.

Guests indulged themselves with poached oysters, smoked salmon with a vodka cream cheese, beluga caviar, and foie gras. Smooth jazz blended with contemporary R&B served as background to the buzz of conversation. Throughout the evening immaculately dressed white-gloved waiters served Dom Pérignon–filled champagne flutes.

Morgan wore a long, two-layered backless gown with thigh-high slits on either side. The top layer was silky sheer black chiffon, which covered a burgundy floral underlayer, giving the dress a dreamy antique-burgundy hue. When she walked, the fabric shimmied seductively back and forth, showing long, shapely legs that ended in black, four-inch Prada evening shoes. Miles looked fabulous in a black velvet Calvin Klein tuxedo with a formal bow tie and black velvet slip-ons.

"Morgan, you and Blake have outdone yourselves," Denise declared as she raised her champagne glass. "To . . . Caché!"

Miles mingled with guests, many of whom he knew from the incestuous and close-knit entertainment industry. At the moment he, Morgan, Dakota and Parker were listening to an aspiring R&B singer whose objective tonight was clearly to jump-start her stalled career. Given the vast amount of purchased cleavage on display, it was apparent this mission would be accomplished by any means necessary. Adeptly, Miles dismissed the budding starlet-to-be in such a seamless way that she left thanking him, though not quite sure why.

"You are too smooth." Dakota chuckled. She had on a long gray sheath with thin rhinestone straps and sexy gun-metal Manolo Blahnik evening shoes. She looked stunning. Parker wore a tailor-made imported black gabardine suit with a gray shirt and tie that matched Dakota's gown perfectly. "Homegirl isn't sure whether you offered to make her a star or told her to get lost."

"Speaking of lost . . ." Miles cocked his head in Blake's general direction.

"If Blake has one more glass of champagne, he'll be sweating bubbly," Morgan whispered to Dakota as her gaze fell on her flamboyant but charming business partner.

Blake was wearing a black Armani three-button tuxedo over a cream silk T-shirt with crushed-velvet evening slippers. Together he and Morgan were elegance personified, and as business partners they appeared to be the perfect complement to each other. She the smooth marketing talent and he the engaging operative.

Downing his fifth glass of champagne only fueled Blake's animated gesturing as he floated through the party, charming women and flirting with men along the way.

The four watched as he suddenly swooped an older society matron onto the dance floor and began an exaggerated waltz to

Dr. Dre's song "Been There, Done That." Caught completely off guard, the poor woman glanced nervously at her husband, an ultraconservative senior v.p. of CitiBank, for a rescue attempt. As he and everyone else watched in astonishment, the dance floor cleared and guests formed a semicircle around the improbable pair. Unexpectedly, Blake led the lady of society into a dramatic dip that unceremoniously dislodged the hairpins from her stiff bouffant. The crowd roared in approval. Before it was over, Lady of Society and Blake St. James were doing the bump in the middle of the floor.

Eventually he sauntered over with a dark, handsome hunk who currently topped the R&B charts, making him an overnight sex symbol and ladies' man. But given the sparks flying between him and Blake, one would guess the baritone actually sang soprano. As Blake approached the group, he made a grand sweeping gesture, bending his leggy frame to gather Morgan in outstretched arms. "Princess, the party is fabulous," he said with an appraising once-over. "The party is beyond my expectations . . . and you know how high they are."

"Do tell," Morgan replied, pinning Blake with a steady gaze of her own.

Not answering, Blake swept off again, and Dakota turned to Morgan. "One thing is for sure. He is certainly in the right business. He's always the life of the party."

"You're right about that."

"Excuse me. I have to freshen up the war paint," she said to Morgan, glancing over at Parker. "I have to look good for my man."

Dakota headed upstairs to the dimly lit master suite of the penthouse, since the powder room on the main floor was occupied. Besides having the best bathroom in the penthouse, the suite also had a huge picture window that framed a stunning view of the city. The portrait started at Central Park, spanned the New York skyline and across the Hudson River to the Jersey Palisades and, to the north, the George Washington Bridge. Since she was alone, Dakota stood taking in the breathtaking view for several minutes. Finally she headed into the bathroom, closed the door and began applying a fresh coat of lipstick.

Dakota didn't hear the door to the master suite open, but when she finally came out, there Parker was, standing in front of the sofa facing the large picture window, enjoying the same view she had admired only minutes before. Maybe she should really give him something to admire, right here in the master suite. After all, they were alone, and he had obviously followed her up here. He was probably planning to seduce her. As her passion escalated, she could feel her nipples firming while she moistened at the thought. She could hardly contain herself.

Parker hadn't noticed her yet, which was good, so she slipped off her shoes and tiptoed toward him. He was sipping champagne and seemed to be completely lost in his thoughts. She eased up behind him and slowly reached around to stroke his love organ. But she was in for a nasty surprise. Just as she looked down to see what her hand had touched, Parker snapped out of his trance, turning in shock. She couldn't believe what she was seeing. She must be drunk. She blinked once, twice. Her eyes *must* be playing tricks. But, alas, the trick was on her. There on her knees was Shelby.

For a second the three of them were a frozen tableau. Shelby, frozen with Parker's melting penis lodged deep in her throat. Parker, eyes wide, staring at Dakota. And Dakota frozen at the lewd and lascivious sight of the two of them.

"Parker, how—how—how could you?" she stammered, shaking her head in denial. Before he could answer, she slapped him across the mouth.

With a nasty smirk, Shelby answered for him. "It was easy."

"You bitch," Dakota snarled.

"It takes one to know one," Shelby shot back. "And by the way, I told you to enjoy it while it lasted. I sure did," she said, licking her sticky lips.

Meanwhile, with Dakota's ring print emblazoned on the side of his face, Parker fumbled with his dick, trying to get it back into his pants. Dakota was tempted to go completely ghetto, but she only had to look down at Shelby, on her knees with lipstick grossly smeared on her mouth, to know that she didn't need to go there.

Dakota snatched up her purse and shoes and ran for the stairs, stopping and stumbling midway in her attempt to put her shoes back on. She made her way, zombielike, to the hall coat closet to grab her wrap before escaping from the nightmare she'd walked into.

"Dakota, what's wrong?" Morgan had seen her as she'd descended the staircase.

"Parker . . . Shelby . . . upstairs," she managed to get out before dissolving into tears. Morgan grabbed her and held Dakota until the onslaught of tears passed.

"Dakota, let me get you a car. You go home and I'll call you the minute I get in. Okay?" Still in a trance, Dakota nodded.

Morgan glanced back over her shoulder as she held open the door for Dakota. She caught sight of Shelby slinking down the stairs looking like the cat who'd swallowed the canary and Parker looking like Tweety Bird.

Once inside the confines of the plush Town Car, Dakota threw herself on the seat and wailed for what was and what could have been.

44

Morgan's mind was still dwelling on the drama from last night's party as she absently went about sorting the mail. When she came across the American Express bill, she immediately noticed that it was thicker than usual. Pulling out the statement, she was shocked by the high balance. More shocking was the fact that she didn't recognize any of the larger charges. Opening her MasterCard bill was even more shocking.

Slowly she began to make the connection. Those charges had all been made during times when Blake had her cards. The first was when she gave it to him for Karen to imprint for the Caché house account, and the second was when he lifted her Master-Card at the Paramount Hotel bar. The fraudulent charges totaled well over ten-thousand dollars and included an Armani tuxedo, a Donna Karan suit, formal shoes, flannel PJs by Frette, china and assorted dinners and lunches at trendy restaurants. He had even bought groceries from Zabar's. The phone rang.

"Hello."

"Hey, girl," came Dakota's despondent tone.

"Hey, how are you doing?" Morgan asked. She had talked to Dakota well into the wee hours the night before, trying to calm her down. Understandably, she had been devastated by Parker's scurrilous betrayal.

"Girl, I'm still shocked. Parker's been calling all morning trying to explain. He keeps saying that Shelby means nothing to him."

"Then what was he doing? Flossing her tonsils?"

"He said he had too much to drink and went upstairs to use the bathroom. She followed him up there, and the next thing he knew she was unzipping his pants."

Morgan sat at the table, shaking her head. "So basically, he's telling you he couldn't help it? That is such bullshit!"

"I know. I asked him, if he loved me so much, how could he have hurt me like that? And with Shelby, of all people! It's a nightmare. We were so happy," Dakota said, trying to hold back tears of pain.

Morgan took a deep breath, exhaling slowly. "What are you going to do?"

"I don't know. I do still love him, but I can't trust him anymore. And without trust, what is love?"

"I know what you mean," Morgan said, thinking about how lack of trust had almost wrecked her marriage.

"Whatever I decide, I know one thing."

"What's that?"

"I'm not giving back the ring, under any circumstances," Dakota said, starting to sound firmer. "He owes me at least that much."

"Yeah, girl, keep the ring," Morgan said, mimicking Chilli in TLC's song "Bitch Like Me."

Dakota let out a long sigh. "Girl, I don't want to talk about him anymore. It's too depressing. Aside from busting Parker, I think the premiere was a success. Don't you?"

"It was," Morgan said, frowning, "but you won't believe this. I just opened my American Express and MasterCard bills to find out that Blake has charged over ten thousand dollars' worth of stuff on my cards."

"What! You've got to be kidding—that's credit-card fraud."

Morgan stared dumbfounded at the list of charges. "I wish I was kidding, that lying, cheating, sniveling son of a bitch! Maybe I should just pay a little visit to his father and let him know he'll be visiting young Blake on Rikers Island unless he writes a check on the spot."

Dakota was happy at the idea of a distraction. "That sounds good. I'll get dressed and meet you at the penthouse."

Morgan threw on some clothes and hailed a taxi over to 235 Fifth Avenue. Dakota was waiting outside when the taxi pulled up to the building. Morgan talked their way in by telling the doorman it was urgent that they speak to Dr. St. James immediately—it concerned his son Blake. He relayed the story to Mattie, who instructed him to send them up. They took the elevator to the top floor and were greeted at the door by the maid.

"We're here to see Dr. St. James," Morgan said brusquely.

"May I ask what this is in regards to?"

"Just tell him it's about Blake, and if he won't talk to us, maybe the police will."

The maid quickly showed them into the library. They looked around at the tastefully decorated and stately penthouse.

Without hesitation, the burly Dr. St. James walked in, demanding, "What is this all about?" With a smooth, dark complexion and gorgeous salt-and-pepper hair, he was indeed a very distinguished older man, just as Blake had described.

Morgan was not the least bit intimidated by his forceful manner. "I know that you met with Blake this morning, but I felt that I had no choice but to personally speak to you about Caché and the money Blake owes me." Either he could straighten things out, or she would be more than happy to, with the help of the NYPD.

"What money are you talking about, and what the hell is Caché?" Dr. St. James wore a puzzled, if not annoyed expression.

Not to be put off by his claims of ignorance, Dakota jumped in on her best friend's behalf. "I'm sure Blake explained that to you."

"I have absolutely no idea what you are talking about, young lady, but Blake should be here any minute. I'm sure he will explain."

"The sooner the better," said Morgan, tersely.

Just then the door to the library opened. "Blake, you're

right on time. These two young ladies seem to have some misunderstanding with you."

Morgan and Dakota both had tongues poised to give Blake a lashing. When they turned around, their mouths dropped open in confusion instead. The man standing before them was nowhere near six-two. In fact, it wasn't Blake.

"Who are you?" Morgan asked.

"Blake St. James. And you are . . . ?"

Morgan and Dakota were speechless. What the hell was going on? Feeling as if they were trapped in Wonderland, they uttered incoherent apologies and made a hasty retreat toward the exit, running past Mattie, whom Morgan now realized was not the maid who had cleaned her house.

"What the hell is going on here, Blake?" his father demanded.

"I don't know," Blake said, bewildered.

"You don't know those young women?"

"No, I've never seen them before in my life."

"Well, they sure seemed to know you—that is, until you walked in. Anyway, I don't have time for this nonsense. You said you wanted to meet with me."

"Father, I finally have my business proposal completed," Blake said, taking the document out of a leather folder.

"Let's have a look," Dr. James said, putting on his reading glasses. He perused the proposal, then looked up and said, "It appears you put tremendous effort into this. I didn't know that you had an interest in opening an art gallery."

"I figured I would combine my art history and business backgrounds. I have a space on hold at Madison Avenue and Sixty-sixth Street. I gave the realtor a thousand dollars earnest money, but unless I can give them a full deposit, I'll lose it."

"So, this is what you have planned for your trust?"

"Yes. I didn't want to show you the proposal until I had the financial projections worked out."

"From what I can see, this looks good. I must say, I'm proud of you, Blake."

"Thank you. If you have time, I would love to show you the space. It's not far from here."

"I would love to see it." He clapped his son on the shoulder. "Well done, my boy."

45

When Morgan and Dakota returned to the apartment, the phone was ringing urgently. Morgan snatched it up. "Hello."

"Hi, princess. It's me, Blake. Just checking in. I wanted to remind you that you don't have to worry about the money. When Denise gives me the check, we'll take care of your debt right away." He still sounded very much like the charming, sophisticated guy who lived in a penthouse on Fifth Avenue.

"So, tell me how much might that be . . . including the unauthorized charges you put on my card?" Even though she was stretched to snap, Morgan's common sense took over. *Careful, careful,* she told herself. There was no telling who this character was or what he was capable of. Images of Andrew Cunanan flashed through her mind as she remembered the day "Blake" and Mattie, or whoever she was, were alone in the apartment. Not to mention that time he'd spent the night with her alone in the house! The memory brought about a deep shudder, causing Morgan to hold the countertop for balance. There was no end to the documents he had had access to: bank statements, credit reports, insurance documents. . . .

"Morgan, I really didn't think you would mind. You know I'll pay you back. My family is worth millions," he said, using that arrogant, rich-boy tone.

"I know. Listen, I'll call you back later. I was just heading out the door when you called," she lied. Anything to get him off the phone.

"Okay, princess," he cooed, before hanging up.

Morgan had called Miles from her cell phone after racing out of the St. James penthouse. Worried, he immediately left the office, arriving just after Morgan hung up with "Blake." She and Dakota were both ashen with shock and fear. Morgan recounted the conversation she had just had with the impostor.

"Don't speak to him when he calls. Check Caller ID, or let the machine pick it up," Miles insisted.

"Okay, but who the hell is he?" Morgan asked, looking from Miles to Dakota.

"Jeff, my second cousin, is an NYPD detective," Miles said. "Let me call him and see if he can help us get to the bottom of this."

"I need to call Denise and warn her. Who knows what this guy is up to?" Morgan said, quickly dialing Denise's number.

"Hi, Denise, Morgan. I hope I didn't catch you at a bad time, but I need to come by and talk with you. Something very important has come up."

Dakota, Morgan and Miles headed uptown. The conversation with Denise was not easy, but ethically she had no choice. So Morgan brought Denise up to speed, starting with the money issues and ending with the events that unfolded that morning. Afterward she apologized for getting Denise involved to begin with. But Denise was very understanding and told Morgan to let her know if she could be of any help.

Detective Jeff Nelson, Miles's cousin, was the best. That evening he met Morgan, Miles and Dakota at their East Side apartment. After sitting down with a beer in hand, Jeff turned to Morgan and Dakota. "Miles filled me in on some of the background, but why don't you two tell me exactly what happened?" he said, pulling out a notebook.

Morgan and Dakota looked at each other. Morgan began, "Well, we met Blake, or whoever he is, at a bar on the West Side back in the summer. He seemed really nice and was very charming." She shook her head in wonder. "He pretended to be this

ole biddy if she wanted to make some extra dough. She said, "Baby, is fat meat greasy?" So he told her to play like she was his live-in maid at his family's penthouse on Fifth Avenue. She looked at him like he was half crazy. But when they got there, she almost blew it by gushing about how nice Morgan's place was. He knew Morgan was thinking, "Now, why is she trippin' over this place when they live in a penthouse?"

But the coup de grace was convincing Miss High Brow Morgan that he had a four-million-dollar trust to start a company. The beauty of it all was that she did practically all of the work. His kinda deal—eighty-twenty. And after getting her fired, she'd had enough time to make it a nice round hundred percent.

He had even thought of a sympathy ploy for when his shit started to stink. The phony cancer story bought him some time because Morgan's dad had died of cancer. His only problem was Morgan insisting on being paid back before he could get the check from Denise. If he could have brought Kathleen in, that problem would have been solved. But uppity Miss Morgan said Kathleen was a slob and started talking about some good-ole-black-girl network. Who knew what that had to do with anything? She'd started off being such a sweet little Georgia peach, all innocent and pure. Then she turned into the bitter bitch from hell, demanding her damn money. Like she needed it. Shit, it was only a few grand, which was a trip to Gucci for her.

But for his biggest payday, he had to look the part. After all, it wasn't every day someone like him toted around a check for fifty grand. He was dressed in his new charcoal-gray suit, which he wore with a black turtleneck and black square-toed buckle-up shoes, all courtesy of Morgan and her MasterCard. He even carried the splendid Gucci master calf briefcase they had given him for his "birthday." What a joke, considering that it was really months away.

When he arrived at Denise's office, the guard showed him into the guest library, telling him Denise had stepped out but would be back shortly.

"Hello, Blake. Excuse me for being late," Denise said, rushing into the room.

"No problem."

"Where's Morgan? I thought the two of you were coming by this afternoon," Denise said.

"Uh, Morgan is across town meeting with typesetters," he lied.

"Well, here's the check to get started on the Christmas party. You'll get the balance afterward."

"Thank you very much for the business, Denise. I'm sure you'll be pleased with the outcome," he said, knowing full well that he had no intention of planning anybody's party—except for his own going-away party. Now that he had the check for fifty grand, he was going to head abroad. Maybe Gstaad.

"And thanks again for arranging tonight. It's been a while since I met a real nice man."

Smiling, Denise said, "It's my pleasure."

"Well, I gotta run and get ready for my big date."

He was meeting Claude Renault, a wealthy art dealer from Paris, at Le Cirque 2000. The opulent, upscale restaurant in the landmark Palace Hotel was art-deco-meets-early-circus. The wood-paneled asymmetrical room was juxtaposed with intense colors and neon lights. A nobody needed six weeks minimum to get a reservation, since the space was created and reserved only for the ultrachic, up-to-the-minute hip, drop-dead gorgeous, superpowerful or, best case, those loaded with dough. After getting his first look at Claude, "Blake" guessed he covered all five categories.

Claude wore a gray Savile Row worsted cashmere suit with an oyster-white dress shirt and a silver ascot. His shoes, which of course said everything about a man, were Italian hand-crafted lace-ups and polished to perfection. He wore a Vacheron Constantin watch to complete the sophisticated look.

Not surprisingly, Claude seemed to recognize him as he approached the table. After all, how many six-foot-two handsome black gay men graced the halls of Le Cirque? Standing, he said, "*Bonsoir*, you must be Monsieur St. James. Denise told me great things about you."

Claude had the sexiest French accent he had ever heard. "Really?" Blake smiled. He avoided using French. Otherwise Claude would most certainly exhaust his list of ten key phrases.

"I was told you were delightful and quite handsome, which I am happy to confirm," Claude added, with a twinkle in his pale blue eyes.

He is a god, thought "Blake." He was about six feet, with broad shoulders and a very solid build for a man in his early fifties. The full head of thick, dark hair with tinges of gray at the temples gave him a very distinguished look. The best part was that Claude didn't live in New York, since it was definitely time to exit stage left.

"We'd like a bottle of 1985 Dom Pérignon rosé," Claude ordered. *"Parlez-vous français?"* he inquired.

"Although I lived in Paris for several years during my youth, my French is inexcusably rusty, so I'd have to say *un peu.*"

Throughout dinner he amused Claude with funny stories of growing up the young, high-spirited, and impetuous son of wealthy black parents. He also found out more about Claude. His father was a prominent French banker and his mother a direct descendant of the first Prince Rainier of Monaco. Claude had been born and raised in Marseilles, near the Riviera. Quaint villages in the area like Saint-Rémy and Aix-en-Provence had stirred Claude's keen interest in art.

"Blake" could feel Claude's strong passion for art and claimed a similar passion for food and wine. This could be his new meal ticket. They would make a perfect pair, traveling the world, appreciating fine art and gourmet meals.

Enjoying the last sips of a thirty-year-old port, Claude took him by the hand and whispered seductively, "Would you care to join me at my Park Avenue pied-à-terre for a nightcap?"

"I would love to," said "Blake," his pulse quickening.

Claude settled the check with his American Express Platinum Card, which Blake noticed was not alone in his wallet. He had every major card you could imagine. Yes, this was definitely the meal ticket.

As they walked out onto Madison Avenue, Claude raised

his hand to signal his driver. A long, sleek black limousine pulled up directly in front of the two men. The driver hopped out to open the door for them. *Now, I could get used to this,* thought "Blake." Once they were settled into the soft leather interior, he leaned closer, purring, "We should have a little dessert before our nightcap, and I have just the thing," he said, unzipping Claude's pants.

Claude reached into a compartment in the side panel. "So do I," he said, pulling out a set of silver handcuffs.

So Claude has a freak streak, "Blake" thought. He was prepared to do whatever it took to reel in this catch.

At that moment Claude turned to him and said in a heavy Brooklyn accent, "Tyrone Nathaniel Thomas, you are under arrest for credit-card fraud and solicitation. You have the right to remain silent. Anything you say can and will be used against you . . ."

Tyrone first thought this was a sick practical joke, until he saw the silver badge that suddenly materialized from "Claude's" breast pocket. While he sat stupefied, the driver replaced his black driver's hat with one bearing the familiar emblem of the NYPD.

Out of the corner of his eye, he caught sight of Morgan, Miles, Dakota and Denise stepping out of a police van. He correctly assumed they had eavesdropped on the entire dinner. They had come to watch the whole humiliating spectacle of his arrest. Infuriated, he yelled out of the window, "You fucking bitch, don't you *know* who I am?"

Morgan had a satisfied gleam in her eye as she calmly replied, "Now I do, Tyrone."

Just as calmly, Tyrone spat out the menacing threat: "Remember this, bitch—revenge is *best* served cold."

47

Sitting on an old blanket on the bare floor in the cold, empty house, Morgan took a bite of the cinnamon raisin bagel, then said to Miles, "Well, it's certainly a long way from the Upper East Side."

"Yeah, but I feel closer to my homeboys already," Miles said, turning his baseball cap backward. After the Blake debacle, Robert had come through and secured a mortgage in spite of Morgan's Global problem. Morgan was able to finish the Christmas party for Jon Atkins without Tyrone/Blake, and since Denise had put a stop payment on his check, Morgan was the sole recipient of the total fee. She was planning on using the money to open her *own* event-planning company.

The brownstone was one of the once-magnificent homes left over from Harlem's Renaissance. At one time they couldn't be given away, but were now going for well over four-hundred-thousand dollars, before renovations. Theirs was a four-family brownstone with an English basement. It sat on Harlem's glorious Convent Avenue. Built of brownstone, the exterior displayed fine hand-carved ornamentation and intricate metalwork. Though the interior had once housed elegant cut-glass chandeliers, rich cherry and mahogany paneling, marble fireplaces, stained glass and elaborate molding, like the rest of the brownstones in Harlem, the beauty had been hidden under years of neglect and abuse. So they had a lot of work ahead of them, but they were both looking forward to it.

Hearing the buzzer startled Morgan; she went to the door and looked through the peephole to see Dakota and Denise.

"What are you guys doing here?" Morgan asked, giving them both big hugs.

"That's some way to greet your friends," Dakota said, handing Morgan a bunch of multicolored tulips that instantly brightened the room.

From behind her back, Denise presented a 1990 vintage bottle of Dom Pérignon.

"Thank you," Morgan and Miles both said.

"I love the place!" Denise said, taking in the rich original detailing in the molding and hardware.

"So do we." Morgan was beaming. "Look at the crown molding. Do you know that there's gold underneath! And the stained glass is at least one-hundred years old."

"It's beautiful," Dakota said, enjoying Morgan's delight.

"Wait until we're done with it," Morgan said, imagining the finished product.

"Let's pop the bubbly," Miles said, beginning to open the bottle.

"Is it cold?" Morgan asked. "You know it *is* best served cold."

"Sorta like revenge, don't you think? It really hits the spot when you never see it coming," Dakota said, smiling slyly.

EPILOGUE

At the quaint table for two near the far window, Morgan sat awaiting the arrival of her dinner guest. She was expecting Percy Harrington III, a senior vice president for Seltex, which was a multibillion-dollar telecommunications company. Seltex spent on average two-point-five million each year entertaining clients, prospective clients, and employees. Gazing at the snow-capped mountains in the distance, she thought about all that had happened since the Caché premiere ten months ago. Because of the bizarre turn of events, she had to make a few changes, but all for the better. Now *she* was the sole owner of Caché and was determined to make it successful.

The product was certainly compelling, and the marketing collateral was brilliant. They featured a series of illustrations like those seen in *The New Yorker* and often featured in many Barneys advertisements. The black-and-white sketches portrayed sophisticated women and debonair men in elegant surroundings, enjoying dry martinis and stimulating conversations. Below the illustration there was always a clever tag line, like, "The most important events always have . . . Caché."

As the maître d' led him to the table, Percy wished he'd gotten rid of his five-o'clock shadow and splashed on a little after-shave before leaving the office. Morgan Nelson was a *very* attractive woman. Her short haircut accentuated chiseled features and engaging brown eyes. She wore a stylishly elegant black wool crepe single-breasted pantsuit. The tailored jacket was worn over a tight, baby-blue cashmere sweater that immediately drew his attention to a pair of full, firm breasts. *Nice packaging,* he thought.

"Hi, I'm Percy Harrington. You must be Morgan Nelson." He smiled broadly, offering his hand, while at the same time wishing he had removed the gold band from his left ring finger.

"I am. Thanks for joining me. Please sit down," she said with an inviting smile.

"Thanks for the invitation. I'm eager to hear more about your company. It certainly sounds impressive."

"I've actually prepared some information that we can review after dinner. But first let's get you something to drink," Morgan said, motioning for the wine steward.

After making several recommendations from the menu, which Morgan knew intimately, she selected a robust cabernet to complement the braised rack of lamb and beef Wellington, ordering in French. Percy was very impressed with how smoothly she orchestrated the evening. She was a seasoned expert on food, wine and how to flirt innocently with a middle-aged man. If this was any indication of her ability to wine and dine, he was sold.

"Morgan, I don't mean to be forward, but what perfume are you wearing? It's absolutely intoxicating," Mr. Harrington said, leaning in for a better whiff.

"It's Annick Goutal, one of my favorites," she answered, flashing that gorgeous smile again.

When the check was settled and they stood to leave, he was surprised by her height. "You look like a model. But I'm sure that you get that comment a lot. How tall are you?"

"Six-foot-two . . . and mostly legs," Morgan answered.